LAST CHANCE

Also by Chuck Barrett

Jake Pendleton Series

The Savannah Project
The Toymaker
Breach of Power
DISRUPTION

Gregg Kaplan Series

BLOWN
Last Chance

Stand Alone

Dead Ringer (eBook only)

Non-Fiction

Publishing Unchained: Revised 2017

LAST CHANCE

A Novel

CHUCK BARRETT

SWITCHBACK PRESS

Edited by Debi Barrett

Cover by Kelly Young at Mary Fisher Design, LLC.
www.maryfisherdesign.com

FIRST EDITION

ISBN: 978-0-9985193-3-3 (Print)
ISBN: 978-0-9985193-4-0 (Digital eBook)
Library of Congress Control Number: 2018905460
Barrett, Chuck.
LAST CHANCE / Chuck Barrett
FICTION: Thriller/Suspense/Mystery

SWITCHBACK PRESS

Published by Switchback Press

www.switchbackpress.com

For Debi

Listen to the whispers and you will not have to hear the screams

PROLOGUE

The middle of nowhere.

Gregg Kaplan sat on his motorcycle idling at the end of a driveway outside the Township of Grass Lake, Michigan somewhere west of Ann Arbor and east of Jackson. Grass Lake was probably a place where everybody knew everybody, and people never locked their doors or cars.

When he rode through town, he saw an average-sized lake with aquatic grasses clumped in the middle—thus the name Grass Lake he reasoned—with a small town built around its shoreline. Like a lot of small towns he had ridden through there wasn't a lot going on, which suited him.

He had stopped at a gas station in town to get directions to the home. His burner flip phone had spotty coverage and the paper map he had used to travel across the country didn't have enough details to guide him to his destination.

The house sat a few car lengths back from the county road and as far as he could tell, wasn't heavily traveled.

Window boxes full of purple and white flowers added spark to the brick exterior of the otherwise plain brick home. Next to the home and slightly behind stood a barn almost the size of the home. Parked under the canopy of three large trees sat a restored classic 1952 Ford F-1. Beside it, an orange tractor. Further back, an open field planted with rows of crops. The home had an old aerial antenna attached to the side instead of the now commonplace preponderance of satellite dishes and underground utilities. A double-lined row of spruce trees bracketed the sides of the home providing privacy from neighbors. In mid-September, there was already a coolness in the Michigan air as autumn signaled its arrival.

This marked the end of his search for her.

His chance to uncover the truth behind the disappearance of his former partner. It had been an exhaustive search with more than its fair share of roadblocks and dead-ends.

The first, and biggest roadblock came from his employer, the CIA. Although it was obvious the Director of the CIA knew his partner's whereabouts, the DCIA had refused to provide him with any information about her location and the reason behind her sudden disappearance.

He had assumed she was sent on a last-minute covert op. But, she never returned and the DCIA refused to brief him about her mission. She had vanished without a word and all he got was a warning to back off or risk the uncertainty of future employment with the CIA.

This day had been a long time coming and his journey had crisscrossed the bulk of the country more than once. It had even taken him overseas to Belgium where he was summarily turned away from every lead he pursued. In one instance, he was physically escorted out of a building by armed guards. He felt then he was close, but in short order every lead evaporated leaving him to start over from the beginning. It wasn't until he persuaded his old handler to covertly search through the terabytes of CIA archives to help narrow down his search, that he made any headway. It seemed his former partner, Isabella Hunt had only one living relative in the database.

That led him to this place.

A perfect place to escape the outside world.

The woman standing in the window looked like she was expecting him.

His throat tightened at the memory of her. Not the woman peering out the window, but the woman he came to find.

Was the answer to his search really in front of him? Or was this another dead-end?

He knew there was only one way to find out. He drew in a deep breath and let it out slow and even to calm himself.

Kaplan shifted his Harley in gear and rode up the driveway.

CHAPTER 1

Two Months Earlier, Mid-July
Montana-Wyoming Border

The Cowboy had planned this job with meticulous detail.

Calculating times of death and locales in order to confuse law enforcement proved more difficult than originally anticipated. But, not impossible.

Ideal locations were the most difficult to pinpoint. One was simple, it belonged to the targets. The other proved to be logistically challenging. Ultimately, the decision came down to the random selection of a remote farm located on the Crow Indian Reservation just a few miles north of the Montana-Wyoming state line. Somewhere between the Little Bighorn River and the Lodge Grass Storage Reservoir. Fifteen miles southwest of Wyola, Montana and ten miles north of the small town of Last Chance, Wyoming.

The Cowboy pulled the rented 4x4 Ford F-250 to a stop and then backed the trailer to the drop off spot. Next came the task of unloading his prey and readying the scene for its eventual gruesome discovery.

One by one, each target was dragged into a barn. The first three were shot, one bullet each to the back of the head—execution style. The fourth target, bound and gagged, was dragged into place. This one must appear to be the main target, he reasoned. He stared down at the Native Crow from under his wide-brimmed hat and reveled in his superiority. He slipped the gun back in its holster, a bullet was too good to waste on this one.

The Cowboy pulled out a surgeon's knife, grabbed the target by his long ponytail, placed the surgeon's knife below one ear lobe and sliced a perfect crescent across the man's neck, deep and precise. Warm, sticky blood spurted across his gloved hand before he could remove it. He lowered the body face down into the large red pool. The man twitched violently and made pained gurgling sounds for several seconds before he went still.

Next The Cowboy gathered his brass, another critical part of the plan, and sealed them in a Ziploc plastic bag.

He closed the barn doors so the July heat would bake the bodies until they were found. Putrefaction was critical to his scheme's success.

The Cowboy retraced the same route back to Sheridan, Wyoming and drove into a car wash, where both the inside and outside of the trailer and the exterior of the truck were cleaned with a high-pressure wash. Tomorrow, the trailer would be returned to the vendor and the truck to the rental car company.

After the second stage of this job was complete, the finger-pointing would begin. The Feds would inevitably be called in as the scope of the crimes would rapidly outgrow the capabilities of local law enforcement as well as the Crow Tribal Police force.

Now, the wheels were in motion.

There was no turning back.

CHAPTER 2

Friday Morning
Four Days Later
Last Chance, Wyoming

It wasn't the double-barreled shotgun aimed at Kaplan's chest that worried him the most.

It was the two rookies behind him.

He kept his hands flat on the counter and his eyes trained on the reflection in the mirrored wall behind the cook. The cook's hands were steady as he kept the shotgun's stock tucked firmly into his shoulder. Judging by his age and the tattoos on his forearms, Kaplan knew he was former Marine and Vietnam vet. It was a safe bet the cook would remain calm and do nothing stupid. He couldn't say the same for the two rookie cops behind him. They looked nervous with their service weapons aimed at his back. Unlike the cook, this could be their first rodeo.

The Last Chance Diner was long and rectangular and fashioned like it was time-warped from the 1950s. The exterior was shiny silver, like an Airstream trailer, but the L-shaped inside was long overdue for an upgrade. Cheap red plastic swivel seats lined the counter. Most of the seats were cracked with age and coated with a film of settled grease from years of frying food. Across from the counter, matching booths with Formica tabletops lined the walls. Each booth with its own window. In the South, they were called *greasy spoons*. Here in the West, he had no idea what they called them—probably the same thing.

The diner was located next door to a gas station and had seemed like a good place to stop. Two birds with one stone, he thought. Gas and food, one stop. Actually, three birds, his bladder needed emptying as well.

He was minding his own business, just passing through with the intention of making one all-important stop. There was someone in town he needed to talk to. Then, depending on the outcome of that conversation, he might stay a few days and explore the area.

At the service station, a Native girl had approached him and asked if he could spare some change. She was young, maybe high school age, he thought, perhaps older but only by a year or two. She held out a small tin cup. He refused to give her money but before she turned away he offered to buy her breakfast. She looked half-starved and perhaps a little strung out. He was surprised how quickly she accepted his offer.

After topping off the fuel tank of his black Harley-Davidson Fat Boy S, he rolled his bike thirty feet where he parked it in front of the diner's plate-glass windows. They went inside, found a booth next to the large windows and ordered breakfast. The young girl gave him the impression she had been living on the streets. Her clothes were typical of a young person. Tight blue jeans with frayed holes in them, tan oversized sweatshirt with sleeves cut short and navy tennis shoes. Only her clothes needed a bath, just like she did. He almost suggested she clean up before their food came but decided against it.

She was memorable, to say the least, with her painted face and feather adorned hair. She had a thin blue mask painted across her eyes, much like a Lone Ranger mask, but smaller, along with blue feathers clipped to her hair behind each ear.

He was right thinking she was hungry. She dived into her food like she hadn't eaten a good meal in weeks. Perhaps she hadn't.

After they finished eating she thanked him and left the diner. He was about to pull out enough cash to cover the check when he saw what was happening outside. His uneventful day had vanished.

"I don't want any trouble, deputies," Kaplan said while trying to analyze the situation.

"Doesn't look like that to me," growled the taller officer. The one with brown hair. "Why don't you tell that to Mark and Scott Pearson while they wait for the ambulance."

The two men outside were bullies who needed to learn to fight. One, unconscious—the other with a debilitating leg injury, neither going anywhere soon under their own power.

Now, staring into the mirror, he knew the shit-storm had just begun.

"Fellas, I didn't start this fight." Kaplan studied the reflection of the two jittery deputies and then the cook.

After a quick assessment, he decided to change tactics.

"Marine?"

The cook didn't answer, just nodded.

"Army. Delta." He wanted to roll up his sleeves, let the cook see his own Special Forces tattoos in hopes that might abate some of the tension in the room. At least with the cook, anyway, who was Kaplan's best chance in this situation. Perhaps his only chance.

"That was a long time ago," the cook said. "I saw what you did. Figured you were ex-military. I don't know you, but I do know the two guys behind you. They don't see much action around here, so I'd advise you to do as they say."

"They do seem a bit jumpy." He kept his palms flat on the counter and said over his shoulder, "You boys are making a big mistake."

"Save it for the town marshal," one of the deputies called out. "Now, put your right hand behind your back. Nice and slow."

The cook lifted the shotgun slightly, remaining just out of harm's way, and nodded a reminder for Kaplan not to try anything lest it be the last move he ever made.

While locking eyes with the cook, Kaplan obliged the young deputy. A metal handcuff clamped tight around his wrist. He felt a tap on the left shoulder.

"Other hand. Just as slow."

He rolled his eyes at the cook.

After the second cuff clamped tight, he was spun around where he stood face-to-face with the two young men. Mid-twenties, tops. One was taller, Kaplan's height with brown hair cut high and tight, buzzed on the sides and longer on top. He had a slim to medium build, unlike the clean-cut ginger deputy who could have been a weightlifter. The red-headed deputy was shorter by a couple of inches and stocky. His arms, neck, and face were freckled which matched his hair. Not a true carrot-top, more reddish brown. He was the jumpier of the two and probably Kaplan's biggest threat. Cocky and antsy—a loose cannon ready to explode.

"Not such a tough guy anymore, huh?" said Brown Hair.

"You know, kid." The word kid made Brown Hair's face turn red. Kaplan continued, "The two guys outside are the ones who should be in cuffs, not me. They pushed over my bike and knocked an innocent young lady to the ground."

"Scott claims you started the fight."

"Which one is Scott?"

"The one who is conscious. The one with the busted leg."

"He lied. I asked those two idiots twice to pick up my bike and help the girl to her feet. That's when one of them took a swing at me with a stick. I just defended myself. The cook can back me up."

The cook shook his head. "Sorry, man. All I saw was you take those two out."

Ginger holstered his weapon and puffed his chest. "You know what I think?" He didn't give Kaplan a chance to answer. "I think you're in some kinda biker gang just looking for trouble."

"I never look for trouble. If I wanted trouble I would have taken both of you rookies down."

Both deputies burst out laughing. "We aren't like those two outside. We've got weapons."

"They had weapons. A ninja stick and a knife. One day your carelessness will get you both killed. Ask this man here." He motioned to the cook. "He'll tell you. You," Kaplan chin-pointed at Ginger, "holstered your weapon leaving yourself unarmed." He eyeballed the other deputy, "You were standing too close. I watched your every move through the mirror. Before you cuffed me, I could have taken you and your gun." He returned his glare to Ginger. "Then, it would have been just you and me. One on one. And you would've lost."

Brown Hair looked over Kaplan's shoulder at the cook. "Is this guy for real? You think he really could do all that?"

"Pretty sure he could. Now, how about you and Doug get this guy out of my diner?"

CHAPTER 3

Kaplan sat on the cot in a ten-foot square jail cell with both feet planted on the floor.

Outside the cell, a small table and a single chair were pushed against a concrete block wall. On the table, his motorcycle helmet, leather jacket, keys to his Harley, and his wallet. In the chair, one of the deputies, the young clean-cut ginger. The one the cook called Doug. His head down reading a magazine, *Guns & Ammo*. Fitting. Above the table, mounted on the wall, was a dry erase whiteboard with the name Martin Joseph Wade, Kaplan's alias, written in black marker in the space under cell #2.

Kaplan propped his elbows on his knees and massaged his wrists. The over-zealous rookies had clamped the cuffs on too tight. He was glad when they were removed. His thumbs and fingertips had started going numb.

The deputy raised his head, closed his magazine, and placed it on the table. "Hey tough guy, how does it feel to be taken down by a couple of rookies?"

Kaplan said nothing.

After twenty seconds of silence, the deputy let loose an exasperated sigh and stood. "Maybe you'll talk to the town marshal. She don't take shit from no one." He rotated on his heels and marched out of sight.

Kaplan hoped the town marshal was more reasonable than the rest of the people he'd met in this town so far. With the exception of the Native girl, people in this town seemed to have a burr up their collective asses. He thought about the two neophyte deputies who arrested him at the diner, their lack of situational awareness might one day get them both killed.

Solitude had its way of allowing introspection.

Sitting alone in the jail cell his thoughts replayed the journey that had led him to this town.

His first Fat Boy, the one he'd owned for many years and had put over 200,000 miles on was destroyed a few months ago in Mayflower, Arkansas at the home of one of his childhood friends. Destroyed, as in bullet-riddled and burned. Months? *Shit.* In retrospect, it had been longer than months, it had been almost a year.

His job in the Clandestine Service of the CIA had all but ended. Officially, he was still on the payroll. *Paid administrative leave* the DD called it. Next, the Deputy Director took his creds and had a guard escort him to the compound exit—all the way to the gate. A government thank-you for getting the job done. He guessed his old friend was right, he didn't like following orders.

He'd been riding his Harley ever since.

A drifter to most, he had a nice home in Tyson Corner, Virginia along with a couple of fat bank accounts he had stockpiled while a covert operative. He'd learned a lot about small towns during his travels. When locals would hear the distinctive roar of his Harley rolling down the street, they'd stop and gawk. He imagined they judged him by his rugged appearance, a leather jacket covered in road dust, a bandana around his neck, worn boots and a beard in need of a barber. Some locals would say to him, "sweet ride," but others avoided him.

Not wanting to end up on the front page of the local newspaper, he minded his own business and, most times, was left alone. But, there was the occasional cop who stopped him and questioned his intentions for no apparent reason. He didn't mind the profiling too much. It was a tool he used in his career.

Kaplan wondered if the people in these small towns ever thought about why they could boast about having safe streets. What if the locals knew how many times he'd put his life on the line, so their cushy lives could go on being cushy? Or the number of people he'd killed in the line of duty to protect their freedom and rights? He was getting tired of trouble always finding its way into his life. And for whatever reason it always did.

And now, following a tip that led him to Last Chance, Wyoming, he was in trouble again. This time behind bars. At least for now, but his intuition told him it might be short-lived.

After several minutes, Deputy Doug finally returned. Along with him, a woman with smooth light brown skin and dark hair. She was dressed in snug blue jeans, a starched tan uniform shirt and a duty belt in a basket weave border patrol style with a brass buckle. Kaplan imagined she had the physique of an athletic woman by the way she held her broad shoulders and her small waist. Toned and firm, Town Marshal Christine Cavalier was an attractive woman. Aviator sunglasses on top of her head held her hair back like a headband. The muscles in her long face were rigid. A woman with a lot on her mind and in need of sleep. She reminded him of Isabella. His former partner. The woman he was searching for.

She strolled to the bars and studied him. Her dark eyes

roamed over him like a cop's probing eyes should. A threat assessment. One that all cops should make, but many didn't. Like what her two deputies didn't do when they confronted him at the diner. Doug the deputy handed her the driver's license he'd taken from Kaplan's wallet. She studied it, raised her head and locked eyes on Kaplan. "Says here your name is Martin Joseph Wade of Dubuque, Iowa. Turns out the only Martin Joseph Wade from Dubuque, Iowa was a one-term U. S. Representative who died in 1931." She handed the license back to Doug who placed it on the table next to Kaplan's wallet. She rested both hands on her hips. "Why don't you tell me who you really are?"

Kaplan hadn't moved from his seat on the cot. He turned away from the woman and didn't speak.

"We may be a small town, Mr. Wade, but I'll find out the truth one way or another."

In his peripheral he watched her spin around and storm out of the room, but not before saying, "Doug, take his prints and run them through AFIS."

CHAPTER 4

Town Marshal Christine Cavalier was careful not to lean back in her office chair since it was held together with rubber bands and duct tape. Budgetary constraints she was told. Her desk had been sanded, stained and painted so many times it was ready for the next garage sale. Besides a few file cabinets, this was all the furnishing that fit in her small office located inside the Last Chance Police Department and Municipal Court building. The pale-yellow century-old brick building was the only public building the Town of Last Chance owned. It consisted of three rooms—her office, a common room with two desks for three deputies and stackable chairs along the walls, and a 20 x 30 room that housed three 10 x 10 jail cells. And it provided a multitude of functions. Once a week, the common room served as Municipal Court presided over by a county judge who drove over from Sheridan—the county seat. Last Chance was part of the Sheridan, Wyoming Micropolitan Statistical Area. *Micropolitan?* Metropolitan she'd heard of, but micropolitan? As she later found out, there were both Micropolitan and Metropolitan Statistical Areas and Divisions, all part of some Office of Management and Budget Census Bureau government crap. Something the mayor, who also owned the saddlery shop, said was important to small communities in order to get federal funding. Without it, he said, the town would wither and die.

Four buildings, which lined Main Street housed four

different establishments. Immediately to the north of her office was the Crazy Woman Saloon, convenient on the nights when unruly patrons of the saloon were escorted by her out the front door of the saloon and directly to the jailhouse. North of the saloon was a saddlery and a pawn shop.

She was a woman in a man's world of law enforcement. She had worked her way through the ranks of the St. Louis Police Department, an uphill battle made even steeper by her heritage. In spite of the fact that her father was a retired police chief from the same department, she was female *and* a minority. Of sorts, anyway. Her father was white, and she was the product of an interracial marriage, which shouldn't make a difference in this day and age, but sometimes the lines of prejudice and bias run deep.

Cavalier prided herself on going the extra mile, putting in extra time and effort every day in her job. She had to in order to be seen as an equal to her male peers. And that's the best she could ever achieve. Equal. Although she outperformed her peers, her superiors always stamped *satisfactory* on her performance reviews. Until she made her first mistake. Then, she was no longer equal or satisfactory. She was inferior. Working in the good ol' boy system was so ingrained in her line of work, it was difficult to stay upbeat. The repercussions others had received for even greater gaffes were less severe than hers for something she didn't even believe was an error on her part, but rather her partner's.

After she filed an appeal and lost, she was *let go*. And that meant every law enforcement job application she submitted from that moment on was tainted by her past.

Her goal to follow in her father's footsteps had whittled down to this, a job as town marshal in the small foothills community of Last Chance, Wyoming. Not sheriff, not police chief, but town marshal. A title she didn't even know existed anymore. But, this was the West where traditions died slowly. The entire Last Chance Police Department consisted of the town marshal and three part-time deputies. Last Chance didn't have a budget to support a single full-time deputy. She was it, the only full-time employee in the police department as well as the only full-time employee of the entire municipality of Last Chance. And to make matters worse, two of the three deputies were actually supported by the city of Buffalo some forty-five miles away in Johnson County immediately to the south. And that was as the crow flew. By highway it was at least sixty miles. Fortunately, the two deputies rented a room above the saddlery next door, paid for by the city of Buffalo. The mayor called it a temporary *internship* training program. It was a deal worked out by her predecessor a couple of years back, shortly before he died of a massive heart attack while screwing Poppy's wife while Poppy was minding the Last Chance Diner. In Last Chance everybody knew everybody's business. The established place to trade gossip was Debi's Nail and Beauty Shop.

Now, Cavalier had to put up with the day-to-day routine of life in a rural foothills community. Her duties might range from investigating a fender bender to taking a complaint about a neighbor's dog pooping in someone's yard. There was one benefit to her job. Location. With serious four-season appeal, Last Chance was beautiful most of the year. Nestled in a wedge on the eastern slope of the Bighorn Mountains, Last Chance was surrounded on three sides by cliffs and craggy rock faces. The Pioneer River extended from somewhere up on Bruce Mountain to the west, down the Bighorn Mountain range, through Last Chance, and meandered aimlessly south-eastward for miles where it seemed to just vanish, gobbled up by the parched earth of the dusty high-desert plains. Except in the spring when snowmelt from the Bighorn Mountains raged down from the hills and the Pioneer River plowed all the way to the North Platte River.

The wedge at the southwest end of Last Chance was highlighted by a V-shaped canyon carved into the mountains by the Pioneer River. During the periods surrounding the Spring and Fall Equinoxes, the sun would set down the middle of the V, offering the most spectacular sunset she had ever seen.

The town of Last Chance was a little more than one-mile square with a U. S. highway called Main Street, running through the heart of town from north to south. To the north, Interstate 90 was only a ten-minute drive. To the south, the highway turned west and almost immediately transformed into a series of switchbacks as it ascended toward Sunset Pass.

There wasn't much to do in the tranquil town of Last Chance, but like most small western towns, it had everything the locals needed, one corner grocery store, a community church, a saddlery, a pawn shop, nail salon, and a post office open on Monday, Wednesday and Saturday. North of town, at the confluence of the Pioneer River and the Little Pioneer River was Pioneer Falls, a series of small waterfalls dropping a total of twenty-four feet and ending near Riverbend Park, the *official* social center of Last Chance.

The town had two restaurants—and that was stretching it—the Last Chance Diner at the center of the town's crossroads, and the Branding Iron Cafe and Campground at the edge of the mountains. Across Main Street from the Branding Iron were the Sunset Mountain Bar and the Sundown Motel. Like any descent western town, there were two watering holes. In addition to the

Sunset Mountain Bar with its balcony views of Sunset Canyon, the Crazy Woman Saloon to the north on Main Street provided variety to those seeking to slake their thirst or boredom.

Cavalier eased her chair back from her desk, stood and strolled over to the window. She gazed across the street not really looking at anything in particular. She settled her hands on her hips and thought about the stranger in her jail. The man who had beat up two of the town's bullies showed no defense wounds on his face or hands even though the odds were not in his favor. Mark and Scott Pearson were no strangers to her jail. Matter of fact, all of the Pearson sons, with the exception of the youngest, had frequented her jail over the past few months. They liked to drink too much and would end up escorted from the Crazy Woman Saloon to a jail cell. The Pearson family patriarch, the legendary land and cattle baron Drew Pearson, the single father of four boys, had the mindset that this was his town and local laws didn't apply to him, and by extension, his sons. Drew Pearson epitomized the image of the Western cowboy with his expensive handmade leather boots, Stetson hats and fleet of Ford pick-ups with plenty of horsepower under the hood to handle most of his large ranch duties. The eccentric man had been known to actually ride his horse into town, hitch it to the post in front of the saloon, and spend the afternoon inside drinking. His sons and ranch hands liked to make an entrance in town as well. They all looked like they had stepped out of an old western with their hats, chaps and spurs.

She didn't know all the circumstances surrounding the brawl outside the diner, but she was sure the two Pearson brothers deserved everything they got. According to Poppy, the owner of the diner and the cook as well, after the two brothers allegedly assaulted the young Native American girl,

Lucy Raintree, the stranger had moved with lightning speed and debilitating force. Poppy said about the stranger, "Kinda figured he was government trained." Poppy should know. He was a Marine in the Vietnam War.

There was something oddly familiar about the stranger, she thought, and it troubled her that she couldn't put her finger on it. He had dark features, dark eyes, and black hair that was starting to gray around the temples. He looked muscular and solid. His whiskers were thick and heavy, like the type of man who could grunt out a full beard in two or three days.

Her deputies had searched the bags strapped to his motorcycle and found nothing. They frisked him and found the man's wallet, which contained a driver's license, two matching credit cards, a prepaid cell phone, six hundred thirty dollars in cash, and a pocket knife. Nothing suspicious or out of the ordinary. Except that the name on his identification didn't match anything in the databases—not in Dubuque, Iowa anyway.

Her thoughts were interrupted when Doug walked into her office with a printout in his hand.

"Whatcha got, Doug?"

"I ran Mr. Wade's prints like you asked." He held out the piece of paper.

"They hit this fast?" She edged closer to him.

"Yes, but you're not gonna like what I found."

"Let me guess, his name isn't Martin Joseph Wade?"

"Don't know for sure." Doug shifted from foot to foot.

"What do you mean you don't know?" She pursed her lips. "What did AFIS say?"

"Restricted access."

She snatched the paper from Doug's hand. "Restricted access? How the hell can his fingerprints be restricted?"

"If he were —"

"Shut-up, Doug, I know how his identity can be restricted. It was rhetorical." She retreated to her desk, sat down and studied the printout. "Guess I'm going to have a come-to-Jesus talk with Mr. Martin Joseph Wade," she mumbled to herself.

CHAPTER 5

An hour had passed since Deputy Doug had taken his fingerprints. Kaplan sat on the cot in his cell and leaned his back against the cold concrete wall, waiting. She'd be back, and he knew she wasn't going to be happy. He heard the cell-block door unlock and sat up on the edge of the cot. The town marshal entered first, flanked by Deputy Doug.

"Well, Mr. Martin Joseph Wade," she said as she stormed toward his cell. "Seems we have something new to talk about. Please step to the bars and turn around."

He didn't move, waiting for the impatience to show on her face. Taking his time, he stood and ambled to the cell door keeping his eyes trained on the woman he'd traveled so far to see. Of course, not under these circumstances. And certainly not while he was behind bars. Her name tag simply read:

C. Cavalier

Town Marshal

Last Chance, Wyoming

The name his handler had found in his covert search. He could see the family resemblance, it was too strong not to. He liked her voice. It sounded familiar and made him think of the woman he had spent the past two years searching for.

"Now turn around and put your hands behind your back," she instructed.

He knew what was coming next. If he hadn't wanted something from her, he might not have been so compliant. Sometimes, like at the diner, resistance wasn't always in his best interest. He needed something from the marshal. Information. Perhaps he could persuade the town marshal to share. He *wanted* an explanation, but he'd settle for just about anything.

He turned around and backed up to the jail cell bars.

"Done this before, have you?" she asked.

He said nothing.

"Okay, Doug," she instructed. "Cuff him."

He felt the metal handcuffs clamp onto his wrists, one at a time, and squeezed snugly so they couldn't be removed without a key.

"Sit down, Mr. Wade," Cavalier said behind his back. He returned to the cot and sat, hands cuffed behind his back. "Open up, Doug."

"You're not going in there, are you? You heard what the witnesses said. He's fast and dangerous."

"Something tells me Mr. Wade will behave himself," she said. "Isn't that right, Mr. Wade?"

Silence.

"Doug, open the door," she repeated.

"But—"

"Dammit Doug. Open the goddamn door."

Doug had an expression of wide-eyed disbelief. He inserted the jail cell key and unlocked the door. Cavalier pulled the door open and paced to the cot where Kaplan sat and hovered over him.

"Lock it up, Doug. And if he makes a move, shoot him."

"Yes, boss," Doug said. "Gladly."

Cavalier sat on the cot across from Kaplan and leaned

forward resting her elbows on her knees. She opened her palms and said, "Here's my predicament, Mr. Wade or whatever your name really is. You beat up a couple of Last Chance's citizens and put both of them in the hospital over in Sheridan. I'll be the first to admit both are unsavory characters, but nonetheless, was that level of violence necessary?"

He peered into her eyes, which seemed to have hardened for the moment. She was taking some sort of diplomatic angle, but he knew her true purpose was not finding out what happened at the diner. "I gave them an out," he muttered.

"An out?" She sat up straight. "Please, do tell."

"All they had to do was pick up my bike and apologize to me and the young Native Indian girl."

"The Indian girl is Lucy Raintree. She was orphaned when she was thirteen and has run away from every foster home for the past four years. She just turned eighteen and is basically a drifter. She refuses to stay on the Rez, says it's not safe."

"The Rez?"

"The Crow reservation, five miles north of town just over the Montana line. And she's right, it isn't safe. Now, she lives on the streets or the town shelter in the winter. Disappears for days, sometimes weeks at a time, then just shows back up. She's no stranger to trouble herself. Sometimes when she returns, she's been beaten up, but I can't get her to talk about it or tell me who did it. Or even where it happened for that matter. I've picked her up a number of times for petty thefts, mostly food or clothes. Never arrested her for it. The diner's owner said you bought her breakfast. That was kind of you, probably the best meal she's had all week. When I interviewed Lucy, she stated she walked outside the diner one of the Pearsons kicked over your motorcycle and that's when they assaulted her. Your involvement is what got Poppy's attention."

"Poppy?"

"The diner's owner. Lucy seems to like you for some reason, Mr. Wade. When I asked what you two talked about, she said she was the only one doing any talking. She said you didn't even give her your name." She shifted sideways, pointing her knees toward him. "Speaking of names," Cavalier continued. "What is you real name? I know it's not Martin Joseph Wade from Dubuque, Iowa. I also know we were denied access when your prints were run through AFIS. Care to explain?"

He said nothing.

In the background, he heard the phone ring and was answered by someone who sounded like the other deputy, the one with the brown hair.

He raised his chin at Cavalier taking note of the pin with her name on it. "What does the C stand for?" He already knew the answer.

The deputy in the other room slammed the phone down on the receiver so hard it startled Cavalier and Deputy Doug.

She turned her attention to the cell-block door. Keeping her focus on what was happening outside the cell, she answered Kaplan, "Christine."

The deputy burst through the doorway.

"Jesse, what is it?"

"The Branson ranch house," Jesse sounded like he'd been running up a flight of stairs. "It's on fire and the LCFD volunteers are on the way."

Cavalier stiffened at the news. She stood, walked to the cell door and commanded, "Doug, open up."

Kaplan leaned forward and said, "Forgetting something?" He twisted his back and raised his cuffed hands.

She ignored him, locked his cell, then she and the deputies left the cell-block. He heard the lock on the cell-block door clank.

† † †

It was times like these when he questioned why he ever got involved in other people's problems. It usually only got him in trouble…or more trouble. It was Friday the 14th, although it felt like Friday the 13th with the luck he was having. Then again, bad luck had found him many times over the course of the past few years. Why should today be any different?

The town marshal and her two deputies had been gone at least a couple of hours. He had tried sleeping on his sides, to no avail. Every time he stretched out, the binding from the handcuffs tugged on his shoulders to the extent where sleep was impossible.

As he was thinking of what to tell Cavalier when she returned, he heard the cell-block door lock clank. The door flew open and in came a skinny young woman with blue paint around her eyes. Her jet-black hair was pulled back in a single braided ponytail. A blue feather hung on each side of her face. With a backpack slung over her shoulder, she plodded a deliberate path to his cell door, inserted a key and swung it open. As she walked toward him, he noticed her eyes, a striking light amber that didn't fit her native Indian heritage.

Lucy Raintree.

CHAPTER 6

By the time Town Marshal Cavalier had arrived at the Branson ranch house fire, the structure was fully involved. She was in the only town-owned vehicle, an older model white Ford Bronco that had seen better days and was now on its third town marshal. Her two intern deputies, Jesse and Doug, parked behind her in Jesse's brand new black Toyota Tundra, equipped with all the bells and whistles. A new truck his doting father recently bought him. The same father who thought it would be funny to name him Jesse, after the infamous outlaw, since their last name was James.

The large ranch home was built in the 1950s and was half brick and half weathered wood siding. The Branson ranch was approximately 1650 acres, give or take, large by many people's standards unless you were from Wyoming or Montana where it was considered a *hobby ranch*. Branson had a half a dozen horses, about a hundred head of cattle and acres upon acres of pigs. He bought the ranch as a foreclosure and had only owned it for a few years. The livestock were part of the foreclosure deal. She didn't understand why Branson bought the place, since he had allowed the ranch house to fall into disrepair from lack of maintenance and the livestock had dwindled in number.

She had arrived moments after the Last Chance Volunteer Fire Department and was promptly informed by the department's lead volunteer, that without a water supply or nearby hydrant, there wasn't much the small pumper could do until the fire started burning itself out. Strong winds were blowing smoke in their direction. She pulled a bandana out of her pocket and tied it around her face to keep the smoke from choking her. Flames had already spread across the roof and were ravaging the old home.

"Anybody inside?" she asked.

"Don't know, Marshal. Fire's too hot to send anyone in and the roof could come down any second. We're all going to have to sit here and wait. Make sure the wind doesn't cause a secondary grass fire."

She had been to this house on rare occasions. Richard Branson and his adult son, Stanley, shared the home and it was a well-known fact around town that their respective temperaments clashed, especially when they had been drinking. She had been called to break up a couple of father-son brawls, most times at one of the town's bars. Neither ever pressed charges against the other. No telling what caused this blaze, but her best guess was that alcohol played a factor.

As the fire spread, more flammable objects and furnishings ignited creating a denser plume of hot air and smoke. It took over two hours for the blaze to burn itself down enough for the pumper to start dousing the remnants with its limited amount of water stored in the tank. The roof of the two-story farmhouse collapsed at the thirty-minute mark. At one hour, burning exterior walls started to fall away from the main structure, what was left of it, which was nothing more than two interior walls and three brick fireplaces and chimneys.

She leaned against her Bronco, crossed her arms and watched the volunteer firefighters as they attempted to extinguish the smoldering flames of what was left of the farmhouse. She prepared herself for what she might learn. The possibility that people might have died didn't seem to faze her deputies. Jesse and Doug sat on the tailgate of Jesse's truck playing cards.

At the hour-and-a-half mark, lead firefighter—LCFD Chief Mike Hayes, a 50-year-old life-long resident of Last Chance—shouted that they had found two bodies on the floor and a handgun. As was procedure, something she was avidly going to follow, she immediately called the County Coroner's Office in Sheridan, Wyoming. He informed Cavalier he'd be there in thirty minutes. He instructed her to ask the fire department to vacate the structure as soon as feasible to prevent potentially disturbing any evidence. Cavalier yelled to her deputies, "Hey, get over here. Make yourself useful and find Fire Chief Hayes. Tell him to pull back until the coroner arrives. My orders."

"Coroner?" Jessie and Doug said in tandem.

"Two bodies inside. Probably the old man and his son."

The deputies exchanged puzzled glances and stood still.

"Go," barked Cavalier. "You two quit standing around wasting taxpayer money."

Thirty-five minutes later, a white van with the words SHERIDAN COUNTY CORONER painted on the side parked next to Cavalier's Bronco. She coughed from a cloud of dust the van had kicked up from the long two-track road that served as the Branson ranch driveway. The coroner opened the door and climbed down from the van.

Sheridan County Coroner Matthew Davidson was an older man, probably sixty-five, tall, thin and a little bit awkward. He had a head full of silver hair underneath his ten-gallon hat and a matching handlebar mustache. He didn't dress the part of a coroner, wearing cowboy boots, Levi's, and a blue-jean shirt. She had worked with Davidson in the past and considered him competent and a straight-shooter—meaning he hated interference from anyone with a political agenda.

She gave him a quick briefing before he went to work. He opened the side cargo door, replaced his cowboy boots with black work boots, slipped on a white lab coat, grabbed a small backpack and headed for the burned down farmhouse. Twenty minutes later, he returned and gave Cavalier his preliminary findings.

"Appears both victims suffered gunshot wounds to the head. Likely the cause of death, but I won't rule anything out until I've completed the autopsies in the lab. I took the liberty and called my office and have someone on the way to pick up the bodies to take them to the morgue. There's a weapon on the floor next to one of the bodies, looks like a .38, and the wounds on the victims are consistent with that type of weapon. Normally, I'd suspect murder-suicide except neither head wound appears self-inflicted, although not impossible. I also found five shell casings on the floor."

After Cavalier asked Davidson a few questions, she put two fingers in her mouth and whistled at Jessie and Doug. Both deputies were back sitting on the tailgate of Jesse's truck still playing cards. They jerked up their heads.

She hollered, "Let's go boys, we've got work to do."

CHAPTER 7

Lucy Raintree held up a metal ring with keys dangling from it and said, "Get up. This is a jailbreak."

Kaplan sat on the edge of his cot and smiled at the young girl. "I appreciate what you're doing, Lucy, but there's no need for you to get in trouble. I'll wait till the town marshal returns."

"No." Her voice was shaky. "We have to go now. It is not safe here. They are coming…and they will hurt me and probably kill you."

"Who? The town marshal? I doubt very seriously…"

Lucy shook her head. She fumbled with the keys and held up a different one. "The town marshal might not be back for hours. You are defenseless in here. He knows you put his sons in the hospital. He knows I am the reason you beat them up. He will come for revenge. We must go." She unlocked the cell door and pulled it open.

Kaplan shook his head. "You leave. I can take care of myself."

"Not in here you cannot. They will bring help. You cannot fight that many. I know what they are capable of. He has hit me before…this time he might hurt me. And he *will* want revenge for what you did to Mark and Scott."

Kaplan saw the desperation on Lucy's face. "Who are these people?"

"Please, mister," she pleaded, "we do not have much

time. We have to get out of here. I will explain later, when we are safe."

He ran through his options. He needed to talk to the town marshal, preferably alone, and breaking out of her jail wouldn't win him any favors. However, he was unarmed, behind bars, and presumably with a mob of angry men headed to the jail to get him. He couldn't let anything happen to Lucy. He stood and rotated around. "All right Lucy, unlock the cuffs. But, if I'm going to protect us, we do things my way from here on out. Understood?"

She waited a beat and replied a weak, "Yes."

After his hands were free he said, "Okay. Give me the keys." He held out his hand and she dropped the keys in his palm.

"Go stand watch by the front door while I get my stuff." He hurried out of the jail cell and over to the table where Deputy Doug had put his belongings. He shoved his wallet in his back pocket, grabbed his motorcycle keys and pocketknife. He headed toward the front door where Lucy was keeping watch. This was not playing out at all like he had planned. He still needed Cavalier's help. Without it, he might never get the answers he was searching for.

Lucy was waiting for him by the front entrance, peering out the window from side to side, no doubt looking for signs of trouble up and down Main Street. "Is the coast still clear?" he asked.

She nodded.

"You wouldn't happen to know where they put my bike, would you?"

"Probably the impound lot behind this building." She twisted and pointed. "Through that door."

"I'll be right back," he said. "You keep watching the street."

"Where are you going? Do not leave me here."

He let his hand rest on her shoulder. "I won't." He rushed through the back door.

It led to a small fenced-in area, perhaps forty feet wide and fifty feet deep. An eight-foot fence with a roll of barbed wired draped across the top. On the street corner side of the fence was a gate with an oversized padlock. On the opposite side was his motorcycle. He fished around in his pocket and pulled out his keys and unlocked his seat. Lifting it away, he reached down and twisted a metal plate out of the way revealing a keypad. He punched in a six-digit numerical password on a customized secret compartment. Inside the compartment was a bag wedged tight in the small space. He lifted the bag, grabbed the contents he needed, then stuffed the bag back into the compartment and reversed his previous steps, ensuring the compartment was locked before he rotated the metal plate back over the keypad. He went back inside, placed his motorcycle keys on the table in the cell room where he found them and joined Lucy.

"Anything yet?"

"Still all clear," she replied.

For the first time since they had met, he realized just how slightly built Lucy really was. He doubted she was five feet and no more than a hundred pounds. She had high cheekbones, a delicate face and amber eyes. She smelled as bad as the grungy clothes she was wearing looked. Life on the streets was a tough life, much more so for young people.

"Lucy, you know this town, I don't. Is there a hotel or someplace nearby where we can get a room?"

"You got money?" she asked.

He was surprised by her question. Her tone made it sound like she thought he was a drifter. Lately, he hadn't stayed in one place very long, but he did have a source of money.

"I bought you breakfast, didn't I?"

Her eyes narrowed, and she said, "I am not going to sleep with you, mister."

"Lucy, I won't hurt you. Of course, you knew that or you wouldn't have come to break me out of jail. If what you said is true, we need to get out of sight before trouble does arrive."

She lifted her chin. After clearing her throat, she said, "I am just scared, okay mister?" She wiped her eyes and nose with the back of her hand. "The only motel is on the south end of town, right before the highway goes into the canyon. There is a bar next door and a cafe across the street."

"Best way to get there and not be seen?"

"All the streets run parallel," she said. "I think we should go a couple of streets west off Main and head south. From there, it is only a fifteen-minute walk to the motel."

CHAPTER 8

The first problem Kaplan saw with Lucy's plan was a total lack of cover getting out of the municipal building onto Main Street. The second was the direct line of sight to the Last Chance Diner and the cook was outside sweeping the front walkway. Every few seconds he would scan the street toward the police department building. Perhaps he had seen Lucy go in and was watching and waiting.

"We need to go out the back," Kaplan said.

"The outside gate is probably locked."

Snatching the keys from the marshal's desk, he jingled them toward Lucy. "Lucky for us you found these. Now, wait here." He rushed out the back door into the impound lot and to the gate with the oversized padlock. He fumbled through the small keys searching for the right one. After a few short seconds he found a key with the name brand of the padlock, unlocked it, and cracked the gate open.

He went back inside and returned the keys to the exact spot where Lucy had originally found them. "Follow me." He led her to the bathroom and motioned to the sink. "Wash your face and take the feathers out of your hair."

"What for?"

"Trust me. Just do it."

Lucy blew out a puff of air, rolled her eyes and stomped over to the sink. After a minute of splashing, she walked back to the door with a hand towel held to her face. "What do I do with this?" She held up the towel, now stained with blue paint.

"There's a dumpster out back. You can toss it in there."

She followed him out the back door into the impound lot where he locked the door behind them. He guided her to the gate, swung it open, and pushed her through, locking the gate behind him. "Change of plans," he said. She twirled and was about to speak when he cut her off. "We go east first, then south. Will that work?"

"It will get us past the diner, if that is what you are wondering."

"That's all I care about at the moment." He grabbed her hand. "Let's move it."

It felt too hot for northern Wyoming, he thought, even though it was July. The sun seemed to be sizzling his exposed skin. He assumed that since Last Chance sat at an elevation of 5100 feet, there simply wasn't as much atmosphere to filter the sun's harsh rays. Hot and windy. He'd heard that the wind never stopped blowing in Wyoming, now he believed it.

The first north-south street was Broadway. He could see it only went one block north before it came to a dead-end. To the south, it seemed to go several blocks before stopping at a large building. The next street to the east was Boardwalk. To the north, the street seemed to end at a grove of trees. He pointed, "What's that way?"

"Boardwalk leads to Riverbend Park at a boardwalk that winds along the Pioneer River.

He glanced to the south. "Doesn't look like Boardwalk goes very far this way."

"It does not. Eventually we must go back to Broadway until it ends at the Last Chance Mercantile. Next to the Mercantile is a wooded open space with a path that leads south and west over a foot bridge that crosses the Little Pioneer River and comes out behind the campground and cafe."

Without a word, he began walking south. Within a few seconds, Lucy fell in beside him. "You know, mister," she said, "sometimes you are bad company."

"So, I've been told."

"So, no friends?"

"Not many. I travel a lot."

"You never even told me your name."

"Is that important to you?"

"See what I mean, bad company."

He replied, "Kaplan."

Squinting against the glare of the sun, she made eye contact with him and said, "What's your first name?"

"Most people just call me Kaplan."

"Okay. Mr. Kaplan it is."

"Just Kaplan," he replied with a hint of a smile.

A block later they went south on Broadway. Last Chance Mercantile was about two blocks away and he could see that it was one of the larger buildings in town. On the side lot, there were racks of lumber, ranch supplies, fence posts and several rolls of fence wire. Parked in front of the store was a row of 4-wheeler style ranch utility vehicles. Across the front facade of the building was a slogan — If we don't have it, you don't need it!

As they approached 7th Street, he saw something that stopped him dead in his tracks.

He recognized it immediately. He'd seen one, maybe this one, earlier this morning before he arrived in Last Chance. It was a black Dodge Charger with an orange stripe on the side with words written above the stripe. He knew from his earlier sighting the words said Wyoming Highway Patrol. The

Charger, with its light bar flashing, pulled to a stop in front of the Last Chance Mercantile. A trooper got out and hurried inside the store.

Kaplan grasped Lucy's arm and tugged her to his right.

She whispered, "We should turn here."

"Never a good idea to push your luck."

Not only was there a state trooper at the Mercantile, he spotted the town marshal's Bronco going north on Main. "Damn."

"What is it?" Lucy asked.

"Trouble." He pointed ahead toward Main. "Actually, double trouble."

Holding her arm, he directed her down the alley between Main and Broadway.

"Kaplan, what was it?" She yanked her arm free of his grip.

"The town marshal just drove by." He indicated with his thumb. "That way, toward the station. I'm guessing we have less than five minutes before the marshal knows I'm missing and then the dragnet will go out."

"Dragnet?"

"Search."

"That was going to happen sooner or later."

"I was hoping for later." He jogged down the alley hoping Lucy could keep up. When he turned to check on her, she was so close they almost collided. Not only was Lucy fast, she ran with stealth, like a cat. No pounding footfalls like his. No sound at all.

When they reached South Fork Avenue, the entrance to Cougar Rock Open Space was directly across the street.

She tugged his hand. "Follow me." Without bothering

to observe traffic, she led him across the street and onto the trail.

He threw a look over his shoulder toward the state trooper's car and was glad to see the man had not come out of the store. He knew that very soon the trooper would be searching for him too.

CHAPTER 9

Cavalier parked her Bronco on the grass space next to the police department building. She got out and stepped over the horseshoe impressions in the concrete sidewalk that led to her office door. A remnant from the past when a previous town marshal, rode his horse over the damp concrete leaving hoof prints indelibly stamped on the sidewalk. She wasn't sure why, but she stopped and did a quick look up and down Main Street before entering. All quiet on the home front, she thought. She walked in, made her way through the common room and to her office, placed her weapon on her desk, and sank down in her rickety chair.

She massaged her temples with her fingers and replayed the whole Branson ranch fire situation in her mind. The coroner told her that Richard Branson and his son, Stanley, had both been shot in the head, execution style. No way it could have been anything other than a double homicide in her opinion. Troubling her was that the coroner found five bullet casings on the floor but told her each of the Bransons had been shot only once. One bullet to the back of the head. The intensity of the fire, kindled by the old dry wood framing of the farmhouse, had destroyed most of the evidence. Locating any bullets from the other fired rounds had thus far proven futile, even with the metal detectors Jesse and Doug had used before she left the scene.

She thought they would find evidence of alcohol, but the Branson residence was completely devoid of any liquor bottles or beer cans. Strange, since she knew they both drank. It was almost as if the Bransons were attending AA. She snickered at the idea of those two at an Alcoholic Anonymous meeting.

On a more troubling note, the killer, whoever that was, had cleaned the scene before lighting the arson fire. That was what the Last Chance Volunteer Fire Department chief had ruled—arson. According to Fire Chief Hayes, the arsonist had used gasoline as the accelerant, leaving the emptied gas cans inside to be destroyed.

Adding to her worries was something the coroner had said. Davidson had indicated that due to the extreme heat of the fire, it was unlikely that the charred remains of father and son Branson would produce much information from an autopsy. According to Davidson, the fire was so hot that it was virtually as if the two Bransons had been cremated. Tissue samples, what little there were, would be used to obtain toxicology reports. Davidson said identification would now rely mainly on dental records and Cavalier doubted if any dental records even existed. The Branson men looked like they had never stepped foot in a dental office.

Jesse and Doug were still at the Branson ranch taking pictures and cataloging any evidence they could before cordoning off the property with police flagging. The entire crime scene weighed heavy on her mind. This was the first major crime in Last Chance since she took over from the previous town marshal. There had been plenty of smaller crimes, especially since the town was close to the Crow Indian Reservation. Natives and non-natives, for the most part, were like oil and water, they didn't seem to mix in society. At least not around these parts.

In northern Wyoming, there was plenty of petty

criminal activity that didn't involve Natives from the Rez. Ranch hands from surrounding cattle and horse ranches had the same issue. Cattle ranchers hated horse ranchers and vice-versa. The Crazy Woman Saloon next door to the jail seemed to be the melting pot for the ranch hands. She had to break up the usual two or three brawls per week, almost exclusively on the weekends when the ranch owners gave the wranglers a couple of nights off.

Even though the Branson father and son combo had been in trouble with her office in the past, she considered them no more than a nuisance. There had been no indication of any involvement in a major crime. *So, who could have killed them and what could possibly have been the motive?* The Bransons typically stayed out on their ranch, only coming to town for supplies and the occasional night out at the Crazy Woman Saloon. They both liked to drink and fight. On rare occasions, other patrons besides the Bransons would get dragged into a big fight, or *fur ball* as Jesse liked to put it, with Richard and Stanley Branson. But, never anything worth killing over.

For the two of them to be shot execution style and their ranch house set on fire, the Bransons must have gotten involved in something bad. She let out a long sigh. Solving these murders was her chance to prove she could handle something more than the petty crimes around town. Yet most of the evidence had been destroyed. First, she needed to get a positive ID on the victims.

ID.

Dammit, in all the excitement, she had completely forgotten about the man from the Last Chance Diner with the fake ID. It had been several hours since she, Jesse, and Doug responded to the Branson ranch fire. She skimmed her log. It had been well over three hours. And she had left him handcuffed this whole time. For that, she knew she should apologize, but that would never happen. After all, he did hospitalize Mark and Scott Pearson.

At that moment, Drew Pearson, three of his ranch hands and sons Stevie and Evan burst through her office door wielding baseball bats and crowbars. She leaped to her feet.

Speak of evil and it will appear.

"Where is he?" the Pearson patriarch shouted.

She reached for her weapon, but Stevie lunged and got to it first. He tossed it out of arm's reach.

"What is the meaning of this?" Cavalier's voice was high-pitched.

"Is he in there?" Drew Pearson pointed to the lockup room with his Louisville Slugger bat.

"Mr. Pearson, I'm warning you. Before you break any laws, I suggest you and your lynch mob leave my office and I'll forget you came barging in here and took my pistol. Otherwise, expect to wind up in jail yourselves." She aimed her finger at each man. "All of you."

"Sit down, missy," Pearson said. "And you won't get hurt. An eye for an eye. That's all this is, Marshal, an eye for an eye." He held his hand out. "I'll take those jail keys."

"Go to hell."

Before she could move, the two larger ranch hands grabbed her shoulders and slammed her down in her chair. She heard the rubber bands on the chair lever break. Stevie Pearson produced a roll of duct tape and held it front of her face. "Be still, Marshal, and you won't get hurt," Stevie said.

"I'll see that all of you go to jail for this."

While the two ranch hands held her down in her chair,

Stevie strapped band after band of the tape around her arms, pinning them to the chair's armrests. Next, he strapped her torso to the back of the chair so tight she felt her chest constrict. He leaned over to tape her legs when she kicked Stevie in the face with all her strength. She heard the crunch and saw the Pearson boy's nose wrench to the side. A cascade of blood gushed out. Stevie cocked his fist to strike her, but old man Pearson was fast enough to grab him. "I said no hitting, dammit."

"But—"

"Don't *but,* me. I told you, no one hurts the Marshal." He faced her and curled his lips upward. "Except me."

In a flash, Drew Pearson's swung his arm out and backhanded her across the face with such brutality that her head snapped to the side. She let out a loud moan. Her lip split open and she tasted blood in her mouth. Cavalier raised her head and said, "I'm gonna put your ass in prison for that, Pearson."

"Shut her up, will you?" Pearson motioned to the third ranch hand who strapped duct tape over her mouth. "Now find those keys and let's get what we came for." He shoved a ranch hand toward the desk.

Within seconds, the third ranch hand dumped the contents of her desk drawer onto her desk. Stapler, pens, paper clips, notepads, and the rattle of keys. "Got 'em."

While one of the ranch hands held her chair, and Stevie went into the bathroom to clean his bloody face, the other four stormed into the lockup. She imagined what was about to happen. The stranger might have been able to handle the two Pearson boys outside the diner with no problem, but this time he wouldn't stand a chance. Not against three vengeful men with bats and crowbars. And certainly not with his hands cuffed behind his back. She hoped they wouldn't kill him.

Last Chance was a town where people like Pearson got away with breaking the law. The cattle baron believed he owned this town and had connections in high places. Right now, she needed her deputies to show up.

As soon as old man Pearson entered the lockup area, she could hear him swearing. "Where the hell is he?"

Drew Pearson came back in her office and got in her face. She was puzzled at what was happening. Where was her prisoner? Drew's bad breath had the powerful smell of chewing tobacco. He ripped the duct tape from her mouth.

With gritted teeth he said, "Dammit, Marshal, where's the man who beat up my boys?"

With each word, the brown liquid from the tobacco dripped from his mouth down his chin and onto his shirt. He wiped his mouth with his hand and dried it on his sleeve.

The stranger wasn't in his cell? Only one of two possibilities, he escaped, or someone let him out of his cell. Her first thought was it must have been her other part time deputy Ken C. Standing Bear, KC for short, who took the prisoner. KC was a nickname he was given during his football days at the University of Wyoming in Laramie before a knee injury sidelined him during his senior year. KC was Southern Cheyenne, raised in southeast Montana, not too far from Last Chance. The Southern Cheyenne Reservation was just east of the Crow Reservation.

KC had the day off and was supposed to be taking his wife to Lander to visit her mother on the Wind River Reservation before he started his vacation. Perhaps his plans changed. There might be a good reason he removed the prisoner from his cell. He could have come back to town early and caught wind of the

Pearson's plan to break into the jail. If so, he would have taken a proactive move to insure the prisoner's safety. However, KC would have radioed her first, she reasoned. That couldn't be it.

Doug had run the stranger's prints through AFIS and was hit with a restricted response. Did that set off some sort of signal? If the stranger was some sort of government agent with a top security clearance, the FBI could have had ample time to have taken him. Or freed him. The only other option—the stranger had managed to escape her jail.

Pearson pounded his fist so hard on her desk, her muscles tensed. "I'm talking to you, bitch. Where's the man who beat up my boys?"

Cavalier needed to stall in hopes a few more minutes would give her deputies time to get back. She lied. "I knew you might do something stupid like this, Pearson, so I moved him to the Sheridan County jail for safe keeping. And the sheriff knows to keep an eye out for you."

The veins in Pearson's temples bulged and his face turned red. He shook his fists in the air and screamed, "You. Fucking. Bitch."

A deafening thud, then her head snapped back. A quick flash of darkness enveloped her senses and her body shut down.

CHAPTER 10

The Sundown Motel seemed fitting for a town the size of Last Chance.

On the southwest edge of town, the motel sat back from the highway, a rustic one-story strip motel with fifteen rooms that opened outside toward the road. The office was at the southern end, next to the Sunset Mountain Bar. Beyond the bar, was the end of town where the highway turned into a visible series of switchbacks as it climbed into the Bighorn Mountains.

Lucy had led Kaplan through Cougar Rock Open Space at a quick clip, slowing once the two of them reached the cover of several oversized cottonwood trees that lined the Little Pioneer River. A forested trail led them from the footbridge, through the Branding Iron Campground and out to the highway next to the Branding Iron Cafe. Across the street sat the Sundown Motel with a sign advertising rooms as low as $49 per night.

Kaplan gave Lucy $300 and explicit instructions on booking a room for three nights with extra cash in case a deposit was required. He stayed out of sight and waited for her to return with a key. Room thirteen, near the north end of the motel. Perfect, he thought. He walked to the back of the building and waited for Lucy to open the back window, something he had already checked out prior to sending her to get a room.

The space was standard for a cheap motel. Two full-size beds, a small bathroom with only a shower, a dresser with a television sitting on top, a mini-fridge, and a two-person dinette table with two chairs facing each other next to the rear window and overlooking the Pioneer River in the distance. The mottled pine paneling had probably been there since the '70s. The carpet had an unwelcome smell of cigarette smoke, as did the drapes on the front and rear windows. Not a *chocolate on the pillow* kind of motel. He'd stayed in much worse in the past, he thought, so it would do.

Kaplan and Lucy took turns watching the parking lot for any signs of the town marshal or her deputies. So far, nothing, which was good and bad. Why hadn't the marshal been alerted to his disappearance? Since he left his motorcycle locked up in the impound lot, the motel should certainly be one of the first places they searched, and Lucy Raintree should be one of the first people questioned. After briefing her on what to expect when the marshal finally tracked her down, she would no doubt convince the marshal and her deputies that she knew nothing of his whereabouts and had used the money he gave her at the diner earlier in the day to pay for the room. She rehearsed the lies and had not only sounded convincing but lying seemed to come naturally.

"When do you think they will come for us?"

"I'm surprised we haven't seen them already. When they do show up, stick to the plan." He inspected her face and clothes. "Do you have any clean clothes in that backpack you lug around?"

"What is wrong with what I have on?"

Kaplan scrunched up his nose. "For starters, you don't smell like a rose garden. You need a shower and a clean change of clothes."

She rolled her eyes. "Like you Kaplan, I also travel a

lot. She held the backpack tight against her chest. "This is all I have. I do not have a wardrobe."

"Does the Mercantile carry clothes?"

"They have everything at the Mercantile. You saw the sign."

He fished around in his pocket and pulled out his money clip. Unclasping the clip, he peeled off two hundred dollars in twenties and handed her the bills. "I want you to go buy some clothes and pick up an extra-large t-shirt for me."

Lucy eyed the roll of money, "Seriously?"

"Yes, seriously. You look like you—"

"Like I am homeless?"

"I was going to say you look like you could use some new clothes."

"Well, I am homeless, Kaplan."

Kaplan nodded. He could see the sadness in her young eyes.

She continued, "Homeless is probably the one thing I am good at. I know where to find the best free food in town. I made friends with a couple of owners and managers who let me use their bathrooms. Not the public bathrooms, but the clean ones in the back. It means a lot to have a clean bathroom to use. There are a lot of us homeless Indians. We are so common in towns near a Rez that we are invisible to most white people. We remind them of how horribly we have been treated by the white man. I am living proof of what the white man has done to Skins."

"I'm sorry Lucy. People can be cruel." He motioned toward the door. "When you get back, you can clean up."

"Do I smell that bad?"

He looked at her. "I've smelled worse." He pushed the

money in her hand and said, “But, I’ve also smelled better. Now, go buy you some clothes.”

“What if I run into the cops?”

“You know what say.”

“What about the Pearsons? What if I see them, or they see me?”

“Try not to let that happen. But if it does, get back here as fast as you can.”

“And if they follow me?”

“You just get back here. I’ll handle everything else.”

“Like you did at the diner.”

Kaplan gave her a sharp stare. “If I have to, yes.”

† † †

Lucy Raintree strode out of room thirteen at the Sundown Motel and made her way across Main Street. Just south of the Sunset Mountain Bar was theend of town and Main Street became a U.S.Highway again. At least, by name. Last Chance was small, like a mile from end to end and side to side. She had walked all over this town many times. She could cover every street, including all the neighborhoods, in just a few hours.

Last time she was at the Mercantile, the owner ran her off for panhandling. She was told not to come back unless she had money. This time she had money. It felt good to hold her head up high and show that asshole owner she could purchase what she wanted. She could not wait to see the look in his eyes when she laid down cash at the register.

Kaplan told her she smelled bad. She lifted her shirtsleeve to her nose and took a deep breath. It smelled okay to her. While she hiked through the Cougar Rock Open Space, she remembered how fast Kaplan had moved at the diner when those two Pearson boys knocked over his motorcycle and pushed her down. It was not her first run in with the Pearson brothers. She had never had anyone stick up for her like that before, especially a stranger. Kaplan was different.

For some odd reason, she felt safe with him. He was not very talkative, but when he did talk, there was confidence and authority in his voice. It made her relax. Maybe because he reminded her of her grandfather back on the Navajo Reservation in northern Arizona. Before he died, he was Chief of the Navajo Tribal Council and had been for as long as she could remember. Even though he died when Lucy was only ten, when she concentrated she could still hear his voice beckoning her. He called her Tadita, *one who runs*. A name that had proven prophetic. He said she always ran and hid when she did not get her way. What she was really running from was her parents' nonstop arguing and fighting. Sometimes her dad hit her mom, usually when he was drunk.

There was truth in what people said about Native Indians not being able to handle alcohol or drugs. Her parents were perfect examples. One night, when she was thirteen, her father came home from the casino in a drunken stupor and started hitting her mother. She and her siblings cowered and screamed. She could not take it anymore and ran out the back door. That was the last time she saw either of them alive. According to Navajo Reservation Tribal Police, her father shot her mother before turning the gun on himself. She went from foster home to foster home, but the murder-suicide of her parents followed her. She was considered bad blood. So, she ran again. As far from the Navajo Rez as she could. She spent a year on the Wind River Reservation in western Wyoming. She was Navajo and almost all the Natives on Wind River were either Northern Arapaho or Eastern Shoshone.

It was rare when anyone left the Rez and went to college to find a better life. Most young Natives thought education was not cool. It was the white man's way. For a Native to go to college would break with tradition.

When she arrived at the Last Chance Mercantile, the state trooper's car was gone. Good, she thought, unless he was out searching for Kaplan. In which case, not good. She did not want anything bad to happen to Kaplan. There were only a handful of cars and pickups in the parking lot, so she felt safe entering.

The owner stopped her at the door. "I thought I banned you from my store."

"No," she said. "You told me not to come back unless I have money."

"I said don't come back unless you have cash. So, do you?"

She dug into the pocket of her jeans and flashed her wad of twenty-dollar bills. "I just need some new clothes."

"You better not have stolen that money."

She shook her head and lowered it.

He stepped aside. "Get what you came for and get out. And no harassing my customers or I'll have the marshal haul you off again."

She eased past him and wandered to the women's clothes aisle. She had been in here before and was familiar with the layout. The clothes she was wearing came from the Mercantile. She found two new pairs of jeans, Converse tennis shoes, two blouses, socks, and undergarments before heading toward the cash register. Then she remembered Kaplan's t-shirt. She doubled back to the men's clothes and scoured the rack for a t-shirt she felt Kaplan might like. There was a bell on the front door that rang whenever anyone came in or out of the Mercantile. Each time the bell rang, she felt butterflies in her stomach and used the ceiling mirrors to check who had entered the store. She needed to hurry, get what she needed and get back to the hotel. Her hand was moving through the clothes hanging on the rack when the bell rang again. The man who walked in looked a lot like one of the Pearson boys, the oldest, Stevie. He had a bandage on his nose and looked pissed. If he saw her, she was in trouble.

She plucked a t-shirt from the extra-large rack and tucked it under her arm. She waited in women's clothes until Stevie Pearson had moved far away from the register. He went to the back of the store where the firearms, ammunition, and hunting supplies were located. She hurried to the register, took out a wad of cash and placed it on the counter.

The clerk eyed Lucy and crossed her arms under her oversized breasts. "Where'd you get all this money?"

"I am in a hurry, if you do not mind." She forced a smile toward the overweight clerk.

"My, my. Kids these days. Always in a hurry."

Lucy threw a glance over her shoulder toward the back of the store and saw Stevie Pearson at the firearms counter, his back turned to her. Her heart beating so fast, she felt breathless.

The clerk finished ringing the items. Lucy swooped up the bag and her change and dashed for the store door. The last thing she heard, was the clerk yelling, "Don't you want your receipt?"

CHAPTER 11

Cavalier regained consciousness with a jolt.

Disoriented, she kicked and nailed her deputy in the crotch before she was fully aware of her surroundings. Doug groaned and rolled away from the chair.

"Marshal," Jesse said. "Are you okay? Who did this to you?"

"Wha—"

"Marshal? Marshal?" Jesse gave her a slight shake. "What happened?"

"I have no memory of…" Her voice trailed off when she saw all the blood on her shirt and jeans.

Jesse kept cutting the bindings and said, "It was that man. The one we locked up. Wasn't it?"

"Pearson. It was Drew Pearson and his boys," she managed to say in a weak voice. "They came for Mr. Wade."

Doug managed to push himself to his feet and hobbled into the cell room. "Wade is gone," he yelled to Cavalier and Jesse.

Jesse spun Cavalier's chair around and put his hands on her shoulders. "Did Pearson take Mr. Wade? To get revenge for his sons?"

It was coming back to her, the timeline of events. Her vision was blurry. She blinked her eyes. Gradually her mind broke through the fog left by Drew Pearson's fist.

Jesse's voice was unsteady. "Marshal, are you okay? We need to get you to the doctor."

"No." She felt a surge of sharp searing pain in her head. "I'll be okay. Calm down. I need a minute to think." She leaned her elbows on her desk. "Go get the first-aid kit." She was silent a beat and then remembered. "He wasn't in there. That's why Pearson was so angry."

"Who wasn't there?" Doug asked as he walked toward the cabinet that held the first-aid kit. "Mr. Wade?"

She halfway dismissed what Doug had said. "Call KC. See if he came and took the prisoner."

"KC? KC is in Lander. He called Doug about an hour ago and asked if he'd fill in for him tomorrow morning, so he and his wife could get a jump start on their vacation."

"Oh shit, I forgot all about his vacation."

Doug brought the first-aid kit to Cavalier. "Damn, Marshal, Pearson did a number on you. Sure you don't need a doctor?"

"I said no." She looked at Jesse and motioned to the back door. "Check the impound lot. See if Mr. Wade took his motorcycle."

"His helmet and keys are still on the table." He pointed to the cell room. "Right where we left them. "His wallet is gone."

Jesse stuck his head out the back door. "Harley is still here, boss."

"How do you think he escaped?" Doug asked. He put the first aid kit down on her desk.

She processed this new development. "If Mr. Wade had escaped, he would have taken his motorcycle and headed out of town. If he's gone and only his wallet is missing, then someone must have come in here while we were out and taken him. That motorcycle looks brand new. He wouldn't have left it here on purpose. He didn't just escape, someone came and got him."

"Remember his AFIS hit came back restricted," Doug said. "Maybe the feds were monitoring, saw the hit, and came and arrested him while we were at the fire. I mean, it is plausible, right?"

It was plausible, but unlikely. She had even thought about that herself for a fleeting moment before Drew Pearson knocked her unconscious. "If the feds took him, why didn't they contact us?"

Jesse came up to her desk and stood next to Doug. "Maybe they wanted to remain anonymous."

Cavalier and Doug both looked at him. "Anonymous?" she said. "You don't take someone from a jail cell if you want to remain anonymous. Nor would you leave any trace he was ever here. You know, Jesse, like a motorcycle."

She felt her lip crack back open and licked her lips tasting the warm blood. Her face felt tight from the dried blood on her skin. "I'm going to clean up." She picked up the first-aid kit. "How about you two bozos call the FBI in Casper and Lander and see if they came and took Mr. Wade … or at least get a make on Mr. Wade's identification. Hell, give the Denver Field Office a try, too."

"Sure thing, boss," the two deputies said in unison.

She walked into the bathroom, flipped on the light, and closed the door behind her. Her hand touched her face. The cut above her left eyebrow was deep and seeping. The hand towel was missing, she tore off a handful of paper towels from the roll, ran them under warm water and patted them across her eyebrow. She used soap and warm water to clean the wound and the crusty blood from below her eye and her cheek and around her busted lip.

From the first-aid kit she took out cotton swabs, butterfly

bandages, antiseptic ointment and a package of ibuprofen. She immediately tore open the ibuprofen and popped two into her mouth drinking some tap water with her cupped hands. Next, she applied the antiseptic ointment to her eyebrow and used a butterfly bandage to keep it pulled tight.

She had a noticeable contusion above her left eyebrow, the result of the knock-out punch delivered by Pearson. A definite goose egg of a knot. Shiny red and prominent. It would be a few days before the swelling would go down. By then, she hoped she had Pearson and his band of hoodlums locked up in her jail. Or better yet, lying in the morgue in Sheridan.

She tossed the bloody towels in the trash can by the door and returned to her desk. Doug and Jesse were still on their phones.

Jesse cupped his hand over the mouthpiece and said, "Nothing with Lander. I'm on hold with Denver now."

Doug hung up his phone. "Nada with Casper."

She walked into the cell room and studied the area. Wade's handcuffs were left hanging on the cell door, one cuff clasped to a horizontal bar about head-high and the other dangling free. Right at eye level so she couldn't miss it. As if flaunting it in her face. The whiteboard above the table outside the cells had been erased clean.

She retraced her steps back to her desk. Jesse was still on the phone with the FBI's Denver Field office. Doug was twirling his pen through his fingers, something he often did when he was bored...or nervous. "Doug, take a look at the whiteboard and tell me what you make of it."

"Sure thing."

Doug walked into the cell room and, through the angle of the doorway, she could see him standing in front of the whiteboard staring and scratching his head. She heard him say, "Hmm."

Jesse hung up with Denver. "Same dead-end."

"Can you be a little more specific, Jesse?"

"I'm sorry, boss. They don't know anything about a Martin Joseph Wade from Dubuque, Iowa. I put the prints in the database and asked them to run a check. They got the same message as we did. I asked them to elevate the priority. After I explained what happened, they agreed."

"And?"

"And it's above their classification level."

"What?"

"The special agent I was speaking with elevated it and it turns out the Denver Field office of the FBI does not carry a high enough clearance to access the file on Mr. Wade's prints."

Doug returned and interrupted, "Who erased the board?"

She ignored Doug and listened while Jesse repeated his conversation with the FBI to Doug.

Something strange was going on and she needed to figure it out. Or better yet, she needed to find someone who did have a high enough clearance to access the classified file on Martin Joseph Wade. She could only think of one person with an inside connection...and that person was no longer capable of helping her out.

CHAPTER 12

U. S. Marshals Service Office
Chicago, Illinois

The alert popped up on his computer.

Senior Inspector Pete Moss raised his arms above his head, interlocked his fingers turning his palms toward the ceiling and stretched till he let out a heavy sigh. It wasn't like he was desensitized and ignored the warnings, he was just used to them being issued. Part of the job. Most alerts signaled the apprehension of one of the many fugitives on the loose, usually not even his cases. Every now and then though, the signal was about one of his witnesses, which meant he would be required to mobilize to locate and then relocate them.

Lowering his arms and relaxing in his chair, he scanned the new alert.

His muscles tensed, particularly in his neck. Squinting, he leaned closer to his monitor and reread the message.

It had been nearly a year since he'd loaded the information and hoped he'd never see an alert on this man.

This alert had nothing to do with the WitSec program.

This one was personal.

The fact that he had used U. S. Marshals Service resources not associated with the Witness Security program could see him facing a forced retirement or worse. Not that retirement would be a bad thing. He was past eligibility and had actually filled out his paperwork. He just found too many damn excuses not to submit his retirement paperwork to HR.

Number one on his excuse list was money. He liked Uncle Sam's lucrative salary and the benefits. Good health benefits that came in handy last year in his cross-country chase from Little Rock, Arkansas to Washington, DC after a witness's identity was breached. A chase that ultimately ended with a bullet in his leg. Fortunately, that wound had healed. So had his standing at the Marshals Service.

That was when he met the spook. The spook was a patriot who had served this country and saved countless lives in so doing. One of the elite in the Army's Special Forces and then a top agent for the CIA's war against terrorism. It was rumored terrorists considered this spook their number one threat. And rightfully so.

Moss always wondered if fighters were born or made and he was sure this man was both. The man could hit his opponent quick, hard and with little effort. Joking, he asked his friend if he had been trained by Bruce Lee. Power and speed he'd never seen before...or since. And all with deadly accuracy. The spook could take out his enemies before his enemies even knew he was a threat. Moss witnessed him organize and execute a raid against what appeared to be an impenetrable fortress on a rock of an island in the Caribbean. A lethal warrior.

Now, the very same agency the spook served had taken steps to all but disavow the man's very existence. And like so many of the duplicitous decisions the government made, it wouldn't completely sever the ties with him either. No, they put him on *extended administrative leave*. Government lingo for don't call us, we'll call you. Sooner or later they would call him when nobody else could get the job done. In the meantime, he was ordered to keep a low profile. Moss knew how that worked. Keep his nose clean, stay off the grid, and stay on the payroll.

And the man had done just that.

Until now.

Moss clicked on the alert. The alert was attached to every piece of information he had on his friend Gregg Kaplan. Fingerprints, name, and aliases—the ones he knew about anyway. This alert originated somewhere in Wyoming. A municipality called Last Chance, wherever that was. Hell, he barely knew where Wyoming was, much less Last Chance. Out West somewhere. Far west of Chicago that was for damn sure. He opened his web browser, loaded Google Maps, and typed "Last Chance" in the search bar. He had two choices for towns, one in Colorado and one in Wyoming. He clicked Wyoming and the application zoomed in on a speck of a town just south of the Montana line and just east of some mountains. Last Chance, what kind of town name was that? He hoped for his friend's sake the name of the town wasn't prophetic.

"Come on, Kaplan, what the hell are you up to now?" Moss said out loud. He read the inquiry. Turned out the name associated with Kaplan's prints was a Martin Joseph Wade of Dubuque, Iowa. This was a new one for Moss, not an alias he knew anything about. The physical description was a perfect match for Kaplan, right down to the tattoos on the man's arms.

For Moss, to get involved now meant he would probably be forced to retire when this was over. Furthermore, would Kaplan even want his help? The man was certainly capable of taking care of himself. They had developed a bond last year and kept in touch with a few phone calls over the course of many months, each time saying they needed to get together again but never did. Those phone calls slowly tapered off. No one to blame, they were equally guilty of not following up. He realized it had been almost three months since the two had last spoken.

He had to admit it, as dangerous as last year's run with Kaplan was, it ranked as the most exhilarating time of his life. He learned a lot from the spook and developed a new respect for covert operatives. Perhaps, he was even a little jealous. That was something Kaplan did every day in his job and Moss had only done it once. Sure, his job as a WitSec Inspector had its moments, but nothing like what he had encountered when he met Kaplan. No life or death situations. Mostly paper pushing to get witnesses into the program and transporting them to their relocation areas. Determining safe zones and hostile zones. The occasional follow-up and once in a rare occasion, a breached detail that had to be dealt with, like the one that brought him and Kaplan together in the first place.

Moss knew several PODs who had been involved in heavy gunfire incidents, but the basic job description of the *plain ole deputy* was different than the WitSec Inspector. Many times, PODs were called in to assist WitSec, but not the other way around. Moss' career had been, for the most part, uneventful. Until last year. He attributed a lot of it to his size. At 6' 4" and a solid 275 pounds, most detainees didn't give him any resistance. But, on rare occasions, it did happen. Moss slapped his belly a couple of times, maybe not rock solid anymore.

Another alert popped up on his computer screen a while later. This one also had to do with Kaplan. More alarming than the first one. Seemed his friend was abducted from his jail cell and whereabouts unknown. He read the circumstances as reported by law enforcement in Last Chance, Wyoming. The hair on the back of his neck stood up. Kaplan could be in serious trouble. The report was submitted by Christine Cavalier, Last

Chance's Town Marshal. He didn't even know there was a such thing as a town marshal.

He kept his eyes focused on his computer screen, mapped the location of Last Chance, clicked the "Directions" icon on the Google Maps display and entered his location. *Damn Kaplan, can't you get in trouble a little closer to Chicago?*

Fastest route, seventeen hours nonstop driving. Eighteen if he was lucky. Probably closer to nineteen by the time all was said and done. He clicked print. If they still had town marshals out west, then there might not be a lot of cell towers he reasoned. He tried to call his friend but got no answer.

In nineteen hours, a lot could happen to change the dynamics of the situation, but he knew he couldn't sit idly by knowing his friend's life could be in danger. He had to help… somehow. He checked airports and flights. Even at nineteen hours, it was just as quick to drive. And that meant driving all night. Traffic would be lighter, but he'd be driving across some desolate country. He'd need to load up on coffee.

He picked up his phone and made a quick call to his Supervisory Inspector. Five minutes later, Moss had locked his desk and was headed for the exit with the next two weeks of leave approved. As he rode the elevator down he mumbled, "Hang in there buddy. Help is on the way."

CHAPTER 13

When she thought of Martin Joseph Wade and his restricted access AFIS file, Cavalier's sister, Isabella came to mind.

Her file was probably restricted as well.

She and Isabella were a year apart in age yet in high school most kids thought they were twins. They were almost exact photocopies of each other. It aggravated her when her teachers who had taught her older sister called her the wrong name. Even in college at Amherst they were mistaken for each other. By then, she didn't think they looked alike at all.

Although they favored each other, their personalities were not the same. Cavalier loved music, especially jazz. Mostly, she liked playing musical instruments. Her favorite were horns, particularly the saxophone. She even found herself in a couple of jazz bands during college.

Isabella, on the other hand, was a bookworm and a history buff. One day her sister brought home a library book about ancient ciphers. She seemed fascinated by them. Most were too complicated for Cavalier, but not Isabella, the more complicated the better. That's why it came as no surprise when Cavalier found out that Isabella was hired as an analyst with the CIA. It was right up her sister's alley. Later, she became an operative. Isabella's life always seemed exciting, jetting to so many exotic foreign cities.

Jesse's voice interrupted her thoughts. "Marshal, what do you want us to do?"

Cavalier blinked several times, focused and saw the time on the wall clock. It had been barely six hours since Jesse and Doug had arrested the stranger. It had been over four hours since she left him locked in his cell alone. Four hours was a long time. Whoever came and got him out of jail could be hundreds of miles away by now. She couldn't sit idly by. She needed a dragnet.

"Jesse, you and Doug check the campground and the motel. See if anyone fitting Mr. Wade's description checked in. And check Sunset Mountain Bar."

She typed on her computer and Jesse and Doug's phone dinged. "That's Mr. Wade's photo."

"You want us to warn people he's dangerous," said Jesse.

"No," she said curtly. "We don't have reason to believe he's dangerous. The Pearson boys weren't innocent in that fight. I don't want to put the town on edge. Your job is to locate him, nothing more. If you see him, call me. Do not engage him. Understood?"

Jesse and Doug nodded.

Rolling up her sleeves, she continued, "Also, check the Branding Iron Cafe while you're down there. When I'm done here, I'll handle Crazy Woman and the Last Chance Diner. I'm sure Poppy will be thrilled to hear that Mr. Wade is missing."

Again, Jesse and Doug nodded their understanding and left the marshal's office.

Cavalier walked two doors down to the Crazy Woman Saloon and showed the bartenders the picture of Mr. Wade. They shook their heads and told her the man had not come in the bar. She left instructions to call her immediately if they saw him. Next, she went across the street and down a block to the Last Chance Diner. The ibuprofen had worn off and now the pain had returned.

She entered the diner door. The owner of the diner, who did most of the cooking, was sitting behind the counter on a bar stool reading the *The Sheridan Press*. "Hey, Poppy."

He raised his head. "Damn Marshal, what the hell happened to you?"

"Drew Pearson came for the man we arrested in here this morning. He did this."

"Who did? Drew or the man you arrested? I mean, I saw what he did to those two Pearson punks in the parking lot. Did that sonofabitch do that to you?"

"No, this is Drew Pearson's handy work. And when I do find that sonofabitch, I'm gonna lock his ass up for a long time." She grimaced. Her anger made the pain in her head feel like a drum roll.

"You okay, Marshal?"

"Just a headache. Got some water?"

She reached in her shirt pocket and pulled out another packet of ibuprofen. Poppy handed her a glass of water and she washed the pills down.

"Thanks."

"What'd he do to your prisoner?"

"That's what brought me here. Seems my prisoner was removed from his cell before Pearson came for him. That really pissed old man Pearson off." She reached inside her jean pocket, retrieved her phone and showed him a photo of Mr. Wade. "You haven't seen him again, have you?"

He reached under the counter, brought out his shotgun and placed it on the bar. "Nope, but I'll be ready for him if he comes back in here."

"That won't be necessary. First of all, that's my job.

Second, if you do anything illegal, I'd have to arrest you, too."

He shook his head and was about to speak when she interrupted. "Besides, I don't think he's a threat. You yourself said it looked like he was defending Lucy Raintree. The Pearson boys probably started that fight. Mr. Wade just finished it. Those boys are just like their father. Bullies and hoodlums."

"You're right about that, but that guy isn't somebody you want to mess with. I got an uneasy feeling about him. He's ex-military all right but I never seen anybody fight the way he does."

"Like I said, let me handle Mr. Wade."

"Mr. Wade? That's his name?"

"That's what his driver's license says."

"But?"

She hesitated a second, cleared her throat and said, "If you see him, call me ASAP."

"Will do, Marshal. But just so you know, I won't be having any trouble in my diner." He patted his shotgun.

She handed him back the glass of water, glanced at his shotgun and said, "Thanks for the water."

CHAPTER 14

Lucy had been gone over thirty minutes.

Kaplan parted the curtains and looked out the window through the sheers. Not that he was worried. Not yet anyway. He let his internal clock calculate the time it took for the two of them to walk from the Mercantile to the motel. A good fifteen minutes, give or take. His military career had taught him an important lesson in life—be patient. He'd give her another fifteen or twenty minutes before he would be concerned. He had given her specific instructions and made it clear that the longer she was in the open where she could be seen, the more likely it would be that someone would remember seeing her.

Being alone gave him an opportunity to dissect what was going on. He liked small towns, however he wasn't sure they liked him. What had started as a manageable situation had already escalated. Not yet out of control, but well on its way. Once again, he was a wanted man. And once again, reluctantly dragged into someone else's problem.

This time, it was Lucy's problems. The young girl could probably take care of herself as far as being street-wise, but she wouldn't stand a chance of staying out of harm's way if that many men came after her.

If?

That was the crux of the matter.

If Lucy was telling him the truth about Pearson's men.

If there even were any men. His extensive training

and experience gave him a built-in lie detector for reading people. His boss had told him he was better at it than most FBI profilers. It was true, until he discovered the limitations of his own mind. Until that one time when he didn't want to see the truth, so he didn't. It had cost lives. Now he was accused of lacking emotion. That wasn't true. He just no longer allowed himself to trust anybody. That was why he was still breathing.

Even though Lucy was young, she was no different. He would keep his guard up around her. She was afraid of something or someone, that he could tell. He believed there was some element of truth in what she told him. How much was another issue altogether.

Now that he was considered an escaped prisoner, the town marshal would be less likely to listen to him or help him—and he still needed her help. First, he had to neutralize the threat, if there was one. He would know that soon enough.

He would go along with Lucy's story for now, until he had reason not to. His gut told him this situation was going to get messy. His Beretta Px4 Storm 45 was tucked in his pants in the small of his back and his Walther PPK 22 was inside the special holster sewn into his right boot. Although a small caliber weapon, the PPK was a good backup and had bailed him out on more than one mission. Besides, caliber didn't matter as much as accuracy. Its biggest drawback was accessibility. He had to lift his pants leg to retrieve it. Practice made perfect and unfortunately for many, he was quite adept at quick retrieval of the small weapon.

He watched out the window as a large black pickup cruised through the parking lot toward the front office. Across the street he noticed Lucy coming from the trail next to the campground. She stopped and stood next to the highway waiting for a semi rig to drive by, the same semi that had been unloading boxes at the Branding Iron Cafe for the past thirty minutes. The rig passed by and Lucy ran across the street. As she turned toward the room, the black pickup stopped in front of her, blocking her path to the motel room.

Kaplan drew his Beretta.

† † †

Lucy froze when the pickup skidded to a stop between her and the motel. She knew the truck. It belonged to Jesse, one of the Last Chance deputies. She had seen the two deputies in it many times. Both doors opened, and the two deputies got out and approached her. She nervously glanced at her motel room and back at the deputies.

"We have some questions for you, Lucy," Jesse said.

"I do not have to answer your stupid questions."

"Are you trying to hide something?" Doug asked.

She held the bag of clothes tight to her chest. "Like what?"

"For starters, what's in that big bag?" Jesse propped his hands on his hips. He looked at the motel. "And where are you going?"

"I do not see where that is any of your business."

Doug held up his phone. "Remember this guy? The man you said came to your rescue this morning? Seems he's missing."

"You wouldn't have seen him since this morning, would you?" Jesse asked.

"Good for him," she said sharply. "His only crime was protecting me, and you two bozos threw him in jail. Those

Pearson boys got what they deserved."

"Well, those Pearson boys' father came to get Mr. Wade this afternoon and bloodied up the marshal pretty bad. Fortunately for this man." He held up the picture again. "He had already busted out of jail…or was busted out of jail."

"What about it, Lucy? Know anything about it?" Jesse pressed.

"Nope."

"Then I'm sure you won't mind us looking in that bag, will you?"

"Yes, I do mind." Lucy squeezed the bag tighter.

Doug stepped forward and ripped the bag from Lucy's arms. "Well, we're gonna do it anyway. If you have a problem with that, take it up with the marshal."

Doug took the bag to the truck and emptied the contents on top of the hood. "Let's see what we've got here," he mumbled. "Two pair of pants." He held them up. "Damn, these are small. Socks, tennis shoes, panties, two women's shirts and—"

"Blouses," Lucy interrupted.

"What?"

"They are blouses. Men wear shirts, women wear blouses."

He rolled his eyes. "Whatever." Doug held up the dark blue t-shirt. "What's this? Certainly not your size. So, Lucy." Doug smirked at her. "What are you doing with a man's extra-large t-shirt?"

She stepped to the hood of the truck and grabbed the shirt. "Have you ever heard of a sleep shirt? It is more comfortable than wearing pajamas."

Jesse looked at the motel again and back at Lucy.

"Where are you going with this stuff?"

"I do not have to tell you anything." She curled her fingers into her palms. "Now, give me back my clothes."

Jesse grabbed her arms from behind and held her tight. "Search her for a key," he said to Doug.

She twisted, kicked and screamed, as Doug patted her down and forced his hand into her back pocket. He pulled a key from her back pocket and held it in the air. "Room thirteen."

Jesse relaxed his grip and she jerked her arms free. "Can I have my stuff back now?"

Jesse winked at Doug. "Let's check it out."

Lucy stuffed the t-shirt along with the rest of the clothes she had purchased from the Mercantile back into the bag and protested as the two deputies dragged her all the way to the motel room door.

Doug unlocked the door to room thirteen, swung it open and both deputies entered her room. After a twenty-second search, including under the beds, all the drawers, and the bathroom, Jesse faced her and asked, "How'd you get the money for the room and clothes? Don't tell me you won the lottery."

"What business is it of yours?"

"You can answer here or down at the marshal's office."

"If you must know." She motioned at Doug's pocket where he stuffed his phone. "That man in the diner this morning, he gave me money. He said I smelled bad, needed a shower and some new clothes. I told him I did not have any money, so he gave me five hundred dollars."

"Whoa, that's a shitload of money," said Doug. "He's right, you do stink and those ratty clothes you're wearing need to be burned. Riddle me this, Lucy Raintree, why would someone you just met give you that much money?" He stared at her and raised an eyebrow. "Unless he wanted something in return?"

"I told you. He was a nice man, unlike some people I know. I guess he felt sorry for me or something. Then you two assholes had to throw him in jail. For nothing. His only crime was helping me." She walked over to the phone on the nightstand and said, "Now, get out of here and leave me alone or I will call the marshal myself."

Jesse paused and gave a one-shoulder shrug. He turned his head slightly toward the door and motioned. "Come on, Doug. There's nothing here. We still need to check the campground and cafe."

The two deputies left the room. Lucy closed the door behind them, eased to the front window, and peeked through the break in the curtains.

That was a close call.

CHAPTER 15

Cavalier checked her watch again and wondered why her deputies hadn't returned to the station. They had been gone over an hour—enough time to scour the town twice. It was approaching 4:00 p.m. and she wanted to get Doug and Jesse and what small arsenal they could gather and go arrest Drew Pearson, his two boys, and three ranch hands. Fortunately, her head wasn't pounding quite like it had earlier and it seemed the swelling of the goose egg on her forehead seemed had gone down.

Several minutes later, Doug and Jesse walked in the station.

"Where the hell have you two been?" she asked.

Jesse said, "We were doing what you asked. No one at the Branding Iron, Sundown, or Sunset has seen Mr. Wade."

"We ran into to Lucy Raintree," Doug added. "At the Sundown. Seems Mr. Wade was kind enough to give her $500 for a motel room and some new clothes."

Cavalier suppressed a groan. Doug had been known to hit on Lucy from time to time. And every time, the girl shot him down. Cavalier spun her head toward Jesse instead, the older and more mature of the two deputies and asked, "Say what?"

Jesse repeated the story Lucy told them at the Sundown Motel, including the fact that, without her permission, they'd searched Lucy, her belongings, and the motel room. "The only thing out of the ordinary was that she bought a man's extra-large t-shirt."

"And that didn't set off any alarms in your head?"

"Yes. That's why we searched her room. She said she bought it as a sleep shirt."

"That's not as uncommon as you might think," she explained."

Cavalier twisted back and forth in her chair. Most of the story sounded legit, except for the part where Mr. Wade gave Lucy $500. That was a lot of money to give away to a charity case, but Cavalier didn't know anything at all about Mr. Wade, except that was not his real name. Maybe he had a soft spot for charity cases or maybe he gave her the money for another reason.

"You didn't find anything suspicious in the hotel room?"

Both deputies shook their heads.

Cavalier had a dilemma. Her revenge mindset was to get Jesse and Doug and head out to the Pearson spread and arrest everyone. Her concern was she knew Drew Pearson would be expecting her and wouldn't go peacefully. If she started something with him now, a standoff might drag into the night, or all night. Her logical mind told her not to poke the bear and leave Pearson for another day. It wasn't likely he was going anywhere anytime soon. Her number-one priority was to locate Mr. Wade. Or at least figure out what happened to him and how he managed to get out of her jail.

And then there was the matter of Lucy Raintree. How did she fit into all of this? Maybe Lucy got lucky and the man was just being kind. But no. There was more to it. She could feel it. She realized she needed a face-to-face with Lucy Raintree.

"You two take the rest of the night off but keep your phones on in case something comes up."

Doug stood and tucked his thumbs in his front pockets. “Aren’t we going after that asshole Pearson?”

She knew to be careful with her words. Her two naïve deputies wanted revenge for what Pearson had done to her. “I don’t think we should plan a raid on the Pearson ranch this late. Daylight is better, and we won’t have much of that left. You two know Drew Pearson. You can bet he isn’t going to let us just march in there and arrest him, his sons, and his ranch hands without a fight.” She rubbed her tongue over her busted lip. “I don’t want either one of you going out there tonight. That’s an order. Do we understand each other?”

Jesse and Doug nodded.

“Now get out of here and I’ll see you in the morning. At that time, we’ll work on a strategy to take down the Pearsons.”

† † †

Cavalier cruised behind the back of the Sundown Motel and parked her Bronco in front of room thirteen. The curtains on both rear and front windows were open and she could see Lucy Raintree’s small silhouette through the sheers. She was tousling her hair with a towel.

She patted her gun, a subconscious habit. Before she left the station, she’d put on her tan baseball style cap and tucked her hair through the sizing strap on the back. It was the official cap of the Last Chance Police Department, including a sewn-on patch brandishing their office logo. She stepped out of the Bronco, walked to the door and knocked.

A few seconds later, she heard a chain rattle and Lucy cracked open the door. Her hair was wet. She was wearing her new clothes, skinny leg jeans, a t-shirt and black, low top

Converse tennis shoes.

Cavalier saw the shock on Lucy's face before she could hide it.

"What do you want?"

Cavalier removed her aviator sunglasses and hung them on her shirt. "Lucy, I'd like to ask you a few questions about Martin Joseph Wade."

"Who?"

"The man who helped you this morning."

"You already did that. And so, did your deputies, about an hour ago."

"I know. That's why I'm here. I have some follow-up questions if you don't mind. May I come in?"

"What if I do mind?" Lucy raised her chin.

"Simple." Cavalier gestured with her thumb toward her Bronco. "Either talk to me here or down at the station. I'll let you make that call."

"What is it with you people? If someone does not want to talk, you just haul them to jail?"

"Well, yeah. That's kind of how it works."

"Fine." Lucy stepped back and waved her in. "I hope you are happy now."

Cavalier stepped in and took careful notice. Two beds, one piled with clothes and the other untouched. No tell-tell-sign that anyone other than Lucy had been in the room. She gestured to the table by the windows with the two chairs. "Why don't we sit there and have our chat?"

Lucy hesitated a bit, flipped her wet hair back with her hand and said, "Fine."

Cavalier repeated the same questions that Jesse and Doug had asked earlier. Lucy's answers seemed consistent with the deputies' version. Too consistent. As if her answers had been rehearsed. And if that was true, Lucy knew more about Mr. Wade than she was letting on. One thing was clear, there was no indication the man had ever stepped foot in this room.

"Why do you think a man you had just met and didn't know from Adam would give you $500?"

"How should I know? He hardly said a word. I was nervous and just kept rambling."

"What about him made you nervous?" Cavalier asked.

"I never said *he* made me nervous. I was nervous because Mark and Scott Pearson were sprawled out in the parking lot. Sooner or later someone was going to see. Actually, Mr. Wade made me feel safe. He and KC are the only people in this town who have ever stuck up for me."

"How did you know his name?"

"Seriously? You just said his name when you came in. Not five minutes ago."

"I did, didn't I?"

"Honestly Marshal, you are not giving me a warm and fuzzy feeling right now."

"Well, Miss Raintree, I've had a pretty tough day, so I'm not in the mood to take any shit from anybody."

Lucy's face twisted. "Did old man Pearson really do that to you?"

"Yes."

"Why are you not out arresting him instead of giving me a hard time?"

"Drew Pearson will get his in due time. Right now, I'm concentrating on locating Mr. Wade before Pearson does."

"Mr. Wade can take care of himself. I saw what he did to Mark and Scott."

"And so did Poppy at the diner. I'm the town marshal and it's my job to not only apprehend someone who escaped from my jail, but also to keep him safe while he awaits arraignment."

"What makes you think he is not long gone?" Lucy asked.

Gut instincts were something cops have relied on for years. Cavalier's father had always told her, "Never buck your gut." She studied Lucy. Her gut told her Lucy was lying…and telling the truth. Figuring out which part of teh story was which would be a challenge.

"Let me tell you what I think, Lucy. I think some things about your story don't add up. I don't think Mr. Wade left town. I think he's still in Last Chance. I think you know more about Mr. Wade's whereabouts than you're letting on." She got up and stared down at the girl. "And, if I find out you've been helping him, I'm going to throw your tiny ass in jail too."

CHAPTER 16

Cavalier sped away from the Sundown Motel seething, tires of her Broncos spraying gravel ten feet behind pinging off other cars in the parking lot. She didn't care. She had spent too much time with Lucy and didn't like being strung along. It was getting dark fast. The sun had set behind the Bighorn Mountains while she was talking to Lucy and she watched the street lights turn on one by one as the photoelectric cells activated by the lack of sun light.

It had been one hell of a day. First, a stranger had come into town and beathad up two brothers. Not that they didn't deserve it. By all witness accounts, he might have done her a favor by putting them in the hospital in Sheridan and keeping them off the streets of Last Chance for a few days. Next, she found out the stranger's identity was restricted. Or, at least protected, for some reason.

Next, the Branson ranch house burned to the ground and the bodies of Richard Branson and his son Stanley were found inside with gunshot wounds to the head. According to the Sheridan County Coroner, they were shot execution style.

She returned from the fire only to be attacked and beaten by Drew Pearson. And on top of that, her prisoner was nowhere to be found. And, of course, Lucy Raintree.

Lucy was hiding something. Her bet was on the whereabouts of Mr. Wade.

"She slammed her palm against the steering wheel.

Her head started throbbing again. She hadn't eaten

anything since breakfast. She was tired, hungry, her headache had returned, and now she was pissed. How could this day get any worse? Not only did she need to concentrate on finding the stranger, she needed to devise a plan to arrest Drew Pearson and his gang without getting her or her inexperienced deputies killed in the process. And, she needed to follow-up on the Branson Murders.

Cavalier pulled her Bronco in front of her home on Eagle Rock Road on the east side of town. She had been renting it since she moved here. It belonged to the previous town marshal and his wife before he died of a massive heart attack. Apparently, his heart wasn't up to the strenuous activity of screwing the wife of the Last Chance Diner's owner, Poppy. The widow blamed Poppy's wife, calling her a hussy. The wife claimed she couldn't live in a house filled with bad memories of the dead husband she now despised. But, there must have been enough good memories not to sell the place. The widow wouldn't sell no matter how much Cavalier tried to persuade her. Instead, she rented it to her. The lease term would expire 30 days after Cavalier was no longer town marshal. No other provisions. No stated year or time limit. As long as Cavalier remained town marshal, the lease would stay in effect. The widow had kept the home in immaculate condition. The older ranch style brick home had only 1200 square feet on the main level and a full finished basement, doubling its size. Two bedrooms, two baths on the main level and one bedroom plus one bath in the basement along with a media room, game room for the grandchildren and home office. The basement was the most recent renovation, within the last ten years or so, according to the owner. The main level had been modernized about fifteen years ago. It was way too big for Cavalier's needs, but the price was right. Her biggest beef with the home was its lack of an enclosed garage. Especially in the middle of winter, the covered carport did little to stop the snowdrifts, making it miserable to go out and start the Bronco on bitter mornings.

She parked in the carport, switched off the ignition and crawled out of the seat. Out of habit, she locked the Bronco and headed to the carport door that entered into the kitchen. She had forgotten to leave a light on for the days when she worked late. It was dark inside and a musty smell filled her nostrils. The mid-July temperatures had been pleasant, and the air conditioner rarely ran except at night when she lowered the thermostat to get a slight chill in the house for sleeping. She flipped on the light switch, gasped and fell back against the door. Her keys dropped from her hand and bounced across the floor.

A man held a gun aimed at her.

CHAPTER 17

Kaplan noticed Cavalier took several deep breaths and held her trembling hands up in surrender.

Good. The last thing he wanted to do was get into a scuffle with her, or worse, a shootout. In the fluorescent light of the kitchen, she looked uncannily like her sister.

"Marshal," he said matter of fact. "It's time we had a chat."

"Mr. Wade, you son of a bitch, how the hell did you get out of my jail and what are you doing in my home?"

"Slow down Marshal. The last thing I want to do is hurt you, so please ease your pistol out of your holster and place it and your cuffs on the counter." He motioned with his Beretta. He saw how rigid she was standing. "And try to relax. If you still feel I belong back in your jail after we talk, I'll go quietly. You have my word."

Her shoulders drooped, and she gave him a slight nod. She removed her gun and cuff holsters and placed them on the black marble kitchen counter. He again motioned with his Beretta. "Now, sit."

She didn't move.

He said, "Please sit Marshal."

She walked over and slid out a chair on the other side of the table from him, sat down and folded her arm. He figured she felt safer with a barrier between them.

She started, "Did Lucy let you out of my jail?"

"Let's leave Lucy out of this," he replied.

"Did you give her money?"

The woman didn't give up easy. He decided to throw her a bone. "Five hundred bucks. She needed a break. I gave her money for food, some new clothes, a bath. Also, she could use a few good nights' sleep in a real bed."

"Quite the generous guy, are you?" she said. "Do you make a habit of giving that kind of money to someone you don't even know?"

"I know homeless."

"How do you know she won't spend it on drugs or alcohol?"

"I'm a pretty good judge of character. Sometimes we all need a second chance."

"Like you, Mr. Wade or whatever your name is? Are you looking for a second chance?"

"From you? No. What I want from you is something entirely different."

"What would that be?" she asked stiffly.

"In due time, Marshal, but suffice it to say you might be my last chance."

She paused, her toe tapped a staccato rhythm. Finally, "Why are you here?"

He ignored her question and cocked his head. "Looks like someone got a little rough with you. I heard you had a run-in with the father of the boys I put in the hospital."

She leaned back in her chair and smirked. "Run-in? More like a beating at the hand of Drew Pearson."

"Because I wasn't in the jail cell?"

She placed her finger on her busted lip. "He did this because I broke his son's nose." Next, she touched the knot on the left side of her head and the cut on her eyebrow. "He did this because you weren't in your cell. And it's a good thing you weren't…or you'd be dead right now."

"I'm sorry, but the actions of Mr. Pearson will not go unaccounted for." He stared intently at her face. "Perhaps you should put ice on it."

"Mr. Wade, what exactly do you want from me?"

"I want you to trust me."

She laughed, then moaned and placed her hand on her forehead. "Please no jokes." Her gaze zeroed in on his. "After everything you've done? Why shouldn't I just throw the book at you?"

"That would be unwise. Surely, you know that if I had no intention of returning, I wouldn't have left my Harley in your small impound lot."

"I wondered why it was still there. I assumed someone came and took you from my jail. Guess I was wrong."

"I can fix this."

"You caused it. How are you going to fix it?"

"Let me ask you this, Marshal. Other than not currently sitting behind bars in your jail, what crime have I committed?"

"For starters, you sent two men to the hospital."

"Except you have witnesses who can verify it was self-defense. You'd be forced to drop those charges, or a judge would throw them out…and you know it."

He could see she was considering what he said.

"Okay, I'll give you that one. But, you did break out of my jail."

"In reality, other than that knot on your head, I saved you a lot of paperwork and embarrassment, perhaps even your job. If I had been in that jail cell when Drew Pearson came in with his lynch mob and they hauled me off, with your past, you'd never find another job in law enforcement again…ever. So, as far as breaking out of your jail, I say no harm no foul."

She gaped at him. "How…how do you know about my past?"

"I know a lot more about you than you might think. So, instead of you sitting here and us getting into a pissing contest, how about we talk about what I can do to help?"

† † †

Wyoming was the fifth state Moss had driven in since he'd left Chicago. Mid-afternoon traffic in Chicago had been heavy, but as he drove west, fewer cars. After loading his destination into Google Maps, he'd chosen a southerly route to keep him out of Wisconsin and Minnesota due to numerous construction zones and avoiding traffic in Rochester during rush hour. His route took him through the heart of Iowa along Interstate 80 where he joined Interstate 29 north of Omaha, through Sioux City and into Sioux Falls. There, he merged onto Interstate 90, which should take him all the way to Sheridan, Wyoming. After Sheridan, it appeared to be about a thirty-minute drive to Last Chance.

Moss was tired. Except for last year's cross-country adventure with Kaplan, this was the first all-nighter he'd pulled in many years, as far as driving was concerned. He'd been downing coffee for the last four hours and stopping every forty-five minutes to relieve his bladder. And since he seemed to be driving in the middle of nowhere with very few exits and even fewer roadside facilities, sometimes he pulled over and relieved his bladder on the side of the road.

The scenery in Iowa was basically a whole lot of

nothing. He'd like to see their welcome center brochure. He imagined it had a picture of a cornfield stretching as far as the eye could see.

It was already dark by the time he reached South Dakota and dawn didn't lighten the skies until just west of the Wyoming state line. He missed the Badlands and the Black Hills because of the almost moonless night. What little he did see were merely shadows and silhouettes. The only upside was that he'd never seen so many stars in his lifetime. As dawn approached and he was convinced he would have to pull over and nap in his car, he came across the Coffee Cup Fuel Stop in Moorcroft, Wyoming where he decided to stop for gas and decided to grab breakfast at the *Deli Depot* inside the fuel stop.

Moss immediately felt out of place. At the pump, his black Cadillac Escalade was surrounded by a plethora of American-made pickup trucks—Silverados, F150s, Rams—all covered in dirt and dust, with off-road tires, truck beds filled with hay bales or ranch equipment. One had steer horns mounted on the hood and a big dog in the bed of the truck.

Stepping inside the café, he knew it wasn't just his vehicle that looked out of place. He was an oversized black man dressed in business casual clothes surrounded by men of all ages dressed in jeans, boots and western work shirts. Some wore leather chaps. Some wore vests. All sported cowboy hats. A few even had spurs on their boots. Their skin was weathered and worn from hard work and too much time in the sun. He noticed a few of the cowboys sizing him up and then dive back into eating breakfast and drinking coffee.

This place was not where he needed to linger, but he was desperate for a break from driving, just long enough for a quick bite to eat.

While he ate, he watched the sky lighten and the sun's rays streak across the barren Wyoming earth. Around 6:00, he got back in his Escalade and worked his way toward the interstate. His GPS said an hour fifty-five to Sheridan and an additional thirty-five minutes from Sheridan to Last Chance. Eight-thirty, quarter to nine he should arrive at the town marshal's office.

Wyoming was unlike any place he'd ever been. So far, there'd been nothing but flat land and tumbleweed. To top it off, the wind wasn't just persistent, it was annoying, bordering on dangerous in his opinion. Some gusts were so strong they rocked his Escalade causing him to swerve slightly in his lane.

Hopefully the town marshal, a woman by the name of Christine Cavalier would give him the scoop on what was going on with his friend Gregg Kaplan, or as mentioned in the alert he received in his office, Martin Joseph Wade.

CHAPTER 18

Cavalier sat at her desk and reflected over last night's conversation with Martin Wade. Her headache was worse and the fog in her brain refused to lift. Last night in bed, when everything was quiet, there was a slight ringing in her ears. Damn that Pearson. He would pay for this.

Wade's arguments about her legal standing with him were accurate. In this case, eyewitness accounts would be enough to exonerate him from any criminal culpability with his run-in with Mark and Scott Pearson, self-defense in the eyes of the law. She knew a county judge would see it that way too. As far as breaking out of jail, that would constitute a crime for which he would, and perhaps should be held accountable. But, he was correct, if he'd been in that jail cell when Pearson came in, and if harm had come to him, she would have had hell to pay. She almost didn't get this job in the first place and retaining it might be her last chance to remain in the world of law enforcement and reestablish her name in good standing.

She chuckled out loud. Last Chance was her last chance.

"Can you let me in on the joke?" An unrecognizable voice boomed from in front of her.

She jerked her head up. Standing in the doorway to her office was a very large black man. Bald, with an amicable face and dimples when he smiled. He could be a linebacker in the NFL, except for his age. Past football player prime, but still brawny, not fat. He was dressed in khaki pants and a button-down dress shirt that was wrinkled from wear. He looked beat, drained of energy.

And he was armed.

A leather holster with his sidearm snapped inside. On his belt, the badge of a Deputy U. S. Marshal.

She rose and welcomed him inside. "May I help you?"

"Are you Marshal Christine Cavalier?" He had a deep strong voice, almost thundering strong.

She gave a sharp nod.

He reached inside his pocket and pulled his credentials and handed them to her. "Senior Inspector Pete Moss, U. S. Marshals Service. I'm here for Martin Joseph Wade."

I knew it. Senior Inspector—that meant WitSec, Witness Security, or witness protection as most people called it. And he was looking for Wade. Dammit, she knew something wasn't right with his prints having restricted access. That had to be it—he was in the witness protection program and her inquiry with AFIS must have triggered an alert and now the feds had shown up. In her little town. And, with the worst possible timing. She glanced at her watch. Wade had told her he would arrive at 9:00 a.m. That was ten minutes from now.

"What do you mean *you're here for Mr. Wade?*" This was a wrinkle in the plan she hadn't expected. Especially after she and Wade reached a mutual understanding and agreement last night. He was going to help her apprehend the Pearson clan. But, with the United States Marshals Service here, that would change things. And not in a good way, for her.

"I know you searched the print database for him," he said. "And I know you later reported he escaped custody. I think I can help you locate him, but first I want to talk to you about the charges levied against him."

Just then, Doug and Jesse plodded in dressed in their

Buffalo County issued khaki pants and shirt uniforms. She'd told them to come in at 9:00.

"Who's this?" Jesse asked.

Moss held up his credentials for the two deputies. "Senior Inspector Pete Moss, U. S. Marshals Service."

Both deputies walked across the main room to their desks.

Cavalier led Moss into the common room and stood in front of the deputies.

"This is about Wade," Jesse said. "Isn't it?"

Moss glanced at her and back at Jesse. "That's right, I came to talk to the town marshal about locating Mr. Wade."

"That shouldn't be too difficult," a voice said from the doorway behind her.

Wade.

Jesse and Doug both leapt to their feet and drew their weapons. Cavalier held up a warning hand. "Stand down, boys. Mr. Wade and I have already had a discussion and he is here to turn himself in. Isn't that right, Mr. Wade?"

Wade ignored her. Instead he was staring Moss down. "What are you doing here?"

"Thought I'd come save your worthless ass…yet again," Moss said. His lips curled up. His dimples grew larger.

Moss stepped toward Wade as did Wade toward Moss. Neither man moved, staring each other in the eyes. Cavalier was worried she was about to have more trouble when Wade smiled. The next thing she knew, the two men were hugging.

"Goddamn, it's good to see you brother." Moss patted Kaplan on the back. "And all in one piece, as well."

"You too," Wade said. "How'd you know to find me here?"

She watched slack-jawed. She had no idea what was going on. These two obviously knew each other and, had some sort of past together. With as much authority as she could muster in her voice she said, "I hate to break up this love fest… but what the hell is going on?"

The two men looked at her and smiled. They were enjoying their respective surprises but weren't sharing what was going on.

Wade cut his gaze at Doug and Jesse, then back at her. "Can we talk alone? Just the three of us?"

"If this is official law enforcement business, they stay," she said. "I don't keep anything from them."

"Not this time, Marshal," Wade said. "You can brief them *after* we talk to you if you'd like."

"Probably a good idea we do this his way. He's not very good at taking *no* for an answer."

Cavalier didn't like inside jokes. She leaned forward and eyed her deputies. "Jesse, you and Doug give us a few minutes."

"But, Marshal—" Doug started to protest until Jesse jabbed him in the ribs.

"Come on," Jesse said. "Let's patrol the town while they talk."

Doug grunted as Jesse escorted him to the door.

"Wait," she called out to the deputies. She looked at Moss and Wade. "Fifteen minutes enough?"

"Make it thirty," Wade said.

She said to Jesse and Doug, "Be back in thirty unless you hear different from me on the radio."

"Sure thing, Marshal," Jesse said and both men left the building.

She narrowed her eyes and glared at Moss and Wade.

"I'll ask you two one more time. What the hell is going on?"

† † †

Kaplan was more than a little surprised when he saw his old friend Pete Moss standing in the Last Chance Police Department. Moss was the last person he expected to see. It didn't take him long to figure out how that came to be. As much as he was glad to see Moss, this wasn't his fight, nor his business.

Moss looked at Cavalier. "Can I have five minutes to talk to Mr. Wade in private?"

She didn't try to hide the aggravation on her face as she indicated the jail room. "You two can go in there. Wade, you should feel right at home."

Moss and Kaplan walked in and closed the jail room door. Kaplan spoke first. "Moss, what the hell, man? I mean, it's great to see you, but I hope you didn't come all the way here just to rescue me."

"Yeah, I kinda did," Moss said. "This is the first time your name has come up since last year's Little Rock incident. I figured you needed backup."

"This isn't your problem."

"I'm making it my problem."

"Why?"

"Because I needed a change of scenery." He cut his eyes toward where they had left Cavalier. "And it's already looking a lot better since I got here. Besides, my job has been boring lately. I think I was hoping for a little excitement."

Kaplan could use a good friend about now. Especially one who knew his way around Kaplan's dangerous world. "Be careful what you wish for, Moss. This time you might get more than you bargained for."

"I'm a big boy." Moss slapped his stomach. "Tell me, Kaplan, why are you here?"

"All right, big boy. Remember when I told you about Isabella?"

"How could I forget? Did you get a lead on her?"

Kaplan raked his fingers through his hair and stroked his two-day old stubble. "Town Marshal Christine Cavalier is Isabella's sister."

"I see," Moss said. "That explains the alias. She is a looker. Any resemblance to Isabella?"

"Too much. Like seeing a ghost."

"Well, the marshal is a good-looking woman." He paused. "I guess Isabella was too, huh? So, tell me, how long are you going to be Wade and not Kaplan?"

"I thought about telling her, I just don't know how she'll take it."

"You gotta tell her soon," Moss said. "The longer you wait, the worse she'll take it."

"You're right, I know." He ran his finger across his forehead. "You see the bruises on her face?"

"Looked like she was on the wrong end of a fist."

"I promised to help her bring in the man who did that to her." Kaplan explained the situation with Drew Pearson and his sons and how he came to be arrested in Last Chance after taking down the two Pearson boys. "In return, she promised to answer some questions."

"It's only fair you tell her."

"Okay," Kaplan said. "Let's do it. I just hope it doesn't backfire."

† † †

The two men had over stayed their five minutes in the cell room. After ten minutes, Cavalier heard the jail room door open and footsteps approach. Both men walked in her office and stopped in front of her desk. She stood when they entered and set her hands on her hips. "Okay," she said. "Let's hear it. What's this all about?"

Moss made a motion for Wade to speak. "The floor's all yours, buddy."

"My name isn't Martin Joseph Wade."

"No shit, Sherlock. Tell me something I don't already know. So, what is your real name?"

"Gregg Kaplan."

The name sounded familiar. He looked familiar, but she couldn't put all the pieces together, not with the fog still rolling through her brain.

"Last night you asked how I knew about your past," he said.

"And if I recall, you said *in due time*."

"I know many things about your childhood, including that your childhood nickname was Danni."

She felt flush. Only one person had ever called her Danni. Her earlier recognition of his appearance and demeanor made sense now. And the name unlocked another flood of memories. Some good, most bad. "Oh my God." She cut her eyes at Kaplan. "It's you." She collapsed into her chair and rested her chin in her palm. "Isabella," she mumbled.

At that moment, her radio blared. "Marshal?"

It was Jesse.

She was still processing what Wade...Gregg Kaplan had just revealed.

"Marshal, Marshal." Jesse persisted, his voice full of urgency.

She eyed the radio. "Go ahead," she finally answered into the microphone.

"Marshal, there's been a shooting at the Sundown Motel. The Pearsons were here. They took Lucy, and Doug's been shot."

CHAPTER 19

Kaplan's jaw clinched when he heard the panicky deputy on the radio.

Had he heard Jesse right? Had Lucy been taken by Drew Pearson?

Cavalier's lips almost touched the mic of the radio. "Hang tight, Jesse, I'm on the way." She stepped around her desk and faced Kaplan and Moss. "You and your friend stay here."

"Not a chance," Kaplan replied.

He said to Moss, "You drive."

While Cavalier rushed to her Bronco, Moss motioned at a black Cadillac Escalade with dark tinted windows. "My new ride. How do you like it?"

Kaplan folded himself into the passenger seat and snapped his seatbelt. "You've moved up in the world. Beats the hell out of that Crown Vic you were driving when I met you in Virginia." He pointed down Main Street. "That way. Hurry."

Lights flashing and siren wailing, Cavalier shot out of her parking spot running code toward the Sundown Motel.

"I think we should let the marshal take the lead," Moss said. "I'll just follow her."

A minute later they arrived at the Sundown Motel. A crowd of bystanders had gathered, and more were coming from the trailer park across the street. Might be the most excitement this small town had ever seen, he thought. Jesse was trying to do crowd control with outstretched arms. Cavalier skidded her Bronco to a stop next to a black Toyota Tundra bringing with her a cloud of dust that blew across the gravel parking lot. She was out of her Bronco almost before it came to a full stop, running in the direction of a body face down in the gravel parking lot. Moss parked his Escalade next to Cavalier's Bronco.

Kaplan sprang out and ran toward room thirteen when he heard Cavalier shouting, "Wade…Kaplan. Over here."

Kaplan stopped, feet sliding across the loose gravel. He twisted around to see Cavalier waving him over. He needed to check the room. He rubbernecked back and forth between her and the motel room.

"Hurry," she yelled. Her high-pitched voice sounded full of fear.

Kaplan sprinted over to the body and dropped to one knee next to Cavalier. It was Deputy Doug. His red hair now matted with blood. He lay motionless in the gravel.

"Flip him," Moss said.

Cavalier and Kaplan pushed Doug's body over onto his back.

"Jesus," Moss said.

"Oh my God." She cupped her hand over her mouth and turned her head away.

Jesse ran up. He stood biting his lip and trying to hold back tears. It took a few seconds, but he finally found his voice, "He took it point blank. It was that asshole Stevie Pearson." He looked at Cavalier. "The one with the broken nose."

"Looks like a shotgun blast," Kaplan said. He raised his head to face Jesse. "Was it?"

"I think it was a Taurus Judge," Jesse said.

Kaplan faced Cavalier. "So, a 410 or a .45 round. Probably a 410. Either way it makes one hell of a hole in its target." He said to Jessie, "What happened to Lucy?"

"Stevie, took her." Jesse's voice cracked. "We tried to stop them. Doug saw Stevie had Lucy and was pulling her toward the Rocking P truck. Before I could stop him, he jumped out of my truck and ran toward them shouting. Stevie opened fire. Doug never got a chance to draw his weapon."

"Did you return fire?" Moss asked.

"I tried, but Stevie kept firing. I couldn't get off a clean shot." Jesse used the back of his hand to wipe the tears rolling down his face. "Is he dead?"

The gaping hole in Doug's chest left little doubt the young police officer was dead. Kaplan placed his fingers on Doug's neck feeling for a pulse. When he removed his blood-covered fingers he said, "He's dead, Jesse, I'm sorry."

Jesse's chin dropped to his chest. Cavalier walked with him back to his truck, her arm around his back.

Moss asked Kaplan, "Are these the same guys who beat up the marshal?"

"Yep." Kaplan wiped the blood off his fingers using Doug's sleeve. "And now they're dead men." He paused. "First, I'm going to get Lucy back." He raised up and looked at Moss. "If they hurt her, it will be the last person they hurt."

"I have a question. Who is this Lucy you're willing to risk your life for?"

He started to give Moss the abridged version about the Native Indian girl and how he met her but was interrupted when Cavalier received a phone call. She looked distressed by the call. The blood drained from her face, what little was left after seeing her deputy lying dead in the parking lot. She stuffed the phone in her jeans back pocket and stormed toward them, leaving Jesse leaning against his truck.

"Shit, this can't be good," Kaplan said.

She took a direct path to him and came to an abrupt halt just inches from his face. "Kaplan, I'm altering our deal." She reached down and wrenched Doug's badge from his belt. She held it up in front of her. "Doug is dead. Jesse is worthless, and I just got a call from Tribal Police Chief on the Crow Rez. Seems someone discovered four bodies on a farm just north of here. All shot in the head, but one. That one had his throat slit. Two of the men live here, one is non-Native, and one is a partial Native. The other two are Natives. Both Crow. One of those dead men owned the farm. If you are half the man my sister described, then you can help me in a big way." She cleared her throat and continued, "Let me deputize you. Go with Jesse to the Rez. Take Inspector Moss with you. I'll wait on the coroner and wrap things up here and head up your way." She thrust the badge at him. "Deal?"

"If I say no?"

Moss elbowed him in the ribs. "What's your problem, man? Take it."

Cavalier continued, "If you don't want the deal, go back to the station, get your belongings and get the hell out of my town. Forget about Drew Pearson. Forget about Lucy Raintree. And you can forget about ever talking to me." Her nostrils flared, and she stepped closer to him. "Do I make myself clear?"

† † †

Two miles north of town, where the U. S. highway made its turn toward the northeast, a dirt road forked left to the north. Long, straight, and dusty. Buffalo Run Road was the name on the sign. Cavalier referred to it simply as *Buffalo Run*.

Five minutes out of town they came to a sign that read:

Entering Crow Reservation
Montana State Line

Kaplan could hear the constant sound of gravel crunching under the tires interrupted by Moss complaining about his new Cadillac getting dirty. He'd only had it a few weeks and now it was riding in the dust cloud kicked up by Jessie's over-sized truck tires.

"Quit your bellyaching," Kaplan said. "It'll wash off."

Jesse turned right off Buffalo Run onto Aberdeen Road and right again on Arrow Pass Road. A quarter mile further Kaplan saw two white Suburbans with blue and gold markings and law enforcement light bars, still flashing. As Moss drove closer, he could read the markings on the side of the Suburbans—Crow Tribal Police. Next to one of the Suburbans was a white pickup truck marked as belonging to Bureau of Indian Affairs.

Moss and Kaplan met Jesse at his truck. The young deputy's eyes were bloodshot, and he kept wiping his runny nose with the back of his hand.

"Listen, Jesse," Kaplan said. "Get it together. Learn from your partner's mistake. I need you to have a clear head. Otherwise you could end up like Doug." Kaplan untied the bandana around his neck and handed it to Jesse.

Moss added, "Law enforcement is a tough gig. Officers die on the job every day. We don't want you to be one of them."

A man of Indian heritage approached their vehicles wearing a blue uniform. His hair was long and black with silver streaks and pulled back in a ponytail. With him was another

Native man with the *Bureau of Indian Affairs* and the name *B. Kickingbull* embroidered on his shirt. Jesse made introductions. The man in teh blue uniform was the chief of the Crow Tribal Police, Joseph Silverheels, brother of one of the victims. His brother, Frank Silverheels, had apparently struggled with drug addiction for the past several years.

Silverheels gave Kaplan, Moss and Jesse a briefing. Turned out the Crow Boy Scout troops were about to gather on the farm of Graham Stillwater for their annual jamboree. The next morning, over two hundred Scouts from the Black Otter District of the Montana Council would pile onto the expansive farm, pitching tents, building fires, and going through all the rituals necessary for the ensuing scout competitions. On the last day of each year's Jamboree, Stillwater hosted an annual dinner and award presentation ceremony in his barn.

The bodies were discovered by one of the troop scoutmasters who came down a day early from Crow, Montana with his assistant scoutmaster to help set up for the event. The scoutmaster's major concern was whether he should cancel or relocate to a more secluded portion of the farm. BIA wanted the event cancelled so no one would taint the crime scene during the investigation. Crow Tribal Police wanted to relocate to another section of the farm, preferably somewhere along the Little Bighorn River.

According to Silverheels, the two men from Last Chance were identified as Mark Leatherdale and Tony Mason. Leatherdale was half Crow by blood quantum.

"Blood quantum?" asked Moss. "What does that mean?"

"In the simplest of definitions," Silverheels said. "It is a registry to determine how much Native American blood people have. It was a system started by the white man's federal government in an effort to limit citizenship. Now, many tribes use blood quantum as a requirement to be a member of a tribe. In today's world, 100% blood quantum is rare and getting rarer. By blood, Mark Leatherdale is only 25% Native, but two years ago when his grandfather died, he was willed another 25% giving him 50% blood quantum."

"Willed?" said Kaplan. "You can will your blood quantum?"

"Yes. It is our way," said Silverheels.

The Bureau of Indian Affairs officer, Kickingbull, explained how Crow Tribal Council could strip a Native of their Indian heritage by removing their blood quantum, even if they were full-blooded.

Mason, the other dead man from Last Chance was non-Native.

Three of the men were shot in the back of the head, execution style, with what appeared to be a .38 caliber round. The fourth man was the owner of the farm, a Crow named Graham Stillwater. Stillwater wasn't shot, but rather had his throat slashed. All four victims were found in Stillwater's barn. Decomposition had already set in and the initial determination was that the bodies had been there approximately five or six days.

As the men walked toward the barn, the rancid smell of decaying bodies wafted through the air filling their nostrils. Jesse used the bandana Kaplan gave him and covered his nose and mouth. The rest of the men pulled their shirts up over their noses. The smell was like rotting meat — putrid.

At the sight of the carnage inside the barn, Jesse leaned over and started to gag. He bolted out of the barn holding the bandana tight against his face. Obviously, he had never seen or smelled a rotting corpse.

Kaplan had warned Jesse and Doug yesterday during their first encounter at the diner that their inexperience and carelessness could get them killed. His prophecy had already come true for Doug. He hoped Jesse would learn from today's tragedies. He could hear Jesse outside retching. Sounded like the kid was drowning in his own vomit.

After ten minutes in the barn, Moss and Kaplan, along with Silverheels and Kickingbull, went outside to get away from the stench. A cloud of dust could be seen coming down Arrow Pass Road.

A white Bronco appeared ahead of the dust.

Cavalier had arrived.

CHAPTER 20

Kaplan watched Cavalier get out of her Bronco, scan the area and let her sights rest on the barn. She massaged the back of her neck and strolled over to where he, Moss, Silverheels, and Kickingbull were standing. He noticed her breathing—shallow and rapid. Her hair was tied in a ponytail and stuffed through the sizing gap in the back of her cap. Her hand constantly swiped loose strands of hair that didn't get tucked into the hat. She removed her sunglasses and hung them in her shirt. Her posture looked like she had the weight of the world on her shoulders. Her face filled with tension. Everyone had their tipping point and he was afraid she had about reached hers.

Jesse had vomited until he could only dry heave. It was a lot for the young deputy to endure in such a short span of time. His roommate and fellow deputy was shot at point blank range with a Taurus Judge right in front of him and the smell of rotting corpses all in the course of an hour would be a bit much for most people to take. As Jesse walked up to Cavalier, he appeared calmer and over his initial state of shock.

"You might want to snort some soap when you get home," Moss teased Jesse.

Jesse smiled. "Thanks…I think."

"Come on," Cavalier said to Jesse. "We have a lot of work to do."

"I am, but…" He motioned at the barn. "I don't think I can go back in there." Jesse handed his camera to Kaplan. "I just can't, Marshal."

Moss took the camera from Kaplan's hands. "It's okay, Jesse, I'll handle it."

Cavalier's features relaxed and she said, "Tell you what, Jesse. The three of us can take it from here. Go back to the station and hold down the fort until I get back."

"Thanks, Marshal." Jesse headed to his truck, got in and drove off.

Kaplan faced Cavalier and said, "He seems like a good kid, but he's not cut out for this job. You should talk to him when you get a chance. Don't let what happened to Doug happen to him."

"I know how to run my department, so keep your opinions to yourself. You know Kaplan, nothing bad had happened around here until you showed up. Now I have two bodies in a burned-out ranch house, I've been beat up, Lucy Raintree has been kidnapped, one of my deputies is dead, and now this. Does trouble follow you? Or, are you just bad luck?"

"Yes," he said.

"Yes, what?"

"Yes, to both. Trouble does follow me which seems to be my ongoing battle with lady luck."

"After everything that has happened here today, I believe it. Since you met Isabella, you've been nothing but bad luck."

"What's that supposed to mean?" he said.

She waited a beat, her stare making him feel like she had x-ray vision. Moss and Silverheels stood on the side looking like they were enjoying the ass-chewing. She continued, "This is not the time or place. We'll talk later."

"To set the record straight, Marshal." Kaplan shoved his

finger toward the barn. "All this happened *before* I arrived. You already had trouble coming. You just didn't know it yet."

She redirected her attention to Silverheels. "Chief, show me what you got here."

Cavalier and Silverheels headed toward the rotting corpses.

Kaplan watched them plod toward the barn and said to Moss, "What the hell was that all about?"

"I don't know," Moss replied with a grin. "But, I like her."

"You can have her."

Moss was grinning and had crossed his arms over his broad chest.

Kaplan and Moss kept their eyes on Cavalier and Silverheels until they disappeared into the barn. "Have I mentioned that I really like her?" He looked back at Kaplan. "Especially when she's dissing on you?"

"Kinda hard not to notice."

Moss held up the camera and the surgical mask Cavalier had given him. "If you'll excuse me, I have pictures to take."

Kaplan watched Moss lumber toward the barn. Moss stopped at the barn door and hollered, "You coming?"

† † †

The past twenty-four hours were going down as the worst. Not only would Cavalier have to justify the loss of a deputy to the Last Chance mayor and town council, she would also have to explain today's death to the Johnson County Sheriff in Buffalo where Doug was officially employed. And there was never anything enjoyable about dealing with Sheriff Bobby

Franks. He was old school through and through. A crusty old man who had been sheriff of Johnson County at least a decade too long. He was the oldest standing sheriff in Wyoming. For that matter, he was the oldest standing law enforcement officer of any kind in Wyoming and very close to the oldest in the nation. Sheriff Franks was a legend in the West and had been sheriff for over forty years. Born and raised in Buffalo, Wyoming, he was the town's favorite son. A high school football star who went on to sports stardom in college, including a finalist for the coveted Heisman Trophy. In his senior year, after being courted as a potential first round NFL draft choice, he suffered an injury to his right knee that ended any future NFL career. He returned home to a welcoming town and ran for sheriff with no law enforcement experience and won in a landslide victory.

Her issue with Sheriff Franks wasn't that he was a bad sheriff, he wasn't. He was as honest as they come. His problem was that he was too old for the job and refused to step down. According to what she'd been told, when Franks' wife died fifteen years ago, the man changed from the gregarious life-of-the-party man the county had elected, to a cranky old bastard who hated the world and spent most of his nights and some of his days with a bottle. She made an attempt to call him prior to driving to the Stillwater farm, but Franks was unavailable, which usually meant he was in a bar somewhere or passed out at home on his couch. It would have been one thing if it was Jesse she was delivering the sad news about, but it wasn't. It was Doug, Sheriff Bobby Franks' grandson.

Cavalier knew the two of the four victims at the Stillwater farm. Tony Mason was in his late thirties, a relative newcomer to Last Chance and a volunteer with the Boy Scouts. He had earned Eagle Scout when he was a teenager and as far as she knew, had never been in trouble with the law. The second victim was Mark

Leatherdale. He had been tossed in jail numerous times. He'd been busted for possession of pot, cocaine, heroin, and as of late, meth. His family on the Rez kicked him out years ago, actually banned him from the family and told him never to return. Now, he was dead. She knew the Native rituals in his case. No family would claim the body. No family would attend the funeral. The burden of disposal of his body would fall on the town's coffers unless she could pawn it off on the Rez.

As she and Silverheels surveyed the crime scene, she was glad she remembered to bring the surgical masks she kept in her car. No wonder Jesse didn't want to go back inside the barn. She could tell Silverheels was disturbed by the sight of his brother lying face down in his own pool of blood. He handled it with the tough resolve he typically displayed.

One man with his throat cut and three men shot, execution style, in a manner that was remarkably similar to the bodies of Richard and Stanley Branson that they'd discovered yesterday at the Branson ranch house fire. The wounds looked consistent with the same caliber slug.

Moss had donned his surgical mask and was taking pictures, lots of them. Kaplan stood in the doorway of the barn holding his mask. She figured after she lashed out at him, he wasn't going to help her any more. She was wrong. Out of her peripheral, she saw him put on the mask and march towards her and Silverheels. There were no words exchanged. They surveyed the remainder of the crime scene side by side. She appreciated his presence but didn't understand why. Now that he had revealed his true identity to her, she knew why he was here and what he wanted from her.

And that was one secret she'd promised never to disclose.

CHAPTER 21

Back at the Last Chance police station, Kaplan saw Jesse sitting behind his desk. Moss was waiting outside for Cavalier to drive back. Moss wasn't being very subtle about showing his interest in the marshal. Jesse looked up at Kaplan, his eyes swollen, his nose was running, and he kept wiping it with the back of his hand.

He walked over to him, "Jesse, go to the bathroom and wash your face. You need to suck it up. If you want to stay in law enforcement, you have to deal with death. Period. And I mean close friends. Unfortunately, it's a fact of a cop's life. Doug screwed up. He should have stayed behind your truck door like you did instead of running into the line of fire. He should have had his weapon drawn and ready. You gotta think before you act. It's a hard lesson to learn." He motioned toward the bathroom. "Go on, before the marshal gets here."

Jesse nodded and went into the bathroom. At the same time, Moss and Cavalier walked into the station. Moss was on his cell phone leaning into it like he was struggling to hear. He had a finger plugging his opposite ear.

Cavalier asked, "Where's Jesse?"

He pointed with a hitchhiker's thumb. "In there."

Moss mumbled into his phone and Kaplan heard him say, "Thanks, Sheriff. We'll have someone there within an hour." Moss disconnected his call and glanced at Cavalier. "All set."

The toilet flushed, Jesse opened the door and stepped into the office. His face was clean, and his bloodshot eyes were much improved.

"Jesse," Cavalier's loud voice echoed off the walls. She reached into her drawer and pulled out a sealed evidence bag with five shell casings in it and marched over to Jesse's desk. "Take these to the Sheriff's Office in Sheridan. Sheriff Knight agreed to expedite ballistics on these casings and the slugs the coroner extracted from the Bransons. Chief Silverheels is sending the bodies from the Stillwater farm to Sheridan for autopsy. The sheriff will make sure his ballistics lab compares slugs from both cases. It's a long shot, I know, but the killings bear such a striking similarity, I can't afford to let it go unchecked. Stay there and wait for the results. Report back to me as soon as you get them. The sheriff said it should only take forty-five minutes or so."

Jesse got his truck keys from his desk, took the evidence bag from Cavalier and headed for the door.

"And Jesse," Cavalier added. Jesse stopped and did not turn around. "Take tomorrow off. Go to Buffalo and be with your family."

He gave a sharp nod and walked out.

After Jesse left, Cavalier picked up her cell phone and announced, "Now for the call I've been dreading. Telling Sheriff Bobby Franks of Johnson County that his grandson is dead." She walked into the cell room and closed the door behind her and sat down on a cell cot.

† † †

The phone call she'd dreaded making went better than she could have ever hoped. It lasted nearly forty-five minutes. To her relief, Sheriff Franks was understanding instead of angry.

He even said that in the back of his mind, he figured Doug would one day get himself killed. According to Franks, it was just a matter of time. He told her he had even tried convincing Doug to find another, less dangerous line of work.

After the initial shock of the news had worn off, Franks said Doug thought being a cop was like playing a video game. She listened while the old man talked about his love for his grandson and recollected memories of taking him out for ice cream and letting him sit in his lap so he could read him bedtime stories. She listened. Franks needed to remember.

After talking to Franks, she felt better about delivering the tragic news. That sense of a doomed career seemed to diminish. Now, she needed to focus on her other, more pressing issues. Prioritizing them was her quandary. Go after Drew Pearson first or investigate the Branson murders and the similar murders at the Stillwater farm? She knew she should wait for the ballistics report from the County Sheriff Jack Knight in Sheridan before making that decision. She noticed the time on her phone. She couldn't believe it was already 2:30. She hadn't eaten lunch…and neither had Moss or Kaplan.

She peered through the small glass window on the cell room door at the two men, one sitting in Doug's chair, the other sitting on Doug's desk. She could see why Isabella fell for Kaplan. Dark hair and eyes. His five o'clock shadow was heavier than most men's beards after a week of growth. He was strong and commanding. An alpha male. And in many ways, he appeared to be the very dangerous man Isabella had described him to be. Poppy thought the man was lethal. He had impressed Lucy when he beat up both the Pearson brothers.

Shit. Lucy. She had almost forgotten about Lucy. That was her newest priority, had to be. Get Lucy back safe and sound. That probably meant having to take down Drew Pearson and his gang at the same time.

She studied Kaplan and Moss again. The two men had some kind of bond. It was easy to tell from mere observation. Their words were jabs at each other, yet neither got angry. They would just come back with their own zinger. And their minds seemed to be on the same wavelength. It felt reassuring to have them here, willing to help. Kaplan's motivation was plain, the Pearsons kidnapped Lucy, now they had to pay. She knew what that meant in Kaplan terms. He wouldn't hesitate to kill them if it came to that. And she was sure he would if they had harmed Lucy. But Cavalier didn't want Kaplan to get the opportunity. She'd make sure the Pearsons paid for kidnapping Lucy, killing Doug and assaulting her. Adrenaline turbocharged her body as she envisioned the satisfaction of her cuffing the Pearsons and tossing them in her jail. When the day came that Stevie got the needle in his arm, she wanted to watch. She wouldn't let Kaplan deprive her of her revenge.

Whatever brought Moss and Kaplan together must have been a powerful incident forging their friendship. There was mutual trust and genuine caring between them. Moss, without hesitation, accepted the potential danger that Kaplan warned him could be forthcoming. She coveted their close interpersonal relationship.

She focused on Moss. When he walked in her office she felt a feeling she had not had in a long time, self-conscious. Physically, she was drawn to him, especially his Grand Canyon dimples and wide captivating smile. He was tall, burly and had a deep husky voice.

Moss stretched his arms and yawned. He had driven all night just to help a friend. That was a loyalty she envied.

After this was over, she knew, Kaplan would want to move on. She knew what he wanted. He was a straight shooter, she could see that. Sooner or later, he'd come right out and ask about Isabella. She had until that time to think of what she would tell him.

Her cell phone rang and snapped her out of her introspection. It was Jesse.

She saw the time. "Hey Jesse, everything okay?" It had been a little over an hour since he'd left with the evidence bag.

"Sure thing, Marshal. Everything is fine. By the time I got here, the coroner had already pulled the slugs from the victims at the Stillwater farm and sent them to ballistics. Sheriff Knight personally oversaw the rush job on the ballistics testing. By the time he was finished, the coroner had made a quick preliminary. I had the reports emailed to you."

"Which reports, Jesse?"

"All of them. Ballistics on all the slugs from both crime scenes and the prelims from the coroner." There was a long silence. "Marshal, Doug is here. I…I mean his body is here. He was on the table when I got here. I couldn't stay. I had to leave. I'm sorry, Marshal, I just couldn't look at him like that."

"It's okay, Jesse. Go home. Get some rest. Try not to think about today…if that's possible. Take as much time off as you need. Okay?"

"Thank you, Marshal."

"If something comes up, I'll give you a call."

"Marshal. If you catch Stevie Pearson, kill him. For me…and for Doug. Kill that bastard."

Jesse hung up.

Kaplan was right. Jesse wasn't cut out for this job. Had she made a mistake keeping the two rookie cops on her force?

The most crime Last Chance ever saw was petty. Until now. But, she couldn't let Kaplan get in her head. He didn't know this town like she did. Jesse just needed some time to gather himself. She'd give him a day or two to get it together. In the meantime, she needed more manpower. Her other part-time deputy, KC, was on vacation and, as much as she hated doing it, she would have to cancel his leave and order him back to Last Chance.

She scrolled through her contacts and placed the call to KC.

No answer.

She left a detailed message, including what had happened to Doug and an apology for ruining his vacation.

Jesse had informed her that Knight had emailed the preliminary ballistics reports. She walked back to her office and gave Kaplan and Moss a *just a minute* signal with her finger as she strode past them without saying a word. She sat at her desk, opened her email and scanned her inbox. There it was, just as Jesse had said. She opened the files and began reading the reports.

Ballistics matched all five slugs as being fired from the .38 found in the Branson fire. Latent prints were lifted from two of the shell casing. No match had been made with the prints through AFIS.

She really wasn't any closer to the truth. All she knew was that the same gun killed five people.

Now, back to business. She needed to draft a list of duties for KC when he returned, but first, she wanted to get with Kaplan and Moss and develop a strategy for rescuing Lucy Raintree from the hands of Drew Pearson.

CHAPTER 22

Lucy sat on the floor, her knees tucked close to her chest and her arms wrapped around her legs. Her eyes unable to focus. She had been locked in the dark room for what felt like hours.

She had seen a lot of things in her short lifetime, but never anyone killed. The silence in the room let her mind wander back to the most horrible thing she had ever witnessed. Stevie Pearson held her arm tight with one hand and used his other hand to blast Doug in the chest with his big gun. She remembered screaming when she saw Doug's chest erupt in a bloody splash. It felt like a Quentin Tarantino movie, only in slow motion. The blast made Doug fly backwards, maybe five feet. And all she could do was watch. She dropped her head on her knees. It was so nightmarish.

Stevie was dragging her to his truck by her arm when Doug and Jesse arrived at the Sundown Motel. Evan stayed in the truck like a getaway driver. She was shocked to see Evan. He had always been nice to her, taking her horseback riding on the ranch when his father and brothers were gone. Showing her some of the cool rocks he had found near the edge of his father's property. She liked Evan. They had even hooked up a couple times in the stable. A literal roll in the hay. But, today he was different. In the truck, he wouldn't even look at her.

Stevie was holding her arms so tight it hurt. He scared her with his bad temper. The bandage over his nose and black eyes made him appear even meaner. Whatever had happened to him had fueled his anger. Now, Stevie acted like he was crazy.

She had always liked Doug. She had turned down all of his advances, but she still liked the attention. He was cute. Reddish hair and light freckles. Not at all like the Native boys on the Rez. She felt responsible for his death. His fondness for her had gotten him killed. He was a cop, he should have known better than to mess with the Pearsons.

When Stevie Pearson was dragging her out of the motel room she saw Jesse stop his truck in the parking lot. She yelled for help and witnessed Doug jump out shouting and running toward her. She noticed he had not pulled his gun out of his holster. She swung her free arm in an attempt to stop Doug. That was when Stevie raised the big gun and shot him. Why did Stevie have to kill him?

After Stevie shot Doug, he kept firing at Jesse, who had ducked behind his truck door. Then, Stevie pushed her into the back seat of the Pearson's quad-cab ranch truck. He held the big gun out of the window and kept firing while Evan drove away. She did not know if Jesse got shot. It did not look like it, but she really could not see much after being pushed down in the back seat by Stevie. He held her down in the back seat the entire time. When the truck stopped, he put a cloth bag over her head and marched her here, wherever here was. Down a bunch of steps and through a musty smelling tunnel or something that felt like a tunnel or long hallway.

She could see a little bit of her prison. A small bedroom in some old house. A bedroom with no windows, only a single door, which was locked. She could hear faint, distant voices, as if they were coming from down a long hall. She recognized Stevie's when he shouted. It made her muscles tense up. She could not tell who the other people were, but it sounded like several different ones, and they were all men. A few times it sounded like arguing. And each time, she heard Stevie's voice.

Her stomach growled and reminded her she had not eaten. Mostly, she needed to pee. She held it as long as she could. She did not want to make any noise, but she could not hold it any longer. She was getting cramps from holding it so long. She went to the door and knocked. She heard nothing. She knocked louder and yelled, “Can anybody hear me?”

It got quiet. No more voices. She put her ear to the door. After a few seconds, she raised her fist to bang on the door again when she heard footsteps. The footfalls got louder and were definitely coming her way. She stepped back when someone fumbled with the lock. The door swung open. It was Evan.

“What do you want, Lucy?”

“I need to pee. And I am hungry.”

Evan pulled out his phone and glanced down at it. She caught a glimpse as it lit up. 3:05. It had been nearly a day since she had last eaten anything. No wonder she was starving.

“I have not eaten anything since last night,” she said. She crossed her legs while she stood there. “I have to go, or I am going to pee on the floor.”

Evan nodded. “Follow me.”

He led her out of her room and stopped at the first door on her right. At the other end of a long hall she could see a couple of men sitting in weathered leather chairs. She did not recognize either of them. But heard Stevie. Stevie glared at her down the long hall. It gave her chills.

Evan stepped in front of her, blocking her view, and pointed. “Bathroom. Make it quick.”

She went into the tiny bathroom. The window was

painted black and locked with a latch and key. *So much for seeing outside.* She was hoping for some kind of visual reference, so she might have some idea where she was. Even if it was a small glimpse of the Bighorn Mountains or the plains…or something. The toilet was dirty. She laid strips of toilet paper across the seat. She did not want her skin touching that nasty thing. When she finished, she washed her hands but refused to touch the towel, just shook her wet hands dry and wiped them on her clothes.

Outside the bathroom Evan was still standing in the same spot. She walked out, and he steered her back to her room which was at the opposite end of the hall from where she saw Stevie sitting earlier. She stood still. "I said I was hungry. If you are going to keep me prisoner, you have to feed me. You have to do that with prisoners, you know. It is in the Geneva Convention or something. I thought you liked me. Why are you doing this? After all we have done together, why are you not helping me?"

"It's not like I have a choice." He paused, "I'm sorry."

He grabbed her arm, guided her back and shoved her into her room.

"I'll bring you something to eat in a couple of minutes." He hesitated. "I'll talk to my father and try to get you out of here tomorrow."

She knew then he lied. Evan was not going to help her. Why? She did not know. Maybe his brother had threatened him too. It was then she decided she would have to take matters into her own hands if she were to get out of there alive. A plan was already formulating in her mind. She knew what she was going to have to do. How to execute it was a totally different matter.

CHAPTER 23

Kaplan paced and wondered if Cavalier was ever coming out of her office. What was she doing in there and how long was it going to take? The longer he waited, the worse Lucy's situation might become. It wasn't like they didn't have some idea where to find her. Drew Pearson had a grudge.

"How are we doing time-wise?" Kaplan asked Moss.

"3:30."

Kaplan looked back at her office door again. "Dammit, what's keeping her? We need to find Lucy."

"Who is this Lucy?" Moss said. "And what's your involvement with her?"

Kaplan explained everything that had transpired since he'd arrived in Last Chance. It was the first time he'd had an opportunity since Moss arrived this morning. He explained the run-in at the diner, jail, his jail break with the help of Lucy, and his late-night meeting with Cavalier last night.

"So, I guess we know what your Achilles' heel is," Moss said. "Keeps landing you in more trouble than it's worth, am I right?"

"What Achilles' heel?"

"Lemme think." Moss put his hand against his forehead like he was doing a mind reading trick. "Oh, I don't know. Maybe it's that you are always trying to protect people who you believe need your help."

"So, you think Lucy stands a better chance of getting

out of this unharmed if I don't help?"

"Not saying you're doing the wrong thing, man. Just saying that's how you're wired."

Kaplan said, "Lucy's a sweet girl, make it young lady, who just needs somebody to give a damn about her. She told me she grew up Navajo, on the Navajo Reservation in northeastern Arizona, somewhere near Monument Valley I think she said. She's had a tough life. I'd like to see her make a clean break. Get her act together and make a better life."

"Crabs in a bucket," Moss said.

"What?"

"Crabs in a bucket." Moss smiled. "You're a fisherman, right?"

Kaplan shrugged. "Okay, I'll bite."

"What happens to the crabs when you fill up your bucket?"

"They scramble around trying to get out. Climbing on top of the other and knocking each other back down in the bucket."

"Exactly, crabs in a bucket," Moss said. "I heard that phrase from a BIA officer on a reservation in Oklahoma while I was WitSec in Little Rock. I had a witness who went into the program after testifying against a casino owner. The officer said that's the plight of Native kids these days. They are like crabs in a bucket, they keep pulling each other down. Every now and then one gets out, but they are few and far between. Sounds to me like Lucy is one of those crabs."

"She doesn't have to be," Kaplan declared. "And I'm going to do my best to see that she gets out of that bucket… for good. But first, I need to track her down and get her out of there, so she doesn't get hurt by one of the Pearsons. After that, we can deal with Drew. And when we find him, he's a dead man."

"Who's a dead man?" Cavalier said as she came out of her office.

He ignored her question. "We need to go find Lucy," he said.

"Yes, we do," Cavalier agreed. "But Drew Pearson has a very large ranch and he'll be able to see us coming for miles."

Kaplan asked, "Are you familiar with his ranch?"

"Somewhat. I've been out there twice. The main ranch house is pretty big. There are a couple of other houses, barn, stables, maintenance sheds, and a big bunkhouse for his ranch hands. Could be more buildings on other parts of his ranch. He owns upwards of thirty thousand acres."

"Whoa, that's a lot of land," Moss interjected.

"Yeah well, he pieced it together over the years off the misfortunes of others. Foreclosures, bankruptcies, deaths, estate auctions. Anyone who couldn't pay their bills, he bought them out. He started off with only a few thousand acres. I heard he bought an old coal camp from the 1850s, then just kept adding to it. Looks like his neighbors have all kinds of problems. Come to think of it, the Branson farm butts up to the Pearson ranch too. I can bring it up on Google Maps if you want a bird's eye view."

Kaplan nodded. "Do it."

Cavalier went back to her desk and loaded Google Maps on her desktop computer. He and Moss circled in behind her chair while she located the Pearson ranch and zoomed in on the ranch house and surrounding buildings. She pointed at the screen. "This is the main ranch house. Pearson and two of his sons live there. The other two are married…" She shot a look over her shoulder and said, "You remember, the two you put in the hospital? Mark and Scott, and their wives live in these houses." She drew their attention to two small houses. "No idea which brother lives where. This is the bunkhouse. Not sure how many ranch hands he has right now. He brought only three here yesterday, so at least three." She zoomed the map out and ran her finger over a long straight dirt road. "And gentlemen, this is the only way in. He owns everything you see on both sides of the road all the way to here."

"What's there?" Moss asked.

"Montana state line and the Crow Reservation."

"Where we went this morning?"

"Precisely. The terrain is mostly flat land here and it's about a mile from the country road turnoff to the ranch house. You can see here he planted these double and triple rows of spruce trees around all sides of his house to break the wind and winter snow drifts. Gives him a little privacy from his sons and ranch hands is my guess." She pointed to the bunkhouse again. "As you can see, the bunkhouse and all these buildings are outside the spruce rows. I'd be willing to bet someone will be standing guard 24/7 now that all this trouble has started."

Kaplan put his finger on a scar in the land that ran from town northward through the middle of Pearson's property and relatively close to the main ranch complex. "What's this?"

"Pioneer River Ditch number four. It provides irrigation and water for a lot of his ranch. It's probably dried up right now since we had such a dry year so far. The snow melt, which would normally fill these ditches with overflow from the Pioneer River, is long gone. Most of the ditches will be dry until next spring unless we get a lot of rainfall over the summer. Thunderstorms are forecast for tonight, but I doubt they'll pan out as dry as it has been. Even if they do, they won't last long. They never do. But, this is Wyoming, that could change in ten minutes."

Kaplan tapped on the screen. "That's how I'll go in."

"Wait just a damn minute," Cavalier growled. "I won't let you just waltz in there and get yourself killed."

"I won't get killed." He could see beyond the fear in Cavalier's eyes. It was genuine concern. A look he'd seen before. In Isabella's eyes. He forced himself to turn away for a second. He swallowed and said, "I have a plan. Do you want to be pig-headed or would you like to hear what I have in mind?"

CHAPTER 24

Drew Pearson lumbered through the over-sized heavy wooden front door which matched the bulky leather furniture inside his ranch house. He had picked up his two injured sons, Mark and Scott, from Sheridan Memorial Hospital and delivered them to their respective cabins and waiting families. The ranch house was Pearson's pride and joy. He built it thirty years ago shortly after he'd gotten married. He had wanted the heavy log cabin appearance and feel with a post and beam interior, something his wife didn't care for, but in the end, he got what he wanted. Inside were several rustic wooden columns designed to match the structure's horizontal logs interlocked by notching. The walls were his hunting showcase, adorned with mounted animal heads. Mule deer, elk, pronghorn, moose, black bear, and grizzly. Prized hunting trophies. A massive stone fireplace anchored the living room. Pearson spared no expense, after all, it was *his* dream home. When he needed solitude, he retired to his private study, another testament to his ego. The study had its own fireplace, not as large and was lined with bookcases that extended to the ceiling. A ladder on wheels could reach any shelf simply by sliding it around the room on its tracks, his wife's idea. The separate door from the study led to the back of the home where he had installed a heated pool and hot tub. A place to unwind and watch the stars while sipping his favorite whiskey.

His home made him feel important and allowed him to impress people, especially his hunting buddies. Seven bedrooms and nine full baths. Over 6000 square feet plus a full 3000 square-foot basement. A home for the entire family, the big family he wanted and almost got. Four boys to carry on the family name. Something to be proud of, but he had wanted more children. Unfortunately, his wife had died during childbirth with his youngest son, Evan.

He had tried dating again, but there just weren't many women who were willing to live in Last Chance, in the middle of nowhere. So, he settled for the occasional tryst with one of the three local widows in Last Chance or a night with a whore in Sheridan or Cheyenne, or if he felt really high class, that special call girl over in Jackson. She was expensive, but worth every penny. He had resigned himself to raising his four boys on his own.

Mark, the second oldest of the four, had suffered a concussion at the hands of the stranger and was held overnight for observation while Scott, third born, wore a full-leg cast. Scott's injury was more severe. The stranger's kick to Scott's leg broke his left tibia or shinbone in what the orthopedic surgeon described as the *sweet spot.* If the kick was higher, it would have damaged the knee, lower and it would involve the ankle. The surgeon informed Scott he'd be wearing a leg cast for a minimum of eight weeks.

Drew was furious. Thinking about what that stranger had done to his boys made his blood pressure rise. Nobody messed with his boys. For that, the stranger would pay.

A year apart in age, Mark and Scott were inseparable as children, even now as adults that hadn't changed.

His two other sons, Stephen, the oldest who wanted to be called Stevie for some stupid reason, and the youngest, Evan, along with three of his six ranch hands went with him when he learned the stranger was locked in the jail. But, the stranger wasn't there. The town marshal claimed he was taken to the Sheridan Sheriff's Office, but one phone call proved that to be a lie. Something that bitch would regret. If she thought for one minute what she experienced yesterday was the extent of his rage, she was sadly mistaken.

Drew Pearson had pretty much run this town until the previous town marshal died screwing Poppy's wife. Against his objections, the town council voted to hire Christine Cavalier. A woman who had bumbled her way through a less than stellar career in law enforcement with one mistake after another. She had blamed her troubles in St. Louis on racial and gender bias within the police force. She claimed she was railroaded by the good ol' boy system. Allegations not upheld at her hearing. In reality, with her track record, the town marshal job in Last Chance was about all she qualified for and even then she was a piss-poor selection by the town council. The council only looked at two things, she was cheap, and she was desperate. He thought that might work in his favor, but as it turned out, she couldn't be manipulated. He had tried and failed to have her removed last year, but the council didn't see things quite the way he did. No matter what he said and how hard he tried, she just wouldn't look the other way. Now, she was a party to this stranger in town who had beaten up his sons. She had to go down. If the council wouldn't take action, he had no choice. He'd take matters into his own hands.

Mark's and Scott's wives had wanted to come to Sheridan with him to pick the boys up, but he promptly informed them their place was at home. It was his job to fetch his sons and bring them home. A woman's place was to take care of her man. Period. As the Good Book said in Ephesians

22-23, *Wives, submit yourselves to your own husbands as you do to the Lord. For the husband is the head of the wife as Christ is the head of the church, his body, of which he is the Savior.* By God, those women would too.

His two other sons, Stephen and Evan lived in the big house with him. His youngest son, Evan, was a good son. He was always a pleasure to be around. Never caused him any problems. And the kid had book smarts. In school, Evan was placed in advanced classes. A teacher told him Evan was gifted. If he read something once, he never forgot it. The issue with Evan was he was different. Different from his brothers and other boys his age. Drew figured Evan took after his mother. Maybe he'd be okay in a big city where boys didn't like sports such as hunting. Actually, Evan hated guns. Drew had tried to help the boy find a sport he could do. At baseball practice, the coach complained Evan was crawling around in the grass, examining ant mounds. None of this was a problem for Evan so much as for him. But, Evan was smart, intuitive and, most of all, obedient. He was very good with numbers. So much so that he had been in charge of all the Pearson finances for the past two years.

Evan was helpful in another way on the ranch, he was excellent with horses and even helped train most of them. He would ride for hours, most times returning with a bag full of rocks that he had collected somewhere on the property. Evan liked to ramble on about those stupid rocks. Evan was the smallest of the four, in size and stature, with a small frame and a mop of blond hair he got from his mother.

Drew's big issue with Stevie was his oldest son's uncontrollable anger and aggression. He was diagnosed with minor developmental problems when he was in grade school.

Stevie's learning problems in school only exaggerated his behavioral problem. Kids made fun of him causing Stevie to have angry outbursts where he used his fists. Drew spent a lot of time persuading the principal not to expel his son for fighting. When Stevie got older, he tried defying his father… once. Something he better never try again if he knew what was good for him. Stevie was the kind of kid who never learned from his mistakes. Even though he would get a beating for his bad behavior, he would keep doing the same thing over and over. He was the biggest of the four boys, taller and stronger. And always the biggest kid in school. Dark hair that grayed prematurely, just like his father's.

In high school Stevie's bad behavior got worse, ultimately getting him expelled. Missing so much school got Stevie held back, so Pearson hired a tutor for his son to get him to the point where he could pass the GED. Barely.

Drew's biggest problem now was how to protect Stevie from the law since he shot and killed one of Cavalier's deputies. That bitch town marshal would be coming for his son soon with an arrest warrant.

There was the matter of how to deal with the Indian girl. His beef with her was that she was the catalyst that started this whole ordeal. She involved Mark and Scott at the diner by getting in their way. Causing trouble seemed to be all she was good at. Evan didn't want to take the girl, but Stevie gave him no choice. Now, the town marshal would probably have an arrest warrant for Evan as an accessory to the kidnapping. Things had changed in his town. Since when did anybody give a shit about an Indian?

He had his own issues with the marshal, too. She had no doubt already put together a warrant for his arrest after he struck her, not once but twice. He was surprised he hadn't already seen the marshal's Bronco barreling down his driveway with reinforcements. She was probably putting together a posse of sorts to come arrest him, two of his sons, and the three ranch hands who escorted him into town yesterday.

He'd be ready when they arrived.

Stevie, Evan and the Indian girl were hidden away in a safe place. A place no one but him, his sons and ranch hands knew about. Someplace they could hole up for a very long time.

In the meantime, he would handle the town marshal when she arrived. He already had a big surprise cooked up just for her. One he'd enjoy watching. After he finished with her, she'd never again be a problem for the Pearson family.

CHAPTER 25

Cavalier sat silent while Kaplan laid out his plan to her and Moss.

When he finished she said, "I don't like it. Even if you are as good as you claim, I can't let you risk your life like that. It's my job on the line, not yours—"

"Hold on," Kaplan interrupted. "This is my decision. Your job is already on the line. If we...you...don't take this to a successful conclusion soon, you won't have a job Monday morning. Pearson's boy killed your deputy. You, an officer of the law, have been assaulted. And Lucy has been kidnapped. You gotta make an arrest. You know you have no other choice. I guarantee in this town, even this small town, people want to feel safe. They look to you to make that happen and if you can't...well kiss this job good-bye."

"What you're suggesting isn't even legal." She pleaded with Moss, "Tell him."

Moss raised his hands and winked at Cavalier. "I'm just back-up. Here to assist."

"This isn't about legal, it's about right and wrong," Kaplan said. "Let's finish this."

She pushed herself from her chair and eyed Moss. "All right back-up, are you willing to risk your career on this?"

Moss said, "If anyone can do this, he can." He gave Kaplan a quick smile. "Face it, Marshal, you've got more to lose without his help than with it."

"What about reinforcements? Can you get some of your

fellow Marshals Service deputies in here as backup? Make the case that all the Pearsons are fugitives?"

"Sure I can," Moss explained. "But understand that if I make that call, you lose control over this and everything must be done *by the book*. Is that the career exposure you really want? Having the feds come in and take over? And on a low note, at best, it would be morning before anything would get started—"

"And by then," Kaplan emphasized, "Lucy could be dead."

She folded her arms and thought about everything the two men standing in front of her were proposing. They were tag- teaming her, and she didn't like it, but deep down, she knew they were right. Action needed to be taken and taken soon. She finally relented. "All right, since I don't have a lot of options, let's do this." Both men had a cocky expressions on their faces. Right now, she'd go along with Kaplan's plan, but she'd keep her guard up. She kept her face serious and asked, "What do you need from me?"

"Two things to start with," Kaplan said. "How late is the Mercantile open and what time does it get dark around here?"

† † †

Kaplan had been gone over forty-five minutes. He'd said he needed some supplies from the Mercantile that he didn't have in his motorcycle packs. He didn't bother to explain before he left, but Cavalier knew she'd find out soon enough.

Moss stayed behind and made a couple of phone calls. She wasn't deliberately trying, but she overheard him talking. One was to the Sundown Motel to secure a room for a few nights. The other sounded like a business-related call, perhaps to his superiors. Cavalier only caught a few words here and there as Moss kept his back to her and his voice low.

When he got off the phone, he came over and sat in the chair next to her. He said, "What's your story, Marshal?"

"Call me Christine."

He rested his large arm on the edge of her desk. She felt her pulse quicken. Self-conscious she pushed the loose tendrils of her hair back behind her ear.

"I like that name. Christine," Moss said. "I read about you on the way here."

"While you were driving? Wait. What? Read about me?"

"Your file—"

"You pulled a file on me?" Her tone full of disdain. "Why would you do that?"

He shot her a wry grin. "I like to know what I'm headed into and that includes the people involved. You would've done the same thing if the roles were reversed. We're on the same team, Christine."

He was direct and confident. She liked that in a man.

"I'm sure you were a good cop and somehow you got railroaded in St. Louis. What happened?"

She wasn't sure how to respond. He was dragging up memories she wanted to stay buried. "It was a long time ago."

Moss paused a moment as if he was searching for the right words.

She broke the silence, "The report said I failed to exercise good judgement in the line of duty resulting in the death of a fellow officer." She closed her eyes. "My partner."

"Is that what *you* believe?"

"No. Not at the time." She was surprised she was confiding in this man, but her gut told her he could be trusted.

She continued, "I had always been a by the book cop. It was a drug bust. My partner and I had been surveilling this warehouse for weeks. We got a tip our suspect was inside. I didn't want to lose this scumbag. I went in." Her voice faltered.

Moss said, "Listen you don't need to continue."

She could see his face was sympathetic. She never liked being pitied. "You asked and now I'm telling you." It took a few moments before she continued, "I had my partner go around to the back of the warehouse to make sure no one escaped. He was a rookie, just 24 and only three months on the force. He had only seen a few misdemeanors and petty felonies. He was shot in the chest at point-blank range. That's why this thing with Doug…"

"Cops die in the line of duty."

"That's what I told myself, over and over. But Internal Affairs had a field day with this. I was black-balled, and nobody would work with me."

"And you think that was all there was to it?"

No, there was more, but that part of the story she wasn't ready to share.

"I guess so," she said.

A loud banging on the outside door interrupted their conversation. They drew their weapons. Moss held out his arm and indicated she stand on his side away from the door. The banging noise got louder. Moss eased over, twisted the knob and swung the door open aiming his weapon at the source of the noise.

"Nice to see you too." It was Kaplan and his arms were full of bags.

"Good way to get shot, partner." Moss holstered his weapon.

"Glad to know, you aren't trigger happy," Kaplan laughed.

"You buy out the store?"

"Funny, that's what the owner said. I did get everything we'll need and more." Kaplan laid the equipment out on Doug's desk and explained what needed to be done and in what order. "Any questions?"

Cavalier scanned all of it and replied, "I hope you know what you're doing."

"Absolutely. I'll go in at 10:00 tonight."

CHAPTER 26

Last Chance Police Department
10:00 P. M.

Kaplan heard the first crack of thunder rumble in the distance.

Cavalier tilted her head in his direction.

She warned, "This could be a problem. As dry as it's been, almost any rain could mean flash floods." She hesitated. "Maybe we should call this off."

"Stay positive Marshal," Kaplan said. "The rain might just make my job easier."

Cavalier didn't appear convinced. Moss lightly squeezed her shoulder helping Cavalier to stop fidgeting. "Wet ground can be quieter than dry ground and the rain might drown out his footfalls." Moss continued, "Easier to sneak up on someone if they can't see or hear you coming."

Kaplan shot Cavalier a warm smile. "What he said."

Earlier in the evening, as dusk was settling, the three of them had driven by Pearson's property in Moss' Escalade, since it was the closest thing to an anonymous vehicle they had available. Cavalier pointed out Pioneer River Ditch number four, which ran through Pearson's property and close to Pearson's ranch house. Kaplan could see by the fading light that it was indeed dry. His drop-off spot would be on the west side of a small ridge just beyond sight of the ranch, about a mile from the ditch and another mile from the ranch house. Two miles.

He would allow himself thirty minutes to get there, ten on the road, twenty in the ditch.

Last Chance Mercantile didn't have the wireless earpiece technology he was used to and neither did Cavalier, so instead he bought three long-range walkie-talkie type radios with push-to-talk ear sets. The man at the store said most of the hunters in the area used them. The box stated a range of up to five miles, but out here in no man's land, he doubted the range would be more than two and half to three miles at best. That should be enough, unless something went terribly wrong. The owner said it was supposed to rain, and since his weather radar showed several thunderstorms approaching northern Wyoming, he suggested waterproof rain pants and jacket. The owner of the Last Chance Mercantile was proud of his new product line from Duluth Trading Co. and said the products had been flying off the shelves even in this little town. Seemed the town had a lot of fisherman and hunters. They weren't cheap, the owner said, but they were quiet when you moved, unlike most rain gear, and durable to the point they wouldn't rip when snagged. Quiet and durable were good. The Mercantile also had several styles of night vision goggles, all priced higher than he wanted to pay. As long as there was lightning in the area he couldn't use the NVGs, but he hated being on a nighttime mission without a pair. Could make the difference between success and failure.

By the time they reached the drop-off spot in Moss' Escalade, small pellets of rain were splattering the windshield. Lightning flashed in the distance and he could hear the thunder rumble. With the engine still running, Kaplan rehearsed the plan one more time with Moss and Cavalier. There was no room for error. They had to all be on the same page with the plan. They both gave him two thumbs up.

He jumped out of the Escalade, the road still dry, and the temperature dropping fast. He had anticipated the after-dark drop as it happened every year when he made his annual migration to Sturgis, South Dakota on his motorcycle. In actuality, he wasn't too terribly far from Sturgis now. He guessed three hours or so. He wrapped his waterproof balaclava over his head, and tucked his ear set safely inside. He slipped a black ball cap on top in hopes that between the rain jacket hood and the brim of the hat, the rain would stay out of his eyes.

He was dressed in full-black tactical gear and armed. Next, he slipped into his new black Duluth Trading Co. rain pants, pulled on the jacket and sealed the neck, wrists, and ankles. After he stuffed the NVGs in one of the jacket pockets he knew he was ready. He'd been in plenty of situations more dangerous with a lot less.

Moss rolled down the driver's side window. Kaplan saw Cavalier lean over from the passenger seat. "Be careful, lightning kills a couple of dozen people a year in the Rocky Mountains," she warned. "If you need backup, we're only three or four minutes away."

"Hey Rambo," Moss said. "Keep your head low and watch your back."

Kaplan shot back, "Roger that." He checked his watch and footed it toward Pioneer River Ditch number four.

By the time he reached the ditch, it was raining harder and the storm had moved closer. He could smell the petrichor in the air. The wind picked up and he could see a wall of clouds and lightning race across the Bighorn Mountains toward the Pearson Ranch. It took him seven minutes to reach the ditch. *Ahead of schedule.* He jumped into the ditch and started running again.

As the rain intensified, the Wyoming clay in the ditch became slick and his boots lost grip time after time. The ditch filled faster than he anticipated with water cascading down from every direction. What had started as a squish had now transformed into a heavy slosh splashing mud knee-high with each step.

A brilliant flash lit up the sky followed by a sharp loud crack that roared nearby, he felt the ground shake under his feet. Sheets of rain moved from the west and the mountains disappeared. The landscape dimmed ahead, and the air became dense and cool against his face. The sky let loose and he was pelted with raindrops. The night became opaque as the rain formed a veil over the Wyoming landscape.

He pushed forward, but the water's natural drag created a lot of resistance.

Behind him he heard a rush of water. Cavalier had forewarned him about the flash floods. The sound grew louder. There was a crackle in his ear. It was Cavalier.

"Kaplan, do you hear me?" Her voice full of urgency. "Kaplan, answer me."

"Five by five," he replied.

"If you're not already, get out of the ditch."

"I'll lose my cover."

"If you stay, you could lose your life. Get out. Now." Her urgent plea sounded like panic.

Being from the East, he had never experienced a flash flood and wondered just how dangerous it could really be. He'd heard stories of people, and even buildings, being washed away, but he couldn't imagine how something with that much force could form in such a short span of time. He picked up his pace and used the lightning flashes to find a climbable escape from the ditch.

"I'm out," he said. "And totally exposed."

"You can thank me later." The sarcasm in her voice was evident.

Another bolt of lightning broke the blackness and illuminated the landscape. In the distance, he saw buildings and trees. Behind the trees, his destination. As his eyes readjusted to the darkness, he could barely make out lights in two of the buildings. The swooshing sound of water beside him changed into a roar. It was at least two feet higher than a moment ago when he climbed from the ditch. He wouldn't have believed it if he hadn't seen it with his own eyes.

Next came a wave carrying sediment and debris. As she said, he'd have to thank Cavalier later. After the wave, the current stayed swift and the water level continued to rise. The only upside he thought, was the deluge of rain would drown out any noise he would make.

He knelt to one knee and surveyed the landscape. The waterproof rain gear had done its job and kept him dry. The brim of his cap was saturated, and water poured continuously in front of his face like a miniature waterfall. The wind didn't help either. He wiped his eyes with the back of his glove.

He stayed still, allowing each flash of lightning to give him a better look at what was ahead. He had memorized the layout of the compound from the picture Cavalier had printed from Google Maps. It wasn't very detailed, but when he compared it with the satellite view and the location of Pioneer River Ditch number four in relation to the compound, what he was staring at started to make a little more sense. What neither view offered him, was a detailed topography of the area. Something he wished he had so he could use the knolls to hide behind as he approached the complex of buildings. In the darkness, those knolls look as if they disappeared.

Another flash of lightning and he recognized the first two buildings. According to Cavalier, these were where the two Pearson boys he encountered the day before at the diner lived. Neither posed a threat. Regardless, he would still maintain a constant vigil in case some of Pearson's ranch hands were out on patrol.

He pushed himself to his feet and sprinted toward the houses. He was within a hundred yards of the first when another bolt of lightning crashed from above and struck a tree near the ranch house. It exploded and burst into flames. The resounding thunderclap was deafening. There was a flurry of activity as six men ran from different directions toward the burning tree. Four from the bunkhouse and a couple from behind the rows of trees.

"Perfect," he muttered out loud.

"What is it?" Moss asked him through the earpiece.

"That last bolt caught a tree on fire close to the ranch house. All of Pearson's men are out there now trying to put it out."

"You got lucky."

"Yep."

Kaplan seized the opportunity and ran toward the back of the first two houses, which were spaced roughly fifty feet apart. Both front doors opened simultaneously, light spilling out onto the front porches. Log cabins. A couple stepped onto the front porch of the first cabin. The man had a cast on his leg and was leaning against crutches. The woman visibly pregnant. The man at the other cabin stood alone and had a large bandage on his head.

He thought it odd that these cabins and the bunkhouse faced Pearson's ranch house to the east instead of facing the Bighorn Mountains to the west. A wasted view in his opinion, but perfect for him. While everyone was watching the tree burn and the ranch hands were scrambling to put out the fire, he seized the opportunity to peek in the back windows of the cabins for any sign of Lucy.

Nothing.

He raced across the gap between the second cabin and the bunkhouse, about a hundred yards. What he saw as he approached the rear of the bunkhouse stopped him mid-stride. On a covered back porch was a man smoking a cigarette, holding a rifle and looking right at him.

CHAPTER 27

Lucy's stomach growled. Evan had brought her a ham and cheese sandwich, a bag of chips, and a Coke not long after she had asked for food. That had long worn off, and now she was hungry again. The only noise was the steady droning of the television at the far end of the hall.

She banged on the door. Footsteps came down the hall followed by the unmistakable sound of the deadbolt tumblers unlocking. She stepped back.

When the door opened, she jumped back even farther. It wasn't Evan. The man in front of her had a bloodied bandage over his nose and two black eyes.

Stevie.

He held a metal tray with food on it. Same as this afternoon—a sandwich, chips in a bag, and a canned Coke. The smell of alcohol surrounded him.

"Here," Stevie said. He thrust the tray toward her. "This is all you get until morning."

"I need to pee," she said.

"You already went to the bathroom."

"That was a long time ago."

His eyes bore down on her. "You know where it is. Just don't bother me anymore tonight, I have a headache." He staggered down the hall and out of sight.

She could barely believe her good fortune. Did Stevie just leave her unsupervised? Maybe his head hurt too much to notice.

Now, to work on her escape plan, but first she really did need to pee. She went back in the dirty bathroom. She reached up and checked the window lock, secured. With her fingernails, she tried to scrape off the paint to see outside. Hopeful at first, when the paint flaked off, but disappointed when she realized the window was painted on the outside too. She flushed the toilet, washed her hands and peered into the hall.

No one in sight. She tiptoed down the hall past the bathroom. On the right, was what looked like a foyer or alcove about the same dimensions as the bathroom. It had a wooden door, which she assumed led outside. It also had two padlocks on it, one high and one low, just like the bathroom window, only bigger. On the opposite side of the hall was nothing, just a long wall made from wooden planks. No doors, no windows, nothing. The only way out, had to be down the hall where Stevie had disappeared a few moments earlier.

As she crept down the hall, the volume on the television grew louder. She peeked around the corner. Nobody to the right. She swung her head left and saw Stevie sitting in a faded leather chair watching *Big Bang Theory* on a small TV. It was a rerun, she had seen it before. Stevie's head was bobbing up and down, like he was falling asleep. From her vantage point, she could see two small rooms along the back wall on each side of the television. Both doors were open, and shafts of light from the TV room landed on a twin bed in each room.

Around the corner to the left was a kitchen. It extended all the way back and she realized the kitchen was what was on the other side of the wooden plank wall in the hallway. On the far side of the kitchen was another door. This one did not have any locks on it.

Stevie snorted with his chin resting against his chest. Lucy ducked out of sight and padded back to her room. She left the door open and quietly ate her food, all the time watching and listening for any sign of Stevie.

While she ate, her thoughts drifted to Kaplan. Was he okay? Was he looking for her? He made her feel safe and comfortable. Someone who truly cared for her well-being. Someone she could turn to when things went wrong. She wished he was here with her now. He would know what to do. He would know how to handle Stevie and get her out of this god-awful place. She remembered the tattoos on his forearms, they looked military, but she never got a chance to talk to him about it. He did not talk much anyway. The quiet, strong, do-not-mess-with-me-or-I-will-break-your-neck type. She did not know how old he was either. She found it hard to tell with his beard stubble and grayed temples. Old, she thought.

She finished her food, wadded up the chip bag and thought about crushing the empty can with the heel of her shoe. That was what she wanted to do to that asshole Stevie, crush him with the sole of her shoe. The thought of it made her feel good. But, she didn't want to wake Stevie.

Somehow, she needed to get past Stevie and out that kitchen door. She picked up her tray to return her trash. It was heavy. Very heavy, and that gave her an idea. If it worked, she could escape through the kitchen door. If it did not, she would be in big, big trouble.

Holding the tray, she slipped back down the hall toward the kitchen…and Stevie. Her chest heaving up and down. She crouched and peered around the corner. Stevie was slumped in the chair and his chin was still resting on his chest. Asleep, she hoped. Now was her chance. She gripped the tray with both hands, and without a sound approached him from behind. She reared the tray back like a batter setting up for a home run swing. How she truly wanted to bach his head in. On second thought, maybe a quiet escape was the best plan. She started to lower the tray when the kitchen door swung open. She froze. It was Evan. Stevie snapped his head up.

"What are you doing out of your room?" Evan demanded. His voice loud and agitated. She had been caught.

"Just bringing this to the kitchen."

"Well, do it and get back to your room. I'll be there in a minute."

She placed the tray on the counter and hurried back to her room. If Evan told on her she was in deep shit. As she made her way back to her room, she heard Evan scolding Stevie.

"What the hell were you thinking?" Evan shouted at his brother. "Dad said not to let her out of the room."

"What difference does it make," Stevie grumbled. "It's not like she can go anywhere. There's only one way out and she'd never get past the guards."

"You're an idiot."

"Fuck you, Evan."

She heard rustling in the kitchen and Stevie said, "I'm going to bed."

She cowered in the corner of the small room and waited. *How come no one has come to rescue me?* She felt her eyes well up.

Evan appeared in teh doorway. "I saw what you were going to do," Evan said. "Nice try. If you get another chance, you'd better kill him with the first blow. If you don't, you're one dead girl." Besides, you'd never make it past the guards."

† † †

Cavalier and Moss hadn't said a word since Kaplan's last transmission. She noted Moss kept checking his watch and returning his attention toward Pearson's ranch. Every few minutes, he would pick up her binoculars and scan the open range. Rain splattered the windshield and the wipers would cycle every fifteen seconds or so. The engine was off, but the electronics were still active. She felt a chill and reached into the back seat and picked up her jacket. Although it was mid-July, temperatures at night still got chilly, sometimes downright cold. The cool air didn't seem to bother Moss, but he was a large man and had just arrived this morning from Chicago.

He said, "I can run the heater if you'd like. I don't mind. Might take the chill out of the air."

Cavalier slipped into her jacket. "I'm fine."

It was weird to her that a man with such an amicable appearance could be a WitSec Deputy U. S. Marshal. But, why not?

"How long have you been with the Marshals Service?"

"Too long." He twisted in his seat and faced her. "I'm eligible to retire, if that tells you anything."

"Have you thought about retiring?"

"Every single day."

"Why don't you?"

He laughed. "Believe me, it wouldn't take much. I have gone so far as to actually fill out and sign all the paperwork. It's just waiting on a date. There have been days I've had the paperwork in my hands and found myself standing in front of the door to HR...but I always back out."

"What stops you?"

Moss rotated back in his seat and directed his attention

out the window toward the Wyoming high desert plains. A bolt of lightning struck nearby, and the vehicle shook. He didn't answer, but with the flash of light, she saw concern on his face. "Are you worried about him?" she finally asked.

"Naw. Kaplan's a big boy. He can take care of himself."

"Where did you two meet?" she asked. "Did you work together?"

He grinned. "In a sense, we did work together. We met last August in Virginia on one of my cases."

"Virginia? I thought you were based in Chicago."

"I was…and am. Chicago is home for me, I grew up there. I was transferred from WitSec in Little Rock, Arkansas to Chicago Enforcement Division. I was back in Chicago for a whopping total of three weeks when my replacement in Little Rock was killed after a witness's identity was breached. The Administrator sent me back to Little Rock until the Marshals Service could find another replacement."

"How did you get to Virginia?"

"Kaplan was in Little Rock at a restaurant, apparently minding his own business when he detected a hit going down. All that CIA training, I guess. He jumped in and saved our witness, but in the ensuing shootout, my replacement was shot and killed. Kaplan grabbed our witness, threw him on the back of his motorcycle and took off."

She raised her eyebrow. "Why didn't he just call you guys to come get the witness?"

"My replacement, who was a good friend of mine by the way, asked Kaplan with his dying breath to keep the witness safe and get him to a WitSec safe house. Kaplan gave him his word. The man would stop at nothing until he delivered him to the SSOC."

"SSOC? Is that some Marshals Service acronym?"

"The Witness Protection Safe Site and Orientation Center in Alexandria, Virginia. I met up with Kaplan in Lexington after chasing him halfway across the country."

She no longer felt cold. She leaned closer to him. "Why was he running from you?"

"He wasn't. He was running from the mob, who was trying to kill the witness. He took the witness to a CIA safe house in Lexington, Virginia and contacted me. Next, he came up with a hair-brained, albeit ingenious scheme, to not only get the witness to the SSOC but to take down the mob at the same time.

"Did it work?"

He laughed. "Like a freaking charm, if you'll excuse my French."

"Sounds like you enjoyed it."

"There's a lot more to that story, but yeah. It was probably the most exhilarating, yet terrifying, few days of my life."

Moss looked in the direction of Pearson's ranch. The rain had slowed, and the powerful storm showed signs of moving out of the area.

"Seems to me," she said, "you wish you were out there with him right now."

"In a way, but I'm enjoying the present company."

CHAPTER 28

Kaplan came to a grinding halt when he saw the man looking in his direction.

He eased his hand into his rain jacket pocket and drew his Beretta. Even though he was looking in Kaplan's direction, it was apparent the man didn't see him or even realize there was someone standing only fifty feet away from him. Perhaps he was looking at the passing clouds or the next storm to the west, which was moving toward them at a good click.

Kaplan didn't move. Movement was easier to spot than a stationary target. The lit cigarette in the man's mouth glowed as the man took another long drag. The man turned and faced the opposite direction exhaling a cloud of smoke. It was the opportunity Kaplan needed. His objective was to take the man down. Swift and quiet, which meant one thing, take him from behind.

Quietly, Kaplan moved forward keeping his center of gravity low. Even with a rain suit on and the cooler air, he felt a bead of sweat roll down his back. He made it to the edge of the covered back porch without the man noticing. It was times like these when he wished he had brought the sound suppressor for his Beretta. He stepped onto the porch. The man was still facing the opposite direction, all sounds drowned out by the roaring torrent of water in the irrigation ditch only twenty feet away.

Kaplan moved closer, careful to keep his approach quiet. The porch's wooden planks were wet helping to soften his footfalls. But then, a loose plank squeaked under his foot.

The man spun around. Kaplan raised his arms and smashed the butt of his Beretta against the side of the man's head.

The man collapsed, dropping his rifle. Kaplan reached for it, but he wasn't fast enough. The rifle clanked against the wooden decking planks. The moisture absorbed most of the sound, but if someone was nearby, they could have heard it.

Kaplan knelt down on a knee and checked for a pulse. The ranch hand wasn't breathing. The blow should have knocked the man unconscious and nothing more. But, this man was dead, plain and simple.

Kaplan picked up the rifle and threw the man over his shoulder. He carried him to the edge of the ditch and lowered him to the grass. He bent over the man, the rain pelted his back while he reached in his pocket for his Maglite. Another flash of lightning lit up the sky to the west.

The man looked mid-twenties and the side of his head was bloody and the blood was being slowly washed away by the downpour. The body couldn't be found, not now, or anytime soon for that matter. Not until this ordeal was over, Lucy was safe and the Pearsons were locked away in jail…or dead.

The intensity of the wind had increased as had the frequency of lightning. Lightning was cutting crazy zig-zags into the blackened sky. The next storm moved overhead. This one more severe than the previous storm. This one sounded angry. Branches of lightning spread across the landscape making contact with something…a tree, a bush, a fence post, a shed out in the nearby field. The ground shook violently with each flash.

Kaplan knew the danger of staying in the open, yet he had no other choice. He tossed the rifle into the water and rolled the man's body into the flooded ditch. The raging waters would carry the body far enough downstream where it shouldn't be found for a day or two. Not until someone went looking for him. And it wouldn't be tonight with this weather. As much as he didn't like the weather, the storms provided ideal cover. Only a crazy person, he thought, would be out in this weather.

As the roiling river carried the body out of sight, he scanned the Pearson complex. Any direct path to the main ranch house would put him in the open for a considerable distance. And with the glow from the four vapor lights mounted on poles in front of the two cabins and bunkhouse, he would be an easy intruder to spot. And there were plenty of men out by the smoldering tree. Too many to get past without being spotted.

He recalled from Cavalier's map search that Pioneer River ditch number four snaked northward behind both cabins and the bunkhouse before turning northeast. It didn't wrap close around Pearson's ranch house, but it did offer him a different angle of approach, one that should keep him clear of the cabins and bunkhouse. If he kept following the ditch until he was due north of the ranch house, he could come in from that angle, and he recalled, there was nothing between the ranch house and ditch for at least two hundred yards except the barrier of spruce trees.

As he'd encountered earlier, the two-dimensional map didn't reveal the subtle, and sometimes significant, topographic changes he needed to fully understand the lay of the land. It was considered flat land, yet there were still plenty of rolling hills and knolls. He trudged northeastward through the sodden and sometimes slick clay, a rise developed between him and the ranch house. In the beginning, it was irrelevant, now it had risen to an ever-increasing cliff and the face was retreating further and further from the ditch itself. Any hopes of keeping sight of the tree line surrounding the ranch house had now evaporated.

He kept close to the cliff face and continued his trek knowing that at some point he'd have to scale the cliff in order to reach the ranch house. The heavy rain was slowly tapering, and at times, almost stopped completely. To the west, one more thunderstorm rumbled in his direction. Moonlight behind the lone thunderhead created a halo around its stormy edges. To both sides, he could see stars. Lots of them. The Bighorn Mountains reappeared. When this last storm passed, the skies would clear, and his stormy cloud cover would dissipate. It would be easier for him to see…and be seen.

† † †

Cavalier stared out the windshield and watched the storms pass one by one. For the longest time, they were like a chorus line marching across the same swath of northern Wyoming, right over the top of Last Chance and the Pearson ranch. The end of the line was coming, the final storm was lumbering over the Bighorn Mountains and the skies were clearing behind it. This storm that looked like it would pass to the north of where they were parked. The rain had slowed to a sprinkle and the windshield wipers, still on intermittent, made a dry squeak with each cycle.

Her watch read 11:30. Kaplan had been gone a total of an hour and a half and it had been close to forty-five minutes since his last transmission. It was an interesting story Moss told her about his and Kaplan's first meeting. She suspected there was more to it than he was willing to share. WitSec was always wrapped up in secrecy. Everybody had their secrets, she thought. Even she did. She had hoped Moss would open up about his personal life, but so far, nothing but work life.

Here goes nothing.

"Is there a Mrs. Moss?" she asked out of the blue.

He chuckled, and she felt her face flush. "Freight train," he replied with no further explanation.

"What?"

"You accused me earlier of getting right to the point. That is what I call as subtle as a freight train."

Busted, she thought. "I was just making conversation while we wait on your friend."

"Uh-huh." He kept his focus ahead and wrapped his hands around the steering wheel like he needed a place to put them. "Two of them. And both ex's."

"Kids?"

"Nope."

"You know a conversation is more than a one-word response."

She could see him grinning at her now. Her embarrassment shot another heat wave through her body. She removed her jacket. The final diminishing storm was sliding to the north and a few moonbeams found their way past the breaking clouds. "Looks like it's clearing up."

Moss switched off the wipers and yawned.

"You were saying?" she said.

"The first marriage was a mistake. We got hitched on a whim in Vegas. Lasted about three months. She was younger, immature, and expected me to be home every night. That isn't how WitSec works, you know. I came home one night to any empty house and a note on the kitchen counter saying she had moved back in with her parents."

"That had to be tough."

"Not really. Not like you might think anyway. It was the best thing for both of us."

"And Mrs. Moss number two?"

"She was the total opposite. Turned out she liked it best when I *was* gone. After about a year, I got suspicious. Strange text messages late at night. Unfamiliar numbers on Caller-ID. So, I had a buddy tail her during one of my out of town WitSec details. Sure enough, she was having an affair with her personal trainer at the gym."

"Wow, that's sounds familiar."

"What do you mean?" She saw his brow furrow.

"You read my file, you know I'm divorced." After she spoke she realized how sarcastic her tone must have sounded.

"I told you already, I pulled your file only to see what Kaplan was up against. I didn't find those types of personal details, just stats and employment issues." He paused and took a deep breath. "So, you were saying?"

"Touché." She liked this man. "I married a fellow cop on the force in St. Louis. The man of my dreams…or so I thought. He was like an Adonis. He worked out all the time. Heavy weights, too. Everything was great for a couple of years. Then, he bought an old bare bones weight gym, called it a *box* I think. He only opened the gym when he wasn't on duty. In no time, business took off and he either had to sell it, close it, or hire someone to keep it open while he was at work. So, he hired this woman, a real head-turner if you know what I mean. The kind of woman other women hate because she brings out all their insecurities. If he was Ken, she was Barbie."

Moss laughed.

"I didn't like the way she looked at him or the way she always giggled at every damn thing he said. You know, if it feels bad, it probably is bad. I told him to fire her, but he refused. Said she was good for business and knew her stuff. Anyway, to make a long story short, I take off early from work one night. Thought it'd be good to spend a little time together. I was so stupid. I even stopped to pick up his favorite Chinese take-out. When I got home, her car was in our driveway. I sneaked in the house and found them both in the kitchen cooking breakfast… at seven o'clock at night. He was standing in front of the stove in his boxer briefs, and she was wearing one of his t-shirts. She was reaching up to get plates from the cabinet showing off her naked ass."

"That's gotta suck," he said. "What'd you do?"

"What any woman would do, I went totally ballistic."

"Hell hath no fury like a woman scorned."

"You're damn right. I started throwing shit at both of them, plates, utensils, knives, anything I could get my hands on. She screamed, ran out of the room and took off. Still in his shirt, I might add. He made some lame excuse about the steroids being the cause. Swore he would end it. I threw his shit out in the yard and kicked him out that night. Next day I went to a lawyer and filed for divorce."

"Any regrets?"

"Only that I didn't revert back to my maiden name of Hunt. The beauty of it all, about a month later he caught her cheating on him."

"Karma, baby."

"Karma is a wonderful thing," she said.

"You know why divorces are so expensive, right?"

"No, why?"

"Because they're worth it."

She laughed until her sides hurt.

"What about now? Any new prospects?"

"Not really, however, there is this one guy I met today that I find rather interesting."

He grinned. "Freight train."

They both erupted in laughter.

CHAPTER 29

As Kaplan approached the cliff, a strange shape appeared inset in the stone. It looked like a simple pioneer's house, one built into the cliff. The building's facade was old and weathered, like reclaimed barn siding. Above, an overhang provided some protection. It faced the northwest, which in Wyoming, meant virtually no protection from the elements. He could imagine the winter's snowdrifts piling up next to the facade and blocking access for months at a time.

On closer inspection, he believed it might have been an old mine. There was a door, which was bolted from the inside, and a small window locked in the same manner. The window was painted black with no way to see what was inside.

It appeared abandoned.

He thought about breaking the glass, but that would make noise and, if on some outside chance there was actually someone inside, he would be made and his attempts to rescue Lucy would be all for naught. Same thing with the door. The wooden door was heavy, but aged. He considered trying to kick it in, but again, the noise.

If his calculations were correct, Pearson's ranch house should be almost due south of his current position. No easy way to scale the cliff wall from here, meaning backtrack to where the rise started not far from the bunkhouse and potentially risk being spotted now that the skies were clearing or push forward in hopes that the rise receded ahead. He opted to stick with the planned mission and push forward.

His gamble paid off. Three hundred yards farther and the cliff wall did two things, merged close to Pioneer River Ditch number four and dropped to a height where he could scale it with minimal effort.

The top of the ridge was covered with grasses and sage. The smell was unmistakable. The sky rumbled again and spit small raindrops. The last storm was passing overhead. He could almost watch it dissipate as it moved across the arid Wyoming high desert plains and the Pearson property. Lightning popped from cloud to cloud, but no more cloud to ground strikes. A fireworks show in the sky. The rumbles grew weaker and the rain stopped entirely almost as quickly as it had begun. He focused his attention uphill and trotted along the ridgeline.

The clouds cleared and stars filled the sky. The crescent moon brightened the landscape and the silhouette of the Bighorn Mountains grew larger than life. Once atop the precipice of the ridge, directly above the facade, he could see the curvature of the ditch as it laid out in front of him. Maybe it was his distance from it, but the torrent of water in the ditch seemed to have slowed and the rushing sound he had used for cover had quieted. To the southwest, the lights of the bunkhouse and cabins were in clear view. A couple of hundred yards to the south he spotted the grove of spruce trees he knew surrounded Drew Pearson's ranch house. Between them, the unmistakable glow of vapor lights. Thirty feet in front of him as he faced the ranch house, something else. Unexpected. But, it reinforced his decision not to kick in the door or break the window to the facade below.

Pipes. Perhaps, exhaust vents. And currently expelling steam…or smoke. Now he knew whatever was forty feet below him was occupied. It also brought up a few other possibilities in his mind. The place below him would be a great place to hide…or hide someone. Evan and Stevie could be holed up down there, but more importantly, that would be a great place to keep Lucy captive.

His earpiece crackled and came to life with a familiar voice. "How 'bout a SitRep, buddy?" It was Moss.

Kaplan sat on his heels to maintain a low profile and brought Moss and Cavalier up to date. He explained his newfound theory about the bunker, for lack of a better word, and about the possibility of Lucy being held captive in there.

Cavalier spoke next. "You need to find that bastard Drew. Make him tell us where Evan, Stevie, and Lucy are."

"Wrong," he replied. His priorities and Cavalier's were different. "I made myself clear and you agreed. Lucy's safety is number one. After she's safe, we go after the Pearsons. It's not like he's going anywhere anytime soon. He's the type who will dig in and fight to the finish."

"I'm in charge of this operation. Is that understood?" Her voice razor sharp. "If you—"

"Seeing as I'm the one out here with my ass on the line right now, I'm making the calls."

There was a long silence. He knew what was happening, Moss and Cavalier were no doubt involved in a conversation. Cavalier had a personal vendetta for Pearson, and he didn't blame her for that. But, her vendetta would have to wait for the right time, and that was not now. That time would come soon enough.

He knew the best execution for a hostage rescue. The government had trained him. He only agreed to wait and go to the Rez first because he needed Cavalier to give him as much information about the ranch layout as possible. Now he needed to surprise the captors. Once Lucy was safe, Cavalier could storm the castle.

No more discussion was needed. He reached inside his balaclava and switched off his radio. He didn't need any more distractions from Cavalier. No more wasting time. He studied the sky and the remnants of the last storm as it drifted eastward. *Still too early for the NVGs.* He would need to wait until the last of the flashing had stopped or moved farther in the distance to matter. No need in risking flash blindness by using them too early. All he would do was focus on locating and rescuing Lucy.

† † †

She was getting tired of Kaplan constantly challenging her authority. Drew Pearson had to go down tonight. Take out the Pearsons and then they had plenty of time to search for Lucy. It wasn't like the Pearsons had time to take her very far. The girl had to be held somewhere on Pearson's ranch. Disable the threat and search for the hostage. Why couldn't Kaplan understand that?

While Cavalier was arguing with Kaplan, Moss reached out and placed his hand on her arm. She stopped mid-sentence and shot him a look.

"What?" she said.

"Let him do what he does best. Arguing won't get us any closer to capturing the Pearsons or rescuing Lucy. Besides, if Kaplan gets Lucy and brings her back, just think of the good recon information he'll have for you. He's getting an up close and personal inspection of Pearson's entire compound. He'll know exactly where everything is, and more importantly, where everyone will be. His knowledge will make capturing

Drew Pearson and sons much easier, not to mention safer."

"What galls me," she said, "is that he doesn't listen. He just does whatever he wants with reckless abandon and total disregard to anyone but himself."

"That's not true." Moss opened his car door and stepped outside. He motioned for her to do the same. He met her in front of his Escalade and leaned against the grill. "Kaplan doesn't do whatever he wants, he does what he has to. Once he's boots on the ground, he acts and reacts. If anything, or anyone gets in his way, he eliminates the threat. Period. That's how he survives. And another thing, and you should let this sink in, that's exactly the way Isabella was trained. Maybe the problem you have with Kaplan isn't because he's the way he is, so much as he reminds you of your sister. I don't know what happened to Isabella. What I do know about Isabella is only what Kaplan has told me. But, if she is anything like he described, then they are alike in so many ways." He paused and took a deep breath that turned into a yawn. "You know why he came to Last Chance, don't you?"

She looked away. Talking about her sister was never easy. She did know Moss was right about a great many things. She knew why Kaplan was here. What troubled her was how to deal with him when the time came. If she told him what he wanted to know, she would have betrayed her sister's trust.

Indeed, Kaplan did remind her of Isabella. They were a lot alike, too much alike, just as Moss had said. Isabella had confided in her many times about the relationship she had with Kaplan. And the love. But, now things were different. Many things had changed. Somehow, her sister had foreseen that Kaplan would eventually find his way to Last Chance and made her promise never to tell him the truth. And that was making this whole thing so damn difficult to deal with.

"I do know why he's here," she finally said. "He's trying to find Isabella."

"That's right. And he's been searching for her for over two years. He's given up everything to find her. And he won't stop until he does."

She felt it coming on and couldn't stop it. Tears welled up in her eyes.

In a broken voice she said, "That's something I can never let happen."

† † †

Sometimes things went according to plan and other times, well, they simply didn't. One thing the Cowboy hadn't planned on, and had no way of knowing in advance, was the unanticipated arrival of the stranger and the cause and effect his presence had on what he thought was a well-orchestrated plan.

By now, the town marshal and her deputies should have enlisted the assistance of federal law enforcement to help solve the unexplained murders on the Crow Reservation and the fire and murders in Last Chance. It was something he had counted on happening as soon as ballistics linked the two crimes, which by now had surely happened. But the stranger's arrival had caused a chain of events that had taken the emphasis and urgency from solving the murders and redirected it to locating a missing, and presumed kidnapped, Native Indian girl and the capture of a local man who killed one of the Last Chance deputies. It altered the routine behavior of several other citizens of Sheridan County and the Last Chance area, which resulted in a crescendo of criminal activity by an entire family, all of whom were probably in the process of having arrest warrants issued against them. Crimes ranging from kidnapping to assault and battery to murder, and anything else law enforcement could trump up against them.

An unfortunate detour to his plan, but not the end of it, either. Just a delay, and not even a long delay. Sooner or later, the executions on the Crow Reservation along with the fire and murders of the Bransons had to be investigated and that would bring them back around to his plan. When things finally got back on track, he would make his move. Provided, of course, he had the slightest of cooperation from someone, who at the present, was not willing to be cooperative. That would change. If nothing else, he excelled in the art of coercion. Maybe *convincing* was a better way of putting it, something that didn't sound quite as evil.

CHAPTER 30

Kaplan examined the pipes, all three of them, not more than four feet above the ground. By the rancid odor eminating from a straight pipe, it had to vent from a toilet below, just like on the roof of a house. The other two looked more like exhausts, both pipes topped with caps, steam coming from one, smoke from the other. He surmised that one person, or several people, must be in the bunker forty feet below him. A curious place to put a domicile unless it was a relic, like an old mine access converted to a living space. And, if it was an old mine, seeing as the front door and windows were bolted tight from the inside, there must be another access point or points.

He sprinted toward the spruce trees in a low, crouched run, scanning back toward the bunkhouse and cabins for any sign of potential threats, like ranch hands or worse, guard dogs. That thought reminded him of Moss and their covert nighttime invasion of a mob boss hideout on an island in the Caribbean where they'd encountered several Rottweilers guarding the Sicilian's fortress. He remembered the pain of the dog bites, not something he wanted to encounter again anytime soon…or ever. He hadn't heard any dogs bark during the storms or when lightning struck the tree on the southwest side of Pearson's home.

He reached the grove of spruces and saw two ranch hands. They were standing near the tree that had been struck by lightning as if waiting to see if the smoldering skeleton of a tree would reignite. From this distance, he could see the glow of cigars beneath the wide brims of their cowboy hats followed by a ring of smoke billow out from underneath. With the breeze from their direction, the aroma was not to be mistaken for cigarettes. They were laughing, and each held a bottle from which each would periodically take a swig.

Kaplan slipped through the rows of trees until he could see Drew Pearson's ranch house. Pearson had illuminated powerful flood lights encircling the perimeter of his home. Kaplan had to remain tucked in the tree line in order to stay concealed. Pearson's ranch house surpassed the norm in size to be considered a mere home, he had pushed the envelope and defied what most people considered luxurious. The home was massive.

Through one of the enormous windows he could see three people, all men, in what looked like a large study or library. At one end was a cozy fireplace. At the opposite end, a heavy wooden desk. The eldest was doing all the talking. Kaplan wasn't good at lip reading, but this was easy, the two younger men kept repeating the words, *yes sir,* every time the other man spoke. The elder must be Drew Pearson, he concluded, and he was either chastising or barking orders. One of the men was a short man with a Hitler-style mustache, dressed like most of the cowboys around this area except he had opted for a bright yellow shirt. The other man could have passed for Sam Elliot in one of his old western movies. Tall, thin and wiry with a head full of gray hair that matched his bushy gray mustache. He held his hat in both hands in front of him. Both men wore holster belts with handguns that from this distance were shaped like six-shooters.

Another man entered the room and the older man

stopped talking. This new man was young, mid-twenties Kaplan guessed. He strode across the room and sat in a leather chair. His movements seemed comfortable, like he'd done the very same things many times and was content with the older man chastising the other two. Kaplan guessed this new man, the young one, must be Evan Pearson, Drew's youngest son.

The old man motioned to the door and the first two men left the room. Seconds later the two scrambled out the front door and down a lighted path that led through the rows of trees. Kaplan backed his way through the trees, following the track of the two men. They moved into the clearing, lit by the vapor lights, and made their way across the open space past the two cabins and into the bunkhouse.

Kaplan pushed his way back through the tightly spaced Spruce trees and retook the recon position he'd had moments ago. The old man stood at a bar and poured a drink in what appeared to be a brandy snifter. His mood had changed and the scowl that he'd had with the other two men had transformed into a smile. Convinced now that this was indeed Drew Pearson, Kaplan studied the two through the window. From his vantage point, he could see Drew was wearing blue jeans and a tan shirt with a dark vest. Beneath the vest, he could see the man's belt was cinched with a large silver buckle. On a hat rack in the corner of the study were several cowboy hats. The older man had thick silvery hair and a gray goatee. He sat down in a chair next to the young man and crossed his legs. Orange boots, probably the ostrich boots Cavalier had told him about.

Their conversation appeared casual as one might expect from a father and son, if the young one was indeed one of Drew's sons. He fit the description Cavalier had given him. Medium height, slim build, blond hair and a youthful, nonathletic appearance. Nothing like the two ranch hands who'd just left. Evan looked like he belonged behind a computer, not out here in the middle of nowhere on a cattle ranch. He was much smaller than his father, who towered several inches above his son. No way to really tell how tall either one of the men was without some other frame of reference, but his gut told him Drew was a tall man. He even walked with a big man's swagger.

Evan was wearing jeans and a light blue short-sleeve sport shirt, like a Polo or something similar. Not the same Western attire everyone else on the ranch wore.

Not seeing anything that would help him rescue Lucy, and not knowing how long this father-son chat might go on, Kaplan retreated through the trees to continue his recon and hopefully locate where she was being held. His instinct kept telling him the bunker had something to do with it, but how to gain access was a big issue. He'd done recon so many times in his lifetime that he'd lost count many years ago. Most jobs with *The Company* required extensive recon before and after he arrived on site. It was part of his training.

He backtracked his way through the rows of Spruce until he was out of sight of Drew Pearson's mansion. He studied the clearing sky. No sign of any remaining storms. Now was a good time for the NVGs.

The night vision goggles from the Last Chance Mercantile weren't goggles in the traditional sense, like the ones he used when he served in Special Forces in the Army way back when. This particular model was a night vision monocular with a head strap to hold it in place. A rotating eye cup allowed for use on either eye. It was a brand he was familiar with and had used in the past, just not this model. He ended up with the Armasight by FLIR Spark-G model with a head strap. This particular night vision monocular used infrared technology versus thermal. He needed to make use of every bit of available light in order to locate not just hostiles, but outbuildings and structures that might not have shown up on Google Maps, like the bunker.

He slipped the night vision monocular from his jacket pocket, secured the head strap snuggly in place and powered up the unit. He remained crouched at the edge of the tree line and scanned the landscape. With the enhancements in night vision technology, this off-the-shelf model was better than the ones he'd used many years ago in the Army, but not nearly the quality of what he'd used with the CIA, which were even higher quality and resolution than what the Department of Defense issued for the troops. Given all that, it was still a high-quality product.

He knew what was behind him, through the trees, where he'd just observed Drew and Evan Pearson. To his left at a hundred fifty feet was the bunkhouse. Working counter-clockwise from the bunkhouse were the two cabins the middle Pearson sons lived in with their respective wives. According to Cavalier, neither had children, but one had a child on the way. She didn't say which one. Each cabin had a vapor light in front and the bunkhouse had one on each corner. A fifth vapor light marked the garage access to Pearson's log mansion.

To the north, clockwise from the bunkhouse he could make out the three pipes sticking out above the bunker, smoke or steam billowing from two of them. He continued scanning clockwise. In the distance, well past the ridge and across the ditch he could see a fence line. Behind the fence, a dozen or so horses and a stable. The horses were grazing on wet grass. Further to the right and beyond the stable, a barn or equipment shed with a lone tractor parked beside it. The tractor had a bush-hog attachment mounted behind. Way out in the distance were small black specks, hundreds of them. He could detect motion. Cavalier had said Pearson raised cattle, that had to be part of his livestock.

As he searched right, he saw fence lines and rolling hills, all quite a distance from where he was. He spotted another small building, not much larger than an outhouse, about a hundred feet from him. A quick check toward the bunkhouse and cabins to verify the coast was clear followed by a crouched sprint and he was in the open for about ten seconds.

The small building was larger than he originally thought, but not by much. A quick estimate was five feet wide by ten feet deep with a door facing the Pearson's log mansion. And it was unlocked.

Kaplan eased the door open, being cognizant that old hinges had a tendency to squeak. When the door was open just enough for him to squeeze through, he stuck his head inside.

It was empty and dark, but it was his way in.

CHAPTER 31

Kaplan switched on his radio to give Moss and Cavalier a situation report when he heard them taking turns calling him.

"Rambo, you out there?" Moss was making a lame attempt at humor. Probably assuming he couldn't hear him. "How do you read me?"

Kaplan whispered into his microphone. "Too loud, too clear, and too often."

"Copy that," Moss said in a low voice. "Good to hear you're ok."

"It's about damn time," Cavalier said. "Where the hell have you been?"

"This marshal is ready to kick your ass," Moss added. "I've spent the past twenty minutes trying to keep Christine from coming to find you."

"Christine?" Kaplan replied. "So, it's Christine now?"

"Shut up, Kaplan," she said. "What have you found?"

He sat back on his heels behind the building and spent the next few minutes bringing them up to date. He described the men he saw in the Pearson home and Cavalier confirmed the descriptions. The two ranch hands he saw were two of the men who raided the town marshal's office. Her description of the third sounded like the young man he killed earlier behind the bunkhouse. She confirmed the other two men were Drew and Evan Pearson.

"Give me a description of Stevie in case our paths

cross," Kaplan said.

"Stevie is unmistakable," she said. "Stringy brown hair and a scraggly beard. I kicked him hard yesterday so look for two black eyes and a bandaged nose. 5'11", 280. Pretty sure you'll know him when you see him."

"I'll take your word on it," Kaplan said. "I'm going in now to get Lucy. Radio going off. If you don't hear from me in an hour…well, you know what to do and where to look."

"Roger that," Moss said.

Kaplan powered off his radio unit and slipped back inside the small building. He snugged the eye cup close to his left eye and used it to guide him down the wooden stairs. He wanted to make sure, in the event of a sudden burst of light, that his right eye didn't suffer flash blindness. He might need to fire his weapon. Guns make noise and he'd learned a long time ago that the best missions were always ones where he went in and out without anyone being the wiser.

The walls were tight as he descended the stairs, stepping lightly on each to maintain his stealth. Every ten steps, the stairs made a ninety-degree turn to the left. He paid close attention to his relative direction to the log mansion. This stairwell had to lead to a tunnel that connected to the bunker or the mansion, or both. The stairs ended after four turns. Five flights. Fifty steps. Same direction he started. He entered a tunnel that extended to his left and right. To the right, Pearson's mansion. To the left, the bunker.

Nothing would give him more satisfaction than to sneak into the mansion and catch Drew Pearson off guard. But, that was not the plan for the night. This was a rescue, an exfiltration, just like he and his old partner Jake Pendleton made in Sanaa, Yemen a few years back when they rescued

Isabella from her terrorist captors. Only this time, he was going in solo. No fancy electronic surveillance equipment to map the interiors of buildings and location of hostiles. No handler in his ear monitoring his every move and feeding him with vital satellite intel. This time, he was on his own.

Now, to find Lucy.

† † †

Evan Pearson had never challenged his father's decisions until now. Mainly from fear of his father's temper.

Drew Pearson had a reputation in Last Chance, and most of Sheridan County, as a man you didn't want to cross. His wealth, and especially his temper, intimidated most people. He was still pissed off that the council had hired Cavalier. A woman.

Troubling Evan was his father's most recent fit of rage directed toward the Last Chance Town Marshal. His father went too far when he lost control and struck a law enforcement officer. He'd heard rumors. But, this was the first time he had witnessed his father do such a horrible thing.

His brothers had been struck and whipped when they were young, but never Evan. The reason was simple, he always did what his father wanted. Unlike all three of his brothers, especially Stevie, he never got into trouble in school. Always made good grades—straight As—that allowed him to not only skip two grades, but to graduate in the same high school class as his next oldest brothers, Scott and Mark.

Scott and Mark were less than a year apart in age and had hung out together as long as he could remember. For some reason Mark was held back a year by his father. Maybe it was to keep them together in school. Mark always made decent grades in school, so it must have been some other reason than grades. He didn't dare ask his father what it was. Scott and Mark had a tendency for mischief, mostly bullying. And they liked to tag team their prey. As kids, they got into a lot of fights and never lost. Even as adults. Until yesterday, when that stranger kicked both their asses and put them in the hospital. How Evan would have loved to have seen them meet their match.

Evan was the only one of the four to go to college, something he knew his brothers resented. Scott and Mark rarely made comments, but when Stevie got pissed at him, he referred to him as *college boy* thinking that was some kind of dig. In reality, the dig was on him. Stevie got his temper from his father…and then some. Even his father, on his worst days, wasn't as out of control as Stevie.

Which brought Evan back to the purpose of his upcoming conversation with his father. Stevie was out of control earlier today. There was no other way to describe it. Today, Stevie went crazy, almost maniacal. Actually, it was maniacal.

Stevie had seen Lucy Raintree the afternoon before in the Mercantile and followed her to the Sundown Motel. He watched her go into room thirteen and was about to confront her when the marshal pulled up in her Bronco. Afraid she might recognize him, or the Pearson Ranch pickup parked in the lot across the street and try to arrest him, he waited until she disappeared in Lucy's room and drove back to the ranch. That morning Stevie had convinced his father that Evan needed to help him nab Lucy for questioning since his other two brothers were unable to drive. His father had agreed and now he sits here, waiting to talk to his father about Stevie and the cold-blooded, and totally unnecessary, murder of one of the Last

Chance deputies.

When Evan arrived at the *big house*, the family's term for their father's mansion, his father was in his library issuing instructions to two of the ranch hands, Slim and Ropey. Slim got his nickname because he was gangly and was what most people envisioned a cowboy should look like. Ropey was Mexican and got his name because he was the best calf roper anyone had ever seen. Both Slim and Ropey, along with the newest ranch hand Butch, accompanied his father to the town marshal's office when his father decided it was time for a good old-fashion beating for the guy who put Mark and Scott in the hospital. "No one does that to one of my boys and gets away with it," he had said. Stevie had licked his lips, ready to fight but Evan tried to back out. His father held his hand up to silence his protests. This was a family matter.

When the marshal kicked Stevie in the face, Evan felt like Stevie got what he deserved.

Shortly after Evan arrived, his father dismissed Slim and Ropey and sent them back to the bunkhouse. He said they were worried about being arrested. Slim confessed he had an outstanding warrant issued by his ex for never paying alimony or child support. He had come to the Pearson Ranch to work since Pearson paid in cash. Ropey was in the country illegally and everyone on the ranch knew it. He didn't want to get deported. Drew Pearson reassured them both that the marshal couldn't touch them on his land. The last thing he told them was, if worse came to worst, they could hide out in the old cabin west of the property.

The cabin was in the foothills of the Bighorn Mountains close to the southern edge of the Crow Reservation. It was deep in the forest and not many people even knew of its existence.

It wasn't much, a couple of cots and a wood burning stove that served as a heater in the winter when his father used to go on winter hunts for elk, deer, or pronghorn. Outside there was a hand-pumped well and an outhouse. By his father's design, and sole purpose of buying the property, it was only accessible by foot or horseback. No roads. Not even the four-wheelers could get all the way up there, although Stevie had been known to tackle the journey on his dirt bike. His father had built a small barn, really only two stalls for the horses when he rode up there. Behind the cabin was a fifty-foot cliff. Evan had been in the cabin once and that was once too many.

After Slim and Ropey left, his father poured himself a brandy and sat in one of the over-sized leather chairs next to him. "What's on your mind, son?" his father asked.

"It's Stevie, he's gone off the deep end. I mean, like never before. He's gone nuts."

"Stevie's a troubled soul, Evan. Give him time, he'll come around."

"No. You should have seen him today. He was like a crazy man. When that deputy yelled for him to stop, Stevie fired. The deputy didn't even have his gun drawn. Then, that other deputy ducked behind his truck door and shouted. Stevie had wild eyes and he started yelling and shooting."

"Maybe that deputy was being too high and mighty and scared him," his father said.

"He wasn't scared, it was like he was possessed." Evan paused to let what he had said sink in with his father. "You gotta do something about him. I think he's unstable. We might not be safe around him."

"Nonsense." His father ran his fingers through his thick graying hair. "I'll have a talk with him. Where is he now?"

"Where you told him to be, down in the hoist house. He's been drinking and smoking all night. He didn't even bother to lock Lucy back up after he gave her supper. I put her back in her room and locked the door before I left. He said he was going to bed."

"Why did he let her out?"

"Food and bathroom, he said."

"Why didn't he lock her back up?"

"I don't know. He's lazy. Told me he didn't see the point in locking her back up. Said she couldn't go anywhere."

"Stupid kid," Pearson mumbled under his breath. He cleared his throat and said, "I see what you mean, Evan. I'll have a talk with him first thing in the morning."

The alert dinged on the security system informing them that the door to the tunnel access had opened.

"See," Evan said to his father. "What did I tell you? Stevie's gone out for another smoke. This'll probably go on all night, you know. I'll bet he's already walked a mile tonight going back and forth to smoke. Probably grabbed another beer out of the fridge before heading up here." He motioned to the security system monitor. "You're gonna have to listen to that all night."

His father didn't say anything at first. Finally, "I'm just wondering if that marshal bitch is planning a midnight raid."

"You'd know if she was coming. I mean, she does have to get past the front gate."

"What makes you think the cops would use the gate? They'd probably come on foot." He motioned out the window. "That's why I got all those idiots standing guard all night. Go on back to the hoist house and tell that brother of yours to pack it in for the night." His father stood, strolled over to the wet bar and placed his brandy snifter in the sink. "You go on to bed, too, Evan. I promise I'll take care of Stevie in the morning. Might just send him out to the cabin for a few days. He likes it out there anyway."

††††

Moss reached his arms upward toward the sky and backward before letting out a moan. "Damn, I could go for some hot coffee about now," he said when he lowered his arms.

"Does Kaplan usually keep you up past your bedtime?" said Cavalier.

"Matter of fact, he does."

"Come on." Cavalier tapped the hood of the Escalade with her fingers. "We can go sit in your car. You can rest, maybe take a nap, and I'll listen out for Kaplan." She expected him to resist and was surprised when he didn't.

They both got back in his Escalade. Moss reclined his seat and crossed his arms across his belly.

"If I snore, just punch me," he said.

Before she finished saying, "No problem," he was asleep.

He did snore, a light wheezing sound at first. Every few minutes he would snort, readjust himself in the seat and start snoring again.

It had been a long day and tonight was dragging. Checking the time every thirty minutes made her feel like this night was never going to end. She rested her head against the headrest and kept her bleary eyes open. This reminded her of times when she and her old partner in St. Louis went on stake outs. Hours of boredom. Too many times, all for naught. Every now and then, the hours of boredom were interrupted with moments of sheer terror. Like when the suspect they were watching got into a shootout and people came flying out of windows with gaping holes in their chests. Or when their cover was blown and their suspect appeared at their car window with a gun pointed at their heads. That kind of sheer terror.

Tonight was different. She didn't mind the boredom. Waiting gave her a chance to get to know Moss. She rotated her head and ran her gaze over the large man sleeping next to her. She liked what she saw, even his belly rising and falling with each breath. She imagined being wrapped in his large strong arms and feeling safe.

Moss had helped her understand the mysterious man she had locked up and was now working with to catch Pearson. She had tricked Kaplan, letting him believe she would tell him what he wanted to know about her sister. Family blood was stronger than her promise.

Moss, on the other hand, was anything but mysterious. He just laid it out there. No beating around the bush. He was direct and forceful and funny, all rolled into one. As she watched the sleeping giant next to her, she wondered how he would feel about her betrayal to his good friend. She hoped he would understand when the time came.

Right now, she needed to focus on the mission. She wondered where Kaplan was and if he was still safe. She glanced at her watch. It had been thirty minutes since his last communication. He had thirty more minutes. If she didn't hear from him by then, she and Moss would storm the castle.

CHAPTER 32

Kaplan had been in a tunnel very much like this one several years ago in Ireland. That one led from the stone ruins of a castle to an underground chamber where a member of the Irish Republican Army had stashed a cache of weapons. Weapons he planned on selling to an Iranian terrorist.

Using his NVGs, he scoped in both directions. To his right the tunnel was long and straight. He could see stairs at the far end rise up, presumably toward

Pearson's mansion. To the left, the tunnel made a left turn just a few feet from where he was standing. Along the ceiling were bare bulbs strung in both directions and spaced roughly thirty feet apart. A single wire connected the series of lights, all of which were off. The floor, walls, and ceiling were some sort of softer rock or perhaps sandstone. Halfway between each light bulb were wooden braces supporting a beam across the ceiling. He was hit with an overwhelming musty smell and, by the footprints on the floor, an area well-traveled. This raised his hopes that he might be getting closer to locating Lucy.

He turned toward the direction of the bunker. The tunnel was dark, so he kept his NVGs active to help him navigate the way. Fifteen feet ahead, the tunnel veered sharply to the left, more than forty-five degrees but less than ninety. Ten feet later it veered back to the right and he could detect a definite decline in the slope. This part of the tunnel was newer, fresher than the previous section, like it was a more recent dig. Perhaps a section of the old tunnel had collapsed, and this newer section was built to bypass it. Sixty feet farther, the tunnel veered back to the right and joined what must have been the original tunnel. To his right, the tunnel went another thirty of forty feet and he could see it dead-end at an old elevator shaft. Now, his theory changed. There was no collapse. For some reason, the tunnel was routed around the elevator shaft, but back to what appeared to be the original tunnel. Why didn't the two ends meet at the elevator? He checked the time. Only thirty minutes left to find Lucy, get out of the tunnel and make contact with Cavalier and Moss. Time to pick up the pace.

He went left. Ahead, the tunnel was long and straight and at the far end, a door. Pay dirt, he thought, it had to be the entrance to the bunker. He abandoned as much caution as he dared and raced toward the door. When he reached it, he could see a ring of light around its edges. No NVGs needed inside. He pulled the unit away from his eye, but left it powered up. Placing his ear close to the door, he strained to pick up any sound on the other side. Nothing. He twisted the doorknob slowly, and felt the latch clear the strike plate.

No sound. Pushing slightly, he heard the door drag against the ground. He gleaned a look inside through the small opening. No one. He pushed further until he could see most of the room. Light spilled into the tunnel behind him. Clay. No wonder the walls felt soft.

He drew his Beretta, resting his finger against the trigger guard and stepped into the room. It was a kitchen, long and narrow. It was connected perpendicular to a larger room, which in turn connected to two bedrooms on the left. He needed to clear the rooms. Both bedroom doors were open. One room was empty, the other occupied and wreaking of alcohol. In the larger room, the television was on, volume loud, and a 12-pack of empty beer cans scattered across a table top. He could see flames through the door of a free-standing wood-burning stove. He followed the exhaust pipe to the ceiling and knew that was one of the pipes he saw on top of the ridge. The man in the bed had a bandage on his nose. He fit Cavalier's description of Stevie Pearson and he was passed out drunk.

Kaplan deemed Stevie no imminent threat and passed through the TV room to a long hall that ran adjacent to the kitchen. At the end of that hall, two doors and some sort of alcove about halfway down the hall. As he eased his way down the corridor, he passed a wooden door on his left. It was locked from the inside with two large padlocks. A few steps farther and a bathroom appeared on the left about the same size of the alcove. Ten feet to the end of the hall and another door, locked from the outside, with a ring of keys dangling from the lock.

He unlocked the door and slid it open. A faint shaft of light from the hall cast onto a cot in the unlit room. On the cot was Lucy Raintree, and she was sound asleep. He eased toward Lucy readied himself for her reaction. He clamped his hand over her mouth and held her down with his arm.

Her first blow landed on his cheek. He pushed her away at arm's length. She was screaming beneath his hand which allowed only a muffled sound to escape.

"Lucy," he whispered. "Lucy. It's me, Kaplan."

She jerked and squirmed. Flailing and thrashing and swinging. Her eyes full of fear.

"Dammit, Lucy, it's Kaplan."

It took a few more seconds for recognition to set in and she relaxed. He put a finger to his lips and slowly released his hand from her mouth. She raised and flung herself into his chest, squeezing like she hadn't seen him in years. He pushed her away. "Lucy, we must hurry," he used his breath to speak. "Stevie's drunk and passed out." He motioned with his arm. "Stay close behind me."

The two of them backtracked Kaplan's steps, down the hall, through the TV room, across the kitchen to the door that led to the tunnel. Once again, he twisted the doorknob slowly and pulled the door open. What he saw changed everything.

The tunnel lights were on.

Someone was coming.

He made a quick sweep noting the tunnel was empty as far as he could see. He closed the door and motioned Lucy back to the hall. They were trapped. He ran through his choices. He could take out Stevie and maybe whoever was coming down the tunnel. He would have to take them out quietly too. Any gunshots might reverberate down the long tunnel and alert Pearson. So much for his plan to get in and out without anyone knowing about it. The wall that separated the kitchen from the hall was not thick enough to stop bullets unless the slug hit a stud, and even then, that might only slow it down. But with studs typically spaced sixteen inches apart, it would almost be like shooting through cardboard.

Something occurred to him. A possible solution. He whispered something to Lucy causing her to pad back to the room she came from while he took a defensive position in case someone came through the door. If that happened before Lucy had finished what he asked her to do, things could get dicey fast.

He was impressed how quiet and fast Lucy moved. She snuck down the hall, closed the door to the room where she was held captive, used the keys to lock the door. She ran to the wooden door in the alcove in the hall. She was out of sight now, but he heard her fumbling with the keys and the large locks on the door. If he remembered correctly, there were only five or six keys on the key ring, hopefully the keys to the door locks were on that ring.

He heard the sound of a latch clanking open. And then a second latch open.

A loud whisper, "Kaplan, they are open."

Kaplan pointed down the hall. She took off without a sound and put the key back in the lock on the door to her room. He was getting antsy. The kitchen door could open any second. He motioned for Lucy to hurry. She ran back to the big alcove door. He had told her what to do, and in what order. All she had left to do was remove the locks and open the door. He heard her make a grunting sound.

"Kaplan." She stepped back in sight. "The door is stuck," her soft voice full of panic.

He didn't want to leave his defensive position until she had the door open, but they couldn't wait any longer. He tucked his gun in his jacket pocket and jogged on his toes to the alcove. Putting both hands on the door handle, he yanked. The door didn't give an inch. He pulled harder. Nothing. He didn't want to make noise, but he had to risk it. They were trapped if he couldn't get the door open. Lucy wrapped her arms around his waist and together they gave the door a hard heave. The door partially unjammed and opened no more than four inches. And it made noise. He told Lucy to hurry and watch both for the kitchen door and make sure Stevie didn't wake up. She gave him a thumbs-up and took off. He yanked again. Another four inches. And more noise. The wooden door had swollen from the elements and didn't want to clear the wood plank floor beneath his feet. He felt the cool evening air rushing in.

After a few seconds, she gave him another thumbs-up. He yanked again. Another three inches. Wide enough to squeeze Lucy through. He wasn't sure he would fit through. He gave her a come-on signal, and Lucy wasted no time rushing his way. She got her head through the opening, and he shoved her out. He managed to get his upper half out. He was twisting, and Lucy was tugging his arm when he heard a noise over the volume of the TV that he didn't want to hear.

The kitchen door opened.

His adrenaline kicked in and he tugged harder till he was clear of the door. He couldn't leave the alcove door open. He had to get it closed fast and quietly. But, how? He pulled until he felt resistance, lifted the heavy door and yanked again. Less noise. He heard rustling in the kitchen. The wind outside had picked up and was pushing its way through the door opening and inside the bunker. He was running out of time. He lifted the door up and heaved again. The door almost closed, lacking by just an inch. A sliver of light spilled out from the opening into the dark night. He heard footsteps, still in the kitchen he suspected, followed by the sound of the wood being shoved in the stove.

Now or never.

He gave the door one last tug. It closed with a thud.

He grasped Lucy's hand and they darted toward the ditch and in the direction of the bunkhouse. As he cleared the cliff face, the bunkhouse came into view. He froze, jerking back on Lucy's hand. The bunkhouse was lit up with floodlights and there were three ranch hands behind it. He knew what was happening. They were looking for their missing man.

"Plan B," he said. "We have to turn and go that way." He

motioned toward the bunker. "We'll escape to the east. There's another county road about a mile that way."

"No," she said. "I know a better way."

"Where?"

"The stables. Do you see it?" She used her head to cue him where to look. "We can ride out of here."

"Won't they know when horses come up missing?"

"No. We will leave the gates open. All the horses will be out of the corral. The Pearsons will think it is a result of the storms. We will let our horses go when we get to safety. They will come back and rejoin the herd before the Pearsons even find out the gates are open." She motioned into the darkness. "There is a footbridge over there where we can cross the ditch. I know the way out of here." She paused. "Ever ridden bareback?"

"I've never ridden at all."

CHAPTER 33

Her radio came to life in her earpiece, it was Kaplan. And he had Lucy with him.

Cavalier glanced at Moss, still half-asleep in the driver's seat. His snoring had stopped, and he appeared restless. She gave him a gentle nudge on the arm.

"Moss."

His eyes still closed. She thought she heard snoring. She balled up her fist and hit him in the arm.

"Moss, wake up."

He jolted upright in his seat and swiveled his head. "What's up?"

"Kaplan made it out," she said. "With Lucy. They're on the way out now."

Moss rubbed his eyes with his fingers and said, "Hot damn." He checked his watch and keyed his microphone. "Damn, partner, cuttin' it a little close, weren't you?"

She smiled at Moss and keyed her mic. "I don't know what he's talking about, Kaplan, you had a good three minutes left."

"I'll give you a full briefing when we get to your car. Give us ten and we'll be there."

"Roger that," Cavalier said.

Moss opened his car door and stepped outside. She followed suit, walked around the front of the Escalade and leaned against the driver's door next to him. The night air temperature had dropped from where it was an hour ago. He had her binoculars against his eyes and was staring across the open prairie toward the Pearson home. She did the same, no binoculars.

With his eyes still focused toward the Pearson home, he said, "Feel better?"

"Better how?"

"Better knowing that Kaplan got Lucy out safe. Better in the fact, as far as we can tell, he did it without incident."

"I guess so. He seems to be how you described him, as Rambo. I made the assumption all hell would break loose. So, yeah, I was on pins and needles. I do feel better."

"All hell will still break loose." He tossed the binoculars in his seat, turned and beamed. "Just not tonight."

She returned his look. That was a fear she had with Kaplan, but now that Lucy was safe and apparently unharmed, she didn't care if all hell broke loose on the Pearson place. They started this. They killed Doug. If Kaplan didn't unleash hell on them first, she damn sure would.

While Moss was sleeping, Cavalier had received a text from KC. He was at the station. She told him to stay put, take a nap on one of the cots in the cell room if he got sleepy but, under no circumstances was he to leave before they got back. That was almost an hour ago.

She was glad KC made it back. He was part-time and by far her best deputy of the three. Shit. Only two now. Well, three if she counted Kaplan. After this was all over, she'd try to make it up to him somehow. KC had been a dedicated deputy, always trying to work as many hours as he could. It took some doing on her part, but the town council approved up to thirty-two hours a week. In emergency staffing situations, they had approved more. This was one of those times.

KC had been a deputy almost as long as she had been town marshal, just shy of two years, and had proven himself to be a valuable and trustworthy man. He said he played left tackle in college, he was certainly big enough, she thought. He was every bit the size of Pete Moss. When he wasn't performing his duties as a deputy, KC was a fishing and hunting guide.

The Bighorn Mountains and the Bighorn National Forest had long been touted as a Mecca for outdoor sportsmen. When given a choice, KC preferred being a fly fishing guide, but in the winter when everything froze, and the hunters piled into the area, he packed up his fly rods and brought out the big game guns. KC was a popular hunting guide and had a top-ranked reputation as a tracker. Big game, small game, it didn't matter, he could track anything, anywhere, a skill his father and grandfather taught him. He said they insisted he learn the old ways, so he could stay in touch with his true Cheyenne spirit.

Last year, the regional game warden enlisted KC's services to track a grizzly that had found its way from the Tetons to the Bighorn Mountains. It wasn't the first time he'd been recruited as a tracker either, he'd been used by the game warden to track black bear, mountain lion, and elk. As much as he said he enjoyed guiding and tracking, he preferred the stability of his deputy's wage. Another reason Cavalier felt compelled to push the town council for more money.

Moss moved away from the car and stared across the dark prairie lit only by the now clear skies and crescent moon. He pointed. "What's that?"

She stepped forward and stood next to him. At first, she didn't see anything in the dark void. She narrowed her eyes and strained.

"Looks like horses," Moss said.

"Really?" she said still straining to distinguish the shape of the dark shadows.

"I can see them, can't you?" He pulled her closer and used his finger to guide her line of sight.

"Not clearly. Damn you have good eyesight. Are you sure you see horses?"

"20/15, baby. Never wore glasses a day in my life. And yes, two horses…with riders."

She detected a little excitement in his voice and reached inside the open window. She picked up the pair of binoculars and scanned the open range. Sure enough. Two horses, two riders—one man, one small woman.

Kaplan and Lucy.

† † †

Kaplan had never been happier to finish something than he was to get off that horse. Not that the horse was unruly, it's just that he was nervous the entire time he was mounted on the horse's back. He never released his two-handed death grip on the horse's mane. Lucy picked out the biggest horse in the corral. She said it belonged to *Old Man Pearson*, since he was such a big man. He knew nothing about horses and had never had a desire to learn. Lucy, on the other hand, knew a lot about them, including the ones belonging to the Pearsons. She said the horse he rode was a Bay Irish Sport, whatever that was, named Zulu and was over seventeen hands tall. She said she wanted to ride the small *paint*, she called it, but opted for a black quarter horse named Drifter. At first, she resisted when he asked how she knew the horses' names, but after he pushed she admitted she had been out here a few times with Evan Pearson when his father and brothers were off on family hunting or fishing trips. Things she said Evan didn't like and wouldn't do. But, according to Lucy, Evan did like riding horses. She said he even raced them in 4-H competitions when he was younger. And he liked to collect rocks. She said he called himself a *rock hound* and had a huge collection in his room.

Kaplan had determined the angle they needed to traverse to return in a straight line to Moss' Escalade without following the ditch, gave directions to Lucy, who in turn guided the two horses along. His calculations were accurate, and the shortcut saved valuable time. As they made their way toward the car, he kept looking back and watching for any signs of activity at the Pearson ranch that might indicate they knew Lucy had escaped. So far, all was quiet.

When they arrived at Moss' Escalade, Lucy halted the horses about twenty feet from the fence. Moss and Cavalier walked to the fence as soon as they saw them ride up.

After Kaplan dismounted, which was nothing more than merely sliding off the back of the gentle giant, Lucy did the same. She uncoupled the lead rope from Zulu's halter that she used to lead Kaplan's horse since he had never ridden, swatted both horses on their butts, and watched them run off into the darkness.

As the horses clomped away, he was surprised that after all that rain the ground was dry again. Back in the East, the ground would have been soggy for days after that much rain.

The fence that lined the county road was a split-rail fence that Pearson had spared no expense building. Two electric wires strung along the inside of the fence kept livestock from pushing it over. Careful not to touch the wires, Kaplan helped Lucy over the fence with a little help from Moss.

You must be Lucy," Moss said. "Pleasure to meet you."

"Who are you?" Lucy replied.

"He's a pain in the ass," Kaplan interjected as he climbed over the fence.

Cavalier stepped forward and gave Lucy a hug. "I'm glad you're safe." She pushed her at arm's distance but didn't let go. "They didn't hurt you, did they?"

"No, Marshal. Evan made sure no one bothered me. They just stuck me in a dark room and left me alone."

"You must be starving," Cavalier said.

"I had a sandwich and chips a couple of hours ago."

Cavalier held her by the hand. "Come on, gentlemen." She pulled Lucy toward the back seat. "Let's get out of here while we still can."

"I want to sit with Kaplan," Lucy insisted.

"All right."

Cavalier and Kaplan swapped places.

The entire ride to Last Chance, Lucy talked about her ordeal and about the things she had heard. She told them that Evan stood up to his father about her treatment when Stevie wanted to punish her for getting his brothers beat up by Kaplan. She said Stevie acted like a crazed maniac…until he got drunk. She said the beer calmed him down. He drank so much, he finally passed out.

Lucy addressed Cavalier. "Except…"

"Except what, Lucy," Cavalier rotated in her seat and faced Lucy.

"Except he wants to kill you, Marshal. He said you should not have kicked him. Said you will pay for breaking his nose. He said when he sees you again, he will kill you on sight."

"Thanks for the warning, Lucy," Cavalier said. She took

a deep breath. "I can take care of myself. Stevie's going to jail, I'll see to that."

"You do not understand. I heard him tell his father that either you die, or he dies trying to kill you, but he will not stop until one of those things happens. I don't want anyone else to get hurt."

Kaplan put his arm around Lucy. She buried her face in his chest. He raised her face with his hand and wiped tears from her cheeks with his thumb. "Lucy, you believe I keep my promises, right?"

She sniffed, ran her hand across her nose and nodded.

"Don't worry about the marshal. She's as tough as they come. And that big ugly guy driving, his name is Moss by the way, he's kinda sweet on the marshal. So, I promise you that he and I won't let anything happen to the marshal. You have my word on that."

CHAPTER 34

Moss parked his Escalade on Main Street behind a Ford F-250 quad-cab dually. It had an extended bed with a topper attached. On the roof of the cab was a metal rack. The truck was covered in an advertising wrap that said *Dreamcatcher Guide Services.* Kaplan checked the time, it was almost 1:00 a.m. and everyone in the car looked tired.

"KC is here," Cavalier announced.

"Who's KC?" Kaplan asked.

"My other deputy."

"I like KC," Lucy said. "He is always nice to me."

Kaplan opened his door and was surprised when Lucy slid out on his side instead of using her door. She stayed close to him, holding his hand until the four of them got inside the town marshal's office. A large man in a tan uniform shirt was sitting at the desk where Doug sat yesterday morning.

Cavalier introduced KC to Moss and him. KC was a big man, Native American Indian, just like Cavalier had said. Northern Cheyenne. He had thick jet-black hair that fell to the middle of his back. When KC stood, he was tall like Moss, maybe an inch taller. He was rock-hard, with wide shoulders, enormous arms and a neck the size of a tree stump. Definitely someone you'd want on your side of the playing field. KC's voice was low but strong and had the sound of a man with a thick tongue.

"I hear you both had a run in with the Pearsons," KC said to Lucy and Cavalier.

"Just Stevie for me. He is freaking crazy." Lucy sat down in a chair next to where Kaplan was standing. "Evan protected me."

"That is because Evan likes you." KC stated emphatically. "Just like Doug did."

The mention of Doug's name brought the room to silence.

Moss stretched his arms and yawned. It spread. Lucy yawned. Cavalier tried to suppress it, but it was easy to see.

Kaplan interrupted the silence. "We should all get some shuteye."

"First, we need to plan our strategy," Cavalier said with an insistent tone.

"Marshal, it's late. We've all had a trying day." Kaplan glanced at Lucy. "Some of us more than others. No way the Pearsons will come back into town tonight and I'm pretty sure they won't try to leave. They have hunkered down. They'll be up all night thinking you're coming to get them. Tomorrow, when we're fresh, they won't be. We'll have the advantage."

"What about the Branson murders?" KC asked. "And the Stillwater farm on the Rez?"

Kaplan looked at Cavalier. "Something for you to think about overnight, Marshal." He motioned for Lucy to get up and turned his head to look at Moss. "How about a ride to the motel?"

"Wait," Cavalier said. "Be back here at 7:00."

Moss groaned.

"How about a 7:30 strategy breakfast at the diner?" Kaplan replied. Everyone seemed to like that idea.

"Okay." Cavalier relented. "7:30 at the Last Chance Diner. You too, KC."

† † †

Even with the complete darkness inside the hoist house, Evan Pearson woke up early as usual. It was his job to go out to the stable and feed the horses. Normally, he took turns with his other brothers, well, with the exception of Stevie. None of the horses liked Stevie, not even his own. Most animals were a good judge of character, horses were no exception. Stevie had been kicked and bitten more times than he could count. Since two of Evan's brothers were injured and the other sleeping off a drunken stupor from last night, stable duty fell solely on his shoulders this morning. His brothers complained that feeding the horses in the morning was a duty befitting the ranch hands his father had on full-time staff, but his father would have no part of it. No son of his wasn't going to pull his fair share of the weight. His father didn't require the ranch hands to start work until 7:30, and since most of them had stayed up all night keeping watch for the marshal, he knew at least three of them were sleeping.

Last night's conversation with his father could have gone better, but it could have gone worse, too. He successfully talked his father out of an intense interrogation of Lucy. And his father ordered Stevie to leave her alone. Stevie was always a wild card. No one in the family ever knew how he would behave from one moment to the next. Fortunately, his father promised to send Stevie out to the cabin for a few weeks until the heat died down, if it ever would. His father would lie to the marshal about Stevie's whereabouts, even to the extent of giving himself up for assaulting her. The family lawyers had a stranglehold on the judges in northern Wyoming. All of Wyoming for that matter. They would have his father out of jail within a couple of hours of his arrest.

The same couldn't be said for Stevie. This time he had crossed the line. He'd never killed anyone before that he knew of, but with his arrest record, Stevie would be locked up in prison for a long time. That is, if they ever found him. Eventually, he knew, his father would try to move Stevie to safety. Maybe, Idaho where Evan's uncle owned a farm north of Sandpoint, not far from the infamous Ruby Ridge. Or east to a horse ranch in Kentucky where his other uncle breeds and raises race horses.

When he was younger, Evan spent alternating summers with his uncles. His cousins used to do the same at his father's ranch. The Idaho farm was located in one of the prettiest parts of the country he'd ever seen, but he preferred his other uncle's horse ranch in Kentucky. Beautiful horses. And clean. Not like his Idaho uncle's place, which was rundown by comparison. His Kentucky uncle preferred nicer things, like his father. With the exception of this drafty dilapidated hoist house, which was nothing more than a converted played out coal mine, everything on his father's ranch was nice. He did have an aunt who lived in Arizona, but he didn't get to see her too often. She stayed single all her life and lived in a condo in the Phoenix area, a town called Apache Junction. He'd only been there a couple of times. Most times, she came to Last Chance to visit his father. He didn't know any relatives on his mother's side of the family. Apparently, his father cut off all ties with them when she died. He'd only seen a few pictures of his mother. Stevie was the only one who even remembered their mother, he was five when she died…when Evan was born.

He stumbled into the hoist house kitchen with only a

small nightlight to guide the way. It was 6:45 a.m. and even though he was up late last night with his father, he was still expected to feed the horses by 7:00 so the ranch hands could tack up by 7:30. As he stepped past Stevie's bedroom, he heard him snoring. Evan closed his brother's door and flipped on the light. The TV room smelled like a frat house party. Stevie had polished off an entire twelve-pack by himself last night. The coffee pot was set to brew at 6:30 and the aroma smelled wonderful. The hoist house was nice and warm this morning, unlike last night when he returned from the big house and the cold air in the hoist house made him wish he'd put on a jacket. He remembered checking the stove, but it still had logs in it. The hoist house was known to get chilly, especially in the winter when the sun left the sky and the temperature would plunge. Even in the summer the stove was sometimes needed to keep the chill out of the air. He assumed it had something to do with the mine. He did know that cold air would shoot up from the mineshaft from time to time. He thought he heard Lucy making noise when he came in last night, but her light was out, and the keys were still in the door. He checked the door and it was still locked. He peeked inside, and Lucy was in the bed, sheet covering her head. She must have gotten cold too.

He filled his travel mug with black coffee and headed for the tunnel stairs and out to the stable.

He knew something was amiss as he walked across the footbridge and noticed the corral gate was open. *Shit.* All the horses were out. Somehow, the gate got knocked open or left open and all fifteen horses were out in the pasture. On closer observation, other gates were open too. There were horses in the cattle yard and cattle in the horses' pasture. This could take a while. He went inside the tack room and rang the bunkhouse.

Two of the ranch hands were asleep, three were eating breakfast, and one was unaccounted for. Slim told Evan that no one had seen Butch for hours and that something must be wrong with his radio. Evan told Slim to wake the other two and all five get out to the pasture and help him round up the horses.

He thought about calling his father, but that was a boat he didn't want to rock this morning. Not with the mood his father was in last night. He didn't drink brandy that often and only when he was troubled, but last night, he must have refilled his snifter about a dozen times. Today would be a rough day for everyone.

By 7:30, all the horses were back in the corral. He informed the ranch hands that they could herd the cattle back into their pasture later. The horses were his immediate concern. He sent them back to the bunkhouse and followed behind by a couple of minutes. As he came out of the stable, he noticed five ranch hands standing at the footbridge. They looked nervous and upset. As he approached the footbridge, he saw what was troubling them.

A dead body caught in the pilings under the footbridge.

And it looked like Butch.

CHAPTER 35

The first thing the man behind the counter did when Moss entered the diner with Kaplan and Lucy was aim his shotgun at Kaplan. Lucy screamed and ducked behind Kaplan. He stood still, not making a move.

"I don't want no trouble," the man said.

Yesterday, Kaplan had told Moss about his encounter with the owner of the diner, a man Christine Cavalier called Poppy. Moss raised his hands. "Whoa, whoa," Moss said as he opened his blazer and revealed the star on his belt. "I'm a Deputy U. S. Marshal, lower your weapon. This man is with me and no threat to you."

The man hesitated, eyed Moss and lowered the barrel a couple of inches. "Here comes the town marshal," he said motioning out the window with the barrel. "I want to hear from her."

Moss looked out the window, sure enough, here came Cavalier and KC walking across Main Street toward the diner. She looked different somehow. Prettier. Sexier. Her tan uniform shirt was tucked inside her slim cut jeans. Her hair wasn't pulled back into a ponytail like yesterday but was hanging free. When she came through the door, he could tell she was wearing makeup, something he didn't notice yesterday. Her brown eyes were captivating. The knot on her head was almost completely covered up.

KC filled the doorway when he stepped through the frame. His clothes were wrinkled, like he had slept in them overnight.

"It's okay, Poppy," she said. "He's one of the good guys."

Poppy lowered his gun and stashed it behind the counter.

"That was almost like before," Lucy remarked. Moss observed she was still shadowing Kaplan, her savior and protector. He couldn't blame her after the ordeal she'd been through.

Kaplan walked over to Poppy. "Sorry about the other day," he said. Kaplan rolled up his shirt sleeve. "I was hoping to show you these, but I didn't want to move with that shotgun in my face."

"Good thing, too," Poppy said. The cook leaned over and checked out the tattoo on Kaplan's arms. "Figured you to be a soldier."

Moss decided to interrupt the reunion. "I don't know about you folks, but I'm starved."

The five of them ordered at the counter and Moss found a booth against a solid wall where Kaplan could have full view out of all the windows. He'd learned it was futile to sit in the open with Kaplan, all he would have done is insisted on this booth anyway. Moss and Kaplan sat on one side with Lucy squeezed between them. Cavalier and KC sat across from them.

Ten minutes into their planning session, Poppy served them their food. They were already on their second carafe of coffee and, Moss noticed, it was time for a third.

No one spoke much while they ate and what little conversation there was had nothing to do with the day's strategy for arresting the Pearsons. When they finished with their food, Poppy cleared their table except for the bottomless flow of coffee. Cavalier started with her idea of priorities. Naturally, she wanted to go out to the Pearson ranch and arrest Drew, Stevie, Evan and the three ranch hands who assaulted her in her office. Lucy protested about arresting Evan. She claimed Evan had nothing to do with any of it. Cavalier reminded her that Evan was present when Drew struck her and when Stevie and the ranch hands tied her up. Even though Evan didn't participate, he was an accessory to the crimes. Especially in the murder of Doug.

"He did not have a choice," Lucy said while using her napkin to wipe her face. "Stevie said he would shoot Evan too if he did not drive. That should count for something, right?"

"Only if Evan can prove he was an unwilling participant and his life was in danger if he didn't go along."

"That is what I just said," Lucy argued. "I was in the car. I heard Stevie threaten Evan."

"I'm sorry, sweetie," Cavalier said. "But, that's not my call. A judge will decide. I still have to arrest him."

Tears streamed down Lucy's face. She asked Kaplan to let her out of the booth and ran out of the diner.

Moss said, "Kaplan, you might want to go after her. She looks up to you."

Kaplan said, "Not yet. Give her some time. She's been through a lot."

KC, who hadn't spoken much since he and Cavalier arrived, injected, "You know Lucy is sweet on Evan, right? I saw her on the highway one day walking back to town. I gave her a ride. She said Evan had taken her horseback riding while his father and brothers were out on a hunting trip. She goes out there whenever Evan is alone. When I pushed her, she confided that she and Evan had hooked up." He turned toward Cavalier. "Doug knew. I think that is why he hated Evan so much."

Nobody said a word. Everybody appeared to be trying to digest what KC had told them.

Cavalier interjected, "I'm not really good at it, but maybe I should have a girl talk with Lucy."

The men in the booth exchanged puzzled looks and directed their attention to Cavalier.

Kaplan spoke first. "No. You should leave her alone."

"What?" Cavalier's face flushed.

"Now isn't the time," Kaplan said deadpan. "I think we should leave her alone for now. I'll talk to her later. First, we have work to do."

Moss sensed Cavalier was about to protest and knew it would lead to an inexplicable confrontation. He knew the best way to break up the tension was to divert everybody's attention.

"Hey Poppy, how 'bout a refill on the carafe and a piece of that coffee cake you got on the counter," Moss said. It worked. KC yelled to bring him some as did Kaplan and finally Cavalier nodded she'd take a piece.

"All right Kaplan," Cavalier finally said. The acid in her voice was unmistakable. "Let's get to work."

† † †

After the four of them developed their strategic plan to capture the Pearsons, Kaplan walked back to the Sundown Motel to find Lucy. When he entered the room, she was sitting lotus-style on the bed. Her eyes puffy and her nose red.

He didn't have much experience dealing with young people, in reality, none. He had a strong protectionist sense of duty for Lucy and he didn't know why. He had just met the young woman, still a girl in his eyes. He could sense a longing in her for something she didn't have or might never have. He knew she lived a troubled life and her parents tragically died when she was young. Perhaps she had gravitated to him because she felt comfortable…or safe. Like a protective father. Maybe he should've let Cavalier have a girl talk with Lucy. No. Cavalier might have many good qualities but nurturing damn sure wasn't one of them.

Maybe KC should have been the one to talk to Lucy. They had some kind of bond, maybe it was because both were Native Indians. KC had connected with Lucy, certainly more than Cavalier. Perhaps it was because of what Moss had said, *crabs in a bucket.* KC probably saw Lucy as one of those crabs. He had made it out of the bucket and done well for himself. Kaplan was sure KC genuinely wanted to see Lucy escape the bucket too.

He sat down on the bed next to her. The silence between them was uncomfortable. What should he do? Finally, he put his arm around her small shoulders. She leaned in and rested her head on his chest.

"Lucy, while I was in my second year of college, my parents were killed when a log truck ran a red light and t-boned their car."

She lifted her head and he could see the sadness in her large brown eyes. "That had to suck."

"It did. Forced me to drop out of college and head back to my hometown in South Carolina to manage the estate stuff. I used the small amount of money my parents had saved to pay for their funerals. The owner of the local hardware store was a good friend of my father's and gave me a job. Felt sorry for me, I think. I went back to work in the town I had longed to get away from. I was miserable. I was nineteen at the time, only a year older than you are now. I thought if I joined the Army, I could qualify for the GI Bill and finish college. That never happened. I did join the Army and was a good soldier. Maybe too good. The Army decided that we both would be best served if I volunteered for Special Forces. Instead of finishing my 4-year commitment and heading out the door and off to college, I re-enlisted. It served me well I guess, but I never made it back to college. Never used the GI Bill for my education. Since I already had eight years with the government, I applied for another government job and got it. Did that for a few years and then by happenstance someone at the CIA wanted to use my skills. Yet another government job."

"Is this going anywhere, Kaplan?"

"Just be patient. What I'm trying to tell you is sometimes you think you know some people, even a best friend, but you don't. Not really—"

"But I know Evan. He is a good guy. So was Doug."

"Maybe." He paused for effect. "I had been with a woman for several years. I thought I knew everything about her."

"What is her name?"

"I knew her by Annie."

"Knew?"

"Yes, Lucy, she's dead now. I was in love with her..." His voice trailed off as he remembered the bloody St. Patrick's Day shoot out in Savannah, Georgia. "I believed I could trust her, and that she loved me, but I was wrong. She had a dark side. Something that stemmed back to her childhood in Ireland. She wasn't the person I believed her to be."

"Why are you telling me all this?"

"Because you don't have a crystal ball. There is one

promise I can guarantee you about your future. It won't turn out exactly, and perhaps not even remotely like you think it will. Sometimes in life you're dealt a bad hand."

"So, you are saying Evan might be a bad guy?"

"I don't know that yet, just like you don't know. What I'm saying is, there might be more to Evan Pearson than you know. Or care to admit. Just like there was a side of Doug you probably didn't know either. And there is a side of me you don't know about either."

"Like what?"

"Like what I do for the CIA…did for the CIA."

"Did you kill people?"

"Don't ask the question if you don't really want to know the answer."

"Dammit, Kaplan, I want to know." She jumped off the bed and put her hands on her hips. "Did you kill people?"

"Yes. It was my job."

"Were they bad people?"

"Yes. I knew for a fact most of them were bad people. Some were very bad people."

"Most?"

"I followed orders."

"Did you enjoy it?"

"Lucy, only sick people enjoy killing. I did what I had to do to stay alive. I did what I had to do to protect innocent lives… to protect this country from evil."

She went silent and stared him in the eyes. "I can see that," she finally said. "Are you a bad person, Kaplan?"

"I don't see myself that way, Lucy."

"I do not either. You helped me when I needed help. Bad people do not do that."

"I helped you because you needed help. You still do. You deserve better than the life you are living here. You're smart. A quick thinker. Maybe you had more than your fair share of bad breaks, but only you can stop this downward spiral. Get out of Last Chance. Go back to school. I'm sure there are lots of opportunities out there and avenues for you to get help."

"Because I am Indian?"

"No. And yes. Not *because* you are Indian, but I know for a fact there are Native American school preferences and scholarships. I'm sure KC can direct you to the right sources."

Lucy said nothing at first and then, "Why will the marshal not give Evan a break?"

Kaplan grinned at her. Cavalier and Isabella were *by the book*, mostly. That was a personality trait they shared.

"Because the marshal obeys the law, Lucy. She took an oath, just like I did. She can't afford to screw anything up right now. She's under a lot of pressure. If she turns a blind eye to Evan, she gets fired. You don't want that do you?"

She shook her head back and forth. "I do not want Evan to go to jail either."

"This is the marshal's last chance to keep a career in law enforcement."

Lucy giggled. Kaplan got it.

"You want Evan to be safe, right?"

She nodded.

"Right now, there is no safer place for him than in the marshal's jail. In all likelihood, the judge will only give him probation, especially if he'll testify against his brother and father."

"Will he do that?"

"I don't know, but if he turns out to be the good guy you say he is, I think he can be encouraged to do the right thing."

CHAPTER 36

The news of Butch's death distressed Drew Pearson. Butch was his real name. All the ranch hands had nicknames, kind of a western tradition. Butch's nickname on the ranch was Gator, since he hailed from the swamps of Louisiana and had a heavy Cajun accent. Last night's storms were vicious, but Butch wasn't the type to wander off and get himself killed. Not accidentally, anyway. And he certainly wasn't the clumsy type, not this kid. Not the kid who climbed all over the barn's steep metal roof when it was covered in ice and snow. Not the kid who could walk the top rail of the split-rail fence and never lose his balance. There was no way he just slipped, hit his head and fell in the ditch to drown. No, sir. Something was amiss.

Drew knew this was not the time to overreact. That type of behavior typically brought out the worst in people, especially Stevie, who could go ballistic without much provocation. And Butch's death would probably ignite Stevie's temper. He knew he had to send Stevie away. To the cabin, for now. Later, when things calmed down and the marshal had exhausted her search, he'd sneak Stevie off the ranch and out of harm's way. Out of Wyoming, for certain.

He needed to hide Stevie fast. By now, he had expected to see a convoy of police vehicles flying up his driveway.

His youngest son, Evan, had brought him the bad news about Butch while Drew was eating breakfast. He couldn't believe it. The news made him sick to his stomach. His reflux kicked in, so he popped another antacid to quell the burn, even though he'd already taken his morning pill with his coffee.

Drew told Evan to round up everyone except the wives and have them gather in his study in fifteen minutes. The grandfather clock showed that was five minutes from now. He gave Stevie strict instructions to pack everything he would need for an extended stay at the cabin. After the meeting, he was to saddle his horse, load one pack horse and head for the mountains, where he could expect to remain for an indeterminate amount of time. Surprisingly, Stevie displayed no objection.

Drew walked into his study where the five remaining ranch hands, and his four sons had gathered as ordered. The ranch hands were standing, almost at attention, and side-by-side. His sons were all seated.

"I just got off the phone with Max, my attorney," Drew began. "I told him everything." He directed his gaze at his oldest son. "Stevie, Max told me there is nothing he can do to keep you from being arrested. When the marshal gets here, you're going to jail, and you won't make bail. So, I need you to leave right now. I'm sure as the day is long that the marshal will show up any minute and make several arrests." Stevie didn't move. "I'm not asking Stevie. You do as I say now."

Stevie never said a word and didn't look at his father when he got up and marched out the back door.

Drew wasn't happy sending his son away, but he had no choice. He refocused his attention back to the ranch hands. "Frenchie, Will and Sweaty, you men did nothing wrong, so you're safe from the law." Frenchie got his nickname because his real name was Pierre Lord and that sounded French to Drew. Sweaty got his nickname because, well, he was always sweaty. Even when it was below freezing outside. Will was the oldest ranch hand and had worked at the Rocking P Ranch for nearly twenty years.

He looked at Mark and Scott. Mark's bandage was gone, and he appeared none the worse for wear. Scott sat on the couch with his foot propped on the coffee table and his crutches leaning against the armrest next to where he sat. "Mark and Scott, you're out of this too. Max said if the marshal tries to charge you with anything, he can have it dropped with a phone call to the judge. Evan, Max thinks he can get you and me out on bail in no time." He addressed his ranch hands. "Same with Slim and Ropey. Max said when the marshal shows up, we should not resist. Just give ourselves up and let him handle the rest. Do I make myself clear?" He scanned the room and all heads were nodding.

Drew told the ranch hands, "Now, you boys get back to work." He faced his three remaining sons. "Mark, you and Scott go home and wait. One of you will have to coordinate with Max when the time comes. "Evan, stay here a minute."

Mark helped Scott to his feet and handed him his crutches. Drew waited till they left the big house and turned to Evan. "I want you to get that piece of trash squaw and haul her down in the mine. Tie her up where she can't be a bother."

"Oh shit," Evan said as he jumped to his feet. "I forgot all about Lucy." He walked to the bookcase, reached under one shelf, and the bookcase opened revealing the tunnel access from the big house. He flipped on the light and disappeared down the stairs.

Today would not be easy for Evan, Drew thought. His youngest son had never been in trouble a day in his life and now he would probably get arrested for something that was clearly not his fault. It was his older brother's…and now it might land him with an arrest record. Unless he and Max could figure out a way to keep him out of it, it was now a foregone conclusion.

Drew was convinced that the featherhead bitch had put this whole thing in motion. If it weren't for her, none of this would have happened. Mark and Scott wouldn't have been hurt if she hadn't involved the stranger. He wouldn't have gone to the jail looking for the man who harmed his boys, lost his temper and taken it out on the marshal. Stevie wouldn't have shot and killed a deputy. The way he saw it, that homeless piece of garbage should be disposed of. Permanently.

After he dealt with the Indian, he would call the marshal and report Butch's death. He would let the marshal have her day. That marshal bitch would think she had the upper hand. He'd go peacefully instead of resisting, which he knew she'd take great pleasure in, then he would put the rest of his plan in motion. When that happened, Last Chance Town Marshal Christine Cavalier would become nothing more than a memory.

† † †

Evan hurried down the long corridor toward the hoist house. He couldn't believe he forgot all about Lucy. She'd probably been yelling for over an hour. His father blamed her for everything, he knew, but it really wasn't her fault. None of it. If his two idiot brothers hadn't always been bullying everyone in town, none of this would have happened. They got what they deserved. Now, his father wanted revenge against Lucy. He couldn't allow that to happen. He liked Lucy. And she liked him, otherwise why would she have freely given herself to him, not once, but twice out in the stable. She was short and as lean as an alley cat. Her face was pretty with her brown skin, amber eyes and high cheekbones. And she was feisty. He liked her. He could see a future life with her by his side.

He burst through the door into the hoist house. Stevie had already packed his stuff and was gone. The kitchen was still a mess and the TV room still smelled like a frat house. All his crushed empties still littered on the floor. No surprise. Stevie was a slob. He passed through the TV room and rounded the corner to the hall. He headed to Lucy's door, stopped and rapped twice with his knuckles. All quiet, which he thought was unusual, especially given the length of time she'd been in there. The keys were still dangling in the keyhole and the door was still locked. He rotated the key and heard the deadbolt clank unlocked. He opened the door. Lucy was still in the bed, just like when he checked on her last night. No, *exactly* like when he checked on her last night. He was about to shake her when he realized something was dreadfully wrong. Lucy had stuffed the bed with pillows to make it look like she was in bed. He spun around, Lucy was nowhere to be found.

He began searching everywhere. Under the bed, in the bathroom, both other bedrooms. How could she possibly have gotten out of her room? Meanwhile, a thought occurred to him. The last person to deal with her was Stevie. He had to have left the door unlocked and somehow during the night, she sneaked out. He walked back into the hall toward her bedroom. Damn, his father would be pissed.

He caught sight of something out of the corner of his eyes. A sliver of light that usually wasn't there. Barely even noticeable and coming from beneath the exterior door. That's when he saw the locks dangling free from their latches. He tugged trying to pull the heavy door open. It was stiff and wouldn't budge. He spent almost ten minutes trying to pry the door open without success. Finally, he gave up. There was no way he could get the heavy door open. Not even wide enough for Lucy to escape. Which meant Lucy who was smaller and not as strong could not have opened it. At least not by herself.

It was a long way from the big house to the hoist house. A trip he'd made countless times. This time it was taking forever and he was running as fast as he could. It was only a hundred twenty yards, just over a football field in length, but he was exhausted and breathing heavy. His footfalls slammed with each step, reverberating an echo through the long corridor. Each echo pounded in his ears. It was if he was running in a fog, his vision blurred, and his head throbbed. How would his father react to this news? He reached the steps to the big house and stopped, bent over resting his hands on his thighs. His chest was heaving. He needed to catch his breath.

As he climbed the steps, he readied himself for his father's temper.

CHAPTER 37

Cavalier was waiting for KC to return from Sheridan with the search warrant for Drew Pearson's ranch along with arrest warrants for Drew Pearson, Evan Pearson, Stevie Pearson, and John Doe warrants for the three ranch hands whose names she could not provide the judge. Thanks to Kaplan's recon, which was never to be mentioned again, she was able to provide exact details and search locations on the Pearson property. The warrant would include the two sons' cabins, the bunkhouse, the stable, the bunker, tunnel, and the main ranch house. She made an early call to Jesse, explained what was happening and asked him if he could come in and help round up the Pearsons. He sounded less than enthused but agreed and had just entered the office and sat down at his desk.

Once again, Moss sat in the chair next to her desk. Kaplan should arrive soon, she thought, how long could it take to talk to Lucy and calm her down. She was resentful the way Kaplan insisted she not talk to Lucy, but in a way, she was relieved. A woman's biological need to nurture was not in her DNA. Even when Isabella got sick, she didn't know how to comfort her. She never knew what to say or how to act. And that was her own sister for crying out loud. It was nice not to have that burden. That was how she saw it, as a burden.

She was about to speak to Moss when her office phone rang. Caller ID read *Rocking P Ranch*. "Drew Pearson, of all people."

She put the phone on speaker so Moss could hear, mostly as her witness in case that weasel Pearson tried to turn it around on her later.

The voice on the phone sounded angry, but he tempered his words. "Marshal Cavalier, this is Drew Pearson."

"Mr. Pearson, I was just about to pay you a visit."

"As I expected…and welcome."

She knew his choice of words was meant to irritate her, and they did, but she wouldn't let it show. Not now. Not when she was about to serve him with a search warrant and arrest his worthless ass along with the rest of his gang. "What do you want, Mr. Pearson?"

"I'd like to report a death on my property."

She swallowed hard. "A death. Who died?"

"One of my ranch hands was found dead in the drainage ditch this morning. When we pulled him out of the water, he had a large gash on his head."

Her eyes questioned Moss. He shrugged his shoulders and shook his head. She steadied her voice, "No, Mr. Pearson, I have no idea what you're talking about. Those storms were pretty strong last night, probably an accident."

There was a long pause. "Could have been, I guess. My ranch hands retrieved his body from the ditch this morning. We left him on the ground covered in a sheet. I didn't want to be accused of tainting a possible crime scene."

Pearson emphasized the words *possible crime scene*. She clenched her teeth as she spoke. She forced her anger back down and said, "Thank you for being so considerate. I'll have the coroner meet us out there in an hour."

"I'll leave the gate open," Pearson said. And he hung up.

She and Moss exchanged looks. "What the hell do you think that was all about?" Moss asked.

"I don't know, but I think I need to have a chat with Kaplan."

Five minutes later, Kaplan walked in her office. Just like last night, he was dressed in full tactical gear, sans the rain suit. He had his black backpack that he'd removed from his motorcycle slung over his shoulder. He was displaying his deputy badge and looked ready for a mission.

"Look who finally showed up," Moss said.

"Let the fun begin." Kaplan said to Jesse. "You up for this?" Cavalier could hear genuine concern in Kaplan's voice.

Jesse replied, "As I'll ever be, I guess. Thanks for asking."

"I just received a very strange phone call, Kaplan," Cavalier said. "Maybe you can help me out."

"Sure. What is it?"

"Drew Pearson just called. Said he found one of his ranch hands in the ditch this morning, dead. His body apparently got caught under a footbridge and wedged between the pilings. He believes it wasn't an accident. You wouldn't know anything about that, would you?"

Kaplan said nothing at first. Maybe he was caught off guard, she thought, or perhaps he was pissed at the insinuation. Or, he could have been thinking of a lie to tell her.

At last, Kaplan said, "There was one point during those storms last night that the current in the ditch was so strong, no one could have survived if they fell in. And, on top of that, the ground near the ditch was very slick. Get too close, fall in, get washed downstream, drown. Most likely scenario."

What he said made sense. After all, she was the one

who warned him to get out of the ditch last night because of the possibility of a flash flood. Yet, he never really answered her question. She said, "That must be what happened. The coroner will meet us at the ranch in forty-five and he'll take the body."

Moss chimed in, "And we'll take the Pearsons."

They had devised a plan of attack to arrest the three Pearsons and the three ranch hands. There were only the four of them against six, or eight if you count the Pearson brothers who were recovering from Kaplan's hand. A passing thought made her wonder if Drew's call was actually the prelude to an ambush. It didn't make sense if it was. Too many bodies, too many questions. Even the mighty Drew Pearson couldn't get away with killing so many. He had to have another angle.

As the four vehicles turned into Pearson's long driveway, she realized that there was no way Drew Pearson would allow them to come arrest him and his family if he didn't already have a plan.

She led the convoy up the long straight drive to the ranch house. Close behind her were Moss and Kaplan in his black Escalade, followed by Jesse in his black Tundra and KC in his big Ford pickup pulling up the rear. As she topped the last rise, the Pearson ranch complex came into view. It had been over a year since she made her last visit to the ranch. The second of two. The first was a social gathering with the town council and several of the more prominent citizens of Last Chance that Drew Pearson hosted in her honor to toast her as the new town marshal. Which was odd, seeing as he had raised the most objection to her hiring. She knew it was all for show…and the town council bought it.

The second was when he reported vandals had cut

down one of his fence lines and allowed over three dozen cattle to escape into the foothills.

The Sheridan County Coroner had arrived early, and his van was parked in front of the bunkhouse. The side door was open, and Matthew Davidson was leaning against the van putting on his sterile coveralls. It was white and disposable, and he referred to it as a *bunny suit*. His evidence collection kit was on the ground next to him. Drew Pearson was lumbering in his direction.

She parked her Bronco at the entrance of the ranch house and blocked the driveway. Jesse parked next to her. Moss had parked next to Davidson's van and KC left his pickup blocking the exit from the common parking area. Pearson had several other vehicles, all registered to the Rocking P Ranch, as Moss discovered from a quick internet search. Pearson's ranch vehicles were a small fleet of white pickup trucks with oversized tires and his brand plastered on each side of the trucks. None of the Pearson sons owned their own vehicle, at least not registered in the State of Wyoming. The only vehicle other than the fleet of pickups registered to Drew Pearson was a late model Mercedes sedan.

She jumped out, and without shutting her door darted across the gravel parking area toward Pearson and Davidson. Jesse was on her heels. As she reached Pearson, Moss and Kaplan came around Davidson's van from each end, one from the front, one from the rear. Pearson looked genuinely surprised. Prominently displayed were their badges.

Moss held up his credentials and said, "United States Marshals Service."

"My, my," Pearson said. "So, you brought in the feds I see?"

Pearson eyed Kaplan. “And who might you be?”

Cavalier cut him off. “He’s my new deputy.”

By now, a small group of ranch hands and family had gathered to see what all the commotion was about. There were five men standing on the front porch of the bunkhouse, dressed in their cowboy work clothes. Two of them she recognized from when Drew assaulted her in her office. They were the ones holding her down when she broke Stevie’s nose. To her left, were two cabins. A man and woman stood on each porch. She raised her hand and yelled. “Stay where you are. All of you.” She shook her finger at the ranch hands. “That goes for all of you, too.”

“Where’s the other one?” she asked. “The third man you brought to my office?”

“He’s the dead one.”

“Where’s the body, Pearson?” Cavalier questioned.

“Down by the ditch. I can take you there.”

“No,” she said. She faced one of the ranch hands she had never seen before. “You.” She motioned with her finger for him to step off the porch. “What’s your name?”

“They call me Frenchie.”

“Okay, Frenchie, take the coroner to the body and stay there with him. Don’t leave his side. You understand?”

Frenchie waited for Drew Pearson to nod and said, “Got it.”

Frenchie led Davidson around the side of the bunkhouse and soon both men were out of sight.

“Where’s Stevie?” she asked.

“I don’t know,” Pearson replied.

“What do you mean you don’t know?”

“He wasn’t here when I got up this morning and no one

can find him."

"Well, that's pretty convenient, don't you think? I'm sure you're worried about him." She reached into her pocket, pulled out the search warrant and handed it to Pearson. "Maybe we can help you find him."

He studied the document, his eyes narrow and his mouth drawing tighter the more he read. "How did you know about the tunnel…and the hoist house?"

"Seems you had a reluctant guest yesterday who found her way back home last night."

"That goddamn Indian girl, I should have known." He shoved the search warrant back at her. "Knock yourself out, marshal."

"So, you admit to kidnapping Lucy?"

She motioned with her hand, Jesse and KC stepped behind Drew Pearson and clamped handcuffs on his wrists and read him his rights.

"I admit to nothing. I just assumed Evan was screwing her again."

Moss and Kaplan placed handcuffs on the two ranch hands who were part of Pearson's lynch mob and Moss read them their rights.

"Where is Evan, by the way?" she said to Pearson. There was an edge to her tone.

Pearson motioned with his head. "In the big house."

She ordered KC to get Evan and bring him out here with the rest of the men.

Mark Pearson yelled from the porch of his cabin with his finger aimed at Kaplan. "That's the guy. That's the guy who did this."

Pearson put it together fast. His face turned red. He

glared at Cavalier. "This is the guy who assaulted my sons? One of your deputies?"

"First of all, eyewitness testimony proves it was self-defense. He's been cleared. So, yeah, now he's one my deputies... to replace the one your son murdered."

Pearson zeroed in on Kaplan. "When I get out of jail, you're a dead man."

"Is that so?" Kaplan replied. Cavalier liked the sarcasm oozing from his tone. It sounded like a taunt. "Better make your first effort count because that will be your only chance."

KC brought Evan Pearson out with his hands cuffed behind his back and stood him next to his father.

Davidson and Frenchie came into view around the corner carrying his evidence collection kit. He stopped in front of Cavalier. "The victim didn't drown," he announced. "Appears he died from blunt force trauma. Until I do the autopsy, I won't know if it happened before or after he went into the water."

"I bet that Indian bitch did it," Pearson shouted.

"KC, get them out of here and lock them up. Make sure you take prints and mug shots. I'll bring Stevie, when we find him." She looked at Pearson. "Odds are, he's in the tunnel somewhere."

A smile curled on Pearson's lips.

CHAPTER 38

After putting both horses in the small makeshift corral and stable, Stevie unloaded the pack horse and took his belongings into the one-room cabin. It had only been a couple of months since it was last used and was still relatively clean. He, his father and two of his brothers used it during hunting season each year.

It took a little over two hours to reach the cabin from the big house. Actually, it was just over two miles as the crow flew, but the trail was anything but straight, so it was closer to three miles by the time everything was said and done. That last mile was difficult and, at places, downright perilous, full of switchbacks and no real defined trail to speak of, just the horse and foot trail that only the family knew about.

A mile straight across the plains to the tree line, then the terrain became steep and rocky. From the cliff just behind the cabin, he could see the big house and all the buildings on his father's property. Unless someone came from behind the cliff, he would be able to see anyone approaching in plenty of time to take action.

Stevie unpacked his weapons and tossed them on one of the cots. He loved his guns. His favorite was the Barrett 50 caliber sniper rifle his father bought him a couple of years ago. He was a dead eye with the gun. He could plink the head off a prairie dog at 700 yards with ease. He had actually sat on the cliff behind the cabin and killed an elk all the way down in the valley. His mouth watered just thinking about all the animals he had killed. It was always a thrill.

It was even more exciting killing that cop. The way the blast from the Taurus Judge catapulted the deputy backwards was cool, just like in his video game, *The Killing Zone*. And the blood spraying from his chest, wow. Better than any movie he'd ever seen. The deputy wasn't the first time he'd ever killed a person, but it was the most exhilarating. If that marshal showed up, he'd get the chance to do it again.

He finished unloading the supplies and put them away. The cabin was rudimentary by most people's standards, but he liked it. *Kick-your-feet-up* was the phrase he would use. Other than having to go outside to use the outhouse to relieve himself, it had everything he needed. Over this past winter, his father had installed a portable generator and a high-end mini-fridge to keep food from going bad. After the fridge cooled, it would keep food cold for three days before the generator had to be started up again. Between that and his father's three super-expensive *Yeti* coolers, he could stay out here for a long time without needing to restock supplies.

He'd been taught early in his life to live off the land. And, since he was such a good long-distance shooter and the Bighorn Mountains were ripe with game, he never went without food. Good food, too. Elk, moose, pronghorn, mule deer…especially pronghorn, were in abundance. Even the occasional black bear wandered into the crosshairs of his rifle from time to time.

Plus, only fifty feet from the cabin was Dead Horse Creek. It was full of trout. The water was cold this time of year, but he would still bathe in the creek. Dead Horse Creek sometimes brought big game close to the cabin. Like the moose he killed last year. He never had to step off the porch. That stupid cow moose just walked right up to cabin while he was sitting there. One shot from his Barrett at that range and the moose never stood a chance. He wasn't fond of moose meat, or bear meat for that matter. Pronghorn was good, elk better, mule deer best of all.

His youngest brother refused to hunt or fish or do most anything outdoors except ride those ornery horses and look for stupid rocks. He called himself a rock hound, whatever that was, but he did have hundreds of rocks in his room. Some were kinda cool, but still, they were just rocks. His father called Evan a *gentle soul*. A nice way to say Evan was a pussy. He wouldn't even go near a gun. Stevie teased his brother that he was adopted because he was nothing like his father or his brothers. He didn't belong in this family.

The longest Stevie had spent out here in the woods was two and a half months. He hoped his father could straighten everything out before too long. He didn't want to be stuck out here during the winter months. It was okay for a week or two on hunting trips, but it could get miserably cold. He used to think he could have been a mountain man if he lived out here a couple hundred years ago or so, but after two weeks in late January, early February this year, he knew he wasn't that tough...although he would never admit it to his brothers or father.

The last thing on his checklist was to set the perimeter alerts. There were three sets, each defining its own perimeter. It was his father's idea a few years ago. Set to alert when wildlife tripped the warning, it had just as much usefulness in detecting human intruders as well. If one of the tripwires was activated, it wouldn't be by his father or brothers, or small game. It would be big game or another human. If human, he would be ready to dispatch the invader.

† † †

Most of what transpired this morning didn't sit well with Kaplan. His gut told him something was off. After everything Drew Pearson and his family had done, and knowing the consequences, why would he be so cooperative? He was hiding something. He freely gave himself, his youngest son, and his ranch hands up to Cavalier without any resistance whatsoever. Totally out of character for the man who busted into the marshal's office and assaulted Cavalier. He had to have put a plan of action in place prior to their arrival at his ranch. Nothing else made any sense to him. But, what was it?

KC returned to the ranch after locking Drew, Evan, Slim and Ropey in jail. He informed Cavalier that Pearson's attorney was livid that they were being left in the jail cells unattended.

"What did you do with the keys?" she asked. KC pulled out the cell room keys and jingled them at arm's length. "Good. Not that I don't trust his attorney, but, … I just don't trust anybody associated with Drew Pearson."

Cavalier took charge at that point. She had Jesse stand watch outside while she and Moss, KC and Kaplan searched the two brothers' cabins and bunkhouse for Stevie. Those searches came up empty. She suggested they start in the *big house*, as Pearson described it, and work toward the *hoist house*, another term used by Pearson. Kaplan reminded her that he didn't know where in the big house the tunnel came out and suggested that he and Moss start at the hoist house and work their way back to the big house. He suggested she leave Jesse to watch the exit to make sure no one left the premises. She and

KC could search the big house while he and Moss cleared the tunnel.

She was reluctant at first but acquiesced to his suggestion. He went to Moss' Escalade and returned with the radios they used last night. "Keep these active," he said to Cavalier. "I doubt they'll work while we're in the tunnel, but it's better than nothing."

Kaplan lifted his chin toward Moss. "Follow me, big guy."

The walk to the tunnel entrance took five minutes, which was a minute longer than Kaplan wanted, but Moss didn't have the same gate as he did. As the two descended into the darkness following the bright beams of their flashlights, each step Moss took reverberated through the stairwell like an elephant was marching behind him. Kaplan had searched for a light switch topside before they started down but found none. When they reached the tunnel, the beam from his light found a metal hard-plate switch on the tunnel wall. He flipped it up and the stairwell illuminated, but the tunnel was still in the dark.

He and Moss hurried down the long corridor, making the zig-zag detour around the elevator shaft and into the bunker. He didn't understand why Pearson called this the *hoist house* as, if he remembered correctly, a hoist house was typically built above the vertical shaft of a coal mine, not lateral to it. Then again, what did he really know about coal mines? Inside the entrance to the bunker—*hoist house*—was a light switch that turned on the tunnel lights.

He and Moss cleared the hoist house and moved back into the tunnel toward the big house. At the fork where the tunnel wrapped around the mineshaft, Kaplan stopped. "We should check the mine," he said to Moss.

"Oh, hell no, I am *not* going down there." He trained his flashlight beam down the dark tunnel toward the elevator.

"We have to clear it. What if Stevie went down there? No stone left unturned, right Inspector Moss?"

"Yeah, yeah, Kaplan, I get what you're saying, but I'm having enough trouble with this tunnel as it is. There's no way I'm going down that hole."

"Claustrophobic?"

"No…well, maybe."

Kaplan walked toward the elevator shaft. "I'll clear it myself."

CHAPTER 39

After he located the light switch, Kaplan and Moss walked down the short corridor to the elevator shaft. This was indeed an old mine, and by the looks of it, an abandoned coal mine, which verified what Cavalier explained to him yesterday. She had informed him that Drew Pearson started buying property when he was a young man living in northern Sheridan County. His first acquisition was an old coal mining camp that dated back to the 1850s. Then Pearson added to it one acquisition at a time as neighbors with adjoining properties fell on hard times. According to Cavalier, he had expanded his property to the north from his initial purchase to include all of the land up to the Montana border, which abutted the Crow Reservation, and west into the Bighorn Mountains to the border of the Bighorn National Forest. She said it was rumored he bought an abandoned gold mine somewhere in the mountains to the west.

The mine shaft elevator didn't look like it had been used in a long time. The rusty shaft mechanism had a rickety wooden hand crank to raise and lower the cage. The cage appeared to be at the bottom of the shaft, but he had no idea how deep the shaft was. Moss grabbed the handle and started cranking. Pulleys in need of lubrication squeaked as the fat sisal ropes worked its way through. He knew that toxic air could build up in abandoned mines. Carbon dioxide often collected along the floor and movement could cause the bad air to mix with the good. He thought about abandoning the search in the lower mine since there were no visible signs of footprints leading to the shaft. But, if he quit now, the search wouldn't be thorough. There was always the possibility of another way into the mine.

When the metal cage was at the top of the shaft, Moss said, "Tell me you're not crazy enough to ride down in that rust bucket death trap."

Kaplan shrugged.

"Shit, man. Give it up. Ain't no way this thing is safe."

"You know I have to go down and check it out. I mean, what are the odds that both ropes break, right?"

"From what I'm seeing, I'd say the odds aren't in your favor. Look at this place. No way it's been used in decades."

Kaplan stepped in the cage. "Just lower me down will ya?" Kaplan instructed. "Slowly."

"I should mention that rattlesnakes and mountain lions might greet you at the bottom."

"Thanks for the pep talk, buddy." Kaplan gave Moss a thumbs-up.

The cage slowly descended down the shaft. With every squeak and jolt, he braced himself. He was sure if the ropes did snapped the cage would send him on a free fall to the bottom floor. Not a preferred way to die.

Kaplan let out a heavy sigh when the cage touched the bottom of the shaft and guessed he was only fifty feet or so below the top of the tunnel. He didn't feel dizzy or lightheaded, so he assumed there were no toxic gases down in the mine. Just in case Moss wasn't kidding, he scanned his light around the area checking for any unwelcome critters. The area opened into a large cavernous room. Crossing in front of the elevator cage were metal rail tracks leading out of sight in both directions. Roughly east and west, if he still had his bearings straight. The room surrounding the elevator shaft was littered with metal carts used to haul coal back and forth. One of these shafts, he assumed, led to the abandoned drilling site and the other had to lead to the surface—somewhere. But, where? He couldn't recall Google Maps showing any other structures that matched where he envisioned these tunnels led, but he knew there had to be a surface exit somewhere. How else could the coal be removed?

He studied the ground surrounding the elevator shaft. A thick dust had settled on everything. He stepped out into the room and watched his boots kick up black dust and leave deep footprints. His were the only ones. It had been quite a number of years since anyone had been in this mine, which ruled this out as a hideout or escape route for Stevie Pearson. At least it had been checked…and ruled out.

He made his way back to the elevator cage and keyed his mic. "Moss, all clear down here. Haul me up."

The cage began slowly moving upward. He didn't like the sound of the strain on the ropes passing through the pulleys. A troubling thought ran through his mind. Going down, he had gravity on his side. Less strain on these old elevator mechanisms. Going up would be the opposite. Would the ropes hold his weight to the tunnel level? He buried the thought and craned his neck upward as Moss started cranking.

He heard it before he felt it. A loud snap. The right side of the cage dropped, followed by pieces of old sisal rope raining down on him. His flashlight fell from his hands as he clutched both sides of the metal cage. It tumbled through the bars on the cage and out of sight below.

Moss yelled, his voice echoing down the elevator shaft. "Rope broke. You okay?"

He could see the beam of his flashlight glowing beneath the cage. He was at fifteen, maybe twenty feet from the bottom. "Not really, no."

"Should I keep trying to pull you up?" Moss asked.

He thought about it for a split second and yelled to Moss, "No. Don't do anything yet."

Up was no good. The closer to the top Moss cranked him, the further he would fall if the other rope broke. His weight was already too much for two ropes to handle, no way the remaining rope would hold.

The metal cage shifted again.

"Moss," he yelled.

"I didn't do anything. The rope, it's starting to fray," Moss yelled in a panicked voice.

"Lower me down," he yelled to Moss realizing he might only have seconds before the second rope broke entirely. "Slowly."

The cage inched down.

Snap.

Freefall.

The last thing he remembered was his death grip on the sides of the cage.

† † †

When he came to, the cage was laying on its side. A cloud of black dust still hung in the air. He coughed. His brain ran through a quick diagnostic check of his body. The fall was fast, and the ride was rough. He had no recollection of the impact. His left hip and shoulder ached. He was on his left side when he regained consciousness, so he assumed he landed that way. Nothing broken, definitely bruised. He had felt worse.

Fortunately, the cage hit the sides of the shaft on the way down which had slowed its fall, otherwise this could have been much worse. He dragged himself out of the cage on his belly.

As the dust slowly settled, the light from his flashlight got brighter and he could detect the walls of the tunnel.

He called out for Moss several times and got no response. He hoped the big man had gone for help, because he wasn't sure he'd be able to pull himself up the shaft if they dropped a rope.

He rolled and pulled himself to a sitting position and then he saw it. The beam of his flashlight was shining on several small wooden crates lined against a far wall next to the empty metal coal carts. He pushed himself to his feet and stumbled to his flashlight and then shuffled to the crates, kicking up black dust knee-high. The crates were coated in the same black silt, just like what he'd been walking through. He brushed the side of one crate with his hand. In bold letters were written the words:

DANGER: EXPLOSIVES
Dynamite

He lifted the lid to the top crate and checked the contents inside. Indeed, three layers of dynamite sticks separated by straw. Twenty-one sticks per crate. Four crates. Eighty-fours sticks of dynamite. No telling how long they had been stored down here. He reached in and grabbed five sticks, stuffed them in his jacket, and addressed his next pressing issue, how to get the hell out of this mine.

The lower tunnel was at a right angle to the one above. He gathered his bearings and realized, as he entered the Pearson compound last night in the midst of all the storms, there was nothing on the west side that would indicate an exit from this mine. He shone the beam down the empty black tunnel. Nothing. It boiled down to 50% chance he was right and a 50% chance he was wrong. His rationale might be groundless, but he was going east.

He started to run, shining the flashlight beam several feet ahead of him, and following the coal cart rail tracks. They had to lead somewhere, either a dead-end or an exit. His hip ached, and he favored it as he ran, but that didn't slow his sprint. The longer he stayed in this hell hole, the worse his chances of survival. Moss might find KC and Cavalier and return with a rope, but he wasn't going to wait.

It felt like he had run a long time before he saw it. A mere speck of light at first that grew brighter and larger with every step. Sunlight. He burst through the bent metal door and into the fresh air. He was facing east. In the far distance he saw a fence line parallel to a gravel road. A pickup was traveling north at high speed and sending a large plume of dust behind it.

He knew exactly where he was.

††††

Cavalier hadn't heard a word from Moss or Kaplan since they entered the wooden shed that Kaplan claimed led down to the tunnel. Her concern was something happening to them down there and they couldn't communicate for help. Moss had reminded her several times since he arrived that Kaplan could take care of himself.

She and KC had entered the big house through the main door and cleared the mansion room by room. When Pearson called it the *big house,* he wasn't kidding. The place was enormous. No telling how many rooms they had cleared already, and it felt like they were just getting started. They began with the upstairs, locating the second set of stairs and proceeding inward between both stairwells until all the rooms and closets and bathroom had been searched. Of all the bedrooms upstairs, only two looked lived in. Stevie and Evan, she presumed. One room was clean and neat, the other a pigsty. She associated them with clean-Evan, pigsty-Stevie. When she was convinced the upstairs was clear, she gave KC the signal and they each took separate stairwells to the main level.

Fortunately, Pearson liked the open floor plan and the main level had a tremendous amount of open area lending their search easier than the upstairs. Mudroom, laundry room, and a half bath were all connected by a single hallway, which led to the kitchen, which was open to a great room with an oversized fireplace at the opposite end. On each side of the fireplace were doors. One led to a master bedroom, Drew Pearson's obviously by the clothes in the closets and boots on a shelf and hats on a rack. On his dresser was a valet with an assortment of western belt buckles. One thing she made note of was how organized this room was. Everything had its place. His closet, which was bigger than her living room, had all of his clothes separated by style. Long sleeve shirts on one rod, all separated an inch apart. Short sleeve shirts on another rod. Long pants, mostly jeans which were ironed, on another rod. Coats, jackets, suits on still another and covered in clear plastic.

She and KC only had one room left on the main level,

Drew Pearson's office. When they entered, she was amazed at the number of books and bookshelves. He had a small fireplace, a TV on a wall opposite his grandiose mahogany desk. There were several large leather chairs facing the desk and a recliner facing the TV. To one side was a wet bar with an assortment of liquor, most bourbon and brandy.

The sound of a thud behind a bookcase startled her. KC had drawn his weapon and readied it before she could get her palm on hers. *Damn, he was fast.* The bookcase where the sound came from moved outward. She could see the glow of a light around the opening case. She aimed her pistol at the moving bookcase and hollered, "Police, hands up."

Out walked Moss with his hands up in surrender. He was winded and sweaty.

Her shoulders drooped and KC let out a sigh and cussed under his breath. She holstered her weapon and patted KC on the shoulder.

"Dammit. We could have shot you. Where's Kaplan?"

Moss lowered his hands. He wiped the sweat from his forehead and said between broken breaths, "He went down in the mine to see if Stevie was hiding down there. The elevator broke and crashed to the bottom. Last I saw him, he wasn't moving, and the elevator cage was in pieces at the bottom of the mine. I yelled and yelled, he never answered."

"I have rock climbing rope in my truck," KC said. "Two hundred feet of it."

"Let's go get it," she said.

The three of them rushed out the front door of the big house toward the parking area where they left their vehicles.

At KC's truck, he climbed inside the bed beneath the topper, opened a metal box and pulled out two coils of multicolored rope. He handed one to Moss and one to Cavalier while he climbed from the bed of his truck. "I always take some on my guide trips, you know, just in case."

"Let's go back to the big house," she said. "And into the tunnel."

"No," Moss said as he cut her off. "It's faster the way I went in with Kaplan." He indicated the direction of the mid-tunnel entrance. "Follow me."

Moss led the way while she and KC followed close behind. If Kaplan was injured, or God forbid killed, she might as well start packing her bags now. No way the town council would let her keep her job if another deputy died. As a matter of fact, they would probably just fire her on the spot.

Before they reached the tunnel access, the black silhouette of a man appeared walking toward them from over a knoll with a slight limp in his step. He was completely black, like someone had poured tar on him.

But, it wasn't tar.

It was dust.

Coal dust.

And it was Gregg Kaplan.

CHAPTER 40

When she arrived back at her office, she was greeted by three men and Lucy Raintree. Only one of the men she expected to see today, Pearson's fast-talking, high-dollar lawyer, Stewart Whitman. Whitman had first made a name for himself down in Casper working for the state's first injury law firm. That's what they liked to call themselves these days. Her father had always referred to them as ambulance chasers. After a decade in Casper, Whitman moved back to his childhood home in Sheridan where he set up his own law practice. He handled every type of law, from criminal to family, corporate to patent. His reputation from Casper followed him to Sheridan, where he had done quite well for himself since the move fifteen years ago. She had a few dealings with Whitman, mostly when one of the Pearson sons, usually Mark or Scott or both, would have too much to drink at the Crazy Woman Saloon and get in a fight. He'd barge into her office, make a phone call, and she'd get a call from the judge. Always the same. It was like playing a game of ping pong. She'd locked them up and let them loose with no charges sticking and no trial.

This time was different. One of the men standing in her office was the judge. The Honorable Martin Shepard was a Sheridan County circuit judge. The same judge who traveled to Last Chance whenever she had business that required a judge, pretty much like this time. No doubt Whitman had arranged this on Pearson's behalf.

Also in the room was Sheridan County Sheriff Jack

Knight. There was no reason for him to be here, unless Pearson and Whitman were planning to throw her a curve ball. She had an idea what that might be and told Jesse to go to the diner, get Poppy, and bring him to her office. Sitting in a chair against the wall was Lucy Raintree. Cavalier had her suspicions about why Lucy was here but didn't want to jump to any hasty conclusions.

Cavalier spoke first. "Your Honor, Counselor, Sheriff, what do I owe the pleasure?" She gave him a brisk smile.

Whitman, in his typical bulldog fashion, was the first to jump in. "I want to know what the charges are against my clients."

"Which ones are your clients?" she asked.

"All of them," Whitman replied with one hand on his hip inside his suit jacket.

She tossed a look at Moss and Kaplan. "This could take a while if you two want to go somewhere."

Sheriff Knight interrupted. "Afraid not. They have to stay. I have questions for both of them."

Oh, shit, she thought. This could turn ugly fast.

She stood while she recounted the incident with Drew Pearson, Evan, Stevie, Slim, Ropey, and the now deceased Butch when they burst into her office and assaulted her. While she went into the details of being tied up and Drew punching her in the face, she noticed Moss clenching and unclenching his hands, she assumed to keep from swinging at something or somebody. She pointed to her forehead, the swelling had gone down but now there was purple discoloration above her cut eyebrow that still had the butterfly bandage. "Drew did this and this." She added the charge of murder for Stevie and accomplice to murder for Evan.

"Do you have witnesses to this alleged attack by my clients?" Whitman asked.

"As a matter of fact, yes I do. There are three of them in my jail and one on the lam."

"Your honor," Whitman said. "May we bring in the accused?"

Shepard looked at KC. "Deputy, bring those men in here."

Jesse arrived with Poppy. Thirty seconds later, KC brought all four men in the main room, still in handcuffs, Drew and Evan Pearson and the two ranch hands.

"Marshal, will you please repeat your allegations with all present?"

"Your honor," Cavalier said. "Are you going to hold court?"

Shepard held up his hand. "Marshal, if I'm going to set bail, I want to hear from both sides."

"Your honor, I haven't even filed charges yet. I have twenty-four hours."

"Marshal, I'll say this one more time, repeat your allegations with all present."

She knew what was happening. She was being railroaded. The good ol' boy system at its finest, with Drew Pearson leading the charge. This would not bode well for her in the long run. And something else was happening too. It had to do with Kaplan or Moss…or Lucy. But, what?

"Marshal," Shepard said. "We're waiting."

She recounted the events of two days ago when Pearson came in and attacked her, leaving out no details, and specifically relating the actions of each individual involved.

Shepard addressed Drew Pearson. "Mr. Pearson, did

you come in here with your men day before yesterday?"

"No, your Honor."

"Mr. Pearson, do you understand the penalty for perjury?"

"Yes, your Honor."

"Have you ever, at any time, struck Town Marshal Cavalier?"

"No, your Honor." Pearson eyes focused on her. He said, "I have never struck a woman."

Cavalier's jaw tightened. She felt her stomach clench at how good Pearson was at lying.

"Where were you the day before yesterday?"

"On my ranch, your Honor. All day."

Shepard asked the same basic leading questions to Evan and the two ranch hands. Evan hesitated to answer at first after glancing at Lucy, then he denied he was in Cavalier's office and claimed to be at the ranch all day with his father. Both Slim and Ropey claimed the same. *Shit*. Even the judge was in on this.

Shepard addressed her. "Marshal, do you have any witnesses who can corroborate your version of the story?"

"No, your Honor. As I said, I was alone. I'm a law officer sworn to uphold the rule of law. Clearly, these men are lying to protect their boss…or father. What did you expect them to say?"

"Don't get testy with me, Marshal." Shepard raised his voice in warning.

"But, your honor."

"I'm not through, Marshal." Shepard faced Evan Pearson. "Mr. Evan Pearson, the marshal suggests you are an accessory to murder and kidnapping. These are very serious charges young man. Tell me what happened?"

Evan's eyes darted back and forth like he felt uncomfortable but seemed to gather himself. "Stevie wanted to talk to Lucy about the other day when that man," he said as he pointed to Kaplan, "beat up my two other brothers."

Now she knew why the sheriff was here. They're going after Kaplan.

"I tried to talk him out of it," Evan confessed. "I mean, what was the purpose, they probably got what they deserved." He stopped abruptly, like he had said something wrong. He scratched his face and continued. "Stevie doesn't have a driver's license and my other brothers, well, they were still recovering." He looked at Kaplan. As did the judge. "I was the only one left who could drive him into town. I said I'd wait in the truck. Next thing I know, he comes out of her room dragging Lucy by her arm kicking and screaming. I wanted to stop him and ask him what he was doing, but a black pickup came sliding into the parking lot. It was her two deputies." He extended his arm and motioned at Cavalier. "Jesse and Doug. Doug jumped out of the truck and ran toward Stevie. Before I knew it, Stevie fired on Doug and hit him in the chest. Jesse ducked for cover. Stevie pushed Lucy into the back seat, stuck the gun to my head and told me to drive. He turned around and started firing at Jesse."

"Stop right there," Shepard said. "Miss Lucy Raintree."

"Yes, sir."

"You were there, tell me your version."

"Okay. Well, I heard a knock on the door to my motel room. I did not think to look in the peep hole. If I had known it was Stevie, I would not have answered the door. When I opened the door, Stevie grabbed my arm hard and yanked me into the parking lot toward the truck. He had a big gun in his other hand and said he would shoot me if I did not come along. I was scared. That was when Jesse and Doug showed up. I screamed for help. Doug jumped out of the passenger side of Jesse's truck and ran toward me. He was yelling for Stevie to let me go."

Lucy stopped talking, her head hung down, a tear bounced off her foot.

"Please, Miss Raintree, continue."

"Stevie had the gun pointed at me until Doug came out. He lowered the gun. I thought he was going to tell Doug to stop, but he did not. He just fired and hit Doug in the chest. Blood went everywhere, it was so horrible." She began sobbing.

"It's okay," Shepard said. "Tell me what happened next."

"Stevie dragged me to the ranch truck, opened the door, and shoved me inside. He aimed the gun at me and told me not to try anything stupid. Then, he pointed the gun at Evan's head and yelled, 'Get us the fuck out of here.' So, Evan took off driving."

"Do you think Stevie would have shot his own brother if he hadn't done what he said?" Shepard asked.

"I do not know what he would have done. He was like out of control or something. Like a lunatic. When Evan started driving, Stevie stuck the gun out the window and just kept firing. And yelling."

"What was he yelling?" Shepard asked.

"I do not know. He was just yelling. Yelling and firing at Jesse."

Shepard said, "Which one is Jesse?"

Jesse raised his hand.

"Is that the way you saw it, too?" Shepard asked.

"I don't know about the gun to Evan's head. I was too busy taking cover. I saw Stevie dragging Lucy across the parking lot. Doug jumped out of my truck almost before I could get the truck stopped. He ran toward Stevie yelling 'Let her go. Let her go.' And then Stevie just shot him at point blank range." Jesse's head sunk. His voice was low. "Doug never even drew his weapon."

"I've heard all I need to hear," Shepard said. He turned to Drew. "Mr. Pearson, it sounds to me like your son Stevie has serious issues. He's in trouble, big time trouble. If you know of his whereabouts or even think you know of his whereabouts, I strongly advise you disclose that immediately for your sake and his. From these witness reports, I will uphold the marshal's assertion of the charge of murder."

"Your Honor," Drew Pearson said. "As God is my witness, I have no idea where my son is or could be. He just disappeared sometime during the night."

Cavalier knew he was lying. Everyone knew, but it didn't matter. The outcome of this little charade was determined long before she got back to her office. This was a setup. Her gut told her Pearson had orchestrated this whole thing. With help from his slime ball attorney Stewart Whitman. And as her father once said to her, never buck your gut.

"Okay," Shepard said addressing everyone but looking at Whitman. "I'm setting bail at $1000 each. Call the courthouse on Monday morning to arrange payment and I'll set the arraignment for one day next week." He turned to Cavalier. "Marshal, I expect you to have charges filed by noon on Monday. Now, release these men immediately on their own recognizance."

"Excuse me, your Honor," she said to Shepard as he was heading for the door.

Shepard held up his hand. "Marshal, I'm done here. For

your sake, I might suggest you are too. Anything more might be considered harassment on your part directed at Drew Pearson and family. This matter is not up for discussion, do I make myself clear?"

She nodded. There was nothing else she could do at the moment. She was defeated. Drew Pearson had won this round. It was amazing—and criminal—what money could buy.

Both Pearsons, Slim, Ropey, Judge Shepard, and Stewart Whitman all left her office.

Sheriff Jack Knight had stayed behind.

CHAPTER 41

"Did you forget something, Sheriff?" Cavalier asked.

The sheriff directed his gaze toward Kaplan. "I'd like to ask this man a few questions."

"About what?" she asked Knight.

"Concerning the incident two days ago where Mark and Scott Pearson were grievously attacked."

"With all due respect, Sheriff, this in my jurisdiction. As is all the Pearson property. As you know, Last Chance Police Jurisdiction extends all the way to the Montana line, and that incorporates all of the Rocking-P Ranch. Furthermore, I have already done an investigation and ruled the incident self-defense."

Knight reached into his pocket and pulled out three folded pieces of paper. "I had this complaint handed to me this morning from the Pearson's attorney along with these written complaints from Mark and Scott Pearson. They tell a different story about the incident Marshal, so I suggest for your sake and the sake of your job, that you reevaluate your determination."

Kaplan had been noticing Cavalier's stress level rising. It was the same tell-tale signs as Isabella's, splotches on her neck. They were faint, but he could see them. Plus, the tone in her voice pitched up a little. She just had her ass handed to her by the judge and Pearson's attorney. The man who beat her just walked out the door. The judge, who she felt was in Pearson' pocket, had handed down a death sentence on Cavalier's career in law enforcement. The town would likely fire her…and soon. All that worry was showing on her face and in her voice.

"Sheriff, I have two witnesses right here. Why don't you ask them what they saw?"

Knight did. He started with Lucy.

She explained, "While Kaplan was in the diner paying the bill, I walked outside and saw Mark and Scott Pearson push over his motorcycle. I ran to confront them. They pushed me back and forth between the two of them and threw me on the ground and kicked me. Scott had a knife and Mark had some kind of stick. That was when Kaplan came out of the diner and demanded they stop. He told them to pick up his motorcycle and apologize to both of us. They attacked Kaplan. Both at the same time, two on one. Kaplan defended himself."

Knight focused on Poppy and said, "So what did you see?"

Poppy looked at Kaplan and then Lucy then back to Knight. "I saw the same thing, sheriff. Those two Pearson hoodlums started it just like Lucy explained."

Poppy had told the marshal earlier he didn't see who started the fight, just who finished it. Kaplan knew Poppy was lying. Now, it was to protect him. From the expression on Cavalier's face, she knew it too. As did Lucy.

Poppy explained, "Mark got to him first and Kaplan landed his elbow to Mark's chest while taking a smack with the stick across his back. At the same time, Scott attacked him with his knife. He turned to the side, grabbed Scott's hand and turned his wrist inward until Scott dropped the knife. Mark came at him again with the stick. With the butt of his palm, he hit Mark in the side of the head. Mark went down and never got up. Scott took a swing which Kaplan deflected with his arm and made a roundhouse kick to Scott's leg. Scott went down. That was when I called the marshal's office to report the incident."

"I see," said Knight.

Kaplan wasn't sure who was more surprised at what Poppy just said, him or the sheriff.

Poppy stared straight into Kaplan's eyes and finished by saying, "That's how I saw it, sheriff."

"Two eyewitnesses, same testimony…just like what Judge Shepard said to me earlier," Cavalier stared at the sheriff. "Only this happens to be the truth."

"That's all well and good, Marshal." Knight held the complaint papers up and shook them. "But I still have these."

Moss stepped forward. "May I see those?"

"Who the hell are you?"

"Senior Inspector Pete Moss, United States Marshals Service." Moss reached inside his jacket, pulling it to one side making sure the sheriff saw his badge, and retrieved his credentials.

Knight faced Cavalier, squinted and said, "I heard you brought in the feds." He swung his attention back at Moss. "What's your business here, Inspector?"

"My business," Moss said, his voice assertive. "Is none of yours. Now, how about you let me see those papers."

Kaplan detected a slight tremble in Knight's fingers as he reluctantly handed the papers to Moss.

Moss did a quick scan of the documents, raised an eyebrow and said, "You know, sheriff, I'm perplexed. This complaint is from the Pearson's attorney Stewart Whitman, dated and signed this morning." He held up the written statements from Mark and Scott Pearson. "Did you witness these men write these statements?"

The sheriff swallowed, his Adam's apple riding the wave. "No, they," he stammered. "Um, they were given to me this morning."

"Including the complaint written by Whitman?"

"Yes."

"Did you notice these statements were not witnessed or notarized?"

"What the hell difference does that make?" Knight said as a light spray of spit left his lips.

Moss acted like he didn't care. Probably because he was having too much fun with the sheriff.

Moss continued, only this time his lips curled up, "It means these are nothing more than hear-say. Hell, I could have written them for all you know." Moss shoved them back to Knight. "Those aren't worth the paper they are written on, Sheriff. Marshal Cavalier has done her job and done it correctly. So, unless you have something else, I suggest you leave now, so she can get on with her job of capturing a murderer."

Knight rubbed the back of his neck. The man had a defeated look, much like Cavalier had a few minutes ago. Then he did something that caught everyone by surprise. He headed to the door, stopped, and gave Cavalier his full attention. "If you want help tracking down Stevie Pearson, just say the word." He crumbled up the papers and threw them in the garbage can. "Sorry Marshal. I never wanted to be part of this." He opened the door and left.

"I never saw that one coming," Cavalier said.

"Marshal," Poppy said, "If you don't need me anymore, I have a diner to run."

"Yeah, Poppy," she replied. "Go on and by the way, thanks."

Kaplan walked toward Poppy with his hand stretched out.

Poppy waved him off and said, "I don't like those Pearsons. They're no good for this town. You can return the favor, Delta. Find that asshole Stevie Pearson and relieve the world of that scum."

Kaplan nodded.

† † †

At the insistence of Moss, Cavalier agreed to move the strategy meeting to the Last Chance Diner. Moss' argument was that since Poppy had decided to make a stand-up move and corroborate Lucy's story about Kaplan beating up the Pearson boys, the least they could do was give the diner some business. In reality, Moss was just hungry. By the time they finished with the raid on the Pearson ranch, the makeshift bail hearing with the judge and Pearson's lawyer, and Sheriff Knight's bullshit interrogation, it was already 1:30 and his stomach had been growling for over an hour.

What happened in Christine's office amazed him. Was this the way Old West justice worked or did Pearson just own everyone? He damn sure owned Judge Martin Shepard, that was plain to see. He'd met his share of corrupt lawmen before, one being a good friend and coworker in Little Rock who betrayed him and one of his witnesses. After being discovered, his friend opted for death by suicide. What a sad tragedy that was. He'd heard of corrupt judges before as well, but not this blatant. What Shepard did today was outside of procedure and he was sure, outside of the law. One he vowed to address as soon as this situation with Stevie Pearson came to an end.

Inside the diner, Poppy took everyone's order and headed behind the bar to the grill. The young deputy, Jesse joined them. They picked the biggest booth, which was supposed to seat six according to Poppy, but with two giants, Moss and KC, Jesse pulled up a chair and sat at the end of the table.

Jesse was the first to break the silence. "I don't want to sound like a pessimist, but aren't we worse off now than we were this morning?"

"That had to be like, a kick in the balls," Lucy said and giggled.

"Figuratively speaking, Lucy," Christine said. "It was like a gargantuan kick in the balls. I'm not real sure where to go from here."

"Not that either of you have any idea what that feels like, right?" KC said. "Marshal, they were lying."

"Oh, hell yeah, they were lying," she said. "Every damn one of them. And that son of a bitch Shepard wouldn't even let me address the kidnapping charges."

"That would have been worse," Moss said. "They could have found out about Kaplan being there last night and hit him with trespassing and then come after the marshal." He rubbed his chin. "This whole thing has turned into a goat rope, whatever that means." He smiled at Kaplan. "Your phrase, not mine."

"It just means that in this situation," Kaplan explained. "We're back to square one."

"What do we do now?" Jesse pleaded. "We have to find Stevie. We owe it to Doug."

"You've heard this phrase before," Kaplan said. "A chain is only as strong as its weakest link."

Moss lips curved up so far his teeth were showing. "And there is a weakest link."

"Who?" Christine asked. "Evan?"

"Something tells me he wants to come clean but is afraid of his father."

"And his brothers," Lucy added. "He hates his brothers, all three of them."

"How do you know that, Lucy?" Christine asked.

"He told me one time when we went horseback riding on his property," she said. "We rode all the way to the mountains where Black Canyon Creek comes down to their property. He said something about riding up to an old gold mine, but it was getting late and I did not want to walk back to town in the dark. So, he took me to a spot at the edge of the ranch where he dug up some really cool rocks."

"So," said Moss. "We need to have a heart-to-heart with Evan Pearson. But, how?"

No one spoke, they all swung their heads toward Kaplan. And waited.

Kaplan took a slow swig from his coffee mug. "I have an idea, but it'll involve some risks." He looked at Christine. "Especially for you, Marshal."

"How risky?" she asked.

"Life and death kind of risky."

CHAPTER 42

Kaplan deliberately exaggerated the severity of danger in his plan to Cavalier for a good reason. He didn't want her to think it would be easy or let her guard down. There was a slight element of danger with her confronting Drew Pearson on his own turf about the whereabouts of his son, Stevie. Not only did Pearson know where his son was, but he had lied about it in front of his bought and paid for attorney and the judge. Drew Pearson was not a stupid man. He would likely be on his best behavior with a formal investigative visit from Cavalier.

Kaplan had had run-ins with the likes of men such as Stewart Whitman before. In the D. C. area there was a toxic cesspool of corrupt lawyers and politicians. The stench went well beyond D. C. and had found its way into every town in America, including Last Chance. He was sure Whitman's billable hours for Pearson would be more than most average people made in a year. Always on the prowl for another get-rich scam or scandal to profit from. Always lying in wait like vultures for another opportunity to seize on someone else's misfortunes or mistakes. Corruption didn't stop at the doorstep of lawyers and politicians, it had permeated throughout the entire legal system. He had the unfortunate experience of having dealt with corrupt judges before. Judges on the take, or like in this case, bought off by some wealthy land baron.

Our country wasn't alone with this type of corruption. It was actually more honest, as a whole, than the overwhelming majority around the globe. Part of his job description as an operative with the CIA was dealing with corrupt men like Pearson in many foreign countries. Men, usually men, driven by power and money and greed. That included terrorists. They had been easy to deal with, *the company* ordered them dispatched. Quick, easy, and, if possible, make it look like an accident…or possibly a crime of vengeance or passion. A sanctioned hit by the CIA on foreign soil.

Whether he liked it or not, that was his life. And had been for quite some time. Just like Ian Fleming's *James Bond* character, the CIA had given him a license to kill. It was something he excelled at, not something he enjoyed. Killing for hire wasn't a good job, just a good-paying job. Very good at times.

Even though the Deputy Director of the CIA had all but kicked him out, he never severed that tie completely. No, the DD was holding back, keeping him on a leash until he was needed again. Holding back until a job required someone with his special skills and talents, but still allowing the agency to completely disavow having any connection. When the need for someone, like himself, who lived in the shadows and stayed off the grid and was, for all practical purposes, invisible. Illusive. Someone who could strike from out of nowhere and vanish in thin air. That person was him. Sooner or later, he knew that phone call would come. And he was okay with that. At least for now.

Drew and Stevie Pearson fit Kaplan's idea of worthless air suckers, especially Stevie. He knew Stevie was not a person who could be rehabilitated or ever accept responsibility for his actions. Stevie lacked remorse, guilt or shame. No nagging voice inside him that prevented him from repeating his ruthless cold-blooded behavior. He was a danger to society and Stevie's fate was already sealed in Kaplan's mind.

Kaplan gathered everyone in the common room around the deputies' desks. Most of them pulled up a chair and sat down while Moss and KC stood to the side. His plan was a subtle ploy to get Evan alone. It should work, but there had been the rare occasion when one of his plans backfired. This plan required only Cavalier, himself, and Lucy. If it didn't work, he had Plan B.

Cavalier's phone rang. She went to her desk, picked up the receiver and just listened. After a second or two, she hung up.

"Guess I'm being called to the carpet."

"What?" Moss said a little louder than he should have. "Who was that?"

"The mayor. He and the town council want to talk to me right now."

"Should I go with you?" Moss asked.

"No. They were quite specific, they want to talk to me alone."

"Where?" Kaplan said.

"Two doors down." Cavalier pointed. "The mayor owns the saddlery."

She marched to the door and left.

He saw Moss' eyes follow her out.

† † †

The Cowboy sat alone at his desk. His plan had not unfolded at all like he anticipated it would. And now, he wasn't sure he could even salvage it. Not without taking bolder steps. Neither the Last Chance Town Marshal nor the Sheridan County Sheriff had made any attempt to solve the murders of the Bransons. Crow Tribal police chief Joseph Silverheels was the only one doing any work to solve any murders. And that was because Silverheels' brother was one of the men killed. Frank Silverheels was a worthless piece of shit. He had addiction problems, to most everything. For years, he was just another drunken Indian who couldn't handle his liquor. Then he moved to cocaine, heroin and now Meth. The last three years, he'd been a Meth head. His appearance showed it too. Extreme weight loss, pallid wrinkled skin, and half his teeth were missing. Frank Silverheels already had tombstones in his eyes, all the Cowboy did was speed up the Indian's departure to the hereafter…or wherever it was Indians went.

What bolder steps should he take to get his plan back on track? With the stranger in town, everything had changed. Perhaps he could use this man to do some of his bidding. He looked like a dangerous man. From what he did to the two middle Pearson brothers, he had skills, ones he could use.

He had expected the marshal to use her deputies, but she had also enlisted the stranger and a federal agent, a Deputy U. S. Marshal, out of Chicago of all places. What could his involvement be in all this?

The Cowboy had known Drew Pearson and hated him for a very long time. His entire life, as a matter of fact. Pearson was a man with a lot of secrets and a lot of skeletons buried in his closet. He was a man with a temper if he didn't get his way, or if someone messed with one or more of his sons. But now, his oldest son was in deep trouble. Murdering a deputy was not something even the mighty Drew Pearson could fix. Stevie Pearson was going to pay for what he had done. The

Cowboy knew what Stevie was really like. Stevie's issues had gotten worse. He knew there was no way Stevie would allow himself to be captured alive and sent to prison. That would be a fate worse than death. Stevie would do what he had always professed, go out in a blaze of glory. Something the Cowboy hoped he could help make possible.

The murders on the Crow Rez were a ruse. Something meant merely as a confusion factor to muddy the waters of his real motivation. And that was the Bransons. Not the father and son specifically, but the 1652 acres Branson once owned that now belonged to the Cowboy. Richard Branson never even knew what he owned—not what he really owned—or how much it was worth. Nor how much it could be worth to every farm and ranch surrounding the property and the town of Last Chance. Or the economic boon it could potentially have on the region. Not until the end, anyway.

Acquisition of that property gave the Cowboy the leverage he needed to put an end to Drew Pearson's empire. Perhaps even do to Pearson what he had done to nearly a dozen ranchers and farmers over the years, squeeze him out of existence. Take from him everything he had taken from others.

Town Marshal Cavalier had her strong points, but she had her weaknesses. With her failure to jump on investigating the Branson murders, he couldn't rely on her in helping him execute his plan. Not after the legal spanking she took today from Drew Pearson, his attorney, and Judge Martin Shepard, whose campaign a few years ago was 100% funded by Drew Pearson.

Perhaps the stranger was the key to making his plan work. If spoon fed the right amount of knowledge, perhaps this man could eliminate the Cowboy's only obstacle, Drew

Pearson. What the stranger might need were a few well-placed clues. Let him piece the puzzle together. Make him think it was all his idea. The stranger could take the credit, he didn't care as long as Pearson was out of the picture.

He needed to talk to the stranger and he needed to do it today.

† † †

Forty-five minutes had passed, before Cavalier returned to her office. Moss had been pacing the room, clearly concerned that she might have been fired. She had talked about possible repercussions from this morning's fall out with Drew Pearson, Stewart Whitman, and Judge Martin Shepard. Her analogy of the Last Chance gossip grapevine moving with lightning speed was accurate. Of course, Kaplan's money was on Pearson having made the call to the mayor himself. He didn't seem the type to let matters resolve themselves at their own pace, but more the type to lead the charge. Especially if he had something to gain.

"Well?" Moss said as she walked through the door.

"They did everything except pull out the paddle," she quipped on her parting remark about the principal's office. "I'm on probation…with caveats."

"Like what?" Jesse asked.

"For starters, I am to leave Drew Pearson and anyone in his family alone except to investigate and search for Stevie. No more searching the premises unless I get the specific search warrant from, and get this, only Judge Martin Shepard."

"After today, good luck with that," KC said.

"Also," she added. "They gave me one week to track and capture Stevie or lose my job. They want me to assign someone to investigate the Branson murders full time and assist Chief Silverheels with his investigation since the two crimes are connected by ballistics. KC, they suggested you because of your heritage. The mayor and council members think you would be the perfect intermediary between Last Chance and the Rez. I agreed, so consider yourself officially in charge of that investigation. Jesse, I need you to work with KC and I want both of you to make this your priority. Do you understand?"

KC and Jesse nodded.

Kaplan fought the urge to jump in the middle of her handing out assignments. He thought for a minute she might not want to go along with his plan from earlier.

"Kaplan, you work with me. I'm going to need all the help I can get. Inspector Moss—"

"Pete," Moss said.

Kaplan jabbed him the ribs. "Really?"

"Okay, Pete. As much as I'd like to, I can't officially ask you to participate in any manner."

"Doesn't matter," Moss said. "I'm going to anyway. I'm not going to sit idly by and watch Pearson get away with his shenanigans."

"Shenanigans?" Kaplan said holding back a smile. "Really?"

"I know a few big words, too, ya know."

"You two shut up," Cavalier interrupted. "I don't have time for couple's therapy, do that shit on your own time. I've got killers to catch."

"What do you want me to do?" Lucy asked.

"I don't have any—"

Kaplan interrupted. "Marshal, since KC and Jesse are going in one direction, and the rest of us are going in another, don't you need someone to man your office?" He pointed to her dispatch console. "Monitor the radios? Answer the phones? Not having someone in this office this morning allowed the Pearsons to collude their stories. Besides, Lucy needs a job, and something tells me she's a fast learner."

Cavalier arched back in her chair and furrowed a brow, like he'd crossed a line. She glanced at Lucy and her expression changed. "Actually, Kaplan, that's a damn good idea. How about it, Lucy? You up for a job?"

Kaplan gave Lucy a sly wink. "Yes, Marshal," Lucy said. "I am definitely up for it."

Cavalier smiled.

"KC, you and Jesse head up to the Stillwater farm and see what you can dig up from Chief Silverheels. Tell him exactly what I told you and see if between his department and ours, we can't figure out what went on out there. And why."

KC and Jesse picked up the investigation kits and left.

Cavalier shuffled papers on her desk and put them in trays and desk drawers. "Now Kaplan, back to your plan. Moss and I will head up to Pearson's ranch. If all goes well, you'll have your chance with Evan. Maybe you can show Lucy how to use all this equipment?"

"Sure thing."

"You do know how it all works, don't you?" Cavalier asked.

"What we don't know, we'll figure out, right Lucy?" Kaplan said.

"Right," Lucy happily replied.

Cavalier's eyes gleamed, then she and Moss left.

After they went out the door, Lucy ran to Kaplan, threw her arms around him, buried her face in his chest and gave him as close to a bear hug as her small frame could.

"What…?"

She leaned her face back. "Thank you, Kaplan."

He placed his hand on her shoulder. "You're welcome, Lucy."

CHAPTER 43

Cavalier stopped the Bronco in front of the prominent ranch gate, blocking the driveway leading to Drew Pearson's home. The metal ranch gate boasted massive pillars supporting a heavy wrought iron arch, a good twenty feet above them. On top of the arch, Pearson's brand, and inside the arch the words— ROCKING P RANCH. Posted on the side pillar was a sign reading, *Trespassers will be shot on sight.*

"Well," she said to Moss. "Not a very friendly welcome sign."

"At least there aren't any skulls hanging on the gate," Moss said with a laugh. "Not human ones, anyway."

She leaned out the window and pressed the buzzer.

A few seconds later. "Marshal Cavalier." The voice was that of Drew Pearson. "I can honestly say I'm surprised to see you. Are you here to harass me and my family some more?"

"No, Mr. Pearson, I'm not. I'm here with Deputy U. S. Marshal Moss to ask you some questions about your missing son."

"We've already had this discussion," Pearson voice crackled in the speaker.

"Not in an official capacity, Mr. Pearson. But, I think you know that already. If you would prefer to call your attorney and have him present, we can wait."

"That won't be necessary." She heard the speaker cut off.

Cavalier shrugged. Moss crossed his arms.

Now what? she thought. Before she could come up with a solution, the gates slowly swung open. She put the Bronco in gear and drove toward the *big house*. "I guess we're in."

"Showtime," said Moss.

As the Bronco approached Pearson's complex, she saw Drew standing outside in the gravel parking area waving his hand to indicate where he wanted her to park. As they stepped out of her Bronco, Pearson motioned to follow him.

"I hope he's friendlier when we get inside," she whispered.

"Not looking too promising," Moss shot back.

This was the second time today she was inside this massive home. Pearson guided them to his study. Slouched in a leather chair the size of a small cow was his attorney, Stewart Whitman. "As you can see, it wasn't necessary to call my lawyer."

Whitman's presence was unexpected, but not a show stopper. "Before we get started Mr. Pearson, I need you to send Mark and Scott to my office to sign the statements they gave on the incident with Mr. Kaplan the other day."

Pearson glared at Whitman who had straightened up in the chair. "They weren't signed?"

"Or witnessed. Until that happens, Mr. Kaplan will be free to leave town."

"You can't let him go free," Pearson growled.

"I have to follow the law Mr. Pearson. You know that. Just like I had to this morning. So, if you don't send your sons down to the station immediately, I cannot stop Mr. Kaplan from leaving town."

Pearson waited until Whitman gave him a nod of approval. "All right, Marshal, but neither of them can drive."

"Perhaps one of your ranch hands—"

"I have a very large ranch Marshal. Unlike you, my men have real work to do. They got a late start on their duties this morning with all the excitement around here."

"Maybe Evan could take them."

Pearson waited till Whitman gave him another slight nod. He walked over to an intercom panel mounted on the wall. He pressed a button and called, "Evan."

A few seconds passed, and a voice said, "Yes sir?"

"Take Mark and Scott to the marshal's office to sign their statements about that Kaplan fellow beating them up."

"Can't one of the hands do it?"

"No, they're all busy. You do it. And do it now, understand?"

"Yes sir."

Pearson returned to where they were standing. "Deputy Moss, may I offer you a drink?"

Moss squared his shoulders. Pearson was a tall man with a bit of girth but standing next to Moss he didn't look so big. She was glad Moss had come with her. "Thnk you, no. I'm good."

"Let's get on with this, shall we?" Whitman said. "I'd like to get home for supper."

With Moss and Kaplan's help, she had put together a list of questions to ask Pearson. A stall tactic. She needed to give Kaplan time to do his part of the plan, question Evan Pearson.

† † †

Kaplan leaned his back against the wall inside the police station resting his arms on his chest. Lucy sat behind a desk with her hands clasped. There were only two desks for three deputies, both pushed together face-to-face with the radio straddling them next to the wall. Lucy asked Cavalier before she left which desk did Doug work at. She chose the other one to sit at and monitor the radio. He imagined in a town this size with small budgets that the deputies were paid fast-food wages. That was probably the reason the marshal had young deputies without much experience. He heard the noise outside the door and knew the Pearsons had arrived. In walked the Pearson brothers, three of them. Cavalier had done her job. Evan smiled when he saw Lucy and she returned it. Mark and Scott looked like they had just waded into shark infested water.

"What's he doing here?" Mark half shouted.

"Where's the deputy?" Scott said as he fumbled with his crutches.

"I *am* the deputy." Kaplan tapped the shield on his belt. "And I'll be helping you boys with your statements."

"We just need to sign them." Scott said.

Mark moved toward the door. "This ain't right. Evan, Scott, let's get out of here."

Kaplan moved and blocked the door.

"No one's going anywhere. Not yet." Kaplan waited a beat and then commanded, "Evan, you sit in that chair next to Lucy." Evan readily went over and sat down.

He directed his attention back to the older brothers, "You two, in there." He gestured to the cell room.

"You can't put us in jail," Scott said defiantly.

Kaplan smiled. "Not going to. But, that *is* where I'm going to have you sign your statements. Now, move it."

The two older brothers were reluctant at first to comply with Kaplan's demands. But, Kaplan was intimidating and neither brother looked like they wanted to challenge him again, especially after the outcome of a few days ago. When the two brothers entered the cell room, Kaplan shut the door, locking them inside.

He marched over to Evan, hooked his hand around Evan's left bicep and led him out of the police station. "Before I talk to them, you and I need to have a talk." He spun the youngest Pearson around and pushed him against the brick facade of the police department building. "Evan, I know you have something you want to tell me. This is your one and only chance, your last chance. Get it off your chest and come clean."

"What do you want to know?"

"Let's start with where I can find Stevie, then we can talk about your father."

Evan didn't seem to want to talk. Kaplan clutched a handful of Evan's shirt, lifted him to his toes, and slammed him against the brick wall.

"I'm short on time Evan. Tell me what you know," demanded Kaplan.

Evan stayed silent.

Kaplan reared back his fist. Evan raised his hands to protect his face. "No. Stop. I don't know much," Evan cried out.

At that point, something seemed to wake up in Evan and the flood gates opened. And it flowed and flowed, as if he had been preparing for this day. And well prepared at that. Seemed there was a lot more to the corrupt nature of Drew Pearson. Even more than he had anticipated, especially how he had amassed his acreage and the tactics he used to get it. Pearson was a classic example of an anti-social personality disorder. A man with no moral conscience and aggressive behavioral tendencies.

Cavalier had mentioned she heard Pearson grew the size of his holdings off the misfortunes of others. According to Evan, Drew Pearson *was* the misfortune of others. And it seemed Evan had harbored years of pent up anger and hatred toward his father and brothers.

What he expected to take only a few minutes with Evan turned into fifteen. He needed to get back to the brothers before they got suspicious. He instructed Evan to stay put and wait on his brothers to come out. Kaplan stepped back in the police station, signaled to Lucy to go wait with Evan. He went to the bathroom, ran water over his hands, grabbed two paper towels and dried his hands as he opened the door to the cell room, making sure both brothers saw what he was doing.

"I'm really sorry about that fellows, but when you gotta go, you gotta go."

"You didn't have to lock us in here," Scott complained.

"Yeah, I kinda did. You see, I didn't want either of you to think you could leave without talking to me first, get what I'm saying?" He stepped out of the way. "Why don't we go in there and sit down?"

Mark asked, "What did you do with Evan?"

Kaplan pretended to look around. "He was in here when I went to the bathroom. He and Lucy must have wandered off. She told me earlier she was hungry. I'm sure they'll be back in a few minutes." Kaplan picked up a notepad. "You know, I've never really done it this way before." He put the pad back on the desk.

"Done what?" Scott asked balancing on his crutches.

"Interrogated anyone like this."

"We don't understand." Scott eyeballed Mark. "Do we?"

Mark shook his head.

Kaplan pulled a chair in front of the two brothers, sat and leaned forward in the chair, resting his elbows on his knees. "See, normally my prisoners would be restrained. Sometimes ropes, sometimes flex cuffs or handcuffs or even chains. Sometimes tied to the floor or a ceiling joist."

"What do you mean prisoners?" Mark sounded astonished. "We're not prisoners."

"You see, that's what I'm talking about. You aren't prisoners. You're just two low-life scumbags who got their asses kicked by me the other day. Nothing more. Thugs in a small town. Bullies."

"You can't talk to us like that."

"Yeah…I can. And you have to listen to it or I will throw your sorry asses in jail for interfering with a law officer in the performance of his duty."

"Can he do that?" Mark asked Scott.

"I dunno, but I don't want another broken leg."

"How about that? You two *are* coming along. The last guy I interrogated didn't understand how important it was to cooperate. I would ask him a question and he'd rattle off some Arabic gibberish and all that did was piss me off. I even strapped him to a board, covered his face with a towel and poured water all over him, he still gave me that Arabic gibberish…or was it Farsi. I don't know, it all sounds Greek to me."

"Where was that, Gitmo?" Scott asked.

"Gitmo? Please. Torture is illegal at Gitmo. No, faraway places where no one knows or sees anything. Places like Yemen, or the last time, Cyprus."

"Who the hell are you?" Mark shouted.

"As far as you're concerned, I'm a ghost. I don't

exist. Some people call us spooks, I don't care for that name, personally."

"What do you want?" Scott's voice was shaky.

"I came here for a reason and you two clowns got in my way. I just wanted to be left alone. I mind my own business and I expect others to do the same. But, you two didn't. And you didn't listen either. I even gave you a way out. All you had to do was pick up my bike, apologize to me and to Lucy. But, did you do that? No." He faced Scott. "You came at me with a knife. I hate knives. I hate being cut or slashed. Those wounds take weeks to heal. I wanted you to know what weeks of healing feels like. And you." He faced Mark. "You and that stupid ninja stick, you really should learn how to use it before you go after someone."

"We're sorry, man, really," Scott pleaded. "Aren't we, Mark?"

"Yeah, we're sorry. I'm sorry. I've learned my lesson. From now on, no more bullying."

"Tell Lucy we're sorry. Nothing like this will ever happen again, I swear."

"You're right about that," Kaplan said. He put a finger in each corner of his lips and whistled. Lucy and Evan walked in. "Lucy, these two have something they want to say to you." He glared at them. "Your turn, boys."

† † †

Evan was intimidated when the man hauled him out of the police department and started barraging him with questions. Not really intimidated, scared shitless. The man was dangerous. He could see it in his eyes. A cold gaze that locked onto his eyes. As much as he despised his brothers and father, he had a rush of guilt after he threw them all under the bus. Not a big rush. All of them had made his life miserable for as long as he could remember. Always picking on him. Calling him names, referring to him as a *pussy* or *girly-man*. Or worse. He'd been beat up by his brothers so many times he had lost count. And with his father's blessing. That old bastard thought that sooner or later the beatings might turn him into the man he wanted him to be. There was nothing about his brothers or his father that he wanted to resemble in any way. It was a curse to be a Pearson. If he could change his name, he would.

He had asked Lucy while they stood outside the police department if she thought he was bad for betraying his family. Her response sounded so mature, so adult.

"It might be painful," she said. "But, it is never bad to do the right thing. And this is the right thing to do."

Now, he was glad he ratted out his family. Hopefully, the marshal and her deputies would track Stevie down and help rid the world of that vermin. As far as his sleaze-ball father was concerned, it was about time someone did to him what he had done to so many people. No, he had no regrets.

After Mark and Scott apologized to Lucy, the man let them go. At first, his brothers didn't speak in the truck until they passed the marshal's Bronco going in the opposite direction headed back to town.

"Who does that son of a bitch think he is?" Scott started.

"Somebody needs to teach that asshole a lesson." Mark joined in.

"And that bitch squaw, too. Dad should have killed her."

"Yeah, Scott, that's right."

Mark and Scott droned on all the way to the big house, exchanging tough guy challenges. By the time he dropped them off at their cabins and helped Scott cross the gravel lot and up the stairs, his two brothers were scheming the best way to kill the man called Kaplan and the marshal. Typical of these two idiots to never learn a lesson.

He smiled.

Perfect.

CHAPTER 44

The first words out of her mouth when she and Moss returned from Pearson's ranch were to ask Kaplan if he was able to squeeze any information from Evan Pearson.

Kaplan spent the next forty-five minutes detailing his conversations with Evan, Mark, and Scott Pearson.

"You didn't really say that to Mark and Scott, did you?" Cavalier asked.

"You should have seen them when they left," Lucy said with a smile on her face. "I thought they were going to pee themselves. He had them rattled pretty bad."

"When Drew Pearson finds out it was all a ruse to get his boys here, he might show his uglier side." Moss said. "No telling how he'll retaliate."

"You think he'll try something?" Cavalier asked.

Kaplan directed Lucy's attention to the dispatch radio console. "Tell KC and Jesse to get back here now."

He focused on Cavalier. The circles under her eyes were darker than yesterday and her shoulders hunched. He knew the stress of the situation was taking a toll on her.

"Personally, I hope he does try something."

† † †

Drew Pearson had always taken his position as father and protector very seriously. Now, that bitch and her posse had gone too far. She was deliberately trying to embarrass and intimidate his family and he was not going to stand for it any longer. He had gathered his three sons in his study and asked for a full briefing. After Mark and Scott told him which deputy was there to get their signatures on their statements—the same man who put them in the hospital—his emotions were nothing short of a volcano erupting. Nobody, and he meant nobody, got away with doing this to his family. The marshal lied to his face. His boys weren't sent to town to sign statements. They were sent there to be threatened.

This time, the marshal and Kaplan were going down. No more bringing in lawyers or judges. That time had passed. It was time he took matters into his own hands. He glowered at his sons, two of them were idiots, but they were loyal idiots. Neither the marshal nor the stranger will ever bring shame on the Pearson name again.

He had no reason to doubt Evan's loyalty, but he couldn't count on him when things got rough. And this revenge was going to get rough. "Evan, I don't want you involved. Go to your room."

"I'm not a kid anymore."

"I know you're not son, but this is something your brothers and I need to handle. I want to talk to your brothers alone."

Drew Pearson was silent until Evan walked out of the room and closed the door behind him.

"From this moment on," the patriarch barked as he slapped the palm of one hand with the backside of his other hand. "The Pearsons have declared war. Marshal Christine Cavalier is standing in our way boys. I warned the city council she wouldn't be able to keep our town safe. They were too goddamned worried about their budget. Now see what's happened." Drew paced back and forth waving his hands as he ranted to his sons. "It's time to take back our town."

Pearson stopped and noted the cast on Scott's leg. He needed more help. He wished Stevie wasn't so far away. He could use him right now. He glanced at the clock on the wall, 5:00 p.m., plenty of daylight left, he thought.

"Mark, go tell Slim to ride up to the cabin and bring Stevie back here. I'll take Stevie with me tonight, he knows what to do."

Mark looked at Scott then back at his father. "We don't need Stevie. We can do this without him."

"I'm sure you boys think you can, and maybe you can, but Stevie certainly can…he's done it before. I'm not taking any chances. There have been enough fuck-ups. Besides, I have another task for the two of you." He swept his hand in the air. "Now, get the hell out of here and tell Slim to ride hard out there and back."

He waited until his sons left before he collapsed in his leather recliner. This reminded him of years ago, when he wanted the property to the north of his measly 5200 acres. If he could get that property to the north, he would triple his ranch size. But the man refused to sell. Even when he offered the man a more than reasonable amount for the property, almost double what it was worth, the man refused to sell. He couldn't understand the man's refusal, he had no family, no heirs, no one to leave any of it to. Pearson had to have it.

Stevie had always been fascinated with fire and explosions, almost before his voice changed. The boy had shown his sadistic side even earlier. But, Stevie tried to be a good son, he told himself. Stevie helped him solve problems when he needed him. When he told Stevie about the rancher to the north refusing to sell him his property, Stevie killed the man and some of his livestock in a fiery blaze. All he had to do after that was buy the dead man's property when it went on the auction block.

Stevie should have no problem helping him eliminate Marshal Christine Cavalier.

† † †

Evan didn't go to his room as his father demanded. He stood outside the door to his father's study and eavesdropped while his father instructed his two brothers on what to do after he and Stevie took care of the marshal. When his two brothers barreled out the door, he almost got caught. Luckily, they were too mad to notice him duck around the corner.

He couldn't let that happen, the marshal was only doing her job. He had given Kaplan all the information needed to arrest Stevie and his father. But, Kaplan wouldn't be expecting this. And once again, his father would win. Suspicions might be cast, but there would be no proof and no witnesses. That was the way his father operated.

If his father was successful with this attack, Evan knew he would never get out of this miserable life. He would always be under the thumb of his father and his father's empire, and worse, his dumbass brothers. He needed to warn the marshal, but how?

He went to his room and typed out a text message, addressed it to Lucy's cell phone, and hit send.

† † †

KC and Jesse were briefing everyone on their trip to the Rez, when Lucy's phone vibrated. She looked at the message, it was from Evan. That was very strange, he had just seen her. The message was even stranger.

SP. Sorry, can't see you tonight. Family going to town.

She read the message again and glanced up. Kaplan was staring at her.

"What is it, Lucy?" he asked.

She didn't respond.

He repeated the question, "What is it?"

She held up her phone. "It is from Evan, but it does not make sense." She handed the cell phone to Kaplan.

"You were going to meet Evan tonight?" he asked. He passed the phone to Cavalier, she read it and passed it to Moss.

"No. That is what does not make sense."

"Maybe he sent it to the wrong person," Moss said. "It was meant for someone with the initials SP."

"That has to be it," Cavalier said. "Unless it stands for a nickname you use."

Lucy shook her head.

KC and Jesse read the message, shrugged, and handed the phone back to Lucy.

"I don't think so," Kaplan said. "I think he's sending you a warning."

"A warning?" Lucy asked. "About what?"

Kaplan continued, "He started it with SP period, not comma."

"Could be a typo."

"Or, so it would look like it was meant for someone

else. I think he's telling you that Stevie Pearson is coming into town tonight." Kaplan rubbed his hand across his beard. "Since he is wanted by the law, you can bet he isn't turning himself in."

"He's coming after Lucy," Jesse blurted out.

"I don't think so," Cavalier said. "I think he's coming for me."

"Not just Stevie," Kaplan added. "The whole Pearson family, with the possible exception of Evan. You can bet Stevie won't be coming alone." He paused a moment. "I doubt you're the only intended target. To him, the only way to solve this is to eliminate everyone and everything he sees as a threat. Drew Pearson sees us all as threats. Regardless of his target or targets, we are all in danger. This man won't let anybody get in his way." He made a circling motion with his index finger. "And that's everyone in this room."

Lucy was right about Kaplan, he was a smart man. He explained that since Stevie couldn't be seen in public without risking arrest, he would make his move after dark and only where he had the protection of cover. That ruled out the Sundown Motel. The only place fitting Kaplan's profile was Cavalier's home. It was down a dark street on the east side of town. Easy in, easy out.

She was terrified Kaplan might get hurt. Or Cavalier and the deputies. Mostly, she was afraid of Stevie and what he might do to her. It was getting late and would be dark soon and there was no place in town she felt safe. Except with Kaplan. He was about to leave her somewhere because she knew he would never let her go with him to confront the Pearsons.

"You should reply to Evan," Kaplan said.

"What should I say?"

He held out his hand. She handed him the phone and

he started thumbing a reply text message. He handed the phone back to her and said, "Send it."

She read it.

I understand. Family first. Too bad. Maybe next time.

She hit send.

CHAPTER 45

Kaplan's first order of business was to make sure everyone had eaten before the sun set. Even though he was tired of the food, he suggested the Last Chance Diner again for two reasons, it was nearby, and it was fast. And they all needed to eat hearty. It might be a long while before they ate their next meal.

While everyone ate their greasy food, his mind began to forecast the upcoming events and how they might play out. In a way, this was where the chess match moved to its end game. Each move was critical. No more pawns to be sacrificed. No more attempts to trick the opponent. Every move counted. Any mistake could cost lives.

If he was right, Drew Pearson had sent someone to the cabin in the woods to get Stevie and bring him in for this inevitable showdown. Evan told him roughly where the cabin was located, somewhere in the Bighorn Mountains west of his father's ranch. Checking land records and plats meant driving to Sheridan, and those county offices were closed. Tomorrow would be too late. Something was going down tonight. He could almost feel the rumble of bad luck and trouble coming again. This time, it was more than just him involved. This time, there were others. Too many others for his comfort level. One thing was certain, he couldn't very well go after the Pearsons *and* protect the others at the same time.

"Moss," he said. "Give Lucy your room key."

"What for?"

"Just do it." He placed his hand on Lucy's arm while Moss dug around in his pocket. "Lucy, you and Jesse go to Moss' room and stay there. No one but us knows his room number, so you should be safe there. Under no circumstances are you to go back to room thirteen, do you understand? Not for any reason whatsoever." Lucy and Jesse signaled their comprehension. "Jesse, you keep your gun ready at all times. Make sure a round is chambered." Kaplan grabbed a menu and opened it to the breakfast portion. He pointed to an item on the menu. "This is the safe word. If this word is not used, do not open the door. Not for me, not for the marshal, not for Moss. No one. Even if we're under duress. That door does not open without this safe word."

"I understand," Jesse said. The young deputy straightened his back.

"Keep the curtains closed and no noise. No TV. If you sit in a chair, put your weapon in your lap with your hand resting on top. If a door gets kicked in, don't hesitate. A split second of hesitation and you'll end up like Doug."

Jesse's expression hardened. The kid understood. "You two get going. Circle the parking lot twice to make sure it's clear. Don't park near the room. Once you go in, you can't come out until you hear from one of us."

"With the safe word," Jesse added.

Kaplan put his hands on the table. "That's right. Now, go."

Jesse and Lucy left. He watched them cross the street, get in Jesse's truck and drive south toward the Sundown Motel. Daylight was fading fast and the last of the sun's rays could be seen shining on the Last Chance Police Department sign across the street. Main Street was already in the shadows. Darkness would envelop the town soon, and with it came danger.

"KC," Kaplan asked, "how accurate are you with a gun? Moss can't hit the broad side of a barn."

"Hey," Moss said as he dragged out the word. "I resemble that remark." He snickered as he looked at the marshal. Cavalier cut her eyes at Moss and smiled. *Dammit, I need to keep those two apart.*

† † †

Evan heard a commotion downstairs in his father's study. Stevie was back. He rushed down the stairs in order to hear what was going on.

"First, you ordered me to get the hell out of the house," Stevie shouted at his father. "Then you tell me to come back. What the hell is going on?"

Evan walked across the great room toward his father's study. Mark and Scott were in there with him. His father saw him, held up his hand, and told Mark to close the study door, locking him out.

He had seen this exact scenario happen before. The four of them in their little huddle, plotting something illegal, something sinister. And every time this happened, someone died. Maybe a rancher or the farmer next door. Or the banker. Tonight, it would be Town Marshal Cavalier. He knew his father hated that woman. *Loathed* was a better word. His father never wanted a woman for marshal and now, she needed to be dealt with. What his father refused to acknowledge was the problem wasn't a woman marshal. The problem was Evan's father.

Drew Pearson had been a bastard of a father and a bastard of a man. He raised three sons just like him. But, his father's reign was coming to an end. And with it, the end of being terrorized by his messed-up brothers. It was past time for things to change around here. His father had put the wheels in motion, but this time, those wheels would run over the great Drew Pearson.

If he'd learned anything from watching his father's brash and brute style, it was that there were better ways to handle these types of situations. More subtle ways of getting what you want. Something he was destined to prove to his father. He'd been in charge of handling all the Rocking P Ranch's finances for several years now, actually since high school and all through college. His father had put him in charge of the finances for everyone on the ranch—business and personal. His brothers were given money each month, basically an allowance, which most times had to be supplemented before the end of the month. Even his father couldn't manage his own money very well.

But, that was okay. The ranch made money, Evan saw to that.

Now, he had put all the pieces in place. All he had to do was sit back and wait for his father and brothers to self-destruct. That phase would begin tonight.

The meeting broke up. Mark and Scott walked out the front door. His father and Stevie stayed in the study. He heard his father call down to the bunkhouse, apparently Frenchie answered the phone.

"Frenchie," his father said. "I'm giving all of you the next four days off."

There was a pause.

"Yes, paid time off. I don't give a fuck what you do. Go on a vacation, just get the hell off my ranch."

Another pause.

"No, I want all four of you gone in thirty minutes and don't return for four days."

Pearson cleared his throat.

"Dammit, Frenchie." His father was yelling. "Let me make this as simple as I can. Today is Sunday. I expect all four of you back at the gate on Thursday evening at 7:00 p.m. Not a minute sooner. Do I make myself perfectly clear?" His father slammed the phone down.

"Goddamn imbeciles," his father said to Stevie. "No wonder that halfwit Butch got himself killed."

"What do we do now?" Stevie asked.

"Evan," his father shouted. "Get in here."

He didn't know if his father knew he was eavesdropping or not. He waited a few seconds before entering the study.

"Stevie and I are going out. Mark and Scott are at their cabins. You stay here and don't leave the big house under any circumstances, you hear me?"

"Yes sir, but why?"

"Don't question me, Evan. Not tonight. If you need anything, use the house phone to call one of your brothers. I just gave the hands a few days off, until the dust settles around here."

Evan saw Stevie's eyes crinkle at the corners and a sly grin spread across his face. He could swear he saw the devil himself dancing inside in his brother's eyes. Stevie and his father were bad men.

Thank goodness Lucy had replied to his text and apparently understood his message. He just hoped Lucy would tell the marshal and Kaplan, so they were prepared when Stevie and his father showed up.

CHAPTER 46

Kaplan was back at Cavalier's home. Only this time he didn't have to break in. It was dark by the time the four of them arrived. He paced the perimeter twice with Cavalier while Moss and KC cleared the inside of her home. It was a ranch style floor plan with a finished basement. The main floor had three doors, the front, the back which led to a small fenced back yard, and a side door from the carport that fed into the kitchen. The basement was just that, a basement. The mechanical room was separated from the rest of the basement and had its own exit out through masonry encased steps and sidewalls that led to a set of heavy-duty steel egress doors. It had keyed locks on the outside to ward off intruders and on the inside, offered quick unlock and release, lift assisted doors for quick escape in the event of a fire. The basement exit was on the side of the house opposite the carport.

He didn't know how or when the Pearsons would show up, or how many for that matter, but he knew they would show up. Unlike last night's thunderstorms, tonight's Wyoming skies were clear and stars were appearing by the thousands. The moon hadn't shown its face yet but couldn't be too far behind. It was an older brick home, built in the 1950s he guessed, and clearly renovated top to bottom within the last decade or so.

He was good at preparing defenses, as was Moss. After all, a big part of Moss's training with the United States Marshals Service was to protect witnesses.

After finishing at the diner earlier tonight, he had Cavalier unlock the impound lot. He rolled his Harley out and rode to the Last Chance Mercantile and picked up another radio and ear set for KC. He met them back at the police department building, where he had KC leave his truck parked out front and ride with Cavalier to her house. Moss drove his Escalade and parked it one block behind Cavalier's house, backed into a neighbor's carport who was out of town on vacation. Kaplan parked his motorcycle at a house two doors down and across the street.

He and Cavalier met KC and Moss in the carport as prearranged. Both inside and outside were clear. Kaplan explained he wanted two in and two out and the two inside needed to stay together in the basement. As much as he didn't want them distracted by each other, he felt Moss should stay inside with Cavalier while he and KC stayed outside manning the perimeter.

Huddled around Cavalier's Bronco in her carport, he reached into his backpack and retrieved the radios and ear sets and handed them out. Constant communication would be critical from this point on. He had everyone power up their units and run through sound and mic checks.

"Now what?" KC asked.

"Now we wait," Kaplan answered. "Moss, you and the marshal go inside. Leave a light or two on, or however you would have it on any given night. Turn on the TV. Find a secure location in the basement where you can keep an eye on the basement egress door to the outside."

"Actually," Cavalier interrupted. "I think I know a way we can watch the egress door and the stairwell at the same time."

"Perfect." Kaplan led KC around the Bronco to the far side of the carport while Moss and Cavalier retreated inside her house. He walked him away from the carport about fifteen feet to a spot where either Cavalier's landlord or the neighbor next door had planted a row of tall blue Junipers. They towered around twelve feet and were bushy at the base. "Tuck in there just far enough where you can see the backyard as well as the front yard. I'll do the same on the other side of the house by the basement egress. If you see vehicles approaching, call it out. Same thing with pedestrians, dogs, cats…basically anything that moves, I want to know about it. I'll do the same for you."

"What time do you think they will come?"

"It's already after 10:00, could be an hour, could be three or four. Maybe not at all. Just be patient." Kaplan strode across the front yard. "And KC?"

"Yes."

"Don't fall asleep."

"Don't worry. When you hunt, you learn how to wait, I will be fine."

He hoped that was the case. The last thing he wanted to see was another dead deputy. He had grown fond of KC. A big man, certainly fitting Cavalier's description of a college former football player. His skills as a hunting guide might come in handy. And, according to Cavalier and even KC himself, he was a very good shot. Most well-seasoned hunters were calm under pressure, waiting for their prey to get within range or closer before taking a shot. This time, the prey can shoot back.

Kaplan hunkered down in the bushes on the opposite side of the house. He zipped up his jacket, laid on his belly next to a Cottonwood tree and waited. The night dragged on. Clear skies and a quiet night were interrupted by four passing cars, the description of which Cavalier recognized as neighbor's cars, one was a very old pickup truck with a loud muffler which she said belonged to an old man at the end of the street. There were half a dozen people out walking their dogs. Thank goodness the dogs were all on leashes. He didn't want to get into a fight with a scared dog.

Midnight came and went. Most of the night, he had been wearing his NVGs. In the field, they were great, not as much clutter in his field of vision. In this neighborhood, he saw more than he cared to. Like the man walking his dog who decided he also needed to find a tree and take a leak. Or the exhibitionist couple across the street who turned out the lights and opened the curtains while they made love. He heard music coming from the house. A favorite song of Isabella's—Stevie Nicks' Stand Back.

He remembered when the director of the CIA had Isabella and him pose as an undercover couple on a mission. That was when they first kissed, for appearance sake, to strengthen their cover story. He felt something, and he was certain she did too. But she'd played it cool, like she did everything. And even as much as he wanted to bring it up, he resisted. He didn't want to jeopardize the mission…or find out he was wrong.

The next op was different.

They'd spent two hours in a bar waiting for a rendezvous with a source. After they made contact and arranged a meeting the following day, she insisted they stay in the bar and have a couple of drinks.

Later, when they got back to their room, they made love. The next morning, Kaplan knew their relationship had changed. He was in love and so was Isabella. That was before Yemen. Before she was captured and tortured. Before he rescued her from her captors in a midnight raid on the Hajjah Palace. Before she nursed him from the broken leg he got in Spain. Before she disappeared without a trace.

He continued to scan the area when he detected movement. Not a dog walker this time, something else. He saw a figure appear on the side of the lovers' house. Then a second figure on the opposite side of the house. Each was holding something he didn't immediately recognize.

When he did, it was too late.

† † †

Moss was sent inside with Cavalier while Kaplan stayed out to do what he did best.

Moss had Cavalier do what she would normally do when she got home from work. Turn on the same lights, TV, whatever would be expected if someone had watched her routine. Next, they headed downstairs to the basement. From the doorway to the mechanical room, he could see the door to the basement at the bottom of the stairwell. This was the best vantage point to watch both exits. He leaned against the wall and slid down to a sitting position. He pulled out his weapon and placed it next to him on the floor.

Cavalier flipped the light on in the basement bathroom and closed the door just enough to allow a sliver of light to filter into the rest of the basement. She strolled over to Moss, took out her pistol from her holster and slid down next to him. Close enough that their arms and hips touched. Obviously a deliberate move on her part, one he welcomed. She placed her weapon next to her hip on the basement floor.

"You and Kaplan, best friends?" she asked.

He kept his focus on the stairwell but could see her looking at him in his peripheral vision. "If anyone is my best friend, I guess it would be him. When you've been through what we've been through together, you develop a bond. We had to rely on each other on a cliff, under a hail of bullets, just to stay alive. And the weird thing was, we just knew what we had to do without speaking. We just did it. Knowing what the other was going to do and what we had to do. So, yeah, we're best friends. That's the reason I knew I had to come out here. He was in trouble and he's my friend."

"You told me last night it was because you missed the excitement."

"Life's short, Christine. When I check out, I want to be able to say it was one hell of a ride."

Cavalier laughed.

"Kaplan's lucky to have you as a friend. I'm glad you felt the need to come here for him. Otherwise, I wouldn't have met you." She let her hand rest on his leg.

She had his full attention. Her eyes locked with his.

His pulse quickened. He felt the excitement course through his body. A second later, he jerked his head back when he heard Kaplan yell in his earpiece. She heard it too.

"Incoming."

His eyes were as wide as hers as he pushed her down and landed on top of her.

The blast was deafening.

Her house exploded.

CHAPTER 47

When the two figures who appeared on each side of the lovers' house raised what they were holding in their arms, Kaplan recognized them for what there were. Something he hadn't seen used in a long time. RPGs. Rocket propelled grenade launchers.

The two green figures fired in synchrony and Cavalier's house exploded into a giant fireball. A mushroom shaped fireball plumed upward. When he saw the RPG tracers, he ripped off his NVGs and buried his face in his arms. Heat from the explosion singed his exposed skin. Trees next to the house caught fire. After the initial ball of fire tapered off, he searched for the two figures, but they had disappeared into the night. It was still too bright to use the NVGs to locate them, but that was now a secondary concern. The green figures had been distinct and recognizable. He knew who they were and where to find them.

Number one priority was getting Moss and Cavalier out of the inferno.

The concussion wave from the explosion blew out all the windows, fire roiled upward licking its tentacles on the roof. He ran to the basement egress and grabbed the handles. Hot. He peeled off his jacket, wrapped it around the handle and yanked. It was locked. Using his foot, he banged on the doors.

"Come on, Moss," he yelled. "Move your ass."

He stomped his foot up and down, banging again and again.

KC ran around the corner and caught Kaplan off guard. Instinctively, he drew his weapon and aimed it at KC's head.

"Whoa." KC stopped and raised his hands. "Kaplan, it's KC."

He lowered and holstered his weapon.

"We gotta get them out of there," KC shouted over the roar of the flames. "Before the fire gets to the gas lines."

Fire and gas appliances. *Shit. I really didn't think this through.* "Call the fire department," he yelled at KC.

KC nodded and took off running toward the street with his cell phone to his ear.

He pounded again on the door.

Nothing.

He stepped back and to the side, pulled his weapon and fired a round into the lock mechanism. His bullet ricocheted off the lock, then the brick wall, and just missed hitting him. That was stupid, he thought.

KC ran up, huffing and said, "LCFD has been alerted. The firemen will show up in about five minutes, the truck will take ten."

By now, neighbors were piling out of their homes. Men and women in robes, some in street clothes. All gawking at the horror that had just occurred on their street, most still trying to come to grasp with what was happening.

He pounded on the door again. "They'll be dead in five minutes."

† † †

She couldn't move. She was pinned down by something heavy. Her head felt like it had been hit with a frying pan and was now throbbing. Her skin was hot, and she couldn't hear a thing. At first, she couldn't see, but she blinked several times and her vision returned. What the hell just happened?

The last thing she remembered was Kaplan's voice in her ear yelling something. What was it? Then she was hit hard and pinned to the basement floor. *Get it together, Christine.* The heavy object pinning her down groaned and moved.

Moss.

She tried to push Moss off, but he was too heavy. She began twisting and yelling until he finally rolled over on his side and landed on his back. It was coming back to her. She leaned over him and with her hands shook him as hard as she could. "Moss. Moss. Get up." Her voice sounded hollow like she was in a tunnel. He groaned. She slapped his face. "Moss, wake up." She slapped him harder. "Goddammit, Moss, get up." He didn't respond. Smoke filled the basement, making it harder to breath and see. She rubbed her eyes and coughed several times to clear her lungs. Her hand felt wet and slimy. She held them close to her face and saw the glisten of crimson by the light of the flames. Close to his face she saw a gash on his head and blood oozing out. She positioned herself by his head, locked her arms under his big arms and tried to drag him, but he was too heavy. She had to get them out or they would both die in her basement.

She coughed.

The hot smoky air from the fire upstairs was seeping into the basement and getting thicker.

She shook her head. Her hearing was returning from the initial blast. She could hear the cracking of the fire above. The heat had intensified. Sweat streamed down her face. In the distance, she heard a faint banging sound. She coughed again.

Moss. You have to wake up. She pressed her fingers on his throat. Strong pulse. Blood was still oozing from his head wound.

The banging continued. She looked around, where was she? The mechanical room. She leaned her head out and observed the stairwell leading down from upstairs. The fire was working its way down the stairs. Her only way out was the basement egress.

She was suddenly aware of the gravity of her situation. The furnace was located in the basement. Natural gas to heat the home and stove. And now she feared it would explode.

She had to reach the egress. But, that meant leaving Moss. Something exploded above her and the whole house shook. The banging stopped, followed by a loud ping on the metal egress door. The banging resumed.

She pushed herself to her feet, grabbed Moss by his shirt and with short hard tugs edged toward the egress door. She moved him two inches, maybe. She balled up more of his shirt in her fists, grunted and hauled harder. The banging on the door continued. Her head swiveled toward the door. Oh my God, someone was trying to get in. Who was it? Kaplan? One of the Pearsons?

She couldn't move Moss by herself, she needed help. The smoke was getting thicker. She dropped to her knees and swept as much of the floor with her hands as she could. Nothing. She crawled to her workbench, grabbed a hammer, and crawled back toward the egress door leaving Moss fifteen feet behind her. It was a one-handed, lift-assisted mechanism. From the inside, once she grabbed the handle and squeezed the mechanism, the door should automatically unlock, and the pistons should raise the doors open. It had worked dozens of times before. She hoped it functioned properly now.

She grabbed the handle and squeezed. As the doors opened, she readied the hammer in case she needed to defend herself.

As the doors opened, the silhouette of a man appeared, his face illuminated by the amber glow of the fire above.

Gregg Kaplan.

† † †

When Moss came to, there was a crowd of people standing around and a familiar face leaning over him. Kaplan.

"What happened?" Moss asked.

"How many fingers am I holding up," Kaplan asked." He raised three fingers on his right hand.

"Three," Moss replied.

Kaplan stood upright. "He's fine." And his friend walked out of sight.

In the distance, he heard sirens. "Where's?"

"Shh," a woman's voice said. He saw Christine's face lean over him. "You have a nasty cut on your head. How do you feel?"

"I'm fine. What about you?"

"You saved my life, Pete. Thank you."

"How long was I out?"

"Three or four minutes, maybe. Kaplan and KC had just put you here when you came to."

She helped him to a sitting position. His whole body ached. He was sure he'd have felt better if a Mack truck had hit him. His hand ran along the side of his face and felt something sticky and wet, what he assumed was blood.

A woman in a bathrobe came over with a handful of

towels. "I'm a nurse. Let me see how bad it is." She took a wet rag and wiped his face. He could feel the cloth tugging at his wound. She had a friendly expression. "I think you're going to live." She placed a dry towel on his head, grabbed his hand and put it on the towel. "Hold this on your head until the bleeding stops. I heard two of you were in the basement, you're lucky to get out alive."

He looked across the street at the inferno. Christine was standing next to Kaplan and KC. Several cars and pickups had parked nearby, and half a dozen men had gathered in her front yard. A man ran up with some sort of metal rod in his hand and Christine led him to a concrete box at the corner of her front yard. "What's that man doing," Moss asked the nurse.

"Shutting off her gas before her house blows up the neighborhood." She pointed to the men gathered in Christine's front yard. "They are all part of the volunteer fire department. Right now, they're waiting on the pumper." She raised her head and looked down the street. "It'll be here soon."

The sirens wailed louder and louder. The reflection of flashing red lights bounced off the houses, trees and cars. The siren stopped as the truck pulled in front of the burning house.

Kaplan and Christine appeared to be arguing, but then she patted him on the arm and her lips said *Good luck.* She signaled to KC, handed him something and the three of them broke up. While she walked toward him, KC ran next to the burning house, got in her Bronco and backed it out of the driveway. Kaplan ran toward his motorcycle, mounted it, and gunned the throttle as he headed down the street.

He managed to get to his feet as Cavalier approached. "What's going on?" He watched Kaplan speed by. "And where the hell is he going is such a rush?"

"He said something to the effect that if the Pearsons wanted to wage war against Last Chance, he would bring the battle to Drew Pearson's doorstep."

"Let's go then."

He started to push himself to his feet, wobbled and she grabbed his arm. "You're not going anywhere until someone looks at your head," Cavalier quipped.

He nodded to the lady in the robe. "That nurse standing there has already checked me out." He removed the towel from his head. "Told me to hold pressure. Said I was going to be around a lot longer to keep pestering you." He smiled. She smiled back.

"I've been hurt a lot worse than this and kept on fighting. Now, let's stop wasting time and go kick some Pearson ass."

CHAPTER 48

There came a point when enough was enough. That time was now. As he told Cavalier, he was taking this battle to Drew Pearson's doorstep and he planned on leading the charge. She claimed she wanted to be a by-the-book officer, but that hadn't panned out so far. Now was not the time or place for by-the-book. This was a time for improvisation and action. Don't do what the enemy expected, but rather come at them in such a way, they were caught off guard.

With the noted possible exception of Evan Pearson, the rest of the Pearsons were dregs of society. And as for Drew and Stevie, their time on earth was coming to a rapid end. After tonight's attack on Cavalier's home, it was time to put an end to Drew Pearson's tyranny.

Everything he needed was in his backpack or on him. He sped down the road on his Harley and out of town to the north, backtracking the way Cavalier had taken him last night to Pioneer River ditch number four. This time, he didn't park down the county road and run back to the ditch, this time he parked where the ditch went under the road. He pulled his Harley over to the side of the gravel road, reached into his left saddlebag and took out a small plank of wood. He placed it on the ground and propped the kickstand on it. He dismounted and scuffed his boot across the gravel road. It was dry and hard enough to support his bike without the plank, but old habits die hard. He stuffed the key in his pocket and rummaged through his saddlebag, collecting the last of what he might need for tonight's assault. He found his camo sticks and smeared black and gray smudge paint on his face and hands until he was satisfied with the result. A quick check in his motorcycle mirror, only the whites of his eyes showed.

He scaled Pearson's fence, careful not to touch the electric wires, and sprinted toward the compound, much like he did last night. This time at a much faster pace and remaining on the west side of the ditch.

It took eight minutes of flat-out running to reach the cabins. Something was different from last night. Instead of the Pearson compound being lit up like a fortress, all the lights were off, including the vapor lights that lit up the parking area for the ranch's vehicles. There were no lights in the cabins, no lights in the bunkhouse, and no lights that he could see at the big house.

All of that was about to change.

In the distance, he could hear Cavalier's siren growing louder and louder, piercing its way through the silent Wyoming night. Within a couple of minutes, he could see the glow of headlights and the flashing of her Bronco's police light bar.

He worked his way up the ditch until he was even with the bunkhouse, took a running start and jumped the quarter-full ditch. Almost the exact spot where he dumped the ranch hand's body last night. As the two vehicles, bounded over the last rise, he saw that KC's pickup was leading the charge, followed by the Bronco.

Now it was time to smoke out the rats.

† † †

After Kaplan sped away from Cavalier's house, she and

KC drove to the police station to pick up his truck. Moss met them there, still holding the towel on his head. She took him in her office to check his wound. The bleeding had stopped. She pulled out her first aid kit, cleaned his wound. It was a gash across the top of his big bald head. She found a butterfly bandage and covered the cut. The three got in two vehicles, KC in his truck and Moss in the Bronco with her and they headed back to the Rocking P Ranch.

She stopped at the entrance. Pearson' gate was closed. She radioed to KC to lead the way since he had equipped his big dually pickup with a cattle guard across the front grill. He called it his *Mad Max* bumper and claimed he'd never actually had to push cattle with it. But, he told her he did use it once to nudge a couple of bison from the road in order to get to one of the hunting camps nearby. KC didn't hesitate or ease into the gate. He punched the accelerator and smashed through the gate. She followed.

They sped down the mile-long driveway toward the big house. A twinge of Deja vu from this morning—technically yesterday morning—when she came to arrest the Pearsons. She knew Kaplan would be ready, she didn't know what he had planned.

Pearson's ranch was dark, and she sensed they were driving into an ambush. "Heads up, guys. This could be a trap."

As they topped the last rise, it looked like a ghost town. No lights anywhere to be seen, and no one moving about.

And then it happened.

The bunkhouse blew up.

† † †

Kaplan used all but two of the sticks of dynamite he found in the mineshaft yesterday. They weren't duds as he feared they might be. When he had sneaked in the back door of the bunkhouse, he found the entire building empty. Relieved somewhat that he didn't have to worry about anyone getting hurt in the blast.

The inside had a foyer that extended from the front door to the back door. Midway through was a long hallway that ran perpendicular to, and across the foyer. He lit the three long fuses together, tossed one down each hall, and dropped the third where he was standing. He ran out the back door and around to the far side of the cabin fifty feet next door.

The bunkhouse exploded. Windows shattered. Flames blasted through every nook and cranny and swirled upward enveloping the upstairs. Within seconds, the bunkhouse was a raging inferno as the fire swallowed the entire building.

Behind him, a sound caught his attention. A low thunderous sound. He turned around and surveyed across the ditch beyond the open prairie. He recognized the sound, hooves pounding in the distance. He grabbed his NVGs. Confirmed. Two horses, two riders, heading west toward the Bighorn Mountains. And the riders looked like Drew and Stevie Pearson.

Kaplan rotated back in time to watch as two vehicles slid to a stop in the parking area. Expecting a possible assault as they discussed before he left her house, they formed a wedge with their vehicles in the middle of the lot.

Within seconds, gunfire rang out from the two cabins.

Cavalier, Moss and KC had taken cover behind Cavalier's Bronco as it was broadside to the cabins. Responding to the fired shots, each took turns firing over the hood and ducking back down for cover.

The back door to Mark's cabin flew open. Kaplan spun, dropped to firing stance and readied his weapon as someone came running out. It was a woman, flailing her arms and screaming. She didn't see him until she almost ran into him. He grabbed her and pulled her down. She screamed again. He shook her until he had her attention. "It's okay," he yelled over her screams. "I won't hurt you. Is there anyone else inside other than Mark?" She shook her head. He pointed down the driveway. "Run. And don't stop until you get to town. Go to the police department and wait for the marshal." Her eyes wide, she pressed her lips together and took off.

"Someone's running away." He heard KC say in his ear set.

"Let her go," Kaplan responded. "Mark's wife just defected."

The back door was left swinging open in the wind. He had an idea. "Get ready, guys," Kaplan said. "Here comes the first rat."

He lit a stick of dynamite and tossed it as far as he could inside Mark's cabin. Then he ran to the back of Scott's cabin and waited.

He heard Mark's front door open and slam shut.

Another volley of shots.

Mark's cabin blew.

His ear set came alive. It was Cavalier. "Mark Pearson down."

Scott kept firing. Cavalier, Moss and KC returned fire. And everything went quiet except for the sounds of inferno.

"Hold your fire," Kaplan said. "I'll clear the house."

The flames from the bunkhouse, and now Mark's cabin,

cast a bright glow through the parking area. Almost as if all the vapor lights were back on. Kaplan charged and kicked in the back door to the remaining cabin. A woman screamed. Inside, a woman was hovered over a body with a cast on his leg lying face down behind a sofa. She had both hands wrapped around a pistol and trained at the body. "Drop the weapon," Kaplan shouted.

The woman glanced at him, still aiming her pistol at the body on the floor. She looked haggard, hair disheveled, a black eye and visibly pregnant. "I had to," she blurted. "The bastard was going to get me and my baby killed. He deserved to die."

"Lady, it's okay. I'm not going to hurt you. Just drop the gun."

Tears streamed down her cheeks. She dropped the gun, fell to her knees, and buried her face in her hands.

"All clear," he said into his mic. "Scott Pearson down."

CHAPTER 49

Kaplan walked out of Scott Pearson's cabin holding his weapon in one hand and supporting a pregnant woman with his other hand. He helped her down the front steps and to the vehicles where Cavalier was standing next to KC and Moss. She had stepped around her vehicle to meet Kaplan and the woman and turned to inspect her Bronco. During the gun battle with Mark and Scott Pearson, she heard pinging of bullets against the metal frame of her vehicle but didn't realize the extent of the damage until now.

Kaplan motioned with his gun barrel at the side of her Bronco. "Looks like Swiss cheese."

"Better it than us, right?" she replied. "What happened to Scott?"

The woman broke down again. "You want to tell the marshal, or shall I?" Kaplan said to the woman.

The woman threw Kaplan a quick glance, began sobbing and in choppy sentences broken up by short gasps for air told Cavalier what happened. "When the bunkhouse blew up, I told my husband this wasn't worth dying over. We have a baby on the way." She glanced down at her pregnant stomach and rubbed her hand on it. "When bullets started flying inside the house, I begged him to stop. He wouldn't listen. I crawled to him behind the couch where he was hiding and pleaded with him to think about our unborn child. That was when he did this." She touched her swollen eye, that was already discolored. "He's done it before too…plenty of times. I didn't want to die.

But, he didn't care. He said if I didn't support the family, he'd kill me." She wiped her eyes with her trembling fingers. "We have a lot of guns in the house. I found a pistol and went back to force him to give up. When he saw me holding the gun, he jumped up. I thought he was going to shoot me. I don't know if I shot him first or you did. It happened so fast. All I remember was seeing his head explode. I just wanted to protect our baby."

The woman began to wail and was about to go limp when Cavalier caught her and gently lowered her to the ground.

Cavalier heard Moss yelling.

"Freeze right there." Moss had his pistol aimed at a man across the parking area from the cabin walking down the driveway away from the big house.

Evan Pearson stopped and raised his hands in the air. "I'm unarmed," he yelled.

By now, KC and Kaplan had their weapons trained on Evan.

"Move forward slowly," Moss ordered. "Keep your hands where I can see them."

When Evan reached the first vehicle, which was KC's truck, Moss ordered him to put his hands on the hood and spread his legs. He complied, and KC patted him down. "He is clean," KC said.

Evan said, "That's Maggie over there, Scott's wife. She's going to have a baby in less than a month. Can I check on her?"

Moss waited for Cavalier's approval. "Let him go," she said.

Evan hurried over to the woman, kneeled down and slipped his arm around her. "Are you okay. Maggie? Tell me what happened."

Evan listened patiently as Maggie's version of the events

were interrupted with bouts of crying. "Scott can't hurt you anymore," he said. Evan looked over at Mark's burning cabin. "Where's Ann?"

"Shoulder length reddish hair?" Kaplan asked.

"Yes," Evan answered. "Have you seen her?"

Kaplan said, "She ran out the back door before the cabin blew. She's safe." Kaplan motioned with his gun toward the road. "By now she's a quarter mile on her way to town."

"KC," she said. "Take Maggie to the station. Watch out for Ann and pick her up. Get their statements and set them up with a room at the Sundown. Tell the clerk I'll settle up later."

"Sure thing, boss."

Kaplan interrupted. "Can we talk? Just the four of us?"

She addressed Evan and Maggie. "You two stay put."

Kaplan and Cavalier joined Moss and KC and stepped out of earshot of Evan and the woman. "What's this about Kaplan?" she said.

"Before Ann ran out the back door, I heard something behind me in the field back there." He pointed behind the cabins and bunkhouse. "Using my NVGs, I saw two men riding away on horses. They were moving fast toward the mountains. It was Stevie and Drew." He faced KC. "You're a tracker, right? Can you track where they're going? I mean…at night?"

"Sure, I can. If I use a flashlight, it is very easy. Without the flashlight it will take longer, but the upside is they will not see us coming. If we wait until dawn, anyone in those hills will see us from miles away. We would lose any element of surprise. Plus, I hear Stevie is an expert with the long shot. He could pick us off before we made it to the tree line."

"Can we make it to the tree line before dawn without using any lights?"

KC held up his watch. "It is 2:30. It will start getting light in three hours give or take. If we move swiftly, I think we can make the tree line by first light."

Kaplan zeroed in on Cavalier's face. "Either KC and I go now, or we wait until tomorrow night. It's your call, Marshal."

It was her call. And it was a bit of a dilemma. She didn't want to wait any longer than she had to capture the Pearsons. What had happened tonight transcended any marching orders the town council had given her. This had to end and had to end soon.

Hesitantly she said, "Okay, do it. You and KC get your gear and get moving."

"How 'bout me?" Moss asked.

"You're not going," she said. "Not tonight."

"And why the hell not?"

"Because you just got blown up is why the hell not. End of discussion." She stuck her palm out like a traffic cop to keep Moss from challenging her decision. She hastened to the back of her Bronco, opened the tailgate, and removed something from the back. She rushed back to where Kaplan was standing. "GPS tracking unit." She placed it in his hand. "Stick it in your backpack. I can track you with my laptop. Moss and I will find you tomorrow. I know a back way into the hills that should keep us in the woods. And keep your radios on, you know, just in case."

KC went over to his pick-up truck, retrieved a camo backpack, rummaged through some plastic tubs in the cargo bed and filled his pack. Next, he brought out a rifle with a scope and headed back to Kaplan. The rifle had a synthetic camo stock. He handed his truck keys to Moss. "You will need these."

"May I see that?" Kaplan asked as he held out his hand. KC handed over the rifle and Kaplan studied it. "Remington 783 bolt-action .30-06 Springfield. I used to have one just like this. Best gun for the money, in my opinion. Lightweight and can take a beating." He held the scope to his eye and scanned the mountains in the distance. "Top of the line." He handed the rifle back to KC using the shoulder strap.

Cavalier motioned for Kaplan to follow her over to her Bronco. She reached in the back seat and retrieved her Marlin 336W 30-30 lever-action Winchester rifle and a box of ammo. She handed them to Kaplan. "No scope, but it might come in handy. This is the Wild West, after all. And things around here with the Pearsons just might go Western."

He needed no explanation. He took the rifle, stuffed the ammo in his backpack, and he and KC sprinted toward the stable and out of sight.

Tonight marked a turning point from which there was no going back. Two of the Pearsons were dead and two were on the run. She had already lost one deputy and just put another in danger. She noticed Evan was still in the same spot with Scott Pearson's widow. He was comforting her, arm around her shoulders. If it weren't for Evan's warning earlier, everything tonight might have played out differently. She might be dead, for one. No telling what else might have happened.

Drew Pearson was known to use his power and influence for his own benefit, not only in Last Chance, but in all of Sheridan County as well. Somewhere along the way he decided to cross the line. Neither his corrupt lawyer nor bought and paid for judge could help him now.

It might have been worse, she thought, if Drew had involved his ranch hands, then the body count could have likely been higher. It was the only thing he'd done that she was thankful for.

She went over and stood next to Evan and the woman. "Evan, you need to come with Maggie to the station. She might appreciate a familiar face. The other woman will too I'm sure, providing I can find her."

"Sure, Marshal," Evan said. "No problem."

††††

After he and KC reached the stable, Kaplan faced west. "They rode off in that direction." He looked toward the moonlight silhouette of the Bighorn Mountains. "Out there somewhere." He strapped on his NVGs hoping to see any movement in the distance, but there was nothing other than cattle dotting the terrain.

He noticed a red glow on the ground in front of KC. "I thought no lights."

"Red light is difficult to detect," KC explained. "It is what pilots use in cockpits at night to preserve night vision. Even in this darkness, this light cannot be seen at a distance. I think we will be safe using it all the way to the mountains. It just takes longer since it is so dim."

KC began stepping north and south, scanning the ground with his light.

"Now what are you doing?" he asked.

"I am looking for spore," KC replied.

"Spore?"

"It is a word handed down in my family. It means I am looking for anything out of the ordinary. There are a lot of horse hoof tracks out here going in many directions. Right now, I am determining which of these tracks are the most recent, heading west, and carrying riders."

"You can tell that by looking?"

"Yes you can, if you know what you are searching for." KC stopped. "Here. Two sets of tracks, heading west. See how the hoof print is on top of some of these others?"

"I can see that," Kaplan said, not admitting that it wasn't easy to differentiate one set from another.

"These prints are slightly deeper."

"If you say so."

"And this is the biggest sign, these prints show a horse running, not walking. See?"

"I'll take your word on it, KC. I've tracked men in the woods and across deserts, nothing like this though. Even so, I had a modern advantage."

"What kind of modern advantage?" KC asked.

"Thermal imaging satellite recon."

"This way." KC put his arm through the rifle's strap and slung it on his back.

KC hiked west, following tracks only he could see and understand. *Following spore?* Who the hell ever heard of such a thing. KC was a tracker and not just any tracker, but a well-trained Native Indian tracker, who probably knew more about tracking than most white men. Certainly, this white man. Kaplan rested the barrel of the 30-30 on his shoulder and followed behind KC. The farther they traveled, the faster KC moved until they reached a fence, beyond which, were nothing but cattle.

Kaplan caught up and held his NVGs to KC's chest. "Would this help any?"

"I do not know, perhaps." He slipped them on, turned

out his red light, and powered up the unit. "I have used night vision scopes before, but nothing like this." He moved his head back and forth and up and down. He knelt and held his hand to the ground. "Can I keep these on? I can see their tracks very well with these. I think we can move much faster now."

"Hell yeah, lead the way."

KC motioned with his arm and took off running across the prairie, weaving through cattle and jumping cow patties. Kaplan followed his lead…and jumps.

Forty minutes later, they were at the base of tree line. The prairie was behind them, and steep terrain in front. The sky was showing first signs of light in the distant east. It wouldn't be much longer before dawn and he was glad they made it as far as they had before the Pearsons would have the advantage of light and high ground.

From here, he knew from experience, their search got harder.

And more dangerous.

CHAPTER 50

Cavalier caught sight of Mark's wife Ann, running down the county road toward Last Chance, just like Kaplan told her to do. She pulled the Bronco to the side of the road. The woman stopped and shielded her eyes with her hand from the bright headlights. Cavalier stepped out of the Bronco, identified herself and instructed her to get in the Bronco.

Back at the police station, she left Moss in charge and told him she would return shortly, first she wanted to let Jesse and Lucy know the coast was clear.

Cavalier drove into the Sundown Motel lot and parked. She strolled up to room seven, Moss' room. and knocked. No reply. *Safe word, dummy.* She knocked again. "It's Marshal Cavalier, L-C Jack Scramble," she shouted. "Open up."

She heard the door chain unlatch and the deadbolt disengage. Jesse cracked the door. As soon as he recognized her, he swung the door open. "Is it over?" he asked.

"Not quite, but it is safe in town now." She saw Lucy in the back of the room. "It's okay, Lucy. Mark and Scott Pearson are dead, and Stevie and Drew are headed to the mountains. Kaplan and KC are in pursuit as we speak, so you're safe."

Cavalier stepped inside. "We have a lot to do, so I want you to gather your belongings and come with me back to the station. Evan and the two Pearson widows are there with Inspector Moss. Jesse, you drive your truck and Lucy, you can ride with me."

She didn't give them much time before she hurried them out of the room and back to the station. As she drove by the Last Chance Diner, she spotted Poppy flipping the sign from *Closed* to *Open*. Must be 5:30, she thought. She saw several pickups in the parking lot belonging to some of the area ranchers, farmers and cowboys who were lining up for a hearty breakfast before a hard day's work on the ranch or farm. And, it was Monday, beginning of the work week for most ranch hands around here.

Coffee and food sounded good about now. It had been a long night, and everyone was tired, unfortunately there would be no rest for the weary. Not today. And certainly not for her and Moss.

When she and Lucy arrived at the station, Moss had everything under control. The two widows were on a cot in one of the jail cells with their arms wrapped around each other. Evan sat on a cot directly across from them. From mere observation, she couldn't tell if the women were sad their husbands were dead or if they had just been traumatized by the night's events. Abused woman ironically felt guilt and shame. It was hard for her to understand woman who stayed in abusive relationships. She was sure in this case the abusers, the Pearson brothers, used manipulation and fear to keep them from leaving. All these women ever had to do was come into her office, say the word and she would have made sure the battered women's shelter in Sheridan came and got them. Their lives changed tonight and in her opinion, for the better. Mark and Scott Pearson had been a nuisance for her since the first day she arrived in Last Chance. If it wasn't a brawl at the Crazy Woman Saloon, then it was the Sunset Mountain Bar or the Branding Iron Cafe, or their latest unfortunate encounter with Kaplan at the Last Chance Diner.

Until she walked into the jail cell and faced the two women, she wasn't sure what she was going to say. "Ladies," she said. Both woman directed their attention at Cavalier. Their faces full of apprehension. "I know it's been a rough night and I'm not sure there is anything I can say right now to make you feel better. When you're up to it," she said, "why don't you go over to the diner and get something to eat. I'll let Poppy know you might head over. Jesse will take you to the Sundown Motel and set you up with a place to stay for a few days. I can't let you go back to the Rocking P until after the scene has been processed." Both women stayed silent. Just stared up at her with tired, swollen eyes. She thought Maggie might start crying again, but she didn't. The women were obviously in shock.

Evan broke the awkward silence. "Thank you, Marshal. I'll make sure they get something to eat. They can stay in the big house with me instead of the Sundown, we have…there are plenty of spare bedrooms."

"I'm sorry Evan. For now, it's a crime scene and must be treated as such. And that includes the big house. I'll need all of you to stay in town and away from the Rocking P." She waited for Evan to give her affirmation that he understood. After a few seconds, he nodded.

Cavalier left Evan and the widows alone, returned to the main room and stopped in front of Doug's desk. "I think that went reasonably well." Moss, Lucy and Jesse did not seem convinced. "All right you three, back to the diner for a strategy meeting."

As she walked outside and across the street toward the diner, she called Matthew Davidson, the Sheridan County Coroner, and explained what had happened and that his presence was needed out at the Pearson ranch again. Second time in as many days. Fourth call by her in four days. First to the Branson farm, the Stillwater farm, and the Pearson ranch yesterday morning and again this morning.

† † †

The cloudless early morning sky was getting brighter and when he and KC stopped after twenty minutes of climbing, Kaplan was able to see all the way back to Pearson's ranch. Wisps of smoke rose high in the sky from the bunkhouse and cabin fires making it easy to spot the ranch. He knew if he could see it, somewhere above him Drew Pearson could see it too. And that made him smile.

After leaving the prairie below, the terrain pitched up drastically. One of the issues KC struggled with was the horses had taken a route up the mountain that kept the Pearsons mostly out of the trees. KC said it would be easy to follow the horses up the mountain, but by doing so, the Pearsons would likely be able to spot them coming.

"Evan said something about the cabin being near Dead Horse Creek, does that mean anything?" Kaplan asked.

"Yes, I know where Dead Horse Creek is." KC handed the NVG glasses to Kaplan. Kaplan stuffed them in his backpack. "That direction about half a mile or so, through that wooded area and over a couple of hills. Rougher terrain than this, but I can get us to the creek and we can follow it up the mountain. It will take us an hour longer, but we will stay out of sight."

"Out of sight means Stevie can't take a long shot at one of us. I didn't come this far so one of us could get picked off by that maniac. If the woods will give us the cover we need to go in unseen and unannounced, then that's what we'll do. Besides,

I like having the element of surprise on my side."

"Fair warning Kaplan, I have never climbed up the Dead Horse before. I have fished downstream where it drops into the valley, but never upstream." KC pulled out his map from his backpack. "Dead Horse Creek meanders a couple of miles up Black Canyon into Bighorn National Forest before it reaches headwater up in Devil's Gulch. That cabin could be anywhere up there. And the marshal is out of luck. There are no roads nearby where she and your friend will have easy access. They would have to go by foot a couple of miles like us."

"Then it is just you and me," Kaplan said with finality. "I'm following you."

When KC said the terrain would be a little rough, he must have been making a joke. He hadn't had to struggle like this in years. Fortunately, this was the West and there wasn't much underbrush to contend with like in more humid climates. The terrain was steep and on more than one occasion they were forced to detour around impassible cliffs. But, they did make it to Dead Horse Creek. And they made it in a little over an hour. The sun was up and shining through the canopy of evergreens, cottonwoods and aspens. It was the canopy that kept them from being able to be seen very far upstream. Which meant no one could be seen very far downstream either. For now, they were safe from being spotted by the Pearsons.

Kaplan signaled KC for a quick break. He wasn't used to the altitude like KC and all the uphill climbing had him huffing. His mouth felt like he was in the desert. Wyoming was dry, as was most of the West, and for someone who lived most of his life in the East, the lack of humidity took some getting used to. He dipped his hands in the creek and scooped a handful of water.

KC was quick and pushed Kaplan's hand away from his mouth. "I would not drink that," KC warned. "It might look clean, but it could make you sick. Giardia gets in the water from animal feces."

Kaplan wiped the remaining water on his hands across his pant leg. KC reached into his pack and tossed him a reusable plastic water bottle. Kaplan gulped a few swallows and tossed it back.

"Thanks. Guess I wasn't as prepared as I thought."

"It happens more than you think, most of my clients are not prepared for how dry it is out here, so I always carry plenty, especially this time of year when all of my guide trips are fishing. It can get brutally hot up here and most clients are wearing waders and boots."

"Do any get *bear caught*?"

KC laughed. "I did not know you Easterners knew that term."

Kaplan said nothing.

"Some do on rare occasions," KC continued. "Most do not as long as they drink plenty of water. Overheating is easy in this climate especially when you get dehydrated. I have had to take a couple of clients to the hospital in Sheridan because they were so sick."

"What about on hunting trips?"

"Mostly, they just do not dress warm enough. Not enough layers."

"Wildlife?"

KC smiled. "The Bighorn Mountains have many species of wildlife. This time of year, we could see most anything out here. Mule deer, whitetail, elk, moose, pronghorn, black bear, mountain lions, coyotes, and tons of birds from grouse to pheasants to eagles and falcons. Last year, we had a very active black bear population, even had a couple of hikers get attacked. One of the farmers outside of Last Chance who raises goats had a mountain lion problem."

"What about rattlesnakes?"

"Down on the prairie, like where the Rocking P is, you will find them. Up here, not so much. It gets too cold during the winter. Every now and then a hiker might come upon a rattlesnake in the lower parts of the mountains, but even that is rare." He paused. "Speaking of which, you ready to get moving?"

He jumped to his feet. "Yep."

CHAPTER 51

Drew Pearson sat in a deer stand he'd built several years ago attached to a lodgepole pine and scanned the high desert plains to the east of the cabin with his high-powered binoculars. He could see all of his property and much more. After the front passed through yesterday, the air smelled clean and crisp. In the far distance, he could see Devil's Tower and beyond that, Black Hills National Forest in South Dakota.

A little over three miles to the east, smoke had been billowing from his bunkhouse and Mark's cabin for several hours. Now, it appeared to be nothing more than a smoldering pile of rubble. It was hard for him to imagine what had transpired last night. Just as he and Stevie left the stable, the bunkhouse exploded. He was smart to send the ranch hands away or else they might all be dead. Not long after the bunkhouse blew, Mark's cabin exploded too. It caught him off guard. He almost turned around and went back to fight it out but opted to stick to the plan and head for the hills. Hopefully Mark and his wife, Ann, weren't inside.

The explosion had to be the work of that stranger named Kaplan who came to town. The one who beat up Mark and Scott three days ago. There was no way the marshal could have survived the blast to her home last night, so he had to assume Kaplan was seeking retribution.

For Drew, it was the first time he had ever fired an RPG, rocket propelled grenade. The kick from the launcher almost knocked him down. Stevie, on the other hand, had used them before. More than once. It was a crude but effective weapon and most times overkill. Stevie said he got the idea to use them from playing some stupid video game. If Kaplan had indeed killed Mark, he would pay. Hell, he was going to pay anyway.

From his perch, he watched Stevie struggle to get the horses in the small lean-to type stable. It wasn't much, two 15 x 15 stalls that he'd built when his sons were children. They still served the purpose. Stevie liked this place more than any of his brothers. Mark and Scott drudgingly made two or three yearly treks to the cabin to hunt or fish, but they would never stay more than a few days at a time, maybe a week if the hunting was good. They whined about not having all the comforts they were used to on the ranch. He had spoiled those boys.

Stevie, on the other hand, would come and stay for months. Summer or winter, it didn't matter. He claimed it helped him get in touch with his inner mountain man. Stevie was the only Pearson, including himself, who could survive out here by living off the land regardless of season. And now, he would have to.

They would have to.

When he bought this land, it was part of a shady deal with the Bureau of Land Management. A 40-acre parcel completely surrounded by the Bighorn National Forest with no access from any road. Totally landlocked without access to the property, and in the most rugged of terrain. He had hunted here since he was a kid. He knew where the game was. He knew how to get here. From the western edge of his property, which abutted the Bighorn National Forest land, all he had to do was travel west across the county road that bordered his property, and into the mountains. He aimed west toward the year-round snowcapped Sheep Mountain and used it as his initial guide to find the trail to his cabin. Sheep Mountain served as the perfect landmark with an elevation of 9813 feet.

The first part of the route to the cabin was easy, cross an open meadow until the elevation veered upward. Once he located his trail, which was second nature after all these years, he had to climb the open rocky slope leading to the forest. Once in the forest, his trail was covered by the canopy of trees, he followed several switchbacks that led to Elkhorn Creek. Once across that creek, he had one more peak to climb before entering a gulch. After reaching the gulch, he'd had to blaze a trail not far from Dead Horse Creek to get to his tract of land and the cabin site. His cabin was located in the rugged and remote area called Devil's Gulch.

When he built the cabin many years ago, it had taken him nearly two years to reach completion since his access weather window was limited to only a few months. During the winter, there was no construction because everything was frozen and covered in snow and ice. Hauling supplies by pack mule took trip after trip. He had to build the cabin using trees harvested from his property. Cut, notch, and nail. Between each log, chinking, which was hauled in by mule. The wood burning stove was hauled in small pieces and assembled on site. It was a long and laborious ordeal, but it gave him sanctuary before his children were born. A chance to get away from that nagging bitch of a wife. Nagging because she claimed he took her away from her home and family and stuck her out in the middle of nowhere.

It wasn't the middle of nowhere in his mind. This part of Wyoming was where he planned to build and expand his land holdings. She wanted finer things and a social life, neither of which was easily found in Last Chance. She was a city girl and would have probably done better near a place like Jackson Hole. But property in that area was too expensive back then, and now it was ridiculous. He wanted a place where land was cheap and not a lot of people lived.

In his own way, he had loved his wife. She was a good mother until she died giving birth to Evan. He was counting on her to raise the kids and leave him to do what he liked. The cabin had only been finished a few years when she died. Since that time, he had been forced to spend more time raising his sons than he cared to. Evan was a lot like his mother in many ways, soft and social. And the only Pearson with a college education.

Privacy had been his desire his entire life. That was another reason he didn't want anyone other than family to know about the cabin. After he built the cabin, he painted the sheet metal roof the same dull gray and green colors as the surrounding rocks and trees. It was already tucked beneath the canopies of several trees, but he didn't want it to be seen from the air either. His requirement was that it blend in with the land. Now, he and Stevie would be forced to live here incognito for the foreseeable future. Between Evan's business sense and Mark and Scott's ranching ability, he was sure his kingdom would continue uninterrupted without him. If anyone could keep it afloat, it was Evan.

† † †

Cavalier and Moss had been monitoring the GPS signal from the tracking device Kaplan put in his backpack from her laptop, which was mounted to the dash of her Bronco. The signal showed movement very slowly north and west along

Dead Horse Creek. The satellite view put Kaplan and KC in Bighorn National Forest, and judging by the topographic map, gaining altitude with every step. She zoomed in on the latest satellite view marked by where the tracking device put Kaplan and KC. No motor vehicle roads or trails showed up anywhere around them. She zoomed in closer and all she saw were rocky peaks and forest. No signs of a cabin either. Nothing.

The tracking device had logged Kaplan's route from the Rocking P Ranch to his current location. A mile west on Pearson property, over County Road 144 and west into the Bighorn National for another two miles. At first, Kaplan and KC made good time, now their progress up the mountain had slowed. Moreover, as Moss indicated, the elevation change was rapid, and their targets seemed to be moving along Dead Horse Creek. She noted one stop for roughly six minutes with no movement. Since that time, it has been a slow but steady uphill progression.

The closest access point to Kaplan's current position was at the Little Bighorn East Trailhead at the southern end of Forest Service Road 113. *But, where from there?* The Little Bighorn East Trailhead started at the Little Bighorn River and went south and west. She needed to go due east to get to Kaplan and according to her topographic map, it was roughly a mile with an 800-foot climb followed by a 600-foot descent followed by another 600-foot climb over very rough and steep terrain. Kaplan was in good enough shape to be able to keep up with KC.

She shared her look of frustration with Moss. "Kaplan and KC are on their own. We can't get there from here and the closest law enforcement or rescue helicopter is several hours away. We don't have the luxury of that kind of time."

"Maybe not, but we should be able to communicate with them if we get close enough. If not here," he said while he tapped his finger on the spot where their path crossed CR 144 west of Pearson property line. "Then here." He paused. "And if that doesn't work, we use that GPS tracking gadget of yours and follow them in."

She closed her lips tight and eyed the big man. As much as she liked Moss he would only slow her down. He was out of his element. Even though she rock-climbed and jogged at this high elevation, this would be tough for her. Moss wouldn't make it a mile before she'd have to leave him. Either she would need to go in on her own, or Kaplan and KC would have to finish this by themselves.

† † †

The climb had been brutal.

Even KC was winded when he signaled Kaplan to hit the dirt. His signal meant possible danger, but Kaplan was relieved to stop and catch his breath. If indeed there was danger ahead, he needed the break.

KC whispered into the radio. "I thought I heard a horse. Could be we are getting close." KC motioned to his two o'clock position.

His eyes followed KC's hand motion but saw nothing but a forest and a wall of rock. When KC motioned again, Kaplan understood. KC would go left around the rock and Kaplan was to go right. The two would come out at the cabin, if it was really up there, from opposite directions.

He gave a thumbs-up, and KC disappeared around the wall of rock. Kaplan went right, careful not to step on anything that could make noise. No loose rock, no sticks. Every step had to be made with complete stealth.

The rushing sound of water from Dead Horse Creek made enough noise to cover quiet footfalls, otherwise the woods were peaceful and anything out of the ordinary would likely be heard by one, or both, of the Pearsons.

Kaplan realized that in order to get around the wall of rock, he had to climb over it. Although he'd done it before when he was in the military or on a couple of ops with the CIA, he would not consider himself a rock climber by any stretch. As was the norm, he'd improvise on the spot.

The wall was only twenty feet, he estimated, and it certainly looked scalable, but he needed two hands, which meant either leaving Cavalier's 30-30 on the ground below or climbing with one hand. He had other weapons, all handguns which he could use, but experience had taught him never to leave behind a perfectly good weapon. He slipped his parachute cord bracelet over his wrist and unwound the cord. He made a makeshift rifle strap and secured it over his shoulder. It'll do in a pinch. In all the years he'd been wearing the wrist band, this was the first time he'd actually used it.

He started scaling the wall, carefully placing each hand and foot, testing for loose rocks before applying weight. When he reached the top of the wall, he saw a well camouflaged cabin and lean-to type barn about two hundred feet away and tucked beneath a thick canopy of trees. *Just like Evan described.*

In a tree behind the cabin, a platform, much like a deer stand.

Sitting in the stand with a pair of binoculars peering out over the plains, Drew Pearson.

His ear set filled with KC's panicked voice. "Shit, I just triggered a tripwire."

A hail of gunfire erupted and the sounds of bullets ripping through the air.

CHAPTER 52

Cavalier left Jesse in charge of the police station and Lucy manning the radios. It seemed the young lady enjoyed it, and perhaps it gave her a sense of purpose, something Cavalier didn't believe Lucy had ever experienced before.

She and Moss drove to the spot where Kaplan and KC's path crossed CR 144. She eased her Bronco to the side of the road and powered the windows down. She made several attempts to contact Kaplan and KC, but received no response, so she suggested they eat their take-out and try again later. She had Lucy pick up burgers and fries from the diner for them before they left. She was starving but she wasn't sure her stomach could handle Poppy's greasy food. Especially now with all the turmoil surrounding the Pearsons, her house being blown up, and the unsolved Branson murders, not to mention the fact that the town council was breathing down her neck about wrapping these cases up.

Her landlord wasn't at all pleased when she found out that Drew and Stevie Pearson had blown up her house. She had told Cavalier, "Those Pearsons were a pain in my cheating husband's ass, too. Drew Pearson was always pushing the extent of the law and always came out smelling like a rose thanks to that shady lawyer. Nothing ever seemed to stick. My husband thought he was involved in much more but could never prove any of it. He would have been glad to see them all gone."

Moss had already dived into his burger and grabbed

a handful of fries. Obviously, the grease didn't bother his digestive track.

"When this is all over," she said. "Why don't I take you into Sheridan for some decent food?"

"Sounds good." He wiped his mouth with a napkin. "This time I'll pay. You've picked up the bill enough already." He took a swallow of his soft drink.

"Least I can do for all the free labor."

"Free labor? Woman, you have yet to get my bill. This talent ain't cheap, you know?"

Moss laughed. She liked his hearty laugh. "Will you stick around after this is over?" The look on his face made her wish she could take back her words. What the hell was she thinking? It just blurted out.

Moss was silent. He rubbed his jaw. "I'll think about it," he finally said. "Provided you take some time off."

"Seriously?" she raised her voice. "After this, I'll probably have all the time off I want. That's how it is when you don't have a job."

The expression on Moss' amicable face changed. He jumped out of the Bronco and lumbered around to the front of the vehicle. Instinct made her copy his move. She was about to speak when she heard it.

Gunfire.

To the west.

In the mountains.

And it sounded like a war zone.

† † †

Lucy sat at Cavalier's desk inside the marshal's office

and was monitoring the radio while Jesse took the two Pearson widows to the Sundown Motel. Evan stayed behind and was sitting in the chair next to the desk. She enjoyed doing something she felt was worthwhile. It was the first time she had ever had a real job. It gave her a sense of accomplishment, something she had never experienced before. She probably would not even have this right now if Kaplan had not suggested it to the marshal.

She opened Cavalier's handwritten notebook lying on her desk and started reading. There were still two outstanding investigations that had yet to even get started. The Branson farm murders and the massacre on the Rez at the Stillwater farm. According to Cavalier's notes, those were connected. The gun used to kill three of the men on the Rez was the same one used and left at the scene of the Branson murders. How weird was that? What had puzzled Cavalier was the timing. The murders at the Stillwater farm on the Crow Rez had happened days before the Branson murders based on what Cavalier described as putrefaction of the bodies. Not sure what that meant, but it sounded yucky. So, how did the gun used on the Rez also kill the Bransons several days later *and* all the shell casings, as Cavalier called them, end up at the Branson farm? And who burned it down?

The killer could not be someone from the Stillwater farm because they were already dead before the Bransons were murdered and the farmhouse burned down. Murder, suicide was ruled out because of the way the Bransons were shot in the back of the head execution style. Just like the three gunshot victims at the Stillwater farm. What was the connection between the Bransons and those at the Stillwater farm?

She was intrigued by the mystery of it all. Someone

went to a lot of trouble to plan and execute the murders, but why? Who had anything to gain?

Jesse walked back in the station and threw a quick glance at Evan sitting next to Lucy. "Everything's taken care of. The marshal said the widows could stay at the hotel for up to a week. At the expense of the town of Last Chance. They're still kind of rattled and didn't want to be separated, so I just put them up in one room. Save the town a little money too."

"That's not surprising," Evan said. "They always stuck together. Kind of had to. Being out there with all of us men. Mark and Scott tricked them into marriage by promising them all kinds of things, but never delivered. And there was no way my father would ever have allowed them to divorce my brothers. They felt trapped and were trapped. I never knew my mother, but I'm pretty sure my father kept her under his thumb all the time just like he did Maggie and Ann. They were afraid of him and their husbands. My brothers were assholes. I saw both Maggie and Ann with bruises on their faces several times over the years. My father told them they needed to try not to aggravate their husbands. Even though Scott was my brother, I don't blame Maggie for what she did."

It was very strange to hear that Evan hated his family so much, but then again, he was right, they were all assholes. She had experienced that first hand over the few years she had been in Last Chance. How could Evan turn out so different from the rest of his family?

Jesse sat down in his chair behind his desk. Evan got up and walked out of Cavalier's office and went over to the chair next to Jesse's desk and sat down. The open door to Cavalier's office allowed Lucy a view of Evan and earshot of their conversation. She ignored them, she was still intrigued by the Branson and Stillwater farm murders and how they were tied together. She flipped a page and continued reading Cavalier's notes.

Two of the men killed on the Stillwater farm lived in Last Chance, one was half Crow and left the Rez to try to get sober. Alcoholism and drug addiction were rampant on the Rez and Mark Leatherdale knew if he didn't move off the Rez, he would never get out of his downhill spiral. He claimed he had lost his Native identity. Graham Stillwater, the man who owned the farm, gave Leatherdale a job. His property abutted the Wyoming state line, so Leatherdale could come and go and would never be exposed to the influences on the Rez that had gotten him in trouble in the first place.

The other man from Last Chance killed on Stillwater's farm was Tony Mason. He had only lived in Last Chance for a few months and was volunteering to help Stillwater with the annual Boy Scouts Jamboree. Look what that got him. She could not see how either of those men had any connection to the Branson farm or their murders. Both of them were victims of being in the wrong place at the wrong time. The Crow Native on Stillwater's farm was there because his brother, Crow Tribal Police Chief Joseph Silverheels, put him there as part of community service work from a drug arrest. Frank Silverheels had been arrested several times by the Crow Tribal Police, all were drug related petty crimes. His brother thought removing him from Crow Agency and making him stay on the Stillwater farm to help with the jamboree would give him a chance to get clean. His community service was to be an in-resident stay on the Stillwater farm for a little over a week. Nine days, according to her notes. Two before the jamboree, five during and two afterwards to clean up. He had only been there a day when he was murdered.

Cavalier's notes were exhaustive. She had explored every angle. The marshal had even written down her questions. *Who had anything to benefit from these deaths? Family? Heirs?* The Stillwater family was one of the largest on the Rez. According to Silverheels, the Stillwater estate was to be divided equally among his children, all of whom had successful lives of their own without their father's money. Nothing suspicious with any of them.

Richard Branson's only heir was his son Stanley, who was also murdered. There were no other known relatives, so his estate would eventually end up on the auction block and go to the highest bidder. There wasn't much on the Branson's farm, Cavalier had jotted in her notes, except that it did butt up next to Drew Pearson's property. Lucy gasped when she read the next thing Cavalier had written. *Is this another Pearson neighbor with bad luck? Another chance to add to his empire?*

The phone on Cavalier's desk interrupted Lucy's reading. Caller ID indicated Sheridan County Sheriff. She answered.

"Last Chance Town Marshal's Office," Lucy said into the phone.

"This is Sheriff Knight, where's the marshal?"

"She is out in the field, may I take a message."

"I need to talk to her immediately."

"Sheriff, you can try her cell phone, but she might have no service where she was headed." She gave him the number.

Lucy opened Cavalier's notebook and resumed reading when the phone rang again. Sheriff Knight.

"Yes, Sheriff?"

"My call went straight to the marshal's voice mail. I need you to get her a message as soon as possible."

"Okay, I am ready."

"This concerns the latent prints we pulled from two of the shell casings at the Branson farm. Originally there was no match in AFIS, so it looked like a dead-end. Now we have a hit on one of the prints KC logged into AFIS yesterday that matched the prints found on the shell casings. Are you getting all this?"

"Yes, sheriff. I have it all written down. Who does the print belong to?" she asked.

"Drew Pearson."

CHAPTER 53

While the volley of rounds was aimed at KC, Kaplan pulled himself over the ledge onto level ground and ran for cover behind a boulder thirty feet to his right. He had barely cleared the cliff's edge when a spray of bullets peppered the ground around him. So much for the element of surprise.

One of the Pearsons was using an automatic weapon, which sounded an awful lot like an AR-15. And that meant it was either modified for fully automatic or it was equipped with a bump-stock. He took shelter behind the boulder, but he knew he couldn't stay there for long.

"KC," he shouted into his microphone. "Sit-rep."

"I am okay but pinned down," he replied. "Sorry Kaplan. It was a gray trip wire, blended with the rocks. Never saw it till it was too late."

"Keep your head down while I assess our situation."

"Roger that."

One of the things Kaplan noted before KC triggered the tripwire and alerted the Pearsons to their presence was that the cabin was strategically located. Drew Pearson was smart. The cabin was nestled in the densest part of the stand of trees. Their canopies covered the already camouflaged roof making the cabin virtually impossible to spot except close up. Someone could walk right past the cabin and never even know it was there unless they were looking for it. If KC hadn't heard the horses and come to investigate, the two of them would have kept climbing up Dead Horse Creek right past the cabin and never been the wiser.

He took a quick glance around the far side of the boulder back in the general direction of the platform where Drew Pearson was sitting just a couple of minutes ago. The tree stand was empty. There was no way to see inside the cabin with the shutters partially closed. The cabin was crude, but solid. Built to withstand the harsh winters and any wild animals that might want a free meal. Studying the cabin, Kaplan felt he had journeyed back in time. A time when people lived isolated and had skills for survival in the woods. He knew this small rustic cabin did not have the modern conveniences of Pearson's ranch, but it had everything needed for a stand-off.

He saw movement in the front window as a shutter cracked open. Somebody was keeping watch with the barrel of a gun moving side to side. What he couldn't see was where the other man was standing guard. He and KC could wait them out, but waiting was not going to be in their favor. He figured Pearson had the cabin well stocked with food and water. He and KC had few supplies.

His ear set came alive, mostly static, but he recognized her voice. Cavalier.

"Kaplan, KC, what's going on up there?" Pause. "Repeat. Kaplan? KC? Do you hear me?"

"Weak and scratchy, but I hear you," he responded.

"I hear you also," KC said.

"What's happening?" she asked. "Are you okay?"

Kaplan started the situation report. "We found the cabin. It's well hidden and camouflaged. No wonder no one knew it was up here. We have both Pearsons pinned inside. They won't be leaving anytime soon. Not with us waiting for them out here." He craned his neck and searched out over the plains. "Marshal, I can see your white Bronco from here. And if I can see you, you should be able to see me."

There was a long pause and she replied, "Sorry, Kaplan, I got nothing but trees and rocks."

Just then gunfire. He ducked. It sounded like a handgun followed by automatic rifle fire. He didn't like what he heard next. KC made a loud grunt in his earpiece.

"Kaplan," KC said in a strained voice filled with urgency and panic. "Stevie's out. I tried to pin him back in, but his father provided cover fire. Stevie headed for the barn." He paused. "Kaplan, I took one in the leg."

Shit. "How bad?"

"Bleeding like a stuck pig."

"Got a tourniquet?"

"Only my belt."

"Sit tight, KC, and keep an eye out for Stevie."

The tides had just turned. And not in their favor. With KC down, he might need backup. Cavalier and Moss were a couple of hours away at best and that was provided they had no problem finding the trail that led to the cabin. And that was no guarantee. He slung the rifle back over his shoulder and crawled to the ledge, keeping the boulder between him and the cabin. This section of the cliff wall was steeper than where he climbed up but still manageable he thought, until he got close enough to jump. Not knowing how critical KC's gunshot wound was, he hurried down the cliff face as quickly as he could and jumped the last eight feet. He landed on his feet.

Kaplan crouched and bolted, staying low toward where KC had disappeared earlier. He held his Beretta ready. He rounded the area where KC should have been. Nothing. No signs the deputy had been there at all.

"Dammit KC, where are you?"

"Look up."

KC was above him, leaning between a tree and the rock wall of the cliff face. Twenty feet up, maybe more, holding his leg with one hand and a tree limb with the other. If someone from above came to the ledge, he was a sitting duck. Totally defenseless. Kaplan kept his Beretta trained on the ledge.

"Can you get down?"

"I cannot put much pressure on it. I will try."

"Where's your weapon?"

KC pointed to where it had fallen, halfway between KC and where Kaplan was standing. Kaplan located a small boulder and ducked behind it for cover. He kept his weapon aimed at the ledge.

"All right, KC, I've got you covered, work your way down. I can't come get you or we're both exposed."

He could see the agony in KC's face with every move the man made. His normally dark-skinned face had drained of color. The deputy had no choice. If he didn't get off that cliff soon, he was a dead man.

† † †

Kaplan had begun giving Cavalier a situation report when he suddenly went silent. Seconds later the hills erupted in gunfire again. Cavalier repeatedly tried to raise him on the radio, but to no avail. She now had no communication with Kaplan…or KC. The sound of the barrage was unsettling. She could hear it echo through the canyon and by the time it reached her and Moss, it sounded like a rapid-fire rumble.

She scanned to the west into what the locals called Black Canyon. Black because of the thick forest of evergreens that lined the valley and extended up the canyon walls, almost reaching their promontory peaks. To the north of the canyon entrance was Owl Rock, which had a south-facing wall that resembled an owl. Owl Rock looked close but was actually beyond where Black Canyon Creek emptied out of the Bighorn Mountains and onto the plains on its eastward journey to nowhere. During the spring runoff, it would actually make it all the way to the Pioneer River just outside of Last Chance.

To the south of Black Canyon rose a cone-shaped mountain called Bald Dome. The name was a perfect description as the top half of the mountain was barren of trees. Beyond Owl Rock on the north side of Black Canyon was Devil's Gulch. According to the display on her laptop's monitor, Kaplan was currently only a few hundred feet below the peak of Devil's Gulch.

Unless Pearson had a secret way into Devil's Gulch, it could only be reached by the most advanced hikers and technical rock climbers. But Kaplan and KC made it, so Pearson did have a secret way in, how else could he ride in and out on horseback? If a horse could make it to Pearson's cabin, so could she.

Her phone vibrated. It was a text from Lucy with a message from the sheriff. A new revelation in the murders. Her urgency to reach the cabin just increased tenfold.

Moss had been staring through Cavalier's binoculars for a long time. It was hard enough not hearing from Kaplan or KC, but Moss not talking right now made her more nervous.

"See anything?" she said.

He kept peering through the binoculars and replied,

"Not a damn thing."

She shook her head and glanced at Moss and back in the direction of the gunfire. She should have gone with Kaplan and KC. What was she thinking? She was the marshal. It was her duty to be up there helping take down Pearson.

Moss lowered the field glasses and stretched his head back. "We've got to go up there," he said rubbing his hands together. "I got a bad feeling about this."

She agreed, they did need to go. Every minute that went by ramped up her anxiety. If something had happened to either Kaplan or KC, she needed to know. If they captured or killed either or both of the Pearsons, she needed to know. From where they stood, it was two and a half miles to where the tracking device showed Kaplan. One mile of that was relatively flat and the other mile and a half was anything but.

Cavalier tried to raise Kaplan and KC again on the radio but heard only static. She lightly slapped the back of Moss' arm. "Gear up."

It took them forty-five minutes to get to the fork in the road. Hoof tracks veered to the right and up a treeless slope. Kaplan and KC's footprints went to the left into the woods toward Dead Horse Creek. They had already crossed Black Canyon Creek and had entered the bottom of Devil's Gulch by the time they encountered the fork.

"Follow them or the horses?" she asked.

He didn't answer at first. She could see he was assessing their options for going either direction. The big man used his index finger as he appeared to be tracing the route up Devil's Gulch. He pivoted around and looked back down the valley toward her Bronco, then toward where Kaplan and the cabin should be. He held the binoculars with both hands to his face and studied some more.

Without answering her question, he let the binoculars drop, the strap around his neck catching them. He bent down, retrieved the walking stick he'd picked up on the trail to the mouth of Black Canyon and started moving with long strides. "This way," he said with an assured tone.

"How do you know which way to go?" she yelled after him.

"I just do. This is the way the horses went. It keeps us in the open, that's why Kaplan and KC went into the woods. This is our best choice."

She trotted up to Moss, grabbed his arm and spun him around.

"Shouldn't we talk about this first?"

"Nope." Moss sounded amused.

"Why not?"

"Kaplan told me to go this way."

"He what?"

He took off the binoculars and handed them to her. He stuck his hand up toward the hill and pointed. It took a few seconds before she saw what Moss was looking at. Kaplan. Next to him on the ground was KC. And Kaplan was signaling which way for them to go.

CHAPTER 54

Kaplan was relieved to see Moss and Cavalier climbing the mountain toward him. Moss had understood his hand signals and took the path that Pearson had used, not the torturous path that he and KC took. His estimate was they should make it to this spot in an hour, give or take. Cavalier lived here and appeared to be in good physical shape, she shouldn't have any issue with the elevation. Moss, on the other hand, might slow her down. He might be in decent shape, but he'd probably have trouble hauling all that body weight up this mountain at this elevation. He was a lowlander and, according to the GPS unit that KC brought with him, they were currently sitting at just under 8000 feet above sea level.

Help was on the way, but there was still the matter of Drew and Stevie. KC said Stevie had made a run for it and while he was shooting at Stevie, Drew plugged him in the leg. Now, there was no telling where either one of them were.

After KC made the grueling descent from his perch, Kaplan dragged him to a protected spot behind several boulders and trees and put a real tourniquet on this leg. He left KC in charge of pressure management on the tourniquet. Too tight and he could lose his leg, not enough and he could bleed to death. It felt like Drew's bullet hit bone. He didn't know if it broke the bone. The bullet entered on the left side and exited out the front, ripping through a gaping section of muscle. KC had been a trooper, only grimacing when Kaplan felt around inside his leg with his finger.

Next, Kaplan had searched in the tree line and found two workable limbs and made a splint for KC's leg, which he secured with duct tape that he kept in his backpack, a critical component of every go bag. In all fairness, the duct tape was an add-on a few years ago when he was in Yemen and a man named Elmore Wiley had pulled some from his pack to repair a hang glider. "Never leave home without it," the old man had said. That piece of advice stuck with him and he had kept it in his go bag ever since.

He had heard footsteps and movement above him several times since he tucked KC in the inverted v-shaped cave. Not really a cave so much as two slabs of rock leaned against each other, blocked on one end by the cliff wall and open on the other. His job until Moss and Cavalier arrived was to guard the opening. He knew the two men were out searching for them and it was just a matter of time before they searched this far from the cabin. When they did, he'd be waiting for them.

The mouth of the cave faced east and left him with a view of the forested canyon below and out over the plains. Cavalier's Bronco was still in sight, and if he leaned out of the cave, he could see the trail up the mountain. Periodically, he'd check on Moss and Cavalier's progress up the mountain, they weren't climbing as fast as he'd hoped.

"What the hell is taking you two so long?" he whispered into his microphone.

A winded Moss answered. "Give me a break, man, I'm not a damn mountain goat."

"Send the marshal ahead of you."

"I am ahead of him," she replied. "I'm almost to you now."

He peeked over the edge. "Damned if you ain't."

Suddenly, a volley of gunfire erupted in the air and echoed through the canyon. "Duck Christine," Moss yelled. Bullets ricocheted off the rocks above him. "Two men on the ledge, both with rifles."

He heard footsteps above him scrambling for cover followed by a pelting of small pebbles and rocks on the top of his cave hideout.

"Kaplan, was that your head that stuck out of that little notch up there?" Moss asked.

"Maybe. Did it look like this?" He stuck his head out again.

"Yep," Moss replied. "You can thank me later, buddy. The Pearsons were on top of you. You and KC were almost history."

"How far down are you, Marshal?" Kaplan asked.

Moss interrupted. "Ten feet below you, fifteen tops."

"Moss, what about the Pearsons?"

Moss replied, "They both retreated. At least for now, anyway."

Kaplan faced KC. "Keep your weapon ready. If someone comes around this corner without announcing themselves first," he said while tapping his earpiece. "Shoot first, ask questions later. Got it?"

KC nodded.

"Moss can you take cover?"

"Already ahead of you, man. Found this nice little tree to protect my ass."

"I got news for you, pal," Kaplan said. "You ain't getting that big ass of yours behind a *little* tree."

"Can you two cut it out?" Cavalier groaned.

"Not a chance," he and Moss said in unison.

KC snickered behind him.

"Green light?" Kaplan asked Moss.

"Green light."

"Marshal, get up here, now."

It took her two minutes, but she climbed her way up to him. He stood outside the mouth of the cave until she reached him. "Glad you could make it."

"How's KC?"

He pointed behind him with his thumb. "Ask him yourself."

"KC, it's the marshal," she yelled. "I'm coming in."

She stuck her head in the cave where KC was propped up against the rock, his weapon trained at the opening. They talked for a few seconds and she promised to get him home safely.

"Movement above you," Moss whispered in the radio.

"How many?" Kaplan asked.

"I only see one, must be the father."

"Moss, get down," Cavalier yelled. "Stevie's a marksman with the long shot."

Just then a single gunshot ripped through the air. Sounded like a high-powered rifle. Kaplan heard a loud crack somewhere below him.

"Moss? Moss?" Cavalier yelled repeatedly.

"Shit, that was close," Moss said. "My little tree just saved my big ass."

"Moss," Kaplan said. "Get ready to run. Preferably, up the hill. We're going to need the help." He looked at KC. "We're leaving, you're on your own till we finish this."

KC straightened himself against the rock and readied his weapon.

"What are you going to do?" Cavalier asked Kaplan.

"You'll see." He reached inside his backpack and pulled out the last stick of dynamite.

"Guess we're going to see some fireworks," Moss said. "Tell me when."

"You'll know when, I promise you." He cut off most of the fuse with his pocket knife, dug around for his lighter, lit the fuse, and let it start burning down toward the stick of dynamite.

"Shouldn't you be throwing that thing?" Cavalier's eyes intense as she took a few steps away from Kaplan.

He held up a finger to tell her not yet. She kept a steady gaze on the burning wick and backed away a few more steps.

"Kaplan?"

No response.

She repeated louder, "Kaplan?"

Just as the burning wick was about to reach the blasting cap on the dynamite, he swung his arm out and tossed it over the ledge as hard as he could. Another shot rang out from Stevie's rifle. Then the dynamite detonated.

"Now," he shouted. "Run."

† † †

How quickly things had changed, the Cowboy thought, and in his favor.

He had just gotten word that Drew Pearson's fingerprints were found on the shell casings from the Branson and Stillwater farm murders. Even without the marshal's investigation, the evidence was finally discovered. That had taken some creative thinking to get Drew's fingerprints on those two casings. But, he managed and didn't get caught.

As if Drew hadn't already sealed his own fate, this would ensure he got the needle or perhaps the new Wyoming backup death penalty, the firing squad. Every way he looked at it, the kingpin land and cattle baron of northern Wyoming was no longer a factor. Whether he lived or died while on the lam, Drew Pearson would no longer have his way.

If for some unforeseen reason, Stevie Pearson was taken alive, he would join his father on death row. He was no longer a problem either.

Neither were Mark and Scott Pearson. They were the easiest pawns of all, so easy to manipulate. With a little persuasion, he had influenced them to open fire on the marshal and her posse as soon as they pulled into the ranch to arrest Stevie and Drew for blowing up the marshal's house. In no time, they were dead. Ironically, one of them at the hands of his own wife.

With either Drew and Stevie soon to be dead or locked up forever, that left Evan as the sole heir to the entire Pearson empire. He was different from the rest of his family. He had good business sense. It was well known that he had been handling all of Drew Pearson's finances for years. In some people's opinion, he was the only reason the Rocking P Ranch stayed solvent.

In retrospect, he probably could have accomplished his goal without going to so much trouble. This was his first time. He'd never killed anyone before. Growing up he would overhear his father and brothers, especially Stevie, talking about all the bad things they had done. He had to plan and execute this by himself. He actually got the idea for the murder ruse from reading an article about an unsolved mystery that happened up in Alberta, Canada many years ago. He used that information to devise his own plan to frame Drew Pearson for the murders of six people. The sons were no-brainers. All that remained now was to tidy up a few loose ends and let the system do its job.

Soon, the Rocking P Ranch, all the Pearson holdings would be his.

CHAPTER 55

Kaplan went left, Cavalier went right and joined Moss as the big man scurried up the hill. They disappeared behind a rock wall. The same rock he'd scaled earlier before KC got shot.

Kaplan was on the Dead Horse Creek side of the cabin now, not far from where he and KC were when the young deputy heard Pearson's horses over the rippling sounds of the mid-summer flow. He worked his way up the slope until he was even with the cabin and inched his way closer. He needed to find a way to assess the situation and formulate a plan of attack. Moss and Cavalier would be waiting to hear from him, until then, everyone was to maintain radio silence unless there was an overwhelming need to break it, like spotting one of the Pearsons.

He stayed below the ridge circumnavigating the cabin. Coming from behind the small barn might provide the best cover and easier access to the cabin. Getting there without being spotted was a problem. The Pearsons would be on high alert monitoring for any sign of movement. If Moss and Cavalier could remain out of sight until a plan of attack was ready to execute, they stood a chance against the Pearsons' firepower advantage and Stevie's sharp shooter ability. The Pearsons held the high ground, something he needed to change. Behind the cabin was a sheer cliff he guessed a good fifty feet high. It overlooked the cabin and barn. On top of the cliff was where he needed to be to give them all the advantage they needed to defeat Drew and Stevie. Like Moss said earlier, he wasn't a mountain goat, and neither was Kaplan.

His estimation of the location of the barn was dead on when he climbed from out of the woods at the cabin level. He came out behind the barn, like he planned, and could hear the horses getting nervous. They had detected his presence and might give away his position if they made too much noise. He was a hundred feet from the cabin itself, the air was still and quiet and the only sounds were the horses nervously pounding their hooves and the faint sounds of the gurgling creek below. The Pearsons had dug in, the big question was where? It was unlikely that they both retreated into the cabin knowing they could be pinned inside. No, one of the Pearsons had to be outside and on the move. He'd bet money it was Stevie. According to Evan, Stevie would stay up here for months at a time, so the demented man knew the lay of the land intimately. Advantage, Stevie Pearson. He had some sort of automatic weapon. Another advantage point for Stevie.

Kaplan eased in sight of the horses in hopes of calming them down, but he spooked the first one causing the horse to bump into the side of the barn making a loud bang. He ducked, expecting a shot to ring out, but none came. He was now staring at a side of the cabin he hadn't seen before and noticed there was a back door. Behind the cabin, an outhouse. How the hell that was dug through all this rock eluded him.

He spotted movement inside the cabin as a gun barrel protruded from one of the window shutter cracks. It was aimed at him. He jumped to his feet and ran laterally across the space between the barn and the cliff behind the cabin. Harder to hit a moving target moving side to side. Whoever was in the cabin tried, and got close with a couple of shots, but

Kaplan's serpentine running kept the shooter missing. When he made it behind the cabin, he held tight to the back-corner wall. Whoever was in the cabin, which by now he assumed was Drew, couldn't get a shot off at him without fully opening the shutters or coming out of the cabin to do it. Drew wasn't his main concern, Stevie was. Flush against the cabin wall exposed him and made him vulnerable. He broke radio silence and called in his position to Moss and Cavalier.

With Cavalier's 30-30, he kept scanning behind the cabin for any sign of danger. It was quiet, too quiet, and that made him nervous. He heard rustling on the opposite side of the cabin and observed the barrel of the gun disappear from the shutter slit beside him. He keyed his mic. "Cabin occupant moving cliff side," he whispered.

"Roger that," Moss answered back in a whisper. "We're on the wall, he can't get to us."

"Where's the other one?" Cavalier asked.

"Can't tell," Kaplan said. "That's what bothers me. One or all of us are sitting ducks. I think it's Drew inside, makes more sense. Stevie is out here somewhere."

Through the canopy of the trees, he saw a figure moving from left to right across the rocks roughly forty feet above him. It was Stevie and he had taken the higher ground. What he could see in Stevie's hands caused sweat to bead down his forehead. A Colt AR-15 with a bump stock.

He called it in to Moss and Cavalier and advised them to seek cover on the front wall of the cabin opposite the cliff wall. They were on their own. He wanted Stevie to himself. He took off running to his left because that had to be the direction Stevie had accessed the cliff.

He expected Stevie to fire on him, but no shot rang out.

† † †

As much as Cavalier hated to admit it, Kaplan executed his plan with precision. And he did so with no hesitation or second guessing. Somehow, he even had an innate ability to predict his enemies' behavior. It had served him well so far.

When he reported seeing Stevie on the cliff behind them, he took chase and told her and Moss to move to the front of the cabin. As long as they stayed next to the wall they were safe from Drew's gunfire. Keeping low, Cavalier and Moss moved along the wall, remaining below the window line. Standing to the side of the window, she saw no movement of the shutters. Maybe Drew had gone to the far side of the cabin to locate Kaplan.

She signaled Moss to follow. She kept her gun readied and raced around the corner of the front of the cabin. She froze. Her mouth fell open as she saw a shotgun barrel aimed at her head.

It was Drew Pearson and he had the drop on them both.

"Pearson," she muttered. "How did you…?"

He held up a walkie-talkie radio. "It helps to have one of these. Now, drop your weapons," he ordered. "And kick them to the side."

Moss lowered his Glock.

"No," she said as defiantly as she could muster. Fear tightened her chest making her take in short breaths to calm her hand. She didn't know if it was from anger or fear, or a combination of both. "Not this time, Pearson. This time you go to jail…or die."

Moss gave her a surprised look. She kept her gun trained on Drew.

"Always the defiant bitch, aren't you, Marshal? I'm not a patient man. Don't make me splatter your brains all over your friend here. Now, drop your goddamn weapon."

Moss' big hand slowly touched the barrel of her gun and pushed it down. "He's not worth dying for, Christine."

"Listen to the Deputy U. S. Marshal, Christine." Drew smirked.

She lowered her gun but kept her grip firm. "Pearson, you can't escape. Not after everything you've done. Not after you killed six innocent people."

"What are you talking about? I haven't killed anybody."

"We have proof." She explained, "Let's start with Richard and Stanley Branson. You murdered them, probably so you could take their property like you have so many others around Last Chance. You also killed Graham Stillwater, Frank Silverheels, Mark Leatherdale and Tony Mason up on the Rez."

"What the hell makes you think I killed all those people?"

"You were careless Pearson, you left your prints on the shell casings found at the murder scenes. Shell casings that came from the gun that killed five of those six men. Ballistics in Sheridan has confirmed it."

"You're lying. I had nothing to do with those murders and there's no way my prints were on any shell casings. What would be my motive? The Branson farm is worthless land. The only thing on the Branson farm is a creek that runs onto my property. I have two other creeks to draw from. As far as Stillwater is concerned, Graham Stillwater has been a close friend of mine for many years. Hell, he was best man at my wedding for Christ's sake. I have no reason to want him dead." He pushed the shotgun barrel closer to her head. "You, on the other hand, have been nothing but a pain in my ass since you arrived in Last Chance two years ago. You, I do want dea—"

A shot rang out and Drew Pearson buckled at the waist. A dark red plume opened in his lower torso. His eyes grew big and she could see the disbelief wash across his face. He dropped the shotgun and slumped to the ground.

She and Moss spun at the same time searching for where the shot originated. Somehow KC had managed to crawl from the cave, leg splint and all, to the cabin level with his .30-06. He took the shot. And saved her life.

She motioned for Moss to go help KC get in the clear. "Pearson, why did you do it? Why did you kill all those people?"

He coughed. Blood spewed from his mouth when he tried to speak. "Not me, Marshal." He coughed a small laugh. "I told you, you're no good at your job." He grimaced.

Blood poured from his wound like a red Artesian well. KC's rifle tore a massive hole in Pearson's body. There was no way to get him help. He was going to die.

"I admit, I tried to kill you, but I had nothing to do with the others." He grabbed her arm with his bloody hand and drew her closer. "Mark and Scott, are they…?"

"They're both dead. Looks like you weren't a very good father."

The Pearson boys were just like their father. No good. Only Evan had escaped the evil influence of this man lying on the ground dying. She wanted to see justice done. But Drew Pearson was never going to prison. She only wished she'd been the one to pull the trigger, not KC.

When Pearson heard the news of Mark and Scott, he let his head fall to the ground. "It was only a matter of…time. It's…better…this way." His breathing was labored, and he struggled to speak.

"If you didn't do it Pearson, who killed the Bransons?" she asked.

"Stevie is a sick man. He…needs…help."

"Did Stevie kill the Bransons?"

A shot rang out from the cliff behind the cabin. A man screamed. She knew it was Stevie.

Pearson's face turned to sadness. A look of realization and resignation stared up at her. "Pearson," she said. "Tell me who killed the Bransons."

He took a short breath, released her arm, and his head fell to one side.

Drew Pearson was dead.

† † †

The trail to the top of the cliff was easy to see. It was well used by someone, probably Stevie, and offered unlimited views over the prairie below. Kaplan could see why someone would want to come up here and sit or read or just stare out at the majesty of this part of the country. It was peaceful and beautiful. It was Stevie Pearson's downfall. A promontory rock with only the one trail on or off, and he was on it. Stevie was trapped, a critical mistake on his part.

He traversed the path across the rock until he came to a split, one path up to the peak of the promontory, the other a lower trail to a lower ledge. When he saw Stevie through the canopy of the trees, Stevie was on the lower trail. Kaplan's turn to take the high ground. The younger Pearson was planning on picking off his pursuers one at a time. Little did he know Kaplan was above him and had the high ground advantage.

Kaplan was ten feet above Stevie and about ten feet behind. He yelled a warning, "Stevie, don't move. Drop the rifle."

Stevie instinctively swung his rifle toward Kaplan. "Who are you?" he shouted. A shot rang out from below making Stevie focus his attention downhill to the cabin.

Kaplan didn't know who shot who, but that shot sounded like a rifle, not a handgun. "Stevie, I have the advantage, now drop your rifle."

"I won't go alive."

"It doesn't have to end this way," he said, but he knew the outcome. It was inevitable, just like Evan had warned. Stevie wanted to go in a blaze of glory.

Stevie swung around, the barrel of his gun still lowered and squinted at Kaplan. Stevie's chest was in Kaplan's sights.

His Delta motto came to mind—*Two in the chest, one in the head works 100% of the time.*

He stared down on Stevie and could see the look in the crazed man's eyes.

He pulled the slack out of his trigger.

"Don't do it."

Stevie made his move, raising his rifle. Kaplan squeezed the trigger and Stevie's chest erupted in a spray of blood. The AR-15 flew from Stevie's hands as he and his rifle plummeted off the cliff. He would never need his other two shots. One in the chest was all it took.

"That was for Doug."

CHAPTER 56

Both Kaplan and Moss had to help KC mount the horse for the ride down from Devil's Gulch to Cavalier's Bronco.

"Thank you, Kaplan. You saved my life," said KC.

"No problem, KC. It was a tough fight. You're a good deputy," said Kaplan.

"Not today. I failed to remember something my grandfather once told me."

"What's that?"

"He said, 'Listen to the whispers and you will not have to hear the screams.'"

"Sounds like a wise man," Moss chimed in.

"Yes. But today, I was just looking, not listening so the white man snuck up on me."

Cavalier took the reins of the horse with the two dead bodies draped across it and led the way down the mountain. Moss hurried and fell in beside her. KC followed on his horse and Kaplan took up the rear march.

During the arduous two-hour descent from Devil's Gulch, through Black Canyon, and across the meadow to Cavalier's white Bronco, Kaplan admired the beauty of the area. He was glad this fight with the Pearsons was over. And he was glad the people he cared about were safe. Something still wasn't right, he could feel it, but what was it?

KC had told him what his grandfather said, "Listen to the whispers."

The whispers in Kaplan's head were more like screams. And they were screaming that he had missed something. But what?

Who stood to gain and who stood to lose?

The wildcards in all of this were the deaths at the Stillwater farm on the Crow Reservation and their connection to the deaths on the Branson farm. The only clear connection was that the same weapon was used in both crimes, a .38. As Cavalier had briefed him when she and Moss arrived, Sheridan County Sheriff Knight left her a message with Lucy that forensics identified prints on the shell casings found at the Branson farm as belonging to Drew Pearson. Lucy sent Cavalier that information in a text message. Sounded like an open and shut case, but it just didn't ring true. Drew Pearson stood too much to lose to be directly linked to the killings even if he did want the Bransons and Stillwater dead. These crimes didn't ring true. They didn't have Drew Pearson written all over them. The end game was something entirely different. He could see that. He could feel it. Someone else was mastermind of this scheme and using Cavalier to do their dirty work.

The Branson murders and the murders at the Stillwater farm just muddied the waters. Then, it occurred to him, if those two crime scenes were removed from the scenario altogether, there was one, and only one, clear benefactor in all of this. He remembered when he took Evan outside the police station and talked to him. He was surprised how easily Evan gave up his family. Sure, the young Pearson son was hesitant at first to rat on his father, but just like that, the floodgates opened. Like the conversation had been rehearsed, planned. Kaplan heard it and dismissed it. He hadn't listened to the whispers. He had fallen for the mastermind's lies.

Where was Evan?

He needed to get off this mountain fast and back to town.

† † †

Lucy had been intrigued reading Cavalier's investigation notes. What was the point now? Sheriff Knight called with definitive proof that Evan's father killed the Bransons and the people on the Rez.

Why was that not sitting right with her? She listened to Evan and Jesse talking in the main room for what seemed like hours. She had hoped to hear from the marshal or Kaplan, but so far nothing. Evan must have seen her looking, he smiled. She smiled back. She couldn't see Jesse.

It was so strange, she liked Evan, but not like before. She now regretted sleeping with him. Why her feelings had changed toward him, she wasn't sure? She had always felt sorry for Evan. His family was one screwed up bunch of people. Two of his brothers were dead, another brother and his father on the run from the law. One for murder and both for attempted murder. How was it that he was spared all the bad genes and got only the good ones?

Lucy scanned Cavalier's notes. *Why would someone want the Branson farm?* she had written. That was a good question. She logged onto the marshal's computer and did a database records search on the Sheridan County Assessor's website. She entered Richard Branson's name in the search bar. No results. She entered Stanley Branson in the search bar. No results. Whose name was the farm under, she wondered? She found the map feature and located the Branson farm parcel. It was actually two parcels, one 500-acre tract and one 1152-acre tract.

She clicked on one land parcel and found no mention of the Bransons as current owner. That was odd, she thought. She clicked on the other parcel and found the same thing. On both property records L. C. Enterprises, Inc. was listed as the current owner. Richard Branson had sold the two tracts to L. C. Enterprises, Inc. over a year ago. Who the heck was that?

It was curious that the Bransons still lived on a farm they had sold nearly a year ago. Who would buy a big farm and let someone else live on it for a year?

She decided to do a Google search.

She started typing her internet searches. Nothing showed up under L. C. Enterprises, Inc. She tried all variations, with and without spaces, with and without periods, and still nothing. She heard Jesse and Evan get into some sort of heated discussion, but she was focused and tuned them out.

Maybe L.C. stood for Last Chance. She did another search. Search results listed Last Chance Enterprises, Inc. as a Delaware incorporated company, established one month prior to the acquisition of the Branson farm. The mailing address was listed as a Last Chance Post Office box number.

She clicked on *Shareholders*. There was one.

The page loaded, and she saw it. The single shareholder for Last Chance Enterprises, Inc. was Evan Pearson.

How could that be? And why? Realization of the ramifications set in fast as her find could mean only one thing. Oh my God, could Evan Pearson have murdered the Bransons and everyone on the Stillwater farm? Why would he do that, she asked herself? He was sitting in the other room with Jesse acting like nothing had ever happened. If he was the killer, then she and Jesse were in danger.

The phone rang and startled her. She jumped. *Get it together.*

She answered. It was the marshal.

"We're on the way in," the marshal said. "We'll see you in a few minutes. How's it going there?"

She didn't know how to answer. She needed to tell her that she figured out that Evan was the killer, not his father, that Evan was in the office, and she and Jesse were in danger. But if she did, Evan might hear. She glanced up, Evan was looking at her.

"Lucy? Is everything all right?" Cavalier asked.

"Yes."

"Can I speak to Jesse?"

"No."

"What?" Lucy had to pull the receiver from her ear because the marshal was so loud. "Why not?"

"Not here," Lucy replied.

"What do you mean he's not there? I gave him specific orders not to leave until we got back?"

"You think you know some people," Lucy said. "But you don't." Lucy hung up the phone without another word.

When she lifted her eyes, Evan was standing in the doorway to the office. She scrolled the cursor and closed her active web browser.

"What are you doing?" he asked.

She saw the expression on his face. She knew he knew. She stood and tried to pretend she was ignorant to her revelation. "About to come in there with you two."

† † †

Evan leaned over and powered off the computer. "My father was right about you, you don't listen." He grabbed her arm and twisted it behind her back.

"Jesse, help," she cried out.

He pulled out his pocketknife, whipped it open, and held the blade to her throat. He pushed her in front of him as he heard Jesse moving toward the office. Jesse had already drawn his weapon. He held Lucy between them. "Put it down, Jesse." He pressed the blade against Lucy's skin and she screamed.

"Do it now. Place it on your desk and step away." He used his hold on Lucy's arm to guide her into the big room. "You don't want her blood on your hands, do you?"

Jesse eased back. "What are you doing, Evan?"

"Dammit, Jesse. Put the gun on the desk and step away. I won't say it again."

Jesse followed his orders. Evan walked Lucy toward the desk until Jesse's gun was within arm's reach then he shoved her at Jesse while grabbing his gun. He aimed it at Lucy. "Take his cuffs and put them on him…hands in the back."

She hesitated.

He raised the gun. "Do it now, Lucy, or I'll just shoot him. And you too."

Lucy clamped the cuffs on Jesse while he watched. He checked them to make sure she wasn't trying to pull a fast one by not securing them tight around his wrists.

"How could you?" Lucy's voice sounded defiant. "Did you kill the Bransons?"

"You don't understand, Lucy. I did it for Last Chance. Nobody knew what was on that land. It was my opportunity to put Last Chance on the map. The Bransons were stupid pig farmers. They didn't know what they had, but I did. I bought his farm and told Richard that he and Stanley could live there rent free for a year, or until they found someplace else. I paid him twice what he paid for that property. Stanley figured out why I bought it and then they said they would not leave my property and would take me to court. I couldn't let that happen."

"What are you talking about?" she asked.

"Cordierite."

"Rocks?" she yelled. "You killed all those people for rocks?"

"Not just rocks, enough Cordierite to make the whole state of Wyoming rich. Not just Teton County. And it's all on the Branson land and my father's land. Enough to make everyone in Sheridan County multi-millionaires. I found one boulder when I was rock hounding that was nearly 30,000 carats...gem quality stones of that size would rake in over a million dollars apiece. And that was a small one. But, that damn Stanley came out while I was rock hounding and saw what I was digging up. I told him it was worthless and that I just thought it was a cool looking rock, but he went home and researched it. Then he and his father knew why I bought the farm from them and threatened to sue me."

"You killed all those people for rocks? I cannot believe of all people, you would do that."

"Well, believe it Lucy. And I'll kill anyone who gets in my way."

He continued, "You know, most people only think of Wyoming as oil, coal, gas, and wind, but this state has the most diverse collection of documented gems of any state in the U. S. Anywhere from gold, diamonds, jasper, opal, platinum nuggets, ruby, sapphire, and a lot more. This should be the Gem State, not Idaho."

"What about your father? How did his prints get on the shell casings? Did he help you?"

"Two prints, two shell casings. No Lucy, he's too stupid to help. Besides, if he knew what I was doing, he would have tried to take what was rightfully mine. I discovered the Cordierite, I bought the land, and I'm going to mine it. This is my fortune. I will make this town rich, this county rich, and this state rich. This town will name buildings and parks after me. I wasn't going to live in my father's shadow any longer."

"Why your father's prints? Why kill all those people on the Stillwater farm?"

"Simple. If I framed my father, he'd be locked up for good. No court would ever acquit him on that evidence. It was a slam dunk conviction. I run the Rocking P Ranch finances. My brothers were never going to do anything good like me. Look at the trouble Mark and Scott got into when they saw your friend Kaplan ride into town. Those two idiots did all that without me even having to incite them. You see where it got them. When my father and Stevie came into town to kill the marshal, I told Mark and Scott that his orders were for them to kill anyone who came on the property. I was the honest, good son, so they never questioned anything I ever told them. And Stevie, he's just not right. You know that. When I was small, he killed our family dog. Once he made me watch him disembowel a goat. He enjoyed it. That's why we don't have dogs or cats or goats. He killed them all."

"Why did you kidnap me and why did Stevie kill Doug? He did not even have his gun drawn."

"My father wanted to scare you, so Stevie and I came to get you. I told Stevie that Doug had a thing for you, but that I wanted you for myself. Stevie knew how much I liked you. He was going to kill Doug sooner or later. You see, it just all worked out for me. It worked out for us."

CHAPTER 57

Kaplan and Moss had loaded the bodies of Drew and Stevie Pearson into the back of Cavalier's Bronco. For the first time, he felt dog-tired. Kaplan had been up and moving since yesterday morning, but so had everyone else in the car. It had been a long four days since he first rode into Last Chance. He saw a car full of weary faces.

Moss was in the back seat and not happy about the arrangements. Kaplan figured his friend had rather have the marshal's company instead of the two dead bodies behind him. He needed to discuss his suspicions with Cavalier before they got back to the police station.

He walked Cavalier through his gnawing revelations about Evan Pearson. She was still having difficulty accepting his theory. In his mind, this was no longer a theory, this was fact. Evan Pearson instigated everything that had happened, and in his opinion, had been planning it for a long time. Of course, he had no concrete proof, which seemed to be all Cavalier was interested in at the moment. He didn't understand Cavalier's reluctance to accept that it was Evan and not his father, Drew Pearson, who was behind the Branson murders. He didn't blame her, if anyone had cause to despise Drew Pearson, it was Christine Cavalier.

She dropped him off at his motorcycle still parked on the county road where he left it last night before he sneaked into the Pearson compound in pursuit of Drew and Stevie after they bombed Cavalier's home. As she regained cell service,

Cavalier notified Sheriff Knight and explained everything that had happened at Devil's Gulch and requested he send the coroner and an ambulance to meet them at the entrance to the Pearson property.

Kaplan and Moss compared leg wound notes with KC while they were coming out of the mountains in an attempt to keep him in good spirits. He seemed afraid he might lose his leg, but both of them assured KC that it would take a much worse wound than he had to cause him to lose his leg. Of course, they had both lied, but KC didn't need to know that. Their ruse seemed to work, and by the time they reached the ambulance, KC was already talking about his next fly fishing trip.

Kaplan followed Cavalier to the entrance to the Pearson ranch. The ambulance and coroner's van were waiting when they arrived. Davidson, the Sheridan County Coroner took the Pearsons' bodies and the ambulance took KC and headed to Sheridan General Hospital. While she waited for them to load KC in the ambulance and the bodies in the van, Cavalier called her office.

She had a peculiar look about her when she disconnected the call. "That was odd," she said to Kaplan. "Lucy said Jesse was gone. And after I gave him specific instructions to wait until we got back."

"That is weird," Moss said.

"You think you know some people," Kaplan said.

"What did you just say?" Cavalier snapped.

"You think you know some people," he repeated. "But you don't."

"That's exactly what Lucy just said to me. Word for word."

"Oh shit, we gotta go."

Kaplan gunned his bike as he led the way back to town. He stopped his bike next to the curb in front of the Last Chance Police Department sign while Cavalier parked her Bronco on the side of the building where she normally parked. The building was locked, so he waited.

When Cavalier and Moss arrived, he motioned to the door. "Got a key?"

"It's locked?" she asked.

"Yes."

"Not good."

All three of them drew their weapons.

She held up a key ring still holding the key to her Bronco between her fingers. She inserted the key twisted it and pushed. "Deadbolt's locked, too."

She shoved the door open and all three of them trained their weapons inside. Over Cavalier's shoulder Kaplan saw Jesse and Lucy, side by side, with Evan behind. He had one arm wrapped around Lucy's neck, using her as a human shield and holding a gun to her head.

"Let them go," Cavalier shouted at Evan.

"Or what, you going to shoot all of us? Kill Lucy and your deputy? I don't think so." He made Jesse close the gap between him and Lucy using them both as human shields. "Now, I'm pretty sure you're a really good shot, but do you think you can pick me off behind these two? Will you risk shooting a bullet between them to get to me. I mean, that's all of like an inch, don't you think? Come in, close the door, and lock it."

No one moved.

"Now Marshal, why don't you and your posse do as I

say?" He pressed the gun barrel harder against Lucy's head and she shrieked. "Do it now," he demanded.

Cavalier, Moss, and Kaplan moved inside the police station. Cavalier locked the door behind them.

"Good. Now Marshal, remove your weapon and walk to Doug's desk."

Cavalier eyed Kaplan and she followed Evan's instructions.

"Very good. Now remove the magazine and clear the round from the chamber."

She did as he instructed.

"Okay, are those all of your weapons? Raise your arms and turn around."

She complied.

"Marshal, stand over there by the jail room door. You, Deputy U. S. Marshal, your turn. Same thing. All your weapons on the table and emptied."

Moss looked at Kaplan and he gave his friend a subtle nod. Moss followed suit, stepped over and stood next to Cavalier.

"You," Evan said. "Mr. Kaplan, now it's your turn. Same routine except don't empty your weapon."

Kaplan placed his Beretta on the desk. He took off his jacket and removed a Glock from behind his back and placed it on the desk as well. He raised his arms and spun around. "Satisfied?"

"For now I am. Go join your friends."

As he walked toward Moss and Cavalier, he noticed Evan relax and expose more of his head and body.

"Mr. Kaplan, I must thank you for all you've done. Your presence in our little town got the ball rolling even better than

I could have ever planned. At this point, with you here and no prisoners, I must assume you've killed Stevie and my father. Too bad about KC. Who got him? My father? No, probably Stevie, he always was good with a rifle. No loss, right? Just another featherhead."

Lucy's eyes welled up and tears rolled down her cheeks.

"It's a shame that you all have to die." He side-stepped to the desk keeping eye contact with Kaplan, while still holding Lucy in front of him. He put Jesse's gun on the desk and picked up the Beretta in one continuous motion and then jammed the barrel of Kaplan's Beretta against Lucy's head. "A stranger comes to town and goes on a killing spree. That's what you're going to be famous for, Kaplan."

"You know you're a dead man, right?" Kaplan said. "I don't see any scenario where you get out of this alive. Not now, not after everything that has happened and everything you have done."

He pushed Jesse clear, but held Lucy tight. "Join them," he said. "All of you, in the jail room."

Cavalier led the way followed closely by Moss. Kaplan let Jesse go next and stood in the doorway. "Evan, I'm going to enjoy killing you."

"Is that so tough guy?" He pulled the gun barrel away from Lucy's head and aimed it at Kaplan. "I'd like to see you try."

Kaplan stared Lucy in the eyes. "It'll be okay," he said with a wink. "Go join the others. It's all over now."

She took two steps toward where Moss was standing, and Kaplan said, "Times up."

Moss dove, knocking Cavalier, Jesse, and Lucy to the ground.

Evan flinched, then fired.

Kaplan rotated sideways, grabbing Evan's gun with his left hand and jerked the youngest Pearson toward him. With his right hand cupped on the guns' grip, he twisted Evan's wrist inward, hard and fast, until it snapped. Evan's knees started to buckle. Kaplan kept pressing until the gun slipped free of Evan's grip and into his own hand. He side-kicked Evan's leg and felled him to the ground. Evan's face looked surprised as he clearly had no idea what had just happened, but Kaplan showed no mercy.

Three shots.

Point blank range.

Two in the chest.

One in the head.

CHAPTER 58

It took two days before anyone was allowed to leave Last Chance.

Each was questioned numerous times by several law enforcement agencies from all levels, including the Sheriff of Sheridan County, Wyoming Division of Criminal Investigation, FBI and, on account of Moss' involvement, the United States Marshals Service.

The kicker for the investigators was the damaging testimonies of Lucy and Jesse of what Evan had confessed in front of them.

Wyoming DCI contacted a geologist to verify Evan's discovery of Cordierite. His assessment verified that massive amounts of the gem existed on the two properties, but nothing of the monetary value that Evan had described. However, it was substantial enough to make many people extremely wealthy if mined correctly. As it turned out, some of those people were Drew Pearson's brothers who lived in Kentucky and Idaho and sister in Arizona. They became the apparent heirs of Drew Pearson's holdings. The property of the Rocking P Ranch held only a small amount of the Cordierite. The bulk was on the property Evan Pearson bought from Richard Branson in what had been ruled by the courts as a legitimate business deal conducted over a year prior. Investigators found a Last Will and Testament belonging to Evan Pearson in his Post Office box naming the Town of Last Chance as the sole beneficiary of his property.

At the request of the mayor, the town council voted unanimously to retain Christine Cavalier as town marshal if she wanted to stay. Kaplan was surprised she didn't jump on the offer. She told them she would let them know by the end of the week. Cavalier said that after this she wasn't sure she even wanted to stay in law enforcement. Maybe she would leave it altogether like Jesse did. When investigators told Jesse he was free to leave, he placed his badge and weapon on Cavalier's desk and walked out without saying another word. He didn't need to. His face said it all. He'd seen enough killing.

Kaplan was relieved Jesse turned in his badge. Some people just don't have what it takes for law enforcement. KC on the other hand, was a good cop. One of the caveats Cavalier laid on the town council if she stayed was to hire KC full time and allow her to hire another full-time deputy as well. It wasn't like the town of Last Chance couldn't afford to do it any longer. She wanted new vehicles for herself and her deputies. And, a complete remodel of the police department building. Or better yet, a new building. After she gave her demands to the council, Kaplan figured she wasn't exactly on the fence about staying any longer.

The doctors at Sheridan General Hospital released KC the next day. He was lucky. The bullet did not ricochet off bone like Kaplan thought, but had caused muscle damage. His quadriceps sustained the damage, but not enough to be crippling. He was told to expect some long-term physical therapy and a limp. He swore he would exercise his leg until the limp was gone.

Moss called a buddy at the Chicago United States Marshals Service office and had him date and deliver his already signed retirement papers to Human Resources. When HR inquired, he told them his retirement was effective immediately. His plans were to hang out in Last Chance until Cavalier made her decision.

When Kaplan asked Moss about Cavalier, Moss simply said, "When you meet a woman like Christine, you gotta try to make it work."

After the investigators left town, Kaplan and Lucy met Moss and Cavalier at the Sunset Mountain Bar to watch the famous sunset that Cavalier had bragged about. While Lucy ordered a Shirley Temple, he ordered Moss and himself a beer. "Marshal, name your poison," he said.

She looked up at the barmaid and said, "I'll have whatever they're drinking."

"This is a new town now, Christine." Kaplan took a swig of his beer. "It's your town now."

She clasped her hands on the table top. The way she examined him made him think of Isabella.

"You don't mind if I call you Christine, do you?"

"Kaplan, you can call my anything you want. I owe you that much and so much more."

"Give me the one thing I came here to get."

She leaned back in her chair and gazed out the window to the west. "We have the prettiest sunsets in this part of the country that I've ever seen. A month ago, the sun would have set in the middle of that canyon."

"Did you just dodge my question?"

Moss said, "I think she did."

Lucy giggled. "Yeah, she did."

"Kaplan, I made a promise years ago to Isabella. If I tell you what you want to know, I'll have broken a promise to my sister. Do you know what it's like to go back on your word?"

"More than you'll ever know."

"That's how I met him," Moss injected. "Because he had made a promise and refused to break it."

Cavalier didn't say anything. He could tell she went introspective. He did know what it was like to break a promise. He'd done it once and it had cost someone their life.

"I do understand," he said. "And I won't push you anymore. If you ever see fit to tell me, you know where to find me."

"Actually Kaplan, I don't."

He grinned at Moss. "He does."

They talked for another hour until it seemed no one had anything else to say to each other. Moss had started flirting with Cavalier again and he could see by her eyes she was falling for him. Maybe they could make a relationship work…at least for a while anyway.

The clock on the wall above the bar said it was time to leave. He stood and pushed back his chair. "Lucy girl, we have an early start time tomorrow. Let's let these two have at it."

She giggled again and stood. She gave Cavalier a hug and one to Moss. While the three of them exchanged goodbyes and good lucks, Kaplan walked to the door and waited. Cavalier said something to Lucy and strolled over to him. Cavalier hugged him and stood back extending her hand. During the handshake, she slipped a piece of paper in his hand. "I owe you this Kaplan. Isabella should have told you herself." She let her head drop, then lifted it. There were tears welling in her eyes. "I have to warn you, it's not at all what you think."

He slipped the paper in the back pocket of his jeans. "Thank you."

She reached and squeezed his arm tight. "And it won't

be easy."

She walked back to Moss.

† † †

The next morning, he loaded all of his bags and the few possessions Lucy had on the back of his motorcycle. They met Poppy when he opened the Last Chance Diner at 5:30 a.m. and ordered a big breakfast for a long day on the road. After they ate, he situated Lucy on the rider's seat of his Harley and left Last Chance behind them. They rode hard and long and fast with Lucy's arms tight around his waist. She seemed to enjoy the ride for the first four or five hours, then she started squirming behind him.

She had asked him numerous times where he was taking her, but he dodged the question. Kind of like Cavalier did to him last night. When they stopped for fuel, they got food and took a bathroom break at the same time. He had never had children and believed he never would, but if he did, he hoped she would be like Lucy. They had both been through a lot and a lot together. He just hoped she would understand when they arrived at their destination and not be too angry with him. It wasn't a trick he planned, but an opportunity. For her. Her chance to never again be a crab in a bucket. Her chance to get off the street and make a promising life for herself. Never be homeless again. Never have to do without again. Another chance, a last chance for a better life.

Fourteen hours later, he rode into a hotel in Kayenta, Arizona in the heart of the Navajo Reservation.

"Why did you bring me here?"

"Let's get a bite to eat, then I'll explain everything."

While they were eating, two Native Americans approached. "Mr. Kaplan, I presume," said the elder.

"Yes. And this is Lucy."

"Lucy, it is nice to meet you. I am Chief Joshua Brightwater, I knew your grandfather well. We were friends for many years." He acknowledged the man standing next to him. "This is Mike Logan, he works for BIA, Bureau of Indian Affairs. As a favor to Mr. Kaplan, I had Mr. Logan locate your Certificate of Degree of Indian Blood." He handed her a large envelope. "Mr. Kaplan has made all the financial arrangements for you to go to the college of your choice, it is up to you to qualify. I do not know what strings he pulled, but it appears your acceptance is a given if you can pass the entrance exams. He assures me you are smart enough to do so. What financial assistance you get with the American Indian College Fund and federal grants will be supplemented by Mr. Kaplan's source. You will not have any expenses whatsoever. No tuition, books, lab fees, or living expenses. One hundred percent coverage of everything, regardless of degree." The chief paused. "Lucy Raintree, this is not an opportunity most Natives ever get. Are you interested?"

She looked at him and he could tell she was bewildered. "You did all this?"

"I made a few calls, got the ball rolling," he said. "The rest is up to you. What do you say, Lucy? The Chief needs an answer."

"Will I ever see you again?"

"Absolutely. I'll be coming around to make sure you keep up those grades."

She buried her face in his chest.

"Lucy?" the Chief asked.

"Yes, of course, I am interested. I will do whatever I must." She faced Kaplan. "I do not know how to thank you. Nobody has ever been as nice to me before as you have. Nobody has ever cared. You saved my life more than once and now this. You do not have to do this."

"You're right. I don't have to, I want to. Sometimes all we need is another chance. I wanted to give you that chance. And Lucy, you can thank me by making good grades and staying in school."

Lucy sobbed as she hugged him tight.

As Lucy walked away with Chief Brightwater and the man from the Bureau of Indian Affairs, he felt proud…and sad. Proud of how far the young Lucy Raintree had come in less than a week's time and sad to be leaving her behind. But for him, there was unfinished business to attend to.

He reached into his back pocket and pulled out the folded piece of paper Cavalier had given him. Could this finally be it? The answer he'd been in search of for so long? He cautiously unwrapped the folds of paper for the first time as if expecting something to jump out at him at any moment.

And there it was. Another clue. Another lead. Or could this finally be the end?

He stared at the words Cavalier had written and he remembered her warning.

It was simply an address.

In Grass Lake, Michigan.

EPILOGUE

Mid-September
Grass Lake, Michigan

He stared at the red brick home and wondered what kind of reception he would receive. Welcome, not welcome, what would it be? Although the ride from Kayenta, Arizona to Grass Lake, Michigan was only 24 hours, it took him a month and a half to get to this point. Not because there was someplace else to go or from being side-tracked along the way, but because of the warning Cavalier gave him in Last Chance.

"It's not at all what you think," she had said. "And it won't be easy."

What wouldn't be easy? Had she found someone else? Was she dead?

So many possibilities rolled through his brain and he contemplated them the way he liked to best, by simply riding. Peace and solitude was what he needed until the time was right to confront his destiny. If this was indeed his destiny or just another dead-end. Or another clue that led to another clue that led to yet another clue. The continuation of his endless journey. Or was Cavalier telling him the truth? Was this finally the end of his search for Isabella Hunt?

He had never been one to put off what needed to be done, but this time, he just couldn't rush it. As much as he thought he was, he realized he wasn't ready to know the truth. Not yet, so he kept riding. He rode thousands of miles. State after state after state. And bad luck and trouble had not found him since he left Last Chance.

He toured national parks and state parks and avoided cities and crowds. This was his time for introspection. His time to sort out all the possible scenarios surrounding Isabella's mysterious disappearance and what his response to each might be. He even journeyed home, to Tyson Corner, Virginia, where he worked on his bike, took care of those pesky details that come with life, and prepared for his journey to Michigan. He touched base with his employer, the CIA, and got the same song and dance. *Don't call us, we'll call you.*

He called his old friend, Pete Moss, and chatted for quite a while. Moss spent two more weeks in Last Chance before returning to Chicago. He seemed content with his decision to retire from the United States Marshals Service. He said it was time to *reinvent* himself, he just didn't know what that looked like yet. He was still toying with the idea of private investigation. Moss told him Cavalier kept her job as town marshal and the town council agreed to all her demands. He said she was leaving KC in charge and taking a well-deserved vacation, in of all places, Chicago. Moss sounded happy, and for that, Kaplan was glad. Maybe Moss and Cavalier could make it work, but long-distance relationships were difficult to survive.

He received a text message from Lucy in early August, only two weeks after he left her on the Navajo Reservation. She had passed her GED with high scores, and through some Native American string pulling by Chief Brightwater, had been admitted to Arizona State University in Tempe, Arizona. She was in the accelerated degree format for a Bachelor Degree in Criminology and Criminal Justice. She had a knack for it, he thought, and should do well. Their paths would cross again soon.

Maybe.

He reached in his back pocket again and unfolded the paper Cavalier had given him. The address matched. It was now or never.

He pulled in the driveway, parked his bike and walked to the front door. The woman in the home who had watched him through her front window greeted him before he could knock.

"Danni said you were coming. I must admit, I expected you a month ago," she said. "Please come in." She held the door open.

Danni, he remembered was Isabella's nickname for her sister, Christine, short for Danielle.

He stepped across the threshold and entered. The woman had shoulder length brown hair cut in a bob. She stuck out her hand. "I'm Clara and you are Gregg Kaplan. Danni described you to a tee."

"Pleasure to meet you."

She waved him off. "Follow me," she said, and they walked down a hallway that opened into the kitchen. "Isabella and Danni grew up next door." She pointed. "One house over. I live here."

The kitchen opened to a large sunroom filled with hanging plants and a potted tree in a corner. A couch with lots of colorful cushions on one side of the room and two wicker chairs were stationed across from it. Through the open windows he saw a screened gazebo in the backyard. He noticed the shaded silhouette of a woman in the gazebo, a ceiling fan slowly whirling above her head. His pulse ignited. She had to be Isabella.

"Is that—?" he started to ask.

"Let's sit first," she said. "May I offer you something to drink?"

"No, thank you. I'm fine."

He moved to the back window and stared across the yard at the woman in the gazebo. It was Isabella, he would recognize her anywhere.

"Please. Mr. Kaplan. Have a seat and let's have a chat." She waved her hand to one of the wicker chairs. Behind the chair was the largest Christmas cactus he had ever seen.

"I'll get right to the point, Mr. Kaplan. What do you know about cerebral aneurysm?"

"Basically nothing, I guess. I know an aneurysm is a thinned and bulging vein or artery. I know it's a bad thing if it bursts. Is that—?" He stared again at the woman in the gazebo.

Clara interrupted, "It's an abnormal focal dilation of an artery in the brain that results from the weakening of the inner muscular layer of the blood vessel wall."

"That sounds very clinical."

"I'm a nurse, so yes, it sounds clinical because it's a clinical explanation. One I think you need to understand before you go outside."

He wasn't sure what he was feeling inside right now. Confusion mixed with fear. The woman in the gazebo was rocking back and forth in a chair.

"The vessel," Clara explained, "develops a dilation that can thin and rupture without warning. Bleeding from the rupture in the space around the brain is called a subarachnoid hemorrhage. It can lead to stroke, coma, or death."

His insides felt weak and unsettled as the wave swept

through him. "Is that what…?" He couldn't finish his question.

"While you and Isabella were together she started getting headaches so severe she was weak and had vision issues."

"I remember, but I thought that was a result from being held captive and beaten in Yemen," he said.

"No, those were her warning signs of an aneurysm. After she was diagnosed, she struggled with the decision about telling you. In the end, she decided against it. She didn't want you burdened with her recovery."

"That's not fair to me. She should have given me a choice."

"Of course, you would think that, but this was her problem to deal with any way she saw fit." Clara paused. "Her aneurysm was located in a part of the brain where surgery was very risky. And most surgeons deemed it inoperable. But, a doctor in Belgium had developed a new experimental treatment that was having good results, so she flew overseas for a consultation. While she was there, her aneurysm breached and the doctors informed Danni that Isabella needed immediate surgery or she could die. Danni consented."

"What happened?"

"The surgery saved her life. She was in a coma for a couple of months."

"What does that mean?"

"To make a very complex explanation short, there were complications during surgery and Isabella lost much of her memory. Her long-term memory seems to be mostly intact with the small exception of a few holes here and there, like the deaths of her parents, but she remembers me, and she remembers Danni. She even remembers my husband, Jerry."

"What's her long-term prognosis?"

"She's stable. Her aneurysm repair is still intact, and she goes in for regular checkups and scans. She can remember things after you tell her, although she might not have any memory of the actual events. It's like a black hole in her memory." She stood. "Let me show you something."

She took him to Isabella's bedroom. "Isabella lives here now. With me and Jerry."

The walls were covered with pictures, written on the pictures were names and dates. There was a picture of him on her dresser. He stepped over to the dresser and picked it up. It was a picture of him and Isabella several years ago, before she was captured in Yemen, standing in front of the Washington Monument. Kaplan swallowed hard. His thoughts of the memory made him long to recapture that moment.

"Danni mailed that to Isabella a month ago. That was a difficult decision for her. Isabella made us promise never to tell you if something happened to her. But yet, here you are."

"Can I see her?"

"Yes. Go on out, I'll join you shortly." He started to walk out of the room when Clara reached for his hands holding them tight. Her eyes full of sadness. She spoke softly, "Mr. Kaplan, don't expect much."

He found his way to the sunroom and out into the back yard. His walked with a deliberate pace, unsure what to expect after Clara and Cavalier's warnings. So much time and now the end of his search. This was never a scenario he had planned for or even considered. He understood why Isabella didn't want him to know. He would have felt the same way if the roles had been reversed. He wanted her to be the same woman he fell in love with.

He stood at the gazebo door and knocked. "Mind if I join you?" he tried to keep his voice steady.

She didn't answer, just stared straight forward. He opened the door and stepped inside. She appeared different, but the same. Isabella's body was no longer the athletic one she used to have, it was frail, eyes sunken and her skin sallow. He realized how much of a toll her sickness had taken. He stood in front of her and a warm feeling began to rise in his chest. She slowly lifted her head. He watched her eyes scan him as they made their way to his face. There was a fleeting glimmer in her eyes. Recognition perhaps, but no memory.

She stood and moved toward him. He could feel his heart pounding so hard he thought his chest would burst. She placed her hands on his cheeks and rubbed the stubble on his face. "I have your picture," she said. "Danni gave it to me. Do you know Danni?"

"I do," he replied. "She's a good sister."

"She wrote that you were my boyfriend."

"That's right."

She inched closer, until their bodies touched. She leaned her head forward and pressed the side of her face against his chest and took a deep breath. "I don't remember," she finally whispered.

Clara had said Isabella would never remember the past, it had been forever erased from her memory. There were parts of his past he wished he could erase from his memory, but those were the things that made him who he was today. Isabella was not one of those memories he ever wanted to erase.

He prided himself on his ability to accomplish almost any task, but Isabella's health was something he could not fix. He felt powerless.

She pulled away from him and sat down. That momentary glint of recognition he thought he saw in her eyes had evaporated.

He had no idea what the future held or whether he would ever see Isabella again. This was not a continuation of his bad luck and trouble, this was life. An unfortunate part, but life nonetheless.

This was the end of his search.

The Isabella Hunt he once knew was gone from his life.

He walked to where she sat, brushed the hair from her face, leaned over and kissed her on the forehead. He wasn't sure what to say. Perhaps her lack of expression said it all.

He remembered how she used to be, her smile, her laugh, and how she made him feel when they were together.

He whispered in her ear, "Goodbye Isabella."

Kaplan waited for a response, but one never came.

He walked back to his motorcycle.

It was time to go home.

AUTHOR NOTES

Last Chance was different than any of my other books in so many ways. It was also the most difficult (and longest) book I've written to date. I did many things in this book I had never done before.

First things first—Acknowledgements: First and foremost, as always, the first read goes to my wife, Debi (author DJ Steele to many). She is an awesome fact-checker and a harsh critic, but her input always makes my books better. Once again, she claimed *Disruption* would be the last book she would edit and, once again, I groveled, and she gave in burying herself into *Last Chance*. Her input is an integral part of my writing and editing process, one I'm not sure I could do without. I'm certain I wouldn't want to do without. She puts me on the straight and narrow and helps punch up many of my scenes, especially when it comes to character emotion. For that, I am eternally grateful.

With each new book I write, the list of acknowledgements typically grows. I am indebted to those who have graciously volunteered their time and energy to steer this author in the right direction. It's their occupational expertise and/or past experiences that have provided me, through interviews and discussions, with a rudimentary foundation to write about things which I know nothing about. My sincerest gratitude to each of those.

Every author understands the true value of *beta-readers*. Not only are they extra eyes on your manuscript, they are readers who donate their time to provide honest, unbiased, and unabashed input. These are volunteers whose motivation is simply to help me make this the best book possible. Thanks again to Debi Barrett, Cheryl Duttweiler, Terrence Traut, Nancy Mace, Colleen M Story, C.J. "Cos" Cosgrove, & Artie Lynnworth. Also, a big thank you to Mike Shockley for the tour of Wind River Indian Reservation & Deputy U.S. Marshal Logan Bryce for the insight on the Blackfeet Reservation. For the inspiration behind the *rockhound* idea, Erica Shockley.

Special thanks to Mary Fisher of Mary Fisher Design, LLC who always creates awesome covers; again, with the special artistic touch of Kelly Young. She took my ideas and used her talents to take this cover well beyond my expectations.

Lastly, I want to thank you, the reader. It is my genuine hope that you found this story entertaining and that those unexpected twists and turns left you smiling…or perhaps cursing…either way, it works for me.

Is it fact or fiction? — This is something I've tried to include in the back of every novel for those of you who like to differentiate reality from this author's … for lack of better words, exaggeration or make-believe world.

It was difficult creating a make-believe world where all this action could take place. In the past, I used real destinations and made creative adjustments. Not this time. This time, it's all fiction. The town of Last Chance is fictitious, although I used some characteristics of several towns I've visited to create a town in the middle of nowhere. Same thing applies to all the establishments in Last Chance…totally fictitious. There is no Pioneer River in Northern Wyoming, nor is there a Dead Horse Creek, or Black Canyon, or Owl Rock, or Devil's Gulch that I'm aware of.